The Making of a Duchess

Shana Galen

sourcebooks
casablanca

Published by Sourcebooks Casablanca, an imprint of Sourcebooks, Inc.
P.O. Box 4410, Naperville, Illinois 60567-4410
(630) 961-3900
FAX: (630) 961-2168
www.sourcebooks.com

Printed and bound in Canada
WC 10 9 8 7 6 5 4 3 2 1

For Mathew, who has stood by my side through every personal and professional trial and triumph. Thank you for your love, your support, your plotting advice, even your "buck up, young camper" speeches. I love you.

One

France, July 1789

JULIEN WOKE SUDDENLY, HIS EYES WIDE AND FOCUSED on the ceiling above his bed. It danced with color, alternating red then orange then yellow. He stared at the colors for three heartbeats: why should his ceiling flicker so?

His gaze darted about his bedroom, looking for anything else out of place. A low fire smoldered in the hearth across from the large kingwood bed he occupied. But it had been banked by the servants the night before and was almost extinguished. It couldn't be the reason for the flickering light. The light was so bright he could make out the lion's head carved into his headboard.

His eyes tracked over the rest of the room: the armchair in the corner upholstered in dark green velvet, the kingwood armoire, the wash stand in the corner, the bureau Mazarin he used for a desk.

Nothing was out of place, nothing out of the ordinary. He allowed his eyes to drift closed again—

And then he heard the shouting.

He bolted upright, tossing the bedclothes aside and rushing to the window beside the bed. He threw aside the heavy velvet draperies and stared into the night. As the eldest of three sons, he had his choice of rooms, and his overlooked the chateau's courtyard. Normally, it was a pretty picture, lined with benches and planted with dozens of flowers. In July, those flowers burst into swaths of red and yellow and pink. As none but the gardeners typically ventured into the courtyard, Julien was certain he was one of the few to enjoy the view.

Until tonight.

Tonight the deserted courtyard swelled with people. Peasants shouting and brandishing torches streamed into the square. Julien couldn't understand what they shouted, but he understood what was coming.

He turned, ran for his armoire, and pulled out a pair of breeches. Quickly, he shoved his legs into them and rammed his nightshirt in at the waist. Where were his shoes? He should have listened to his nanny and put them away. Julien fell to his knees, searching.

He heard windows breaking now, heard the shouts growing louder, and knew some of the peasants had overpowered the servants and were inside the chateau. In Paris, his parents had tried to shield him from the rumors of unrest among the lower classes, but he'd heard anyway.

Unspeakable things—things he didn't want to think about.

There was another crash and a shout.

Mort à l'aristocratie! That was what the peasants had shouted in Paris before they had torn the nobles apart—massacring them. So many had been killed, even babies were butchered. He had not seen it happen, but he had heard. He eavesdropped on his parents and their friends talking and knew about the fall of the Bastille and the uprisings in the streets. His father told his little brothers this trip to the country was for rest and relaxation, but Julien knew the truth.

And now the truth was inside his home.

Finally! His hand brushed the leather of one shoe, and he snatched it then slipped it on. Where was the other?

Oh, forget it! He had no time. He must reach Armand and Bastien before the peasants did. The twins were only eleven and wouldn't know what to do. He was thirteen. He could defend himself.

He yanked open his bedroom door and immediately threw an arm up. The hallway was already thick with gray smoke, the way to his brothers' rooms obscured. He would have to breathe through the linen of his nightshirt. Coughing and stumbling blindly forward, he grasped at the sword that hung on the wall opposite his door. It had been his grandfather's sword, and he was not allowed to touch it. Julien did not like to break the rules, but he needed that sword.

It was heavy, so heavy that he could not hold it upright for long. He dropped it to the floor and had to drag it behind him as he moved toward his brothers. Julien had been glad when, upon turning twelve, he had been allowed to move into this far wing of the chateau. He'd felt older, mature.

Now he wished he were closer to the rest of his family. The sound of the thirsty fire licking at the chateau walls peaked and merged with the cries of the peasants. They were coming closer, and they would surely kill him when they found him.

Mon Dieu, s'il vous plaît. Aidez-moi.

Julien was sweating, his nightshirt wet and clingy. It was hot, so hot, and his heart was beating like a trapped woodpecker against his ribs.

Behind him, he heard someone running. *Mon Dieu!* They had found him. He whirled, squinting through the gray smoke. But he could see nothing. Inside his chest, his woodpecker heart stuttered and flapped its wings while the rapid footsteps grew closer. Julien raised his drooping sword, attempting to strike. But before he could swing, his mother's face was before him.

"Julien! Oh, thank God. Thank God!"

"Ma mère?"

She was dressed in a long white robe, streaked with blood and soot. Her hair, always perfectly coiffed, now streamed about her white face in black waves, making her look slightly deranged.

Julien focused on the blood. "Ma mère, are you alright?"

"We have no time. Your brothers." She took his hand and pulled him behind her. Julien noticed that beneath the skirts of her robe she wore no shoes. Even more troublesome: her robe was torn in the back.

The heat around them expanded, the air so thick and pulsing Julien could feel the heat singe his lungs. He fought for each gasping breath.

"Hurry!"

They heard footsteps, and she pulled him aside, flattening them both against a tapestry on the wall.

But it was not the peasants. It was a groom and Albertine, his mother's maid. "Duchesse," the maid cried. "You must not go that way. The flames. They are too much."

"Come with us, Duchesse," the groom offered.

"No, thank you. I must reach my sons first."

To Julien's surprise, she spoke calmly and with composure. Despite the chaos and the choking smoke and the approaching cries, his mother managed to appear unruffled.

She put a hand out, touched Albertine's arm. "You go on without me. Get out, and quickly."

Without another word, she pulled Julien past the servants and along the corridor. They were both coughing now, the smoke so thick it was a wall they had to fight through. Julien hardly knew where they were anymore. He was confused and disoriented. His head hurt, his eyes smarted, and he could not stop coughing.

"We're almost there," his mother reassured him. "Don't—"

He heard the shout of angry voices ahead, and his mother slid to a stop, pushing Julien behind her. She retreated until their backs were pressed against the corridor wall. Julien peered behind him and recognized the painting hung there. They were close to his brothers' rooms now. So close.

Through the smoke the enraged voices rose and fell. "Move out of the way."

"Join us or die."

"You think you can protect the aristos? *Mort à l'aristocratie!*"

The last was repeated by all. Julien knew these were peasant voices. They were inside the chateau, right outside his brothers' rooms. He thought he recognized several of the peasant voices as well—Matthieu, who baked bread in the village, and Marie, who washed and sewed for her meager wages.

"S'il vous plaît." That was the voice of the boys' nanny. Julien knew it well. His mother stiffened, as tense as the band of his slingshot before release.

"They are just children," the nanny cried. "Have mercy. Have mer—" Her words were cut off with a scream followed by a thump and a gurgling sound Julien would remember until his last breath.

"Break the door down!" one of the peasants— Matthieu?—cried. "You! Search the rest of the house."

His mother started, seeming to come alive again. She looked at him, and he knew she wanted to go to his brothers.

She would die with them.

Julien closed his eyes, prayed fervently, "Mon Dieu, sauvez-nous." A peace came over him, and he opened his eyes, knew what he had to do.

He would go with his mother. Yes, he still had the sword. He would fight until the end.

But his mother was watching him, and a look of profound sadness marred her features. The expression wavered for a second and was finally replaced by determination. "Run!" she hissed, pushing him back the way they had come and following close behind.

Julien ran, feeling his mother's hand securely on his back. He could hear the voices of the peasants behind him, and at some point his hands, slick with sweat from the building heat, dropped the sword. He would have gone back for it, but his mother pushed him relentlessly on. He stumbled and fell, his lungs unable to steal enough oxygen to keep his legs moving. He tried to rise, but his mother opened a door and wrenched him inside, closing and bolting it behind him.

This was a guest room, one Julien could not remember ever having entered before. The furnishings were draped in white linen, giving the hulking bed and the towering clothespress a menacing, ghostly appearance.

Julien shivered, leaned against the door, and coughed. The smoke had not penetrated this ghost room as heavily yet, and he gulped for air, which only made him cough harder. His mother ran to the window, and Julien struggled to his feet and followed.

The room was at the back of the house. Looking out the window, Julien could see the moon and stars. No peasants were below. They were either in the courtyard or inside the house.

"Help me open this window." She unlatched it and pushed up, and Julien pushed with her. They both drank of the clean air and stared at each other. For a moment, she looked so young, too young to be the mother of three.

Then she looked down, and her youth seemed to drain away.

Following her gaze, Julien peered at the decorative ledge below the window that encircled the chateau. He knew his feet could reach it if he dangled from the window. His mother was taller and would reach it easily, but she had the skirts of her robe and undergarments to contend with.

The drop was not insubstantial.

Something pounded on the door, and they both turned and flinched.

"It's locked! Kick it open!"

Julien looked at his mother. "If we stay on the ledge until we reach the corner"—he pointed to the edge of the chateau—"we can use the cuts in the stone to climb down."

He'd done it before from his own room. Of course, his room was considerably closer to the corner, and he had the cushion of the trees and shrubs in the courtyard beneath him.

They would have no cushion here.

Thud! The door rattled. *Thud!*

The peasants were coming through.

His mother nodded. "You go first. Don't stop. No matter what happens to me."

He frowned at her, but with no time to argue, was forced to swing one leg over the ledge. He looked down accidentally, and the world spun. Gripping the window tighter, he swung the other leg over. He was dangling by his hands now, and his feet felt for the ledge. He'd grown since the last time he had done this, and it was higher than he remembered. Once he found purchase, he released the window ledge and hugged the stone wall. Despite the fire, it was cold to the touch.

Slowly, carefully, he edged along the ledge. Pausing, he looked back at the window. "Mother, hurry!"

It seemed an eternity before one white-clad leg appeared at the window. Soon the other followed. She hung in midair, her feet dangling as they searched for the ledge. She wavered, her grip weakening. But just as Julien feared she would fall, one foot then the other found the ledge. Slowly, she released the window sill.

Julien stared at her in admiration. His mother was no coward.

"Go," she hissed. "They're almost through the door."

He inched along the wall of the chateau—step, slide; step, slide. He moved quickly, watching his mother from the corner of his eye. And yet it still startled him when several heads poked out the window. One of them was, indeed, Matthieu.

"There they are! Get them."

The heads disappeared again, and Julien kept moving. Step, slide. Step, slide. Step—

Something arced out the window and thudded to the ground below them. Julien froze and watched as the vase shattered on the cobblestones. Then another object came at them, this one better aimed. The brass candleholder barely missed his mother's shoulder.

Step, slide. Step, slide. Step, sl—*houp-là*! He'd reached the corner of the house and would now have to climb down. His mother was still sliding closer, and the peasants were aiming the second candleholder at her. It grazed her arm, causing her to flinch and sway.

"Hold on!" Julien screamed. He felt a stab of terror, sharp as any sword blade, pierce his chest.

And then she was steady again.

The peasants booed, and Julien wished he could go back and personally strangle each and every one of them.

But he hadn't the luxury of daydreams, even those

of vengeance. It would take time for the peasants to reach the back of the house, but he knew they were coming. He began to climb down, using the ornate stonework as hand and footholds. He climbed quickly, reaching the bottom long before his mother. She was less agile, and as he stood there, he worried that her white night robe would act as a beacon to any who came this way. Each step down seemed to take forever. How he wished she would hurry. How he wished he could run away.

And then he was ashamed of himself. What would his father think if he knew his son had even considered leaving his mother to fend for herself? Why, no Valère would ever act in such a cowardly fashion.

At this very moment, his father was probably fighting the peasants. He would win, too. The duc de Valère was strong and good. He would beat these peasants and save them all.

His mother was almost to the bottom, and Julien reached up, putting his hand on her back to let her know he was behind her. He looked up just in time to see a half-dozen books rain down, and he grabbed his mother, pulling her around the corner and out of danger. The two of them, mother and son, fell to the ground, leaning against the house for a moment's respite.

On the other side of the wall, the books thudded to the ground, and he heard the peasants in the window yell, "Around the corner! They're getting away."

Julien was on his feet again, taking his mother's hand. They had not a moment to waste. If the peasants caught them—

No. He would not think of that.

"Mother, the stables!"

She nodded, and lifting her skirts, ran beside him. As one, they arrowed for the stables. Julien felt invisible hands grasping at him, but he was too afraid to look over his shoulder and gauge how close the peasants truly were. He could not slow. He could not stop.

They rounded the side of the chateau, and the stables came into view.

Julien gasped. The stables were on fire, and he could hear the horses screaming. Why hadn't the grooms freed them? Without thinking, he ran for the stable doors, slamming into them and pulling them open. He would have to go inside, freeing each horse individually.

"Julien, watch out!"

The attack came from the side. At first he could not comprehend why Claude, one of the Valère grooms, would attack him. Julien raised a hand to fend off the assault. Pain sliced through him as the shovel Claude held came down hard on his arm..

Behind him, the peasants chasing them had caught up. They stood back, cheering the groom on. *"Mort à l'aristocratie!"*

Julien swayed, and the groom smiled.

So even their servants had betrayed them.

Raising the shovel again, the groom brought it down swiftly. This time, Julien ducked, kicked the groom hard, and darted around him. He might not be strong, but he was quick.

"Ma mère, get away!"

She was holding a pitchfork, the look in her eyes maniacal as she waved it at the peasants. Most were armed with only dull knives or fire pokers, and they stayed back. Waiting for their opportunity.

She glanced at Julien, and he raised his arms, nodding to her. She tossed him the pitchfork, and he caught it easily—just in time to fend off another blow from Claude. The handles of the tools clashed together, and Julien pushed back, throwing Claude off balance. Julien struck again, and the groom fell. Grasping his chance, Julien turned the tines of the pitchfork on the servant.

"Don't get up or I'll kill you." He looked at the men and women closing in on the stable. Men and women with hate and bloodlust in their eyes. "I'll kill all of you."

"No, little boy," one gray-haired woman missing several teeth hissed. "We're going to kill all of *you*. *Mort à l'aristocratie!*"

The peasants charged, and Julien threw the pitchfork and ran.

Into the fire. Into the sound of screaming horses.

He ran blindly, hitting a solid wall of warm, trembling muscle.

"Julien, get on. Hurry!" His mother's voice, coming from the right. He could barely discern her white robe and curtain of black hair in the smoky dark. She was atop a dancing dappled mount.

Reaching high, Julien grasped the mane of a large bay gelding and pulled himself up. The horse reared, and Julien held until his muscles felt they would snap from strain. One of the peasants approached, and the gelding skittered. Julien struggled with his nightshirt, tugging it over his head and wrapping it around the horse's eyes. His mother had done the same with her robe and, clad in her chemise and petticoats, she was now urging her blind horse forward, through the open back of the stable.

Julien turned his mount to follow just as the old peasant woman ran for him. She was brandishing the pitchfork now, and he kicked at her with his bare foot. The tine sliced through the tender flesh of his foot, and Julien cried out

With his good foot, he kicked desperately at his gelding. The beast jumped and ran forward. Julien held on with all his strength, trying to steer the horse through the doors. He could see his mother waiting, and just beyond her, the woods beckoned.

If they could only reach the woods.

The gelding veered crazily to the right, and Julien pressed hard with his leg, urging the horse left. They cleared the stable with mere inches to spare, and then he was out in the open, beside his mother. He pulled the nightshirt off the horse's eyes and hunkered down, allowing the beast to gallop for the woods. He would slow the animal when they were closer. Farther from danger.

Their way was lit from behind, the light of the fire making the dark night as rosy as a sunrise. But Julien did not dare look back. He looked only at his mother, who rode right beside him.

They ran through a small brook and into a line of trees. By unspoken agreement, they slowed their mounts, and the duchesse de Valère turned to look at the chateau. Reluctantly, Julien turned to look as well.

The house was engulfed in fire—the bright red and orange flames surging into the sky like angry, grasping hands. Around the fire, the peasants danced and sang a macabre song.

Julien felt ill. His head ached, and he couldn't catch his breath. His foot was bleeding and throbbed white-hot with pain. But it was nothing to the pain of losing his brothers.

No.

"I'm sure they escaped," he said through gritted teeth. "Father saved them."

His mother turned and looked at him. "Your father—" she began, and then glanced down at her bloody nightgown.

"No," Julien whispered. "No!"

She looked away, but not before he saw the heart-rending grief in her eyes. The anguish pulled her face down, etching deep grooves where only faint lines had been the day before.

"No." The word was a mere breath.

"We must go," she said. "Come first light, they'll be looking for us."

Julien nodded. He looked one way and then the other, unsure where to lead—even if he should lead.

"We'll go home. To England," his mother said. "My parents will take us in."

"England?" Julien had heard his mother talk about her homeland, but he had never been there. "How will we travel? We have no money."

"We won't let a small thing like that stop us." She looked away from the fire and met his gaze. "We're Valères. What would your father say?"

"*Ne quittez pas,*" he said automatically. *Never give up.* "You're the duc de Valère now."

Julien swallowed. He was the duc, a heavy burden for a thirteen-year-old. But Julien would shoulder that burden. He would make his father proud.

He would avenge this day, and he would never give up, not until justice was done.

Two

London, 1801

"MA'AM, SIR NORTHROP HAS ASKED FOR YOU."

Sarah looked up from the geography book she and her two pupils were bent over and frowned. "Me?"

The butler did not respond. Wrisley merely raised one salt-and-pepper eyebrow and waited. He was the picture of forbearance, though Sarah knew he must detest errands like this.

She removed her reading spectacles from her nose, leaving them to dangle from the chain around her neck, and dusted her hands on her shapeless, gray gown. It was a nervous gesture, and her teachers at the Ladies Benevolent Society Academy for Young Girls—the Academy, as the girls there called it—had told her countless times the gesture did nothing to improve her deportment. And yet Sarah could not seem to resist the action when she was unnerved.

Why would Sir Northrop want to see her? As she interacted almost exclusively with the lady of the house, Sarah had not thought Sir Northrop knew she existed.

Wrisley cleared his throat, and Sarah stuttered, "Sir Northrop? Certainly. Tell him I will be along momentarily."

Wrisley sighed and closed his eyes briefly, his look pained.

Sarah winced. When she was flustered, she could be such an idiot. Wrisley would want to escort her, of course. She turned back to her charges. Both waited, hands in laps and eyes on her, for the lesson to continue. Anne, nine years old, and Edmund, age seven, were sweet, good-natured children. It had been a joy to tutor them these past two months, and Sarah sincerely hoped her employ would not end today.

Not that she had any reason to suspect it would. She had done nothing wrong.

Had she?

"Children, I must speak with your father," she said, stating the obvious. "It's almost tea time. Why don't you wait for your tea and toast in the nursery? I shall meet you there."

"Yes, Miss Smith," Anne said obediently. She rose and straightened her white and blue gown.

Edmund followed, less concerned with the wrinkles in his clothing. As he passed, he leaned over and whispered, "I'll save you the marmalade, Miss Smith."

She smiled. "Thank you, Edmund."

When the children were gone, she followed Wrisley into the corridor, leaving the clean, bright schoolroom behind. With its solid desks, comforting books, and pretty yellow and white checked curtains, the schoolroom was her haven. She felt safe inside, sure of herself and her position. Outside, she felt uncertain.

The schoolroom was on the third floor of the town house, along with her own tiny room and various other servants' quarters. As the governess, Sarah did not associate with the lower servants. Custom dictated that she might socialize with Lady Merton's maid as well as the housemaid, but she had not been in the Merton household long enough to form much of an acquaintance with these or any of the other upper servants. Consequently, when Sarah was not with the children, she was rather lonely—a strange sensation after years of sharing quarters with dozens of girls at the Academy.

Wrisley had not so much as turned to be certain she was following, and near the stairs that led to the house's lower levels, Sarah felt safe to steal a peek in the gilt-edged mirror that hung there. She blew out a breath at what she saw. The sleek bun she had coiled her hair into this morning was no more. She had taken the children on a nature walk in the garden earlier, and between the wind and the sudden spring shower, her neat coiffure was ruined. She tried to smooth it back into place, but it was hopeless.

And then there was the state of her dress. The serviceable gown was wrinkled and stained at the knees. She should have changed after kneeling in the garden, but it was such a chore that she had intended to save it until dinner. A little soil would not hamper her teaching geography and French this afternoon. Of course, clean clothes and tidy hair were important, but so was digging in the dirt and playing in the rain. The children understood that. Sir Northrop might not be so open-minded.

"Ma'am." Wrisley's voice floated up the stairs, and Sarah rushed to follow him. She was always chastising

Anne for sounding like a herd of horses on her way down the stairs, and Sarah was careful to descend gracefully, though her knees were shaking as she drew nearer to Sir Northrop's library.

Not for the first time, she wished she had just a little of the beauty some girls seemed to have in abundance. It might give her a boost of confidence. But she was stuck with plain brown eyes, drab brown hair, and a freckled complexion from forgetting her hat out in the garden once too often. And she did not want to even think about her mouth. It was much too large for her face. Growing up, she had practiced sucking in those swollen lips to make them look smaller, but the exercise only made her appear stranger. Still, she was tempted to try it today.

How she wished she had just one—*just one*—admirable physical feature!

Wrisley reached the vestibule on the ground floor and turned toward Sir Northrop's library. Sarah hurried to follow, the weakness in her knees spreading so that now her head was spinning as well.

Could she have done something wrong?

No.

Perhaps Sir Northrop wanted a report on the progress of his progeny. In that case, what would she say? Anne's French was quite good, but Edmund's geography was poor indeed.

Wrisley motioned for her to wait as he opened the ornate library door and stepped inside. Sarah took one last deep breath and reminded herself of the Academy's motto: Chin up.

It was a maxim that had served her well both in her employment as a governess and in life. No matter what trials she must face, she could always keep her chin up and her courage intact.

"Sir Northrop, I present Miss Smith." Wrisley opened the door wider, and Sarah entered. She curtsied quickly, catching only a glimpse of her employer seated behind an enormous mahogany desk. She kept her chin high but her gaze on the Turkey carpet, patterned in green and gold.

"Thank you, Wrisley. That will be all."

Sarah kept her eyes downcast as the butler retreated, closing the door behind him.

"At ease, Miss Smith," Sir Northrop said, and Sarah realized she was still curtseying. She rose and saw that Sir Northrop was studying her. His brow was furrowed with intensity, and Sarah wanted to die with shame.

She focused her gaze on the shelves of books lining the wall behind her employer. "I'm sorry about the mud stains, Sir Northrop," she rattled. "I took the children into the garden this morning and was showing them the new dahlias. There was quite an interesting insect on one. It was green and orange and black and had oh so many legs—eight or ten or—anyway, I knelt down to show the children. I didn't realize the ground was—"

"Do you always talk this much?"

Sarah blinked. "No." Resisting the urge to explain further, she pressed her lips together.

"Good." Sir Northrop rose and strode around his desk. He was a tall man, well-built and muscular. Sarah understood he had been in the Royal Navy before retiring to London, marrying, and starting a family. He had been knighted by the King for his service to his country. Because many of his exploits were well known and heralded, he was accepted into the highest social circles.

Sir Northrop passed her, and she fumbled with her hands, finally clenching them in front of her. She would *not* smooth her dress. Behind her, she heard him turn the lock on the door. Sarah froze, not daring to look around.

"Do not be alarmed, Miss Smith."

"I'm not alarmed," she squeaked.

He made a dubious sound then stood in front of her again, his expression grim. She waited for him to speak, but he did nothing except stare at her for what felt like at least five full minutes.

Finally, she ventured, "Is something wrong?"

"Yes." He crossed his arms and leaned back against his large desk. "I have a very serious problem."

She swallowed. "Oh."

So she had done something wrong. It was probably Edmund's geography. The poor boy could hardly identify the main rivers on the Continent.

It had to be Edmund. Unless...

The way Sir Northrop was studying her. The way he was looking at her. He wasn't thinking of...

No, certainly not.

But Sarah did recall that Pippa, one of her favorite teachers at the Academy, had told the girls a story about a former employer who had so wanted the teacher in his bed that he had chased her halfway around the house, finally cornering her in the—Sarah took a sharp breath—library. Pippa had managed to fight the man off only by wielding a fire poker.

Was there a fire poker in this library? Sarah had not thought to check. She turned surreptitiously to glance at the fireplace.

"Miss Smith, I need your help, and this request is—how do I say it?—rather unconventional."

Sarah's eyes fixed on the fireplace. No poker!

"Un—" Sarah cleared her throat. "Unconventional?" There was a clock on the mantel. Perhaps that would serve if she became desperate.

"Miss Smith, I think you'd better come into the music room with me." He gestured to the door at the other end of the library. Sarah and Anne had spent quite a few hours in the music room, and she knew this door from the other side. She had not realized it led into the library. Which meant that Sir Northrop might have spent hours listening to Sarah and Anne practice.

He gestured at the door, and Sarah, relieved, hurried toward it. He was not going to chase her about the house after all. He just wanted... what did he want?

She opened the door and was immediately taken aback. The music room was usually light and airy, the draperies secured to allow sunlight from the garden to pour in. Today the heavy drapes were shut and the French doors closed tightly. In the center of the room, one of the velvet chaise longues squatted before the fireplace, and Sarah could make out a single delicate slipper dangling off the end.

"Is that her?" a female voice croaked from the direction of the chaise longue.

"It's her," Sir Northrop answered.

"Let me see her."

Sarah looked in confusion from the chaise longue to Sir Northrop. Sir Northrop nodded at her. "Go around to the front of the chaise longue. Madam would like to see you."

Madam? Sarah spoke with Lady Merton every day, and this woman sounded nothing like Lady Merton. Lady Merton was young and a bit silly. This woman's voice was smoke and fog. And she sounded pained.

Reluctantly, Sarah inched around the chaise longue until she stood before the woman. The stranger was lying on her side, one hand supporting her head and the other clutched protectively at her ribs. The woman was younger than she sounded; Sarah guessed twenty-seven or twenty-eight. She had glossy black hair and large coffee-colored eyes. Her lips were red, the color matching the burgundy gown she wore. The gown had been loosened, and the bodice fell quite low, revealing the swells of an ample bosom.

She was a beautiful woman, catlike in her repose. And yet instantly Sarah knew something was wrong.

"I'm injured," the woman told her. "I've been shot."

"Shot?" The word burst out of her mouth before she could contain it. "How? Why?"

Sir Northrop stood on Sarah's other side, and the woman looked at him now. "Didn't you tell her?"

"No. You said you wanted to see her. Do you agree now that she'll do?"

Sarah frowned, a chill running up her spine. "Will I do for what?"

The woman was looking at her again, assessing her. "Come closer, Miss—"

"Smith." Sarah looked at Sir Northrop. "Sir, should we not call for a surgeon?"

"I've already done so, Miss Smith."

The woman gave her a wry smile. "No need to worry about me. I'm not so easy to kill. Come closer."

Sarah bent, and the woman reached out and cupped her chin. Sarah saw that her hand had held a towel, and the towel was red with blood. Sarah closed her eyes and tried to ignore the dizziness. Could she not just return to Edmund and Anne and the geography lesson?

Chin up.

The woman released Sarah's chin and looked up at Sir Northrop. "Is this our only choice?"

"Yes."

"Are you certain?" The woman frowned.

"Perfectly. She has patience and intelligence. She's fluent in French, and with a bit of work, she will look the part."

The woman looked dubious. "What about—"

"All our female operatives are on the Continent," Sir Northrop said, interrupting. "I can't wait for one to return."

The woman nodded reluctantly. "I know. If we wait, everything we've put into place is ruined." She looked at Sarah again. "But can she do it?"

Sarah raised a brow. "Do what?"

The woman ignored her question. "Your name is Smith?"

"Yes," Sarah answered reluctantly.

"Is that your family name"—the woman winced in pain—"or are you an orphan?" It was a reasonable question. The custom was to give all orphans the surname *Smith*.

Sarah glanced at Sir Northrop, who nodded at her. "Answer, Miss Smith."

"I'm an orphan," she said, feeling her cheeks heat in shame. "I was left on the steps of the Ladies Benevolent Society. I didn't come with a name, so I was given the name Sarah Smith."

"And you know nothing of your mother?" the woman asked.

Sarah shook her head. She hated speaking of this—how she had been abandoned with only a slip of paper on which the name *Sarah* had been scrawled. And even that had been misspelled.

But although Sarah had been told countless times that she had been left at the Academy as an infant just a few days old, sometimes she had dreams or vague memories of a mother and a father. The feeling of love and happiness was strong in what Sarah called her phantom memories. Yet, she knew they could not be true.

What was true, though no one ever spoke of it, was that all assumed Sarah's mother had been either a prostitute or a loose woman who found herself pregnant and without a husband. Unable to care for the child, she had given her up to charity.

Sarah was, in essence, a bastard. Unwanted. Unloved.

And yet, she had made something of her life. She was a respectable woman—a good governess, too. After all, she had secured this position—though she might come to regret it.

"Whom do you know in London?"

Sarah blinked, surprised at the question. "I... ah." She paused, uncertain how to answer.

"She doesn't know anyone," Sir Northrop offered impatiently. "My butler tells me no one has called for her, and she spends her day off in her room, reading."

Sarah stared at him. Why should he care what she did on her own time? Why should he care if she preferred to retreat to her room—not much more than a closet really—and read about far-off places or daydream that one day she would have a home and family of her own?

"Then you have no friends?" the woman asked.

Sarah straightened. "I have friends." She realized her chin had drooped and raised it again. "I'm close to several of the girls at the Academy, but we all work. Most are governesses in the country, and we communicate through writing."

"But no one in London."

"The teachers at the Academy," Sarah said, trying not to sound defensive.

The woman waved that away. "You're unlikely to meet with any of them." She looked at Sir Northrop. "And you said she had been a governess for another family?"

"Yes. She came with a good recommendation. She was dismissed because the boys went off to school, and she was no longer needed. The family had no daughters."

Sarah stared at him. "Sir, may I ask to what all of these questions pertain? Is there a problem with my work or my family history?"

"Oh, no!" the woman exclaimed then succumbed

to a fit of coughing. When she recovered, she croaked, "Your history is perfect."

"Perfect?" Sarah gave her a long look. She had thought being born penniless, without a surname, and a likely bastard many things over the years, but never *perfect*.

"Miss Smith," Sir Northrop said now, turning to her. "I need your help."

Sarah nodded. "With the children?"

"No. With the duc de Valère."

Sarah blinked. "Who?"

"Julien Harcourt, duc de Valère," the woman repeated. "He's a traitor and an informant, and we need you to spy on him."

Three

"YOU WANT ME TO DO WHAT?" SARAH SPUTTERED. SHE could not have heard them correctly. They wanted her to spy? On a duc? She was a governess. She did not know anything about ducs or spies.

"Calm down," Sir Northrop ordered. He retrieved a chair and pushed it toward the fire for her. "Here, take a seat."

"I'd rather stand, thank you."

"Very well." She saw him glance at the injured woman—was *she* a spy?—before he continued. "I know all this must come as a shock to you, Miss Smith. But I don't have time for niceties. Your country needs your help. Will you do it?"

"No, I can't. I'm a governess, not a spy."

Sir Northrop crossed his arms, and the look in his eyes was dangerous. "I am well aware of your station, Miss Smith, but you have all of the qualities necessary to complete this task. I have watched you the last few days."

Sarah stiffened, feeling uncomfortable.

"I have noted your extensive patience with the children. You must have covered the same geography lesson with Edmund ten different times, and yet you never showed even a hint of exasperation."

Sarah swallowed. So he *had* noted Edmund's poor comprehension of geography. "But, sir, it's my job to be patient with children—"

"Few have that sort of patience, or your quickness of mind. When Anne tried to skirt her writing exercise last week because she was hungry, you persuaded her to write about the food she was craving. She showed me the composition that evening, and the descriptions were impressive."

"Sir, we are speaking of dealings with children. Surely, I do not have the skills needed to spy on a French duc!"

"You are fluent in French, and we do not expect you to act alone. We will give you guidance and preparation. You have been approved."

"Approved?" Sarah looked from Sir Northrop back to the injured woman. "By whom?" There was silence, and Sarah hissed in a breath. "Are you telling me the King has asked for my assistance?" Her hands were shaking now, and she tried to still them in the folds of her gown.

"Not by name." Sir Northrop paused as though considering how much to tell her. "As you know, I was knighted by the King for service to England. What you may not know is that I still render assistance to His Majesty. I work for the Foreign Office, training and overseeing some of our best operatives."

Sarah gawked at him. Sir Northrop—her employer, the man in whose home she resided—oversaw the country's spies?

"This"—he gestured to the woman lying on the chaise longue—"is the operative we had planned to use, but—let's call her The Widow—The Widow was injured in the line of duty. We need someone to take her place. In three days."

The Widow? What kind of name was that? A code name obviously, and one Sarah wanted nothing to do with.

"You're our only hope, Miss Smith," The Widow said. "There are no other operatives free at this time."

"But why me?" Sarah took a step back. "Surely there are many patient, quick-witted women about."

Sir Northrop nodded. "True, but all have a history here in London. You do not. No one in the upper circles of the *ton* will know you are not who we say you are."

"The *ton*?" Sarah felt the panic creep in. The *ton* was the collective name for England's high society—the wealthy, titled, and fabulously stylish. "I don't know anything about the *ton*. I'm just a governess," she repeated. Perhaps if she said it enough, the truth would sink in.

"Nonsense. You live with the *ton*, work for them. You are preparing Sir Northrop's children to live in the world of the *ton*. You know more than you think," The Widow said. "What you don't know, you'll figure out. More importantly, you have the look we need. The duc has been given a general description of me—brown hair, brown eyes, taller than average. You fit that description."

Sarah shook her head. "B-but I don't look anything like you. You're—" She gestured to the woman's bosom, unable to find the words.

"The duc has never met me, so that shouldn't be a problem."

Sarah opened her mouth then closed it again. Every protest she made was met with a counterargument. It seemed futile to point out that she had never met a duke in her life. Why, even Sir Northrop made her nervous, and he was only a knight. And now they expected her to go gallivanting about the *ton* as though she associated with the aristocracy every day?

They wanted her to spy.

On. A. Duc.

Did they know she did not have the stomach for telling lies? How could she lie to this duc? She would be sick all over the man as soon as she said her name.

Oh, and what name was she to give? The Widow?

She shook her head. No, she could not do it. Sir Northrop was watching her, frowning.

"I'm sorry," she said. "I have to decline. I–I'm just a governess. I must return to my charges."

❧

Julien Harcourt, chevalier, duc de Valère, *pair de France*, pushed away the glass of brandy his friend Rigby offered him. "I'm done."

Done with the brandy and done with his club. He glanced about the smoky sitting room filled with men seated in leather chairs, papers in one hand, brandy in the other. The hum of voices was incessant, and beyond, in the gaming room, he could hear the cries of victory and groans of defeat.

Rigby raised a brow. "It's French brandy. Some

entrepreneurial smuggler risked life and limb so we could pay a pretty penny to drink it."

"Penny?" Stover said, interrupting. "That bottle cost more than a penny."

"You finish it, then," Julien offered. "I'm going home to bed."

Rigby and Stover exchanged glances. "Big day tomorrow, eh?" Rigby said. The taller of Julien's two friends, he had auburn hair, fair skin, and still looked eighteen. As the nephew of a marquis who had more money than King George—or King Midas, for that matter—Laurence Rigby had enough blunt to buy a thousand bottles of smuggled French brandy.

Julien rose, and Stover rose with him. Marcus Stover was older and more serious. More frugal, too. His blond brows creased with concern. "You didn't finish telling us about the letter."

"Or the lovely Mademoiselle Serafina."

Julien ignored Rigby's comment. The letter was still on his mind. It was the reason he had come out to his club tonight. The reason he was still here at—he checked his pocket watch—three in the morning.

"Oh, what'd you go and do that for?" Rigby complained. "Don't tell me what time it is. If I don't know, I can truthfully tell my father that the time got away from me."

"You need to get your own flat," Stover informed him.

"Or move in with Valère here," Rigby said, waggling his eyebrows. "His mama doesn't care how late he stays out."

"She'll care tonight," Julien said, deciding he might

as well take his seat again. There was no point in going home yet. He would not be able to sleep. The letter was still on his mind.

"She wants you looking your best for the Mademoiselle Serafina."

"Stubble it," Stover ordered Rigby. "Tell us about the letter."

He handed Julien the brandy, and this time Julien accepted it. He took a long swallow, lowered his voice, and said, "I'm going back to France."

"Are you jingle-brained?" Rigby exclaimed. "There's a war on."

Julien gave him a look, and Rigby sat back. "Alright. I'll stubble it."

Julien turned back to Stover. "I received a letter from someone who alleges he was a servant for my family. In the letter, he claims to know the where-abouts of my brother Armand."

"Where?" Stover asked.

"He won't say in the letter."

Stover looked thoughtful. "It could be a trap. Get you back in France then capture you."

"Are there windmills in your head?" Rigby sat forward. "Of course it's a trap."

Julien turned on him. "And what if it's not? What if my brother is trapped in France right now, rotting in some jail, while I lounge here, sipping brandy?" He slammed the glass down, garnering looks from several men at the gaming tables.

Rigby gave them a wave, and they turned back to their faro. "Calm down, Valère. We're just trying to warn you what this ill-fated venture could cost you."

"I don't count costs," he said through a clenched jaw. "If my brother is alive, he needs me. There's no price on that."

"Have you considered that your brothers are most likely dead?" Stover asked.

"There are no records of their deaths."

"What records would there be?" Stover spoke carefully. "You said yourself your mother believes the boys perished in the fire."

Yes, but Julien wanted proof. He had obtained proof of his father's death. After the duc de Valère fought the peasants, giving his wife a chance to escape, he had been captured and transported to Paris and guillotined as the crowds cheered.

But of his younger brothers, the twins Sébastien and Armand, no account existed. Julien had gone back to France in secret and investigated, but he had gotten nowhere. And then yesterday he received the letter. It was signed by Gilbert Pierpont, their former butler. He wrote that he had information about Armand but couldn't give the information in the letter; it was too dangerous. He wanted Monsieur le Duc to come to Paris—into the lion's den.

"I have to be sure."

Rigby shook his head. "You're going to get yourself killed playing the hero."

"I'm not a hero. I'm just doing my duty." *Ne quittez pas. Never give up.* That had been his father's creed, and Julien had adopted it.

"Well, let me give you another duty. There's a tavern over in Chelsea with the prettiest barmaid—"

"I don't care about some woman."

"That's obvious," Rigby muttered. "Work, work, work."

Julien sighed. It was true. He worked far too much, but he hadn't had the security of a father's fortune like Rigby and Stover. He and his mother had to start over after fleeing France.

"He's not going to meet a barmaid on the same day his fiancée arrives," Stover said.

Julien winced. "Don't call her that."

Stover held up his hands. "You and I and the rest of the *ton* know your mother hopes you'll ask the chit to marry you."

"I'm the one to bend a knee." He rose. "And I'll make that decision."

"You'll do it." Rigby sighed. "Duty and all that."

"Try it sometime."

Rigby frowned. "What's that mean?"

"How long has your family been trying to match you with Miss Wimple? She's rich, has land adjoining yours, and blushes every time you speak to her."

"She has horse teeth." Rigby wrinkled his nose.

Stover laughed. "And you have big ears."

Rigby's hands flew to his ears. "Do not!"

With a laugh and a shake of his head, Julien strode away.

He did not go straight home. He walked until he tired his brain enough that he thought it would finally allow sleep. Three hours later, he stood in front of his town house in Berkeley Square. The sun was just breaking through the clouds, penetrating the thick fog that shrouded the night and engendered damp and cold even this late in May. He hated the English damp. It made his foot throb, the pain like a persistent adversary after all these years.

He stood in front of the house, leaning against the door, watching the last of the carriages rattling along the road. He supposed the occupants were returning from some lord or lady's ball. Had his mother gone? Was he supposed to have attended?

Behind him, the door opened and Luc, his valet, stuck his head out. "Monsieur le Duc, do you intend to stand out here all night?" he asked, voice thick with his French accent.

Julien turned to squint at Luc. "What are you doing up?"

"Eh! *Mon Dieu!* Look at that cravat." Luc gestured desperately at the vestibule. "Come inside, *s'il vous plaît*. Are you certain you are part French? No Frenchman would treat his accoutrements in this fashion." He lifted the wilted cravat with two fingers. "*Au secours!* It is ruined, no?"

Ruined was an exaggeration. The cravat was undone and had a small stain on it, but Julien wasn't going to argue the point. Once inside, he dropped into a pink and white striped satin Sheraton chair, waving away his valet. "I'll buy another."

Luc frowned then bent to remove the neck cloth. "That is what you always say."

"This time he means it."

Julien looked up and saw his mother standing at the top of the steps. Rowena, dowager duchesse de Valère, descended, the train of her yellow morning gown trailing over the steps after her. She was a beautiful woman. Not quite five and forty, her hair was still black, her figure still trim, and her smile still sad.

Once when he and Stover were too far in their cups, Stover had described her as ethereal. Julien could see that now. The grief that accompanied losing two sons and a husband had not robbed her of her beauty, but it had transformed that beauty into something fragile and poignant.

She seemed so delicate now, not the same woman who had scaled a chateau and fought off angry peasants with a pitchfork.

She reached the marble landing and held out a hand. "I missed you at the ball."

So he *had* been expected to attend. "I was with Rigby and Stover."

"Ah."

"Monsieur Bruyere, leave us, please."

"Oui, Duchesse." The valet bowed deeply, and taking the wilted cravat with him, retreated.

She extended a hand. "Come, have tea with me." Julien thought of her with tea cup and saucer, stirring cream and sugar into the cup. She never seemed so English as she did when she took tea. Of course, she was English, and she never tired of reminding him that he was half English. She often said he might as well consider himself fully English as the French certainly did not want their kind back.

"Ma mère, je suis fatigué." Julien spoke the French stubbornly. He would not disavow his origins. A look of sadness crossed her features, and he regretted his words immediately. "Never mind, I'll—"

She held up a hand. "No, you go to bed."

He hesitated and then decided that, at this point, bed was probably best. He turned toward the steps.

"But, Julien?"

He paused, looked back.

"Don't sleep too late. Mademoiselle Serafina Artois is arriving today."

Julien clenched his jaw, nodded. His mother might think she had procured him a bride, but in Mademoiselle Serafina, Julien saw something else.

Vengeance.

Four

SARAH COULD NOT BELIEVE SHE WAS DOING THIS. SHE could not believe she was standing in a modiste's shop, being poked and prodded and fitted.

"Not that one," The Widow said. "Keep her in blue." She sounded annoyed and as though she were in pain. A surgeon had come to tend her at Sir Northrop's, but she had refused to take any pain medication for fear it would put her to sleep. She claimed it was her duty to assist Sarah with these final preparations.

She apparently also felt it her duty to threaten and cajole until she got her way. Two days ago, when Sarah had refused to participate in this... scheme, The Widow told Sir Northrop to fire her, and he had promptly done so. Sarah could see why he had been such a successful naval officer. He was ruthless. He gave Sarah two choices: leave her position and be tossed out on the street with nary a reference nor an opportunity for another position—or spy for the Foreign Office.

Sarah had no illusions about life on the streets of London. She doubted she would make it through the night with her chastity intact. And Sir Northrop said he would make sure the Academy would not take her back. He threatened to write a letter saying she was a disgrace to their good name. As an institution that relied on charity, the Academy considered reputation everything. Even if the teachers wanted to help Sarah, they could not assist her without risking the future of all the other girls.

It was not fair, and it was not right, but life had never been fair to Sarah. She pushed her anger down and agreed to spy. The Widow had promised it would be only for a few days—perhaps a week at most. But Sarah was expected at the duc's residence today—this very afternoon. All of the dresses The Widow had had made up would have to be altered to fit Sarah. As far as Sarah could see, that meant all the gowns would have to be taken in at the hips and the bosom.

How depressing.

"What's going on in there?" Sir Northrop called from outside the dressing room.

"We're fitting her in the blue dress," The Widow answered. "She'll wear that today, and we'll send the others later." She looked at Sarah. "You may tell the Valères your luggage went missing."

Another lie. Wonderful.

The past two days and nights she had done nothing but lie. She prepared hour after hour to play the role of Mademoiselle Serafina Artois, daughter of the comte and comtesse de Guyenne. She had been primped and poked, prodded and pushed. She had been drilled in etiquette, dancing, languages, deportment, and Mademoiselle Serafina's life history.

Sarah's brain felt as though it would explode, and

her head was still throbbing. She eyed The Widow. "Are you sure you're not feeling any better?" Sarah asked her. "If you're well enough to direct all this"—she indicated the modiste and two seamstresses busily measuring and sewing. Sir Northrop had assured her they all worked for the Foreign Office and could be trusted—"then perhaps you could go yourself."

"Yes, I'm sure there will be no small commotion when I faint on the ballroom floor from loss of blood."

"Ballroom? You don't *really* expect me to dance?"

The Widow frowned at her. "You'll be moving in Society, and as this is the Season, there will be balls. We practiced all afternoon yesterday."

And still she felt uncertain. There were so many dances and so many steps to remember. Sarah swallowed, wishing she had practiced with the other girls when attending the Academy. It had just seemed so silly at the time that she had chosen to read rather than learn the steps to a minuet she would never dance.

The Widow sighed. "Try to avoid dancing, if possible. At least your French is good. You speak like a native."

"Thank—ow!" Sarah jumped when one of the seamstresses poked her with a pin.

"Sorry, miss."

"Your facility with French will serve you well," The Widow said, nodding at something the seamstress was doing to the blue dress. "As you recall, the duc and his mother are fluent in French, and your family comes from France. Your parents were friends with the Valères before the revolution."

"You told me, but I still don't understand how the Valères won't know I'm an imposter."

The Widow gave her a look full of forbearance. "We went over this."

Had they? Her head was spinning. "I want to make certain I understand."

With a sigh, The Widow explained, "The comte de Guyenne lost favor with the French court in 1782. They fled with their daughter, Mademoiselle Serafina Artois, when she was but a toddler. The Valères haven't seen Serafina since she was two years old. The families never corresponded until the Foreign Office initiated contact, pretending to be the comtesse de Guyenne, Serafina's mother."

"Wait a moment." Sarah shook her head, causing the modiste to mutter and take Sarah by the shoulders to still her. But Sarah's heart was racing. She had seen a crucial flaw in the story. "How do you know, after all this time, the two families have never seen each other? How do you know they haven't sent portraits? What if this Serafina is short and blond?"

The Widow gave her a long look, perhaps deciding how much to reveal. "We know," she said slowly, carefully, "because the Guyenne family is dead. They were executed after they fled Paris. All of them."

Sarah's stomach roiled. *All of them.* Even little Serafina?

"Their bodies were found here in London," Sir Northrop called. "But it was kept from the public, and everyone assumed their escape was successful. The Valères were overjoyed by the comtesse de Guyenne's letters."

Sarah looked down. The plan felt rotten, and it seemed criminal to exploit the death of a child, even in the name of patriotism.

But that was not why the hair on her arms stood up at the mention of little Serafina's story. Something was so familiar. Had she heard the story? Known another Serafina? No, not Serafina.

Sera...

The Widow must have sensed her hesitation. "I know it seems unethical, but consider with whom we are dealing. If our information is correct, the duc de Valère is a traitor and a spy. He's been selling British secrets to the French for years. If he is not stopped, who knows the consequences?"

"We'll all be speaking French if Bonaparte has his way," Sir Northrop chimed in.

A woman with a brush, comb, and curling tongs came in and gestured for Sarah to sit in a chair. Another woman knelt in front of her and began applying rouge to her lips and cheeks. Sarah had never worn cosmetics, and the powder and rouge felt heavy and stifling. All of this attention made her feel horribly self-conscious. No one had ever taken time to notice her, and now she was suddenly thrust onto a stage. But could she play this part?

"You *can* stop Valère," The Widow said, perhaps sensing her doubts.

"I don't feel ready." And she was a very bad liar. Lying made her stomach hurt.

"You are. Remember that we need information— letters, journals, tidbits from conversations you over-hear. Anything, whether you think it might be of use or not, should be communicated to us. Use Katarina, the maidservant, to relay messages or to send for us if you need us."

Sarah felt perspiration break out on her lower back and between her breasts. "What if I'm caught?"

"Use your wits and you won't be. If that doesn't work"—The Widow lowered her voice—"use your other charms to distract him."

Sarah stared at her. "I'm not going to—"

"Of course not." The Widow waved a hand. "You'll be in the house several days. The duc will undoubtedly be out or otherwise occupied for some portion of that time. Our sources tell us he works long hours. You should have no problem finding an hour here or there to snoop. Very well?"

"Very well."

The Widow made it sound easy, and perhaps it was—for her. But Sarah could easily see herself making a mistake and botching everything.

"Don't worry about contacting us," Sir Northrop called. "We'll contact you."

"Not so much rouge," The Widow instructed the woman with the cosmetics; then she glanced back at Sarah. "Stay in character at all times. You are Mademoiselle Serafina Artois, daughter of the comte and comtesse de Guyenne. You are nobility. The Valères are old family friends, so don't talk too much of your mother and father, lest you say something that contradicts what the duchesse remembers. Talk about your interests, your hobbies."

Sarah frowned. "And what if I encounter a situation for which I'm not prepared? What then?"

The Widow gave her an annoyed look. "Be creative, Serafina."

But she was not creative, and she was not Serafina.

Who, upon seeing her, would ever believe she possessed a name like Serafina?

"All done!" the hairdresser announced.

"Let me see." The Widow tried to rise, winced, and lay back again. "Stand up, Serafina."

Sarah obeyed, and The Widow nodded her approval. "Sir Northrop, come see our Serafina."

The curtains separating the two rooms parted, and Sir Northrop stood in the opening. He gazed at her for a long moment, and then folded his arms and nodded, looking quite satisfied with himself. "Just as I thought. She'll do very well."

Curious now, Sarah turned to glance in the cheval mirror behind her. She searched the reflection for herself. There was The Widow, the seamstress, the hairdresser and...

Was that her in the sapphire blue gown? The woman's jaw dropped, shock and surprise on her face.

Sarah closed her mouth, and the woman did as well.

It *was* her! No, it was Serafina, and she was tall and elegant and—beautiful. Sarah touched her face and her hair in awe. Somehow they had made her look beautiful. Was it the rouge? The coiffure? The diamonds about her neck? Undoubtedly, they contributed to the illusion, but the face that looked back at her was still familiar. It had the same plain eyes, only now they seemed dark and mysterious. It had the same brown hair, only now it looked thick and glossy. And she had the same full lips. Those had not really improved. They still looked too big for her face.

But her body... it looked almost as though it

belonged in this gown. She could feel heat rise to her face at the amount of flesh on display. Somehow it did not seem like her own. Was her skin really so white? Were her curves really so pleasing? The afternoon dress looked as though it had been made for her, and she supposed it had. It was in the latest style, and the robe was fashioned out of sky blue crepe. The petticoat underneath was of the whitest muslin and trimmed with lace. The bodice was cut low, but a tucker provided some modesty. Sarah turned to see the train, marveling that she should wear a gown with a train. It looked so elegant, so regal—so impractical.

But she did not have to be practical anymore. Mademoiselle Serafina hired others to be practical for her.

Sarah turned to The Widow and Sir Northrop, and they both smiled at her. "You see?" The Widow said. "I told you that you could do it. Now, one last small, very small, issue."

Sarah raised a skeptical brow. "Yes?"

"How is your Italian?"

❦

Julien didn't like surprises, so the instant the carriage carrying the comte de Guyenne's daughter arrived, he knew it. It was rather later than his mother had expected, and Julien had seen her lingering about the vestibule and conferring with Cook, undoubtedly on the best time to serve dinner.

Julien's library faced the back of the town house, but it opened into a small parlor his mother often used for correspondence in the mornings. It was a feminine room with pastel paintings on the walls, delicately carved molding on the walls and ceiling, small chairs upholstered in pink and white silk, and fresh flowers in fragile vases.

Julien felt big and cumbersome in this parlor, but it had the advantage of facing the street. Thus, he had found reason to occupy himself there most of the afternoon.

Not because he wanted to see this Mademoiselle Serafina. It was just that his library was… too dark, and he had several documents to review.

He was at the window, document in hand, when the much-anticipated Serafina arrived. He almost dropped the papers when she stepped down from the carriage, assisted by a footman. He took her in quickly. She was tall and slim and wearing a fashionable blue gown with a large hat that obscured her face. But then she glanced up, and Julien took a half step back. She did not look at all as he had expected. She was fresh and wide-eyed and innocent. He caught a quick impression of chocolate eyes and strawberry lips before he registered the expression on her face. Astonishment.

At her reaction, Julien had the urge to step outside himself. The town house had looked quite normal when he had stumbled in this morning. Had something happened to it in the meantime?

As he watched, Mademoiselle Serafina retreated and appeared as though she were going to climb back into the carriage. But behind her a maidservant was emerging, and so Mademoiselle Serafina had no place to go but forward.

Interesting.

Julien allowed the drapes to fall, retrieved his papers, and returned to his library. The comte's daughter had actually looked a little scared and... what was that other expression?

Intimidated. Yes, intimidated by the town house.

Perhaps after they had fled France, the family had grown up in poverty. But if that were the case, how had they afforded travel to London? Passage from Italy was expensive, especially with the war.

Julien heard Grimsby open the door and greet the lady. Using a measure of the self-control for which he was known, Julien stayed moored to his seat. He would see the lady at dinner. If his first impressions were not amiss, he would have no difficulty finding some feature—physical or otherwise—to spark an attraction. And unless she were an ugly shrew, Julien planned to propose.

Julien was the last in his line, and his family name would die—as had been the fate of so many French aristocratic families—without an heir. Mademoiselle Serafina's family faced the same predicament, but they had no son. The best they could hope for was to join their only daughter to another old noble French family—even if the scion was half English.

At five and twenty, Julien had yet to form an interest in marriage, but he did like the idea of thumbing his nose at the revolutionaries who had tried to snuff out the Valères.

He had vowed vengeance, and he would have it. He slid a panel in his desk aside and, using a key he always kept on him, opened the secret drawer there. He extracted the servant's letter from his breast pocket, the letter that had given him hope for Armand, and held it, felt its weight, then secured it back in his desk.

Armand was alive. He knew it. And he would stop at nothing to find him.

∽◈∾

Sarah's stomach was in turmoil. Seeing the duc's town house had sent a surge of panic through her. She had not expected something so grand for a French émigré and his mother. This was most definitely a duc's house. Not an English duke, true, but she could not imagine their houses were any grander. This house was huge, enormous, mammoth, in fact. Outside, the façade was white with black shutters, and it towered over her—over all of London it seemed. Sir Northrop had told her only the duc and his mother lived here. So much space for only two people! Why, the entire Academy could have been housed here and still had space for the Valères.

The interior of the home did nothing to quell her astonishment. The vestibule was black-and-white marble, and it gleamed from the foot of the door all the way up the curved stairs that led to the drawing room on the first floor.

She looked up. The chandelier—was that cut crystal?—gleamed. She looked down. The banisters— were they mahogany?—gleamed. She looked to the side. The vase on the small table—was that Sèvres porcelain?—gleamed.

She looked forward, and even the buttons on the butler's coat gleamed.

Sarah looked down at her own ungleaming self and felt a burning rise in her throat. She had been in many aristocratic homes, but none this grand nor this impressive.

"This way, my lady," the butler said and indicated those gleaming steps.

She took a deep breath and, on wobbly legs, followed. *You are Mademoiselle Serafina Artois.* She swallowed. *Chin up!*

The Italian maidservant Sir Northrop had sent with her was being led in another direction, probably up the servants' stairs, and though Sarah had just met the girl a half hour before, she had the urge to latch on and follow her. The servants' stairs seemed far less intimidating than the marble mountain in front of her.

But Sarah was not certain how much the maidservant, who Sir Northrop had called Katarina, knew about this scheme. Did she know that Mademoiselle Serafina Artois was really Sarah Smith? No matter. No daughter of a comte would sleep in a cot in a bedroom the size of a cupboard.

The butler had paused and was waiting for her to follow. Once again, Sarah had the urge to turn and run the other way. Would life on the streets really be so horrible?

A picture of garbage and rats and men drunk with gin flashed in her mind. The duc's home was certainly superior to that image.

The butler was still waiting, and Sarah raised her skirts and rushed to follow. She had taken two steps before she checked herself, lifted her chin a notch, and began to climb the mountain at a leisurely pace.

Hurrying would not do. That was the kind of mistake that would end with her selling flowers on some street corner. As a governess, Sarah was used to being an outsider. She was not quite a servant and yet, not part of the family. She often had time to observe her "betters." She would have to use the fruits of that observation now.

Sarah had noticed that the upper classes seemed to enjoy making others wait on them. Not that she intended to be *that* kind of aristocrat, but she doubted it occurred to most of them that they were not the center of the universe and that others were waiting, sometimes quite impatiently. This butler would be accustomed to waiting.

Sarah gingerly lifted her skirts, taking one last leisurely look about the vestibule, and then began to climb the mountain. With a nod, the butler continued on ahead of her, and she sighed in relief.

She could do this. She *could* do this.

At the top of the steps, the butler moved forward and paused in front of two towering, white doors. Sarah looked up and up and up. Was this a drawing room or a throne room?

She shook her head. Serafina would not be impressed.

With a flourish, the butler swung the doors inward and announced, "Mademoiselle Serafina Artois, daughter of the comte de Guyenne."

Sarah swallowed and stepped forward, the light from the windows at the front of the room blinding her temporarily. She blinked before being wrapped up in a hard embrace and assaulted by rapid French.

Caught off guard, it took her a moment to translate.

"Dear, dear Serafina! How good that you have come," the woman was saying. She stepped back, holding Sarah at arm's length. "Let me look at you. I cannot believe how you have grown up."

"Duchesse?" Sarah squeaked.

"*Oui!* Do you remember me?"

As they had never met before, Sarah had no trouble answering, "No, Your Grace."

"Oh!" The duchesse's eyebrows rose. "Do you speak English then?" The duchesse had switched to English, her accent that of a native.

Sarah flinched, hoping she had not already made a mistake. She wished she were a better actress, but she must proceed onward now. "Yes. I speak English and French."

"And Italian?"

Sarah clenched her teeth, remembering the tidbit The Widow had dropped on her at the modiste's this morning. "Of course."

"Please, do sit. You must be exhausted after your long journey. Would you care for tea?"

"No. Thank you." She was not yet ready to play her role and attempt nonchalantly to sip tea at the same time. She took a seat on a bright yellow chintz sofa while the duchesse sat across from her in a dainty chair upholstered in cream satin.

The duchesse was everything Sarah had expected. She was regal and poised and beautiful. Small and trim with thick black hair, she had an effortless beauty Sarah would have died for.

The duchesse was smiling, but there was something sad in her face.

For a long moment, the duchesse just stared at her, and Sarah began to worry that she had been found out. She gave her a wobbly smile, trying not to think about the fact that she was sitting in a town house in Berkeley Square. No one but the wealthiest, most prestigious families lived in Berkeley Square. Half of the *ton* would be impressed were they to be invited to tea in this drawing room.

The duchesse was frowning now, and Sarah curled her hands into the fabric on the sofa. Something was wrong. Perhaps she should be talking? But what did a comte's daughter say to a duchesse?

She glanced about the room. Above her was a crystal chandelier; below her was an Aubusson carpet in red, blue, and green; around her was furniture of the best quality. The intricately carved wood shone. Paintings lined the walls, and the cornices were expertly crafted. Behind her was a small pianoforte, and across from her stood a huge fireplace with gold trim and heavy porcelain urns flanking the mantel.

"Th-this is a lovely room," she stuttered. "So—" Luxurious? Huge? Terrifying? "Pretty."

Sarah clutched the sofa tighter. Oh, how stupid she sounded! Her stomach clenched again, and she bit her lip to keep the bile down.

"Thank you." The duchesse smiled. "I am trying to decide whether you resemble your mother or your father more. I think your father, but I see you have your mother's cheeks."

Sarah nodded. "Yes, that's what everyone says." She smiled. Perhaps playing Serafina would not be as bad as she had feared. She need only smile and nod and agree.

"And how are your dear parents? I cannot tell you how overjoyed I was to hear from Delphine and to find out that you and your family had settled in Italy and were doing well. When she suggested you might be open to a visit to London, Julien and I couldn't wait to see you. It's too bad your parents could not come as well. How are they?"

Sarah nodded, keenly aware her instructions had been to avoid the subject of her so-called parents. "They're fine. Thank you for asking."

The duchesse was frowning at her. "But if they are well, why could they not make the trip? Your mother said your father was on his death bed."

Sarah blinked and swallowed. Her stomach gave a threatening heave. "Yes, well, other than that, they are fine."

She wanted to sink into the sofa and hide underneath it. She was such an idiot! The Widow and Sir Northrop had told her that her father was supposedly on his deathbed. How could she have forgotten? She had to take a deep breath and calm down. She had to *think*.

There was a tap on the door, and a woman who was probably the housekeeper entered. Sarah sent up a prayer of thanks. "I'm sorry to interrupt, Your Grace, but Cook needs to see you."

"Oh?" The duchesse stood. "I'm so sorry, Serafina. I will return in a just a moment."

Sarah stood as well. "Please, take your time."

A moment later, the duchesse was gone, and Sarah was alone in the ornate drawing room. She turned this way and that, afraid to touch anything. Oh, how she hated all of this lying and playacting! But the faster she completed this mission, the sooner she could return to life as a governess. Perhaps she could find the evidence Sir Northrop wanted now, and then she would be able to tuck Anne and Edmund into bed tonight.

With new purpose, she moved about the room, looking for a desk or table with a drawer—anything that would hold or conceal papers. She passed a large painting of an Italian noblewoman and then halted and whipped back around. Was that a—no.

She leaned closer. Was that a Titian?

Oh, Lord. Oh, my. Just how wealthy *was* this family? An actual Titian! And then another thought occurred to her—with wealth came power. What would happen if the Valères discovered she was not who she claimed? Would she be thrown in prison?

Even worse, what if the duc de Valère was a spy? If he realized she had found him out, he might see the need to be rid of her. Permanently.

She put a hand to her belly to still its roiling. She could not worry about that right now. She had to keep her chin up and her wits about her. She tried focusing on the Titian.

She wished she could put on her spectacles in order to read the signature, but The Widow had forbidden her to do so unless absolutely necessary. So Sarah squinted and leaned in close, lifting one hand toward what looked like a scribble.

"I wouldn't touch that if you want to keep my mother's favor," a deep voice said from behind her.

Sarah swung around, knocking a bowl off a nearby

side table. It shattered loudly when it hit the gleaming wood floor.

"Oh!" She looked from the shattered bowl to the man standing in the drawing room's entrance.

It was him. She knew it.

This was the duc de Valère. The spy. The traitor. The man who might kill her if he knew what she had been sent to do.

Her stomach clenched again, and grabbing the vase nearest her, she promptly cast up her accounts.

Five

Mon Dieu.

Julien stared as Mademoiselle Serafina Artois was sick in his mother's blue and white Ming vase. The thing had cost him a fortune, and now his future wife was using it as a chamber pot.

Probably as a good a use as any for the vase, but now what was he supposed to do?

"Grimsby!" he bellowed. "Get up here!"

Mademoiselle Serafina raised her head, her face pale and waxy. Julien figured he'd better go to her—he'd better do something.

"I'm sorry," she moaned. "Oh, this is humiliating."

"Nonsense. You were very ladylike." With a flick of his wrist, he loosened his cravat and handed it to her. She frowned at the cloth. "It's the best I can do on short notice," he said.

She grimaced and put the white linen to her mouth. Julien prayed Luc would not see this.

He reached down and put a hand on her elbow. "Let's get you to the sofa. You can lie down."

She didn't protest, just allowed him to help her

to her feet. She wobbled slightly, and he put an arm around her slim waist. At his touch, she inhaled sharply and glanced at him.

As he had noted before, she was tall, the top of her head reaching just below his nose. And he could see now that she had eyes not the color of chocolate but of creamy tea, long eyelashes, and—he inhaled slowly—ripe, full lips.

He looked away quickly, trying not to notice how the swell of her breast felt where it brushed his chest. They reached the sofa, and he settled her on it, both relieved and annoyed to release her.

"Lie down," he ordered, his voice gruffer than he had intended.

She did as he ordered, lying stiff as a board and staring at him as though he planned to chop her head off.

Grimsby entered, and Julien motioned to the vase. "Clean that."

"Yes, Your Grace."

While Grimsby carried the vase out, Julien crossed to the tea service and poured the chit a cup of tea. "Cream or sugar?" he asked, looking over his shoulder.

She was staring at him, wide-eyed and terrified. She shook her head.

He brought her the tea, and she struggled to sit so that she could drink it. Julien pretended not to notice her hands were trembling so badly that the tea cup and saucer rattled loudly.

She was no typical English beauty. Years of life surrounded by those pale, blond creatures had dulled his memory of dark-eyed Gallic women. His mother had told him Delphine, the comtesse de Guyenne, had been ravishing in her day. Obviously, the daughter had inherited her mother's good looks. But there was nothing in her that flaunted that beauty. She seemed almost unaware of it.

She was taller and thinner than most of the women of his acquaintance, but she was far from angular. She was not falling out of her gown, as was a la mode, but she was rounded and curved in all the places a woman should be. Yes, all in all, she was a beautiful package, but he felt something more for her than attraction. He felt longing. His gaze fell to her mouth, her lips poised on the edge of the tea cup.

Those lips gave him ideas.

"What happened?"

Julien turned as his mother and the housekeeper rushed into the drawing room. His mother was beside Mademoiselle Serafina in an instant. "Are you unwell, my dear?" She put a hand to Mademoiselle Serafina's forehead. "You don't feel warm. Come." She urged the girl to stand. "Let's get you to bed."

"That's not necessary," the girl said, her eyes still darting about the room. "I'm fine. I must have eaten something that didn't agree with me."

Julien watched as his mother and the housekeeper escorted the girl from the room. He followed them into the hallway and heard the housekeeper ask, "Where is your luggage, my lady? The footman said there was none in the carriage."

Mademoiselle Serafina stumbled and quickly righted herself. "It's coming. It was—lost."

"Oh, dear!" his mother exclaimed. "What will you do?"

"The—dock… workers are bringing it."

"I see." His mother glanced over her shoulder and met his gaze.

Julien could say one thing for Serafina Artois. She was not boring.

～

Sarah wanted to die. As soon as the duchesse and the housekeeper left her, Sarah dismissed her maid and climbed into the enormous bed. She lay there for a moment, looking about the room. She had made two more mistakes as soon as she set foot in this room. First, she had thanked the housekeeper for showing her the way. Aristocrats did not thank servants, and the woman had given her a quizzical look. The second mistake was asking—twice—if all this were really hers. She had never slept in such a beautiful room, such a large bed, such lavish quarters.

She blinked, certain it would all disappear. But, no, the walls were still lavender, the sheer cream curtains still pulled back from floor-length windows, the white and gold fireplace still crackled with a cheery little fire. Tucked in one corner was a walnut and satinwood armoire, decorated with paintings copied from Greek antiquity and carved with corner finials and rosettes. In another corner was a delicate tulipwood dressing table with a hinged mirror that could be raised when in use. Finally, there was the bed on which she lay—a half tester with matching canopy and bedclothes in blue satin— bedclothes the color of the duc de Valère's eyes.

She pulled the covers over her head and squeezed her own eyes shut.

She was mortified. Humiliated. She was never going to recover from this indignity.

She had actually cast up her accounts in front of a duc! Could anything be worse?

Well, she supposed having sharp needles stuck in her eyes would be worse, but not much.

And he was a handsome duc. Why hadn't The Widow deigned to mention that little fact? The man was a veritable god. Sarah closed her eyes, but she could not strike his image from her memory.

He was tall—that was her first problem. She adored tall men, men who made her feel small and petite beside them. Not that she had ever known a man like that, but a girl could dream. When the duc de Valère had helped her to her feet and put his arm around her, Sarah had felt slight and dainty.

Not only was he tall, he was muscular. His chest was broad, his arms like steel, his shoulders square.

And his neck. When he had removed his cravat, she had seen a good deal of the solid bronze flesh beneath. She liked the way his black hair curled against it. She had rarely seen a nobleman with hair longer than his collar, but she could not stop thinking about the way the duc's hair swept back from his forehead and fell softly until it grazed his collar.

He was obviously no typical nobleman. He had not shaved that day and possibly not the day before. His square chin was shadowed, giving him a slightly dangerous look that Sarah was willing to argue contributed to her nervousness. But what had really done her in were his eyes. They were so blue—and so penetrating. She was certain he could look straight through her and know she was never, and would never be, Mademoiselle Serafina Artois.

Sarah tossed off the bedclothes and lay staring at the ceiling. She had humiliated herself in front of a duc, tossed her accounts in what was probably an expensive vase, and broken a porcelain bowl. She hoped it had not been Sévres.

A disastrous start. But that did not mean this scheme was doomed. For her own sake, she must become Mademoiselle Serafina. She could not afford to fail, and that meant no more nervousness, no more casting up of accounts, and no more mistakes!

There was a tap on the door, and Sarah steeled herself. Slowly, she pulled the bedclothes back into place and composed her expression. "Come in."

The duchesse and her housekeeper entered, the latter carrying a silver tray with two linen-covered dishes. "How are you feeling?" the duchesse asked. "Do you think you could keep down a little soup?"

Sarah gave what she hoped was a stately smile. "Yes. I'm much better now. Thank you for bringing dinner to my room." Especially as she didn't think she could have made it through a formal dinner. Not tonight.

"There's soup and bread and butter. If you feel hungry later, just ring, and Mrs. Eggers will bring more."

"Thank you. This is more than generous."

"Nonsense." The duchesse waved a hand. "I'm sure you're used to far finer."

Sarah gave her a vague smile.

"I do hope you are over this indigestion tomorrow," the duchesse added as the housekeeper set the tray on the bedside table. Sarah was careful not to thank her.

"We've been invited to a ball hosted by Lord Aldon, and I so want to introduce you to everyone. Several of the guests are French émigrés and will have known your parents from before the revolution."

Sarah swallowed and stubbornly pushed down the fear that threatened to erupt again. "A ball?" she said as though that were all she had ever desired in the world. "How wonderful."

"I do hope your luggage will arrive in time. If not, perhaps we can find something of mine that will suit you."

Now this truly was unexpected. "Again, Your Grace, you're more than generous."

"Call me Rowena. After all, you'll be here several months, and I anticipate that we shall become great friends."

Sarah sensed the duchesse would have preferred if she tried out the new name immediately, but she simply could not do it. Not yet. Still, it was a kind and welcoming gesture.

She had a brief flash of one of her phantom memories—a dark-haired woman singing—and then it was gone.

"We'll leave you in peace," the duchesse said, turning toward the door. "Let me know if you need anything. Anything at all."

"Thank you."

The door closed, and Sarah nodded to herself. She had done better that time. Her nervousness was decreasing and her confidence growing, especially if she did not think too much about the duchesse's last words—the duchesse expected her to stay for months.

Months as Serafina Artois! And the sham started with a ball tomorrow night.

A ball!

Sarah had never been to a ball in her life. The closest she had come was encouraging the Jenkins boys—the children of her last employer—to say goodnight to their parents as Mr. and Mrs. Jenkins left for a ball. It was the only one she ever remembered them attending.

But she would have to get through it somehow. If she could avoid dancing and pretend she spoke everyday with viscounts, earls, barons, and marquesses, she would be fine. Just fine.

And then she had an alarming thought. What if the duchesse—Rowena—expected her to dance with her son, the duc de Valère? Surely, he would ask her to dance. It would be rude of him not to.

Oh, no. No, no, no. She would never survive a dance with the duc.

She had to find a way out of this.

She could feign sickness again, but that would not work forever. Eventually she would have to get well and go to social outings. And she did not want to go to social outings. She wanted to be back at Sir Northrop's with Anne and Edmund, looking at insects in the garden and studying geography. Sarah sighed. The only way to return to her charges was to do as Sir Northrop expected: find evidence implicating the duke.

And if she wanted to avoid dancing with the handsome duc, she would have to do so tonight.

❧

Julien sat in his library, brandy in one hand, book in the other. His dark blue coat was wrinkled, and he wore no cravat. The lamp had long since burned down, but he hadn't closed the book or finished his brandy or made any move to go to bed. He was exhausted after staying out all night, but he didn't relish sleep. Sleep brought dreams.

His mind was working now, figuring out how he could slip into France, meet the servant who claimed to know of Armand, and get back to London again. All without being caught by either the French or the English and being accused by one, or both sides, of being a traitor.

The two countries were at war—that much was true, but Julien did not think the situation could be any worse now than in '94, when he had gone back several times looking for Bastien and Armand.

That had been during the Reign of Terror, when the streets ran with the blood of his fellow aristocrats. If he had been caught then, he would have been a dead man. But he had not been caught, and he had not stopped searching for his brothers. After Napoleon seized power in France, the terror quieted, but on each of Julien's voyages, travel between the two countries grew more and more treacherous. Even the smugglers hesitated to risk it, despite the fact that French wines and fashions sold at a premium on London's black market.

Rigby was right: he was a fool to go back. Julien just could not see that he had any other choice. If Armand was alive, however remote the possibility, Julien would risk anything to reach him.

He heard a thud outside the library door and tensed, every muscle in his body straining to hear.

All was silent. It was probably just one of the servants. Probably just the house settling.

But Julien did not relax. The image of a white-haired woman wielding a pitchfork rose in front of him. Julien pushed it away. He really should go to bed. His mind was playing tricks on him.

Then something moved outside the library door. Julien's gaze darted to the floor, and he saw the shadow darkening the thin slice between the carpet and the closed door.

Luc? Grimsby?

Julien did not move. There was a knife in his desk drawer. Should he go for it or wait for the intruder to move first?

The door handle turned slowly, silently. Julien no longer harbored any illusions that it was his valet or his butler. Both would have knocked before entering.

The hinges creaked, and the intruder paused on the other side of the half-open door. He carried no light, but the library was darker than the vestibule, and it would take a moment for his eyes to adjust. Julien knew he could use that to his advantage.

Obviously satisfied he had not been detected, the intruder pushed the door open farther and stepped into the library. He closed the door silently behind him, then without looking right or left, went straight for the desk. The trespasser was short and slight and—wearing a dress?

What the—

Julien stared in disbelief as the woman rounded his desk, sat in his chair, and then felt around the surface of the desk for a lamp.

"The oil burned down," Julien said dryly, the satisfaction of seeing her jump making him smile briefly. "But I can light a candle if you'd like."

"No," she squeaked. "That's quite alright."

That voice, that tall, slim figure—Julien closed his eyes and groaned inwardly. "Mademoiselle Serafina?"

"Who? Oh! Me." She cleared her throat. "Your Grace, I can explain."

Julien set his book and brandy on the side table, rose, and lit a candle on his desk. The warm light flickered over Mademoiselle Serafina's features, making her brown eyes look large and luminous. Her hair was loose about her shoulders, falling in ribbons of silk down her back. She had not changed out of her blue gown. It was wrinkled and falling off one shoulder but still presentable.

He put both hands on the desk and gave her a hard look, this woman who was to be his wife. Did she know that was the plan? It had never been discussed.

He shook his head. Of course she knew. Women always knew.

She cleared her throat again, the slim white column of her neck drawing his attention. "As I said, I can explain."

He waved a hand and went back to his seat on the sofa against the wall. Lifting his brandy, he took a long swallow, almost draining it. "Go ahead. Explain."

"You're not foxed, are you?"

He raised a brow. "Would that be a problem? After all, I'm in my own home, in my own library. And up until five minutes ago, I was quite alone."

She swallowed again. Was her face slightly paler?

"Are you going to be sick again?"

She straightened her shoulders and notched her chin up, looking slightly offended. "I'm fine. Thank you."

"There's an empty decanter behind you. Costs a hell of a lot less than the Ming vase you made use of this afternoon."

She narrowed her eyes at him, obviously annoyed. "A gentleman would not have mentioned that incident again," she said, tone frosty.

He shrugged, not feeling the least compunction to act the gentleman when she was the one who had invaded his library. He took another drink from his glass and studied her. "You don't have any accent," he said finally.

"What?" She frowned at him, probably thinking he was foxed.

"Your English." He sat forward now. "You have no French accent, not even a trace." He was always keenly aware of his own accent, knew no matter how perfect his English, it would always mark him as a foreigner.

She put a hand to her throat. "Well, I was so young when I left France that—"

"For Italy."

"Yes. My parents live in Italy."

"And yet you have no Italian accent."

She opened her mouth then closed it again.

"Say again?"

"We speak English."

"Your parents are French, you live in Italy, but you speak English."

She shrugged, a dainty gesture that caused one

ribbon of hair to fall over her shoulder and caress his desk. He stared at it.

"We're eccentric." She looked him full in the face, daring him to question her.

He raised his glass in a mock salute. "That must explain why you're wandering about my home in the middle of the night, creeping into my library. What were you looking for?"

"Paper and pen," she said rapidly.

"Why?"

"I needed to write a letter. Immediately."

"To whom?"

"My mother. You know that my father has been so ill…" Her gaze drifted to his desk, and he followed it, hoping no important papers were lying about. He noted the envelope containing the letter about Armand. His hand itched to move it, but that would only draw her attention to it.

How could he be such a fool as to leave it lying out? Enough toying with her. He would give her the paper and send her back to bed.

He leaned down, easing open the drawer where he kept the parchment. He reached inside, and something silky brushed over his knuckles. He glanced up to find Mademoiselle Serafina looking over his shoulder to study the contents of the drawer.

She gave him a sheepish smile.

"Here." He handed her several sheets of paper, a pen, and a jar of ink. "Anything else?"

"No."

He gave his desk chair a pointed look, and she rose, clutching the writing supplies to her chest.

"I'll just go back to bed now."

He went to the library door and opened it for her. "Good night."

But as she walked toward him, it occurred to him that this was probably as good a time as any. After all, they were alone, and he did rather want to get the whole business over with so he could concentrate on plans to travel to France.

She reached the door, but he shut it again in front of her. She stopped short and gave him a nervous glance. "What are you doing?"

What *was* he doing?

Vengeance. Think about vengeance and duty, he ordered himself.

"Mademoiselle Serafina, we both know why you're here."

"We do?" The color drained from her face, and he saw now that she had freckles across her nose and her cheeks. She stared at him and clutched the paper so tightly she wrinkled it. "Who told you?"

He frowned. "No one told me. I know what's expected of me, and I have no objection."

Now she frowned, confusion in her eyes. He gritted his teeth. Hell, he hoped she wasn't going to make this more difficult than it had to be.

"So?" he prodded. "What do you say?"

She was watching him closely, looking uncertain. "I… have… no objection either." Her words were slow and measured.

"*Très bien. D'accord.* My mother will want to start the wedding preparations immediately." He turned away from her, snatched the letter about Armand, and tucked it into his coat pocket.

"What?"

He heard her drop the paper and pen and looked back to see her standing stiff and wide-eyed. "What wedding?"

"Our wedding. You just agreed to be my wife."

Six

SARAH FELT HER STOMACH HEAVE VIOLENTLY, FELT THE room sway before her, and reached out for something solid. She closed her hand on the first object she touched—the duc's arm. It was warm and solid under her fingers, and when she looked into his eyes, they met hers.

Heart beating fast, Sarah looked away and released him. Her head was spinning, and her ears were ringing. She could not have heard him correctly.

The duc had not looked away from her. "Are you feeling unwell?"

"Yes. No." She could feel her cheeks burning. *Say it, you ninny!* "Yes. I think there's been a misunderstanding."

He narrowed his eyes. "I see."

"When you were ah—" How to say this? How exactly did one turn down a duc's marriage proposal? "When you were proposing, I didn't realize you were proposing."

He raised a dark brow, annoyance darkening his features. "What did you think I was doing?"

"I-I…" She pressed her lips together. There was simply no getting around the embarrassment. "I don't know. I'm sorry."

He was frowning now, and that made the room spin again. "You said you didn't have any objection."

"I know." How could she explain that she was trying to keep him from guessing she was an imposter?

She couldn't.

The duc raised a brow. "But you do accept." It was more a statement than a question, and he was already turning away from her.

"Not exactly."

He stopped, turned back, gave her his full attention. She opened her mouth, shut it.

What was she doing? Turning down a duc's proposal? Was she mad? She could be the duchesse de Valère.

Of course, if The Widow and Sir Northrop were correct, she would also be the wife of a traitor.

And then there was the minor fact that the duc had proposed to Mademoiselle Serafina Artois, and she was Sarah Smith. Chances were he would notice the name change during the ceremony.

"Not exactly?" The duc crossed his arms over his broad chest. It was an intimidating gesture, whether he realized it or not.

Sarah supposed he realized it. She took a fortifying breath. "I'm afraid I can't accept."

He scowled at her, and she resisted taking a step back. He looked even more intimidating when he scowled. Dangerous as well. "You're refusing my offer."

He seemed to be saying it more to himself than

to her, so she did not answer. He shook his head, locked his hands behind his back, and turned away from her.

Sarah glanced at the door, wondering if she could go back to her room. The duc began to pace, and she said, "I think I'll go up to my room now."

He didn't answer, simply kept pacing.

Very well. She would take that as an affirmative. Besides, she was Mademoiselle Serafina. She did not need to wait for permission.

She reached for the door handle, and he spun toward her. "May I ask why?"

Sarah's hand froze in midair. "Why what?"

His azure blue eyes darkened. "Why you've refused me."

"Oh. Well…" She could hardly tell him the truth, which meant she would have to lie again. Or… tell him part of the truth. "We hardly know one another."

He stared at her, and she awkwardly lowered her hand to her side again, twisting her fingers in her gown.

"Go on."

Sarah frowned. What more was there to say? Who would accept a proposal from someone they hardly knew? Was that not self-explanatory? But he was still looking at her. She needed another reason. "I suppose what I'm saying is that I'm not in love with you."

"Nor I you. But what has that to do with anything?"

Sarah blinked. Of course! She was such a fool. The aristocracy routinely married for money or position, but she could not change direction now. "What does love have to do with marriage?" she scoffed, playing Serafina to the hilt. "Are you that obtuse?" Immediately, her eyes widened, and she clamped her mouth shut. Had she just called a duc obtuse?

Fortunately, the duc did not seem to notice her insolence. He heaved out a great sigh and ran a hand through his black hair. Sarah watched transfixed as it fell in layers right back in place. She wondered how that hair would feel between her own fingers.

"You want romance, is that it?" He sounded quite put out by the idea, which irritated her for her some reason. She was not asking for romance for herself—she was not naïve enough to believe that would ever happen—but didn't Mademoiselle Serafina deserve at least to be courted? Or was this duc so full of himself that he thought women should fall at his feet?

"I don't want anything from you, sir. I just want to go to bed."

His eyes flickered at her words, and she realized the mistake in wording.

She hastened to correct her mistake. "What I meant was—"

"I know what you meant. What I don't understand is why you should come all the way from Italy just to refuse my proposal. Your mother could have done that via the post."

"What do you—" Understanding flashed through her like the sun through clouds. The duc and his mother had assumed she was coming with the intention of marrying Valère. Perhaps all had even been arranged in the letters exchanged between the duchesse and the Foreign Office.

But, no. She had seen the correspondence. No mention of marriage had been made. No *overt* mention—that would be vulgar. But there had been allusions, veiled allusions.

She could kill Sir Northrop and The Widow for not having foreseen this possibility or instructing her how to respond. Perhaps she should have accepted?

The duc was still watching her, irritation making his dark brows a slash over those magnetic blue eyes.

"I-I…" Her mind raced for the correct response, but her thoughts were a muddle. His features darkened, and she took a step back. Why had she not gone to her room when she had the opportunity?

"But perhaps you never had any intention of accepting my proposal," the duc said now, voice icy. "Perhaps you had other motivations for coming."

She raised her brows. "I did?"

"Did you?"

"No." None besides snooping through his personal items and determining whether or not he was a spy. Her gaze traveled to his desk again. She might not be a professional spy, but she had seen the letter with the French markings on it. If only she had been alone, she could have pocketed it, and this nightmare would be over.

"Perhaps you want to survey the field before you make any commitments."

She blinked, dragging her gaze from his desk. "Survey the field?"

He gave her a look that said he knew she understood every word he said. She wanted to laugh, He thought she was being difficult, when in reality, she had simply not been paying attention.

"The other eligible bachelors in the *ton*," he said, voice edged with steel.

"Oh, no." She shook her heard violently. "I don't want to do that." Too late she realized such a firm denial would probably confirm his suspicions.

"Not to worry. You'll have your opportunity tomorrow night at Lord Aldon's ball. I'll chaperone you, of course. Introduce you to London's finest." He reached for the door handle and pulled the door open.

"But I'm not interested in London's finest," she protested, envisioning having to dance with half a dozen men. "I don't even want to go to the ball."

But he was not listening. He stalked through the vestibule and up the marble stairs. Sarah watched until he disappeared. She sighed, already weary of playing Mademoiselle Serafina, but she was not so weary as to forget about the letter she had seen on his desk.

Heart pounding, she turned back to it and hurried across the room. Her gaze scanned the desk quickly. Where was it? Where *was* it? Oh, if only she had her spectacles—

"Mademoiselle, is there anything you require?"

Sarah let out a short squeak and whirled about. The butler, Grimsby, was standing in the doorway, keys in hand. Valère must have sent him back to lock the door.

Sarah cleared her throat. "No. I was just going up to my room."

"Shall I light your way?"

She shook her head. "I'll manage."

⚜

The next day was a blur of primping and preparation. The rest of Serafina's clothing arrived first thing in the morning, and Sarah was awakened by Katarina, her Italian lady's maid, unpacking the trunk and shaking wrinkles out of the gowns.

When Sarah poked her head out of the bedclothes, Katarina began babbling away in Italian. Sarah nodded, pretending to understand. Not long after, the duchesse descended. Intent on playing her part, Sarah was still in bed, sampling from a tray of coffee and scones the housekeeper had set on her bedside table a few moments before.

The duchesse entered, did not bat an eye that Sarah was still abed, and ordered her to take a hot bath. Then she inquired as to whether Katarina would be offended if Serafina had her hair done by Madame Leroix. She was the most fashionable hairdresser in London at the moment, and everyone knew the French had superior talents when it came to coiffure.

"Oh, please don't go to so much trouble on my behalf," Sarah urged, though she knew her protests would be to no avail. But she was beginning to feel guilty at all of the attention being paid to her. Who was she to deserve to sleep on silk sheets, have a maid unpack her things, and a housekeeper bring her breakfast in bed? She was no one—her parents unknown and most likely disreputable. If the duchesse knew who she really was—

Sarah swallowed. No, the duchesse would never know. More importantly, the duc would never know.

"You make use of Madame Leroix, Your Grace. I assure you, Katarina will do well enough for me."

The duchesse smiled benevolently. "You don't want to offend your sweet little maid. I understand. Give me the words, and I'll give her the bad news."

Sarah's gaze darted to Katarina, who was across the room, humming to herself and carefully placing folded garments in the clothespress.

"The words?"

"The Italian. *Scusi, signorina?*"

Katarina turned sharply, her face lighting at the sound of the duchesse's Italian. Sarah wanted to groan in frustration. It was too early for so many complications!

"Un momento, per favore." The duchesse turned back to Sarah. "Serafina, how do I tell her that her services won't be required this evening?"

Sarah gritted her teeth. At the moment, she remembered exactly three words in Italian: *bravo, arrivederci,* and *grazie*. None of those would help in this situation. She was tired, she was irritable, and she was hungry. For a moment, she was tempted to tell the duchesse the truth and end this whole charade.

But then she had a quick image of herself on the streets, huddled in a doorway, fending off a leering, gap-toothed ruffian.

Sir Northrop wouldn't really put her out on the streets, would he?

Oh, yes, he would. Especially if she made a muddle of this assignment. If she compromised national security by informing the mother of a traitor that the Foreign Office was spying on them.

Sarah glanced at the duchesse and wondered how she was going to get out of this muddle. "Your Grace?"

The duchesse frowned.

Sarah gave herself a mental kick. The duchesse had asked to be called by her Christian name. "Rowena," she managed, though it went against all of her training to be so informal. "My maid and I have a…" She glanced at the ceiling, hoping she looked thoughtful, her mind racing for some plausible excuse. "A complicated relationship."

It was vague, but vague was good.

"Would you mind if I spoke with her privately?" Sarah lowered her voice. "I don't want to hurt her feelings."

The duchesse nodded in understanding. "Of course. I leave you to it. I'll have that bath sent up for you right away, and Madame Leroix will be here this afternoon." She turned toward the door, then back again. Her eyes were soft and shining. "Oh, Serafina, I cannot tell you how excited I am. I've been waiting for this day for so, so long!"

And with a quick dab at her eyes, she was gone.

Sarah leaned back on the pillows and closed her eyes. She hated this. She absolutely hated this. After her conversation with the duc the night before, now she knew why his mother was so intent on making her welcome: she thought she would soon acquire a daughter-in-law.

Instead, Sarah was going to be the cause of her losing a son to prison or worse. The penalty for treason was drawing and quartering.

Sarah shook her head. She did not want to think of that, did not want to think of the handsome duc on trial at the Old Bailey, the leering crowd of spectators, each paying a farthing for admittance to the show.

Would she have to testify? She supposed she would. How would she stand tall and keep her chin up then, when she was face to face with the duc and he knew the truth: she was no comte's daughter.

She glanced at Katarina and saw the girl looking at her. If Sarah was not really the daughter of a French comte, was Katarina really a maid? Was she even Italian?

Sinking down, Sarah tried to remember when life became so complicated.

&c&

In his dressing room, Julien tried not to think about how much he hated social outings. He scowled at his valet as Luc held out a dark blue coat and proceeded to stuff Julien into it.

"All in the name of fashion, no?" Luc said, straightening the tight coat.

Julien didn't answer. He tolerated the stuffy clothing necessary for the balls, musicales, and fêtes because his mother enjoyed the outings and because at times they were useful for business purposes. It was far more useful to go to his club or his solicitor and do business there, but it never hurt to put on his finest and be seen in the homes of England's beau monde.

He knew part of his allure was curiosity. Not just that he was a refugee from France—there were many of those in London, especially in the years directly following the revolution. Those who had settled in London had done so very modestly. His counterparts, former comtes and barons and the sons of vicomtes and marquesses, taught French to English schoolboys or attempted to learn professions.

Some, like Julien, were lucky. Julien's father had foreseen the trouble brewing in France and had sent what money he could to London. It was not much—most of the Valère fortune had been in land. But it was enough that Julien and his mother did not have to rely solely on her parents. They were also wealthy, but their money was likewise tied up in land.

The real curiosity for these English was that Julien, due to his efforts, was a *wealthy* French émigré. His mother had been frugal with the money his father had left them, and when Julien was eighteen, he began to invest it.

He began small in proven, low-risk ventures. But gradually, as he became more confident, he took greater risks—and reaped greater rewards. His risks were never foolish. He took the time to investigate each scheme thoroughly, and he found he had a talent for separating the wheat from the chaff.

Now, at twenty-five years of age, he owned a shipping company, several merchant ships, and warehouses. The *ton* had to know the money his father had left him was gone, replaced by money he had earned in trade, more or less. But he had the title and the money that went along with it at one time, and that seemed good enough for them.

"How should I tie your cravat tonight, Monsieur le Duc?"

Julien raised a brow.

"The Oriental? The Mathematical? The Napoleon?"

"No, not that last one. Just knot it. I want to look at some papers before the ladies come down."

"Of course." Luc began to tie the cravat. Julien

prayed his valet would be satisfied with the first effort. He did not have the patience to endure several attempts tonight.

Not that anyone would be looking at his neck cloth. Sometimes Julien felt as though he were covered in money, the way mothers of young, unmarried ladies eyed him. Julien had heard rumors he was worth more than ten thousand a year, which was not true of course. It was more like eight thousand, but if he denied the ten, people would only believe it more. The English were peculiar in that way.

Luc stepped back, observed his work, and frowned. But before his valet could undo the knot, Julien moved away. "This is fine. Thank you." It was a dismissal, but Luc made no move to leave.

"I would have thought Monsieur le Duc wanted everything perfect for Mademoiselle Serafina Artois."

Julien gave him a hard look. "You would have thought wrong."

The valet tapped his cleft chin. He had a narrow face and jet black hair swept back from a high forehead. His clothing was always impeccable. Hell, Julien thought, the man dressed better than he did.

"So Mademoiselle Serafina is not to your taste."

"Not exactly," Julien said, thinking back to her response the night before. Who answered a marriage proposal with *not exactly*? He pulled on his gloves.

He had told himself half a dozen times the night before that he was glad of her rejection. Glad he wasn't going to have to pretend to be madly in love, buying her flowers and writing her love poems.

But if he was so glad, why did he feel so annoyed?

"What do you find not to like?"

Julien scowled at him. He had known Luc for years, but the valet could overstep his bounds. "You needn't wait up tonight," Julien said, leaving the dressing room to walk through his bedroom. "I can undress myself."

"And throw all the clothes on the floor," Luc accused.

Julien shook his head and opened the door. He would attend the ball, do his duty and escort Mademoiselle Serafina, but he would think no more of her than he did any other task which befell him. She was a task. That was all. Not much different than balancing his ledgers. He'd taken three steps down the hall, heading for the staircase, before he saw her.

At that moment he had two thoughts: was her bedroom really that close to his, and had any of his ledgers ever looked that beautiful?

Seven

SHE STOPPED, HER BROWN EYES WIDENING WHEN SHE saw him looking at her. He supposed he was scowling—not the appropriate response—but what else was he supposed to do when hit by a wave of arousal so hard it made his head hurt?

The women had been up here all day primping, and obviously not without benefit. Mademoiselle Serafina wore a tunic of pink silk over a train of white silk. Her sleeves were full and short, though her arms were covered by pink gloves that matched her dress. Her bosom was not so well covered. The evening gown had a rounded neck that dipped low enough to show a tantalizing swell of rounded breasts. Julien could have focused on that creamy display of skin all evening, but he forced his eyes upward—and was not disappointed.

Her long brown hair swept dramatically away from her face. Coiling on top of her head like a dark serpent, it sparkled with what looked like jewels. With her hair pulled away, her fine bone structure was apparent. She had elegant cheekbones, a straight nose, and large eyes.

And then there was the mouth. Someone had rouged her lips, and now they looked moist and ripe as a strawberry. She was watching him, that mouth slightly parted, and he wondered what she would do if he strolled up to her, swept her into his arms, and kissed her thoroughly.

He was tempted to find out.

"Is something wrong?" she asked, glancing down at her gown then back up at him.

"No." He clenched his jaw, annoyed at himself. He was not supposed to be thinking of her anymore.

She smoothed her hands over the pink gown she wore, drawing his attention to it again. It was an interesting choice, as the colors and the style made her look young and innocent. But one look at the neckline and the display of soft, porcelain flesh, and Julien was in no doubt that this was no child. He tried to focus on something else—the way the gown cinched in just beneath that roundness, the perfect lines of the train, the quality of the material.

No. None of that drew his attention as much as that low neckline. Unfortunately, she seemed aware his gaze was locked on her bosom. She lifted a hand, fingering the small diamond necklace she wore. Besides the necklace and dainty earbobs, she wore no other jewelry, which was not the fashion. That was to her credit, as he liked her simplicity. He liked it all—too much.

"I was just going downstairs." She reached down and adjusted the fingers of one glove, her face flushed now, her eyes not meeting his.

"I'll escort you." Before he could think his actions through, he held out one arm.

She looked at it reluctantly, and he wanted to kick himself. Why was he electing to spend time with her? He had done his duty, asked for her hand, and—except for a turn around the ballroom and a dance or two—he could be done with her. If only he could stop imagining his hands freeing that silky hair and watching it cascade over her bare back.

"Thank you." She took his arm, and he moved forward, escorting her down the marble staircase. "Are you anticipating the ball?"

He knew this was idle chatter, something polite to say to break the tension. Something to assure him that she was not going to bring up details of the night before.

But he didn't feel like excusing her that easily.

"I doubt I'm anticipating it as much as you, my lady."

She glanced at him, those milk-and-tea-colored eyes wide with confusion. Was she really that guileless?

"I'm actually not anticipating the evening at all," she said, and he could see it was the truth—not some carefully crafted rejoinder. "I told you I preferred not to attend."

"Ah, but there's no romance here."

He saw her chin hitch up a notch. "Oh. This is about last night."

They reached the vestibule, and she released his arm, moved away. His mother was still preparing for the ball. Now was the time to go to his office, look at those papers. He should leave Mademoiselle Serafina Artois to entertain herself until it was his duty to do so.

He glanced at the library door, closed and locked—as he had instructed Grimsby to keep it from now on—but he didn't move in that direction. Instead, he turned back to her, clasped his hands behind his back. "Marriage is my duty," he said. She had been studying a painting, and he saw her form go rigid at his statement. "I don't expect you to understand this, but I take duty seriously."

She turned to face him. "So your proposal last night was purely a matter of duty. A business arrangement." Her eyes flashed, and he thought he saw a hint of annoyance in her face.

"It's not romantic. Though it is fitting."

She stepped forward. "How so?"

"The goal of the revolution, of Robespierre and his ilk, was to snuff us out. If you and I were to marry, produce offspring, we'd defeat that. We'd beat them."

"You sweep me off my feet, Your Grace."

He could not help but smile at that. The chit had some backbone. "You want to be swept off your feet, you'll find plenty who'll try at Aldon's ball. They may not know much about duty, but then that isn't your concern."

Her eyes flashed at that. Oh, yes, she definitely had some backbone.

"I see. So because I turned down your... business proposal, I now have no sense of duty?"

He shrugged. "It's not generally something women concern themselves with."

Her head snapped up, making her stance regal and indignant. And annoyed. "Oh, really? Why you—" She stopped, making him wonder just what epithet she would have used. "You know nothing about me or my sense of duty."

He crossed his arms over his chest, enjoying the repartee. "I know you want romance."

She stalked closer to him. "And I know you're relieved to be free of the *duty* of marrying me. However, I must point out, Your Grace, were this matrimonial duty truly so important to you, you might have tried just a tiny bit harder to accomplish it."

He stiffened. "Are you that shallow?"

She blinked, close enough now that he could see what looked like gold flecks in her brown eyes. "I'm afraid not. The truth is that no matter how you'd proposed, the answer would still have been no."

He opened his mouth to say he knew not what, and his mother called, "What's this? Is anything wrong?"

Mademoiselle Serafina jumped back as though burned, but he took his time. Deliberately, he turned and nodded to his mother. "*Bon soir, ma mère.* You look lovely." He extended his arm as she reached the landing. She took it, but her eyes were darting from him to Mademoiselle Serafina.

"Were you quarreling?" She addressed Mademoiselle Serafina, who was looking at the same painting again.

Mademoiselle Serafina turned, pretending she had not heard. "*Excusez-moi?* Oh, Your Grace, you look beautiful. *Trés magnifique.*"

"*Merci—*"

"What is that material? Satin?" Mademoiselle Serafina moved closer to admire the dress.

"Why, yes, it is satin. Do you like it? I was afraid the color might not suit me."

"Oh, no. I love burnished copper. It's perfect." Mademoiselle Serafina shot him a sidelong look, and he had to give her credit. She evaded the question better than any barrister might.

That didn't mean he wasn't still annoyed. And after their exchange tonight, he might even notch that up to aggravated. But he would have to put all of that aside for the moment. The ball and duty called.

∽◦∾

Sarah had been at the ball for a good quarter hour before she stopped staring and was able to form a coherent statement. It was not so much that she was impressed by the ballroom or the titled guests, but she could not believe the way in which some of the crème de la crème behaved. The low necklines of the gowns, the men's leering stares, the blatant flirting with anyone other than one's spouse. It was quite a departure from the Puritan values she'd been taught at the Academy.

"Are you feeling well, Serafina?" the duchesse asked for what must have been the third time. "Julien, fetch her a glass of lemon water, *s'il vous plaît*."

Sarah did not think lemon water would fix this dissolute gathering, but she let the duc go. She could breathe more easily when he was not standing beside her.

"I'm fine. A little overwhelmed, I'm afraid."

The duchesse nodded. "These things are always a bit of a crush. Come, let's commandeer those chairs." She pointed to a matched pair of exquisitely carved straight-backed chairs upholstered in what looked like velvet. Behind them the wall was painted to resemble the heavens. The blues and whites were startling, as were the images of half-dressed angels or gods—she was not sure which—who frolicked there.

The ballroom, if not the guests, was exquisite. Sarah had not imagined there were rooms of such size in London. The city she knew was cramped and dirty, but this room was airy and immaculate—or at least it had been until half of the *ton* had descended. Now the polished wooden floors were covered with satin slippers and men's pumps. The huge French windows that overlooked extensive, sculptured grounds were blocked by forms dressed in every shade, from the whitest white to black as dark as midnight. The orchestra was seated in the balcony overlooking the spectacle, and they were just beginning to tune their instruments, causing the already noisy crowd to elevate the volume of their conversations.

No wonder the duc had not objected to fetching her a glass of lemon water. The refreshment room was probably quieter and less crowded. Sarah sat dutifully beside the duchesse and surveyed the enormous crystal chandelier hung from the ceiling. She did not think that one year of her wages would pay for a single crystal on that chandelier, and there were hundreds of crystals and three large chandeliers!

"Their Graces, the Duke and Duchess of Devonshire."

Sarah's head snapped around as the Devonshires were announced. Amazing that she, a simple governess, was at a sumptuous ball with the likes of the Duke of Devonshire! Who would be announced next? One of the princes? The King?

Oh, she did not belong here. She did not belong at all. Any moment, someone—perhaps the Duke of

Devonshire himself—would see her, point, and say, "What's *she* doing here?"

Sarah closed her eyes and tried to calm down. Of course she wasn't going to be exposed. She knew no one here, and even if she had known any of these fabulously wealthy people, they wouldn't have recognized her. She recalled the picture of herself in the glass before she had gone downstairs. She knew her pink silk gown, the color of a baby's lips, was perfectly appropriate for the evening. The modest diamond necklace and earrings she had chosen to wear with it showed wealth without being ostentatious. Madame Leroix—she had not been able to convince the duchesse that her hairdresser was not needed—had done wonders with her hair and cosmetics.

Even Valère had given her an admiring look—or two—when he had first seen her. She felt her cheeks heat now as she remembered the caress of his gaze over her body.

"Are you certain you feel well?" the duchesse asked again. "You're quite flushed."

"I'm fine." She must stop thinking of him! But Valère had looked at her in a way she was not used to. The honest approbation in his eyes made her feel beautiful. And in these clothes and with this hair and these diamonds, how could she not feel beautiful? Perhaps she actually looked as though she belonged at this ball and among these members of the peerage.

"Good. Then come with me," the duchesse said. "I want to introduce you to the Duke of York. He's just arrived."

Sarah balked. "Th-the Duke of York? The prince?"

The duchesse nodded. "Yes. Have you met before?"

Sarah shook her head, eager and nervous at the same time. "No. I-I…" Her mind raced for something to say when she met the duke. *Hello* seemed far too banal.

At the far side of the room, Valère was returning, two glasses of murky liquid in his hands. Sarah seized the opportunity to put off the introduction until she had thought of some witty bon mot. "I think I had better wait for the duc to return with the lemon water. I find my throat is parched."

The duchesse gave her a look, and Sarah wanted to shake her head. No, no, no. She knew what that look meant, and that was not why she wanted to wait for Valère at all.

"Of course. You wait here for Julien. I'm certain you two would like a few moments alone."

"No. That wasn't what I meant."

But the duchesse was already walking away, threading through the crowds toward a distinguished-looking man in military uniform.

Sarah took the opportunity to sink down again into one of the plush chairs. The ball was exciting and spectacular, but in her heart she knew, even if she woke up a duchess tomorrow, she would not belong here. She was a simple girl with simple dreams. She dreamed of a husband and, one day, children. She wanted love and laughter and a happy, uncomplicated life. She did not need jewels or expensive gowns; she just needed a man to know and love her for who she was—Sarah Smith, governess and orphan.

"Buona sera, signorina."

With a frown, Sarah looked up at the tall, red-haired man standing before her. He was dressed impeccably in evening attire. His cravat was a little too large and frilly, and his hair overly styled, but he had a friendly smile.

Why was he speaking Italian to her? Was this some strange aristocratic custom she did not know? *"Buona sera,"* she answered. She held out a hand, and he took it, kissed it.

"Bella. Molto bella." He did not release her hand.

She smiled, hoping whatever he had said was positive. Strange—with his red hair and fair skin, the man did not *look* Italian.

"Ha bisogno di—"

"Rigby, what are you doing?" Valère, holding the two glasses of lemon water, stood behind the red-haired man. The duc was scowling.

"Oh, hello, old boy. I was just introducing myself to this enchanting creature. Mademoiselle Serafina, I presume?" He winked at her.

So he *did* speak English. "Yes. And you are?"

Rigby looked surprised. He turned to Valère. "She speaks English?"

"Perfectly. Mademoiselle Serafina Artois, may I present Laurence Rigby."

Now she understood, and she wanted to groan. This man was a friend of Valère's, and he obviously expected *her* to speak fluent Italian. And with the duc standing right there, she could not exactly tell him that she knew only a handful of phrases. That would give her away for sure. Perhaps this man was also a spy—in league with Valère.

Belatedly, she realized the men were looking at her expectantly. "Oh!" She held out her hand again, and the red-haired man bowed over it. "Pleased to meet you, Mr. Rigby."

He looked up at her, brown eyes twinkling. "And I, you. I've been wanting to practice my Italian."

Of course he did. "Well, I'm the person for that," she said with as much cheer as she could muster. Here she was, masquerading as a Frenchwoman, at a ball filled with Englishmen, and she had to meet the one Englishman who wanted to speak Italian.

"*Magnifico!* How is this? *I cammelli sopravvivono nel deserto senza acqua.*"

Sarah blinked. What had he said? Something about camels? "*Benissimo!* That was perfect." But the man gave her a look rife with disappointment. Obviously, he wanted her to answer in Italian.

"Here." Valère shoved the glass of lemon water at her. Sarah sipped it eagerly. She could not be expected to speak Italian when she was drinking.

"Where is my mother?" Valère asked, his tone sharp and short.

"She went to speak with the Duke of York." Perhaps she should suggest they join the duchesse. Only half a glass of lemon water stood between her and the Italian language.

"Mademoiselle Serafina," Rigby began, "May I have this dance? Or should I say, *Potrei avere—*"

"No." Valère stood with arms folded over his chest. "I've already claimed the first dance."

Rigby nodded, turned back to her.

"And the second," Valère interjected.

Rigby frowned. "You can't keep her to yourself all night."

Valère offered his arm. "Watch me."

Sarah did not really want to take Valère's arm. He made her jittery and he made her angry and he made her feel far too warm for comfort.

But he did not speak to her in Italian. She supposed she should be grateful for small mercies.

"*Arrivederci!*" Rigby called after them. Sarah could not help but smile over her shoulder at him. He seemed a sweet boy.

"*Arrivederci!*" she called back, At least she knew what that meant.

"Don't encourage him," Valère snapped. He was staring straight ahead, leading her toward the actual ballroom, where she could hear the strings finishing their tuning and see couples lining up for a dance.

Sarah had always been slow to anger. Her easy temperament and her high level of tolerance was one reason she made a good governess, but she was at the end of her patience with Valère. He might be a duc, and he might be the most handsome man she had ever met, but he could also be exceedingly vexing and domineering.

"I wasn't encouraging him," she snapped back. "I was simply being polite—a skill, *Monsieur le Duc*—which you have yet to master." She wasn't afraid of him anymore. She wasn't even attracted to him anymore.

"Is that so?" He turned to face her, his eyes burning into her. Alright, then, perhaps she was still a little bit afraid and more than a little attracted. But she was standing her ground.

"It is." Unfortunately, her voice hadn't stood her ground with her. It sounded weak and feeble.

He shook his head, obviously annoyed with her. "Let's dance." He made to pull her forward, but she resisted. Who had been this man's governess? He had appalling manners. He scowled at her. "What's wrong now?"

She resented the *now*. "I thought Frenchmen were supposed to be charming. Did that skip a generation in your case?"

He blinked at her, took a moment to process the statement, and then gave her a dry smile. "I'm half English. That's the boorish side of me."

"Yes, well, even an Englishman can request the pleasure of a dance."

Surprising her, he made a sweeping bow. "*Oui, mademoiselle.* May I have the pleasure of this dance?"

She frowned down at him. He was gazing at her through his eyelashes, his eyes daring her to reject him. People were watching them now. She could not very well say no without causing some speculation among the other guests.

And of course, now that the music began, she remembered that she was a horrible dancer. Oh, why had she encouraged him to ask her in such a way? She should have pled a headache and hid in the ladies' retiring room the rest of the evening!

Now she had no choice but to accept. "Of course."

He rose, made a grand gesture of offering his arm, and escorted her onto the dance floor. They took their place among the other couples, he across from her. She smiled at the others in their set, then leaned over and hissed, "Are you certain you want to dance, Your Grace?"

The couple beside him looked from her to Valère. Valère smiled at them, then her, tightly. The dance was already beginning. The first couple moved down the set. "I asked you to dance, and I escorted you here, so yes, I'm certain I want to dance."

"Oh." She watched the second couple, trying to memorize the forms. Was it a turn to the left and then a step or a turn-step-turn?

He was looking at her dubiously. "Why do you ask?"

The couple beside them began to repeat the forms, and Sarah felt her heart pump faster. Oh, how she regretted not having practiced dancing more.

He reached for her, and she stepped on his toe. "Oh, no reason."

He turned one way, and she went the other. Oh, how mortifying. But she would keep her chin up and get through this. It was no less than the Academy expected.

Valère tightened his grip on her hand. "It's a turn and then a step," he instructed. "Just listen to me."

She did. It was embarrassing that he had to tell her the forms, but she completed them successfully. She even began to smile. She was dancing. With Valère's help, she was actually doing this.

Despite the Italian and the dancing, she might get through this night yet.

And then at the edge of the crowds, frowning at her, she saw Sir Northrop. He held up ten fingers then walked away.

Sarah missed the next step.

Eight

"I'm so sorry," Sarah said for the tenth time as the duc de Valère escorted her from the ballroom. "My father has been ill for some time, and I have not wanted to dance. I'm afraid I'm out of practice." It was a clever lie, and she actually said it rather smoothly. But at that moment she would have given anything to be a better dancer than liar. The duc was limping—very slightly, but she noticed.

"It's fine," he said.

"No, it's not. You're limping."

He gave a surprised look. "Old injury. Nothing to do with you." He paused just at one of the doors of the ballroom, not caring that he was blocking the exit. Sarah squeezed into a corner with a potted plant to make more room. "Would you like me to fetch you a glass of champagne?"

He was still acting the perfect chaperone. Despite the fact that she had tread on his toes half a dozen times, he was going to fetch her a refreshment as was the custom. Obviously the duc could affect good manners when the moment called for them.

"No, thank you. I don't drink champagne."

"Well, I do." And he limped off.

So much for affecting good manners.

But his departure did give her a moment to think. During the dance, Sir Northrop had held up ten fingers. What could that mean? Ten o'clock? She glanced at the longcase clock across the room. It was quarter of ten now. But how would she know where to meet him?

If she were a spy—a real spy—where would she plan to meet? The terrace? The library? The conservatory? Did this house even have a conservatory?

She would start with the terrace. The French doors leading outside were just past the row of potted plants beside her.

"There you are, Serafina."

Sarah glanced up and saw the duchesse leading a man and woman toward her. Not now! She glanced at the clock again. Twelve minutes until ten.

The duchesse stood before her. "Mademoiselle Serafina Artois," she said in French, "may I present the comte and comtesse Poitou."

Sarah curtseyed and glanced at the clock again. "*Enchantè*," she answered.

"The comte and comtesse knew your parents," the duchesse continued in French.

"Really?" Sarah's French was fluent, but between pretending to be Mademoiselle Serafina, worrying about the time, and wondering what Sir Northrop wanted, she could hardly remember her English much less concentrate on this conversation.

"We were so relieved to learn that you and your family made it out of France alive," the comtesse said.

"As I recall, your father vexed the king mightily. If we'd only listened to Guyenne, we might have been spared that so-called revolution."

Sarah frowned in confusion. Had Serafina's father said something that could have prevented the revolution? Something bold enough that the king would exile him? Since it seemed she was expected to say something, she smiled and gave a vague, *"Oui, bien sûr."*

It was eight minutes to ten. Surely, Sir Northrop would wait for her.

"How did you manage to get out?" the comte asked.

The duchesse nodded. "Oh, yes. Do tell the story."

"The story?" Sarah took a quick breath. Now she had to make up a story?

"Delphine gave me a scattering of details in her letters," the duchesse told the comte, "but I'm certain Serafina will tell it better."

Sarah gritted her teeth to keep from screaming in frustration. Could nothing go right tonight? How was she supposed to tell a story she didn't know?—she glanced at the clock—in five minutes and in French, no less!

She was going to murder Sir Northrop.

But the duchesse and her friends were looking at her, their faces rapt with attention. She had to say something. "It began in"—she watched the duchesse—"Paris."

The duchesse furrowed her brow.

"I mean, the country outside Paris."

The duchesse continued to frown. "I thought you were in Marseilles."

"Oh." Sarah nodded. If the duchesse knew the

story so well, why didn't *she* just tell it! "Is that where Mama began the story?"

"Yes. She said you were in Marseilles, all three of you riding in the carriage. It was Sunday, and you were on the way home from—"

"Mass," Sarah interjected with a smile. "That's right."

The duchesse frowned again. "I thought the king sent the news in the evening."

"Um—it was vespers," Sarah said as though this should be obvious.

"Ah!" The duchesse nodded. "I see. Go on."

Go on? She glanced at the ceiling and tried to conjure something else to say. If this story was not believable, it might cast doubt on who she was and alert the duc that he was being spied upon. The consequences would be dire. She *had* to be clever now…

Had not Mademoiselle Serafina been only a toddler at the time of the Guyenne's flight? Yes!

"I fear my memory of the event is somewhat unreliable," she said with a smile. "I was so young."

"Of course you were." The duchesse patted her arm.

"But I believe that after my parents received the king's letter—"

"Mademoiselle Serafina? Is that you?"

Sarah whirled to see Sir Northrop coming across the room, a huge smile on his face. The duchesse, comte, and comtesse turned as well. Sir Northrop's eyes bore into her, and she forced herself to speak. "Sir Northrop, I didn't know you would be here."

He joined their small group, and Sarah introduced him.

"And how do you know one another?" the duchesse asked her.

Sir Northrop looked at Sarah, and Sarah looked back. Apparently, he had not come to save her after all. "We met… in Italy."

"In Italy?" Sir Northrop shot a glare at her.

"Oh, how lovely. I adore Italy!" the comtesse exclaimed, her accented English thick and difficult to understand. "Where in Italy?"

Sarah closed her eyes for a moment and said the first place that popped into her mind. "The Piazza San Pietro. Isn't that right, Sir Northrop?" His eyes were throwing daggers, but she did not care. Let him think on his feet for once. He was the one knighted for service.

Sir Northrop took a long moment to consider then said coolly, "My wife and I traveled to Rome on our honeymoon. We first met Mademoiselle Serafina and her family there. Of course, Serafina was but a child then. Our families have kept up the connection over the years."

"And you didn't know she was in London?" the duchesse asked.

"No idea," Sir Northrop answered, and he almost looked as though he were telling the truth.

"I wrote," Sarah said quickly, not wanting Mademoiselle Serafina to appear rude. "Perhaps the letter was misdirected."

Sir Northrop nodded at her. "Perhaps." He turned to the duchesse. "Your Grace, would you mind if I stole Mademoiselle Serafina away for just one moment? I know Lady Merton would love to see her. I'll bring her right back."

"Of course," the duchesse said. "We'll wait here."

Sir Northrop offered his arm, and Sarah took it. With her upswept hair, rouged skin, and fancy gown, she felt ridiculous beside the man who knew she was nothing more than a governess. But she reminded herself that no one else knew she was a fraud, and she held her head high. Sir Northrop led her across the room, glanced over his shoulder casually, and then opened a side terrace door and slipped out.

The side terrace was small and empty. Chinese lanterns lit the main terrace as well as the lawns, but this section was shrouded from light. Sir Northrop closed the terrace door and leaned against it. Sarah pressed herself against the banister.

"How are you doing?" Sir Northrop asked without prelude. "Have you found any evidence?"

Sarah stared at him, anger building. "Found any evidence? No. I'm too busy trying to remember that my father is deathly ill, my family fled from Marseilles, and that *buona sera* means good evening. I think."

Sir Northrop raised a brow at her tone.

"I'm sorry," Sarah said, "but I'm at my wit's end. Thank God you interrupted just now. They wanted me to tell the story of the Guyennes' flight from France." Her voice was rising, sounding slightly panicked, and Sir Northrop held up a hand.

"None of that, Serafina. I won't have it. Calm down."

"Calm down? I might be able to calm down if I had a fortnight to study my character. If you'd given me more than three days to learn all of this!" She gestured at her gown and then the ballroom. "But how am I supposed to calm down when I have the duc de Valère asking me to marry him?"

Sir Northrop leaned forward, and she could have sworn his eyes glinted. "Valère asked you to marry him?"

She shook her head. "As if you didn't know! As if you didn't arrange it through the letters."

"We didn't arrange it, but we had hoped the idea would occur to the Valères."

Sarah shook her head, exasperated. She could hear her tinkling earbobs sway. "Why didn't you tell me?"

He waved a hand as though her question were inconsequential. "What did you say?"

"No, of course."

"No?" His voice boomed out, and she winced. "Why did you say no?"

"Was I supposed to say yes?"

"Of course!"

"How was I to know that?"

"Any idiot would know that."

She inhaled sharply and straightened her shoulders. "I see. Perhaps you'd like to send someone else to play Serafina. Someone who's not an idiot."

She tried to push past him, to return to the ball, but he grabbed her shoulders and thrust her back against the banister. "This is not a game," he gritted out, his spittle wetting her cheeks. "I—we—don't have time for your dramatics."

Her heart was pounding fast now, fear replacing the earlier feeling of inadequacy.

"Do you understand?" Sir Northrop growled.

She nodded. "Y-yes."

Sir Northrop stepped back again, but that did not diminish the sinking feeling creeping over her. Sir Northrop was not going to help her. In the back of her mind, she had hoped he would tell her this was all over, that she could go back to little Anne and Edmund. But that was not going to happen. She was stuck being Mademoiselle Serafina, and no one could save her.

"You said Valère asked you to marry him," Sir Northrop reiterated, calmer now. "And you rejected him."

She nodded.

"Was he angry?"

"He said he wasn't."

"But?"

She glanced over his head at their shadows cast by the Chinese lanterns in the garden. Behind him, the bricks of the town house flickered red and blue and yellow ominously. "He seemed annoyed."

"Not so annoyed that he didn't ask you to dance."

"Duty is important to him. That's why he asked me to marry him. Duty."

"Good. Then you can get him to ask you again."

"What? No, I can't!" Sarah shook her head defiantly, but the look in Sir Northrop's eyes made her take a step back. "I told him no," she said sternly. "He's not going to ask me again."

"Find a way to convince him otherwise. I need you engaged to Valère."

Sarah felt suddenly exhausted. She was no spy. How could she possibly deal with all these complications? Couldn't Sir Northrop see she was unprepared? Did he not realize the dangers she faced if she failed as Serafina?

She wanted to protest, but something about the

way Sir Northrop glared at her kept her silent. Perhaps Valère was not the only danger.

"An engagement lends more legitimacy to your being in Valère's home," Sir Northrop told her, "and it develops closeness between you and the duc. The closer you are, the easier it will be for you to crack his defenses, find out what he's really up to."

"I saw a letter on his desk." The tidbit was not much, but maybe it would substitute for an engagement. "The writing was French. I didn't get a good look, but I thought it might have come from the Continent."

Sir Northrop nodded, looked pleased, and she relaxed slightly. Afraid of Sir Northrop! Sometimes she was such a ninny.

"Get your hands on that letter. Copy it or bring it to me. Valère and his mother will be going to the King's Theater next week. Make sure you're there."

"And if I can secure the letter, then I don't have to worry about the engagement?" She knew even before she spoke that she was wasting her breath.

Sir Northrop gave her a hard look. "You need the letter *and* the proposal. Is that clear?"

She sighed. "But how do I persuade him to propose again?" She remembered the night before with no small discomfort. If she were Valère, she would not propose again.

"That's your problem. Your orders are to become engaged. Posthaste."

She stared at Sir Northrop, open-mouthed. Was this how the Foreign Office operated? Next they would be ordering her to get married and produce a child.

An image of Valère kissing her, in an effort to

produce that child, flickered in her mind. She saw his hand cup her chin, his fingers caress her cheek. And then those long, aristocratic fingers slid down to the exposed flesh of her neck and shoulders. She could almost feel his light touch skating across the swells of her breasts.

She took a shaky breath. For a moment the thought of starting a family with Valère, the notion of having his children, warmed her—heated her. But she quickly pushed the notion away. Valère wanted Mademoiselle Serafina, not Sarah Smith.

And she did not want him either. No. It was only the idea of children and a family that was affecting her. She could not think where those lustful thoughts had come from.

"Did you hear me, Serafina?"

She nodded rigidly. "Yes." *Find the letter. Get engaged.*

"Good. Now get out there and get to work. Use some of your feminine wiles."

She raised a brow. "Feminine wiles?"

"Exactly." He gave her a pat on the shoulder and opened the terrace door. "Good luck."

And then she was back in the crush of people. She took one step and stared into Valère's azure blue eyes.

❧

Julien had been one second from tearing the terrace door off its hinges and going after her. What the hell was Mademoiselle Serafina doing out on a secluded terrace with that man? He did not know the man's name, and he did not care if he was bloody King George himself.

And now she was back again, her face white and drawn.

Julien grabbed her arm, pulled her aside. "What did he do to you? Did he accost you?"

"What?" She was staring at him, clearly confused. "No. That was Sir Northrop."

"Who the hell—" He paused, tried to wrest control back. "Your pardon—who is Sir Northrop?"

"My empl—a family friend."

Julien narrowed his eyes. There was something she was not telling him. She looked down at his hand on her arm. "Would you mind releasing me?"

He did so, stepping back but continuing to study her. Her face was pale, and she would not meet his gaze. "What's wrong?"

"Nothing at all." She glanced at his empty hands. "Did you have a glass of champagne?"

She was changing the subject, and he supposed he would have to allow it. After all, what she did on terraces with strange men did not concern him.

He clenched his hands into fists.

Julien spotted Stover heading toward them and nodded to him. Stover was just the man to keep him from saying something he would later regret. He already had too much to regret with this woman.

"Mademoiselle Serafina Artois," Julien said as Stover paused and bowed before them. "I present Marcus Stover."

She held out one gloved hand, regal and self-assured once again. The color had come back to her cheeks as well. "Good evening Mr. Stover. How are you enjoying the ball?" She had to raise her voice to be heard over the din of voices and the swell of the orchestra.

"Very much, and you, my lady?"

She smiled. "It's been a whirlwind." She gestured to the couples now dancing. The women were spinning, their gowns belling out.

"Have you had time to see much of London?"

She shook her head. "No, not yet."

"Perhaps Valère will give you a tour. You're in Berkeley Square, and that's not far from Hyde Park."

Julien frowned. Why had he not thought of offering to take her on a tour?

"I've heard Hyde Park is lovely," she said, "but what I'd really enjoy is one of Gunther's ices. I haven't had one of those in—" She paused, glanced at the dancers again. "I mean, I've heard those are delicious."

"I see our reputation precedes us," Julien said. "What else would you like to see? I'll take you when I have a moment away from business."

"That will be never," Rigby interjected, coming up behind Stover. "You should allow me to escort you, Mademoiselle Serafina. We might practice our Italian." He winked, and Julien had to resist the urge to punch the man.

"Perhaps you should take Miss Wimple out and about, Rigby," Stover said. "I'm sure she's on pins and needles, waiting for you to call."

Julien coughed to cover his grin, but Rigby shot them both looks rife with sabers. Then he smiled. "Unfortunately, Miss Wimple is not in attendance this evening." He turned to Mademoiselle Serafina, his eyes sad. "Which means I have no one to dance with.

Mademoiselle Serafina, would you end my loneliness and grant me the pleasure of this dance?"

She blinked, looked to Julien for help, but before Julien could stop Rigby, the man had her on his arm and was leading her away. She glanced back once, her look pleading.

"You should probably cut in," Stover said, watching them go. "Too much time with Rigby and she'll book passage back to Italy tomorrow."

Julien crossed his arms to stop himself from following Stover's advice. He was not going to go after her. "That wouldn't be the worst thing."

Stover raised his brows. "Trouble already?"

Julien stared across the room for a full minute. He did not really want to discuss this, but when no engagement announcement was forthcoming, everyone would be talking about it anyway. "She rejected me."

Stover frowned. "What? I didn't hear you."

"You heard me." Julien kept his eyes on a sconce across the room.

"You proposed already?"

"I don't like to waste time." The music began, and he moved to the right a few steps, so that he had a better view of the ballroom and the dancers. He caught a flash of Rigby's red hair and shook his head. Mademoiselle Serafina was stumbling through this dance as well.

"You might have waited until you'd had a conversation or two."

Julien glared at him.

"Just a suggestion."

"Thanks."

Julien watched the dance proceed, watched Rigby laugh at something Mademoiselle Serafina said. Was she witty? She had not said anything amusing to him.

"What are you going to do now?"

Julien shrugged. "Any suggestions? I don't care about the marriage, but my mother has the whole *ton* thinking we're buying the bridal trousseau."

"It's not that bad."

Julien gave Stover a sidelong look.

Stover pointed to Rigby and Mademoiselle Serafina. "Perhaps that's not such a bad idea. You might encourage more of that. Though"—he frowned as Serafina turned the wrong way—"she isn't likely to attract many dancing partners."

Julien sighed. And just why exactly did that statement please him?

Two hours later, Julien walked into his club. It was crowded as usual. At this time of night, the patrons were raucous and jovial. He wound through the haze of smoke, stopping periodically to converse with an acquaintance. But he refused offers to join any of the parties, foregoing the port and leather chairs for the gaming room

At the entrance, he paused and scanned the green baize tables then arrowed for Rigby, who was standing next to the faro table. He clapped his friend on the shoulder and steered him away. "Hey, wait a moment! I have money on this."

"I thought you were a dancer, not a gambler."

"I can be both," Rigby said, shrugging Julien's hand off. "For what it's worth, old chap, I'm not trying to steal the lovely Serafina."

"Oh, good. I was worried."

"As well you should be." Rigby signaled a waiter and asked for two brandies. "But I wouldn't do that to Miss Wimple, even if I haven't fully committed to the idea of marrying the little mare."

"You're quite the gentleman, Rigby."

"I know, and it's exhausting." He fell into a wingback chair. "All the gallantry and chivalry. It's enough to wear a man out." The waiter reappeared. "Ah. There's fortification now." He swallowed a good portion of the brandy then rolled his head to look at Julien, who had taken the chair beside him. "For what it's worth, your Mademoiselle Serafina has better teeth than my Miss Wimple, but my Miss Wimple can speak Italian."

"So can Mademoiselle Serafina." Julien took a swallow of the brandy. It was cheap, not as good as what he had at home. He could be there now, enjoying far better brandy, sitting in his office… thinking about Mademoiselle Serafina just a floor above him.

That was the precise reason he was not at home.

"I don't think she *can* speak Italian."

Julien refrained from rolling his eyes.

"She didn't say a word to me in Italian during the entire dance."

"Perhaps she just didn't want to talk to you."

"Ridiculous. I think she doesn't know Italian."

Julien sighed. "Yes, yours is the more logical explanation."

"Odd. To be from Italy and not speak Italian."

"Yes." And it would be, if it were true. He spotted Stover across the room and muttered, "Thank God."

Stover saw them and took an open chair. Reaching

into his pocket, he extracted a slip of paper and passed it over to Julien.

"What's this?"

"Name of a privateer who might be able to assist you with those travel plans we were discussing."

Julien stuck the paper in his coat. "Really? How'd you come by this?"

"My sister was giving a dinner party, and she wanted to serve French wine. She had my brother-in-law running about Town for two weeks, looking for some good quality French vintage. He said this is the only man who can acquire it at present. I thought with your shipping connections, you'd be able to find him."

Julien nodded his thanks.

"You're not still planning to go to France?" Rigby moaned. "I thought we'd decided only a cods-head would attempt that."

"Stubble it, Rigby," Julien said and took another swallow of brandy.

"Not to mention, you have the lovely Mademoiselle Serafina to live for."

Julien looked at Stover, and together they said, "Stubble it, Rigby."

Nine

HE WAS OUT. SARAH HAD IT ON GOOD AUTHORITY FROM both the duchesse and the butler that Valère had gone to visit his solicitor and would be out for most of the day.

And then, on top of that good news, the duchesse had gone out as well. She had asked Serafina to go shopping with her, but Sarah had feigned a headache, waiting in bed for three-quarters of an hour after she heard the duchesse depart. In that time, the house had quieted, and Sarah had worked out a plan for breaking into Valère's library.

Her last attempt, two days after the ball, had ended in failure as the library door had been locked. She assumed it would be locked again today, and she could not very well stand in the vestibule and try to force it open. She would not have to use force at all if her plan worked.

Fully dressed, she threw off the covers and rose, then tiptoed to the door and peered out. No one was in the corridor.

She crept down the stairs, her breath a little short and her heart pounding. She was not certain if she felt a surge of energy from nerves or excitement. She feared some part of her was actually beginning to enjoy this game of espionage.

Sarah started down the wide marble stairs and saw the woman she wanted: Mrs. Eggers, the housekeeper. Mrs. Eggers was quite good at her job and bobbed her head at Serafina right away. "Mademoiselle, you shouldn't be up and about. Can I help you with something?"

Sarah put a hand to her head, trying to look sad and pitiful. "Yes, thank you, Mrs. Eggers." Sarah clenched her hand into a fist and dug her fingernails into her palm. Serafina would not thank the housekeeper. Serafina would order, not ask. She *had* to remember that. Sarah cleared her throat. "I find that I cannot sleep and want a book to read. Can you—I mean, please direct me to the library."

"Oh." Mrs. Eggers looked at the library door. It was closed, and from the look on Mrs. Eggers's face, still locked. "It's right there, my lady, but I'm afraid it's locked."

Sarah, the governess, would have given up at that point and crept back to her room without a book. Serafina was not about to give up that easily. "Could you open it for me, please? I mean, please unlock it."

The housekeeper frowned, and Sarah knew that now would be the test. If Grimsby was like most butlers, he had probably nipped out for a quick pint as soon as he realized he would be free of both employers for several hours. He would have left the keys behind, not wanting to risk losing them to pickpockets or carelessness. He would also have given orders that the library should remain undisturbed.

But those rules did not apply to Mademoiselle Serafina, or, if they did, Sarah did not think Mrs. Eggers would risk angering Serafina by refusing what really was a simple, ordinary request. But just in case she was considering it, Sarah raised an eyebrow in what she hoped was an imperial gesture.

"Just a moment, my lady," the housekeeper said. "I'll go get the key."

She moved off, toward the servants' stairs. Grimsby probably kept the keys in his room, and Mrs. Eggers would have to fetch them. Sarah waited, pacing back and forth across the marble vestibule with nervousness.

Hurry. Hurry.

At any moment, the duc, the duchesse, or the butler could return, ruining her plan.

Hurry!

Thankfully, Mrs. Eggers did not know the meaning of laziness, and she was back quickly. Sarah smiled, seeing the housekeeper holding the keys high. She tried not to crowd too close behind Mrs. Eggers as the woman opened the door, but it was difficult not to rush the housekeeper. Finally Sarah heard the lock click, and the housekeeper turned the door handle.

Sarah forced herself to move slowly inside, as though she had never been there before.

"I'll just wait while you choose a book," Mrs. Eggers said.

Sarah had anticipated this as well. She took her time perusing the shelves, studying the varied fiction and nonfiction titles. Sarah would have hurriedly grabbed the first volume she touched and scurried away with it. Serafina was far choosier and in no hurry. It did not matter to her that the housekeeper was too busy to stand about waiting for her.

Sarah tapped her finger to her chin as she surveyed the titles, not seeing the books at all. *Come on,* she pled silently. Surely someone on the staff urgently needed the housekeeper. All Sarah needed was five minutes alone.

The clock ticked by, and Mrs. Eggers waited patiently. Sarah pulled a book off the shelf and flipped through it, not seeing anything between the covers. She paused on a page and pretended to read.

"Mrs. Eggers?"

Finally!

"Yes, Molly? What is it?"

"I was polishing the tea service like you asked, ma'am, and I dropped the pot. I'm afraid I may have dented the dining room table."

"What?"

Sarah covered her mouth to hide her smile. Molly was in a good deal of trouble. Sarah did not wish hardship on the maid, but she knew this was the chance she had been waiting for.

"Mademoiselle?" Mrs. Eggers called.

Sarah looked up, pretending not to have heard their exchange. She feigned impatience. "What is it?" she asked, putting a hand on her hip.

"I'm sorry, Mademoiselle. I need to step away for a moment. You take your time."

Sarah sighed loudly, then looked back at her book and absently turned a page. She felt like the rudest creature on earth, but it was necessary. From what Sarah had seen, the Valères treated their servants well, but they were still aristocrats. They had been served their entire lives and had no idea what it was to serve. They were not intentionally rude, and indeed Mrs. Eggers probably did not think Serafina rude right now, but Sarah knew she was not Serafina.

She listened as Mrs. Eggers's steps retreated, then scooted closer to the door. She peered out and saw the housekeeper entering the dining room. Quickly, Sarah pushed the library door closed and ran to Valère's desk. She set the book on the corner, in case she needed to pretend to read it, and began to rifle through the papers on the top.

Accounts. Correspondence. Ledgers. Nothing that looked promising.

Where was that letter she had seen on her first night? She needed something that looked like it had to do with France.

She finished going through the papers on top of the desk and slid open one of the drawers. Outside she heard one of the servants talking, and her heart lurched. Was it Grimsby returning?

She lifted her book and pretended to read it. Her heart pounded so loudly that she could not hear when or if the servants moved away. Finally she rose and tiptoed to the door again. The vestibule was empty, but she had to hurry. Mrs. Eggers might return without warning.

Sarah prayed for more domestic complications as she peered into the open drawer. This was the drawer Valère had pulled paper and ink out of on her first night, and that looked like all it held. Paper, quills, ink. Drat! Where was he keeping that letter?

She slid that drawer closed and opened another. This one was full of correspondence. She glanced at several of the documents, but they were business–related. If she had time to read them all, she imagined one might prove useful, but these looked benign. No references to France. Nothing in French.

With a frustrated sigh, Sarah sat back and stared at the desk. Time was up. Any moment Mrs. Eggers would return. Sarah was to accompany the Valères to the theater tonight, and she suspected Sir Northrop would approach her for an update on her progress. She had not persuaded Valère to propose again, so she had to give Sir Northrop something.

Confound it! Sarah kicked at the desk, and her slipper thudded hollowly on the wood. Everything in her stilled, and she kicked at the front panel again. Again, the hollow sound.

Sarah leaned down and knocked on the side panel of the desk.

Solid.

She tried another area.

Solid.

She tapped on the front panel again.

Hollow.

"Found it!" she whispered and fell to her knees behind the desk. Her fingers fumbled over the wood, looking for an opening, some way to slide the panel aside or up. When she tried sliding it up, she had success. The panel slid into the desk, and she saw a hidden drawer.

She was breathing so quickly, she felt as though she had run a mile. This was it. She knew it.

She grasped the drawer handle and tugged, but nothing happened.

Frowning, Sarah looked at the drawer more closely. Under the handle, there was a small gold lock. She needed a key—a small gold key.

Sarah jumped up, banging her head on the bottom of the desk in the process, and sprinted to the door, where Mrs. Eggers had left the butler's keys. She ran her fingers through them. There were several small gold keys, but none that would fit the desk.

Drat! Drat! Drat!

Valère must keep the key on his person.

"I will have to speak to Her Grace."

Sarah froze as Mrs. Eggers's voice floated across the vestibule. Sarah jumped back into the office and ran for the desk. She had to close that panel, or Valère would know someone had been here.

She dove under the desk, tearing one of her flounces in the process, and slammed the panel down.

Or she would have, if the panel had moved.

No, no, no!

She tugged harder, but the panel would not close. Sarah climbed to her knees and focused on the panel, pulling deliberately. Perspiration trickled down her back and between her breasts. She was huffing like an old mare.

"I'll see to that in a moment, Smith." Mrs. Eggers's voice was growing closer. In mere seconds, she would step into the room, and Sarah would have to explain what she was doing under Valère's desk.

"God, please," she pleaded. "Please."

The panel slid smoothly down, and Sarah fell back in relief. A second later she was on her feet and dashing across the room to the couch. She threw herself on it, arranged her dress, and closed her eyes.

The library door opened again, and Mrs. Eggers peered inside. "Mademoiselle?"

Sarah sat up. "Oh, Mrs. Eggers. Where have you been? You've kept me waiting."

"Are you well?" The housekeeper looked concerned to see her lying on the couch.

"Not at all, Mrs. Eggers. Help me back to my room."

"Certainly. Did you find a book to read?"

"I'm afraid I'm not feeling well enough to read at the moment."

"I see."

It was only back in her room that Sarah realized she had left the book on Valère's desk. Perhaps he would not notice when he returned.

She sighed and lay back on her bed, a real headache throbbing behind her eyes.

Of course he would notice. She was not that lucky.

❦

King's Theater was crowded as usual. Julien doubted most of the people packing the boxes were interested in the opera to be performed. Most hoped to see and be seen. The women wore gowns of every color, covering themselves in silks, satins, velvets, and lace. Their necks and arms were heavily laden with diamonds, rubies, and pearls, and their ears glinted with garnets and sapphires. In their hands they held elaborate Chinese fans, which they flicked open or closed continuously. Even when Julien could not hear a woman's conversation, her fan spoke volumes.

His mother had told him that women used fans as a secret language. A fan touching the right cheek meant yes, while a fan touching the left cheek meant no. There was more, but Julien had not cared to remember it. Besides, he could read a woman's signals well enough. He knew without benefit of a fan handle pressed to her lips when a woman wanted to be kissed, or if she dropped her fan in front of his feet, she wanted to form an acquaintance. Women were not so difficult to understand.

Until now.

As he led his mother and Mademoiselle Serafina through the crowds lingering in the foyer, up the plushly carpeted stairs to their choice box overlooking the stage, he wished that Mademoiselle Serafina had a fan. She was still a mystery to him. She had refused his marriage proposal, and yet she truly did not seem interested in other men. She was pleasant but formal in her brief conversations with him, and yet at times he caught her peering at him with undisguised interest. Perhaps he might understand better what she wanted from him if she could show him with her fan. But as she didn't carry a fan, he decided to ignore her. Or at least half of him did. The other half...

The theater hummed quietly. The rest of the *ton* had yet to fill in most of the other boxes, and for the moment he could see the bones of the old building. It was the shape of a half circle with boxes for the wealthy lining the upper tiers and overlooking the stage. The less expensive seats were on the ground. Those on the ground might have a better view of the stage than many in the boxes, but those in the boxes did not come to see the performance. The boxes provided a much better view of the others in attendance. In addition, each was equipped with heavy blue drapes that could be pulled closed for privacy.

The drapes in their box were open as he seated his mother then pulled out a heavy blue-upholstered chair for Mademoiselle Serafina. She wore a simple gown of white muslin tonight, paired with a fringed Indian shawl in pale blue. Her hair was piled atop her head and arranged in a wild array of curls. Small flowers created a pretty wreath that wound its way lazily about her head. The current style was a profusion of curls about the cheeks and forehead, but Serafina's face was bare, and the severity showed off her delicate bone structure. She was taking in everything with her usually wide eyes and rounded mouth. What did she see that he did not? "Oh, the ceiling is just beautiful!" she exclaimed.

Julien glanced up at the painting of a chariot and horses. He had seen it many times, and it failed to impress him now. Perhaps he was becoming too jaded, immune to beauty. But then he looked at Serafina and knew he was not immune to all beauty.

"It is lovely, isn't it?" his mother answered. "I'm certain you must have stunning theaters in Italy as well. In fact, as this opera is in Italian, you can translate for us."

Julien was watching Serafina and saw her hesitate before answering. "Of course."

He frowned. Was Rigby right? Did she really not know Italian?

"Oh, look! There's Lady Hawksthorn," his mother said, pointing to a box across the theater. "I want to have a word with her. Will you two excuse me for just a moment?"

Julien fought the urge to say no. He didn't particularly want to be alone with Serafina, but he could not leave her either.

"Bien sûr, ma mère." He rose and held the heavy curtain at the back of the box open for her.

When he returned to his seat, Serafina was watching him. His mother's vacant chair was between them, and he liked that arrangement. He had avoided Serafina after the ball, not liking the feeling he had when she danced with Rigby. He was not going to call it jealousy, but it had some suspicious similarities.

And then last night... there had been that dream.

He shook his head.

"Are you looking forward to the performance?" Serafina asked.

Julien mustered up his reserves, preparing for chitchat. He could handle chitchat. That was nothing to dream about. "I'm not even certain what the production is."

"You don't enjoy opera then?"

Julien shrugged. "The first two hours are tolerable. After that..."

She smiled.

"And you?"

"I've never been to the opera."

Julien stared at her. "Never? But Italy has so many opera houses, so many of the great composers."

She looked away, taking in the scene again. "I think my parents always meant to take me."

Her face was sad, the first time he had seen it so, and he felt like taking her in his arms, comforting her.

He had forgotten that her father was so ill. She must be worried about his health.

But Julien stopped himself from rising and depositing himself in his mother's chair. That was just the kind of thing that would lead to more dreams. Even now, looking at her face in profile, he could remember how soft her skin had been in the dream. How ripe her lips.

He closed his eyes and willed the image away.

Think about something else.

"You forgot your book," he said, remembering the slim volume he had found on his desk after returning from his solicitor's this evening. He had been angry with Grimsby, thinking the man had not kept the library locked, but Mrs. Eggers had confessed that she had allowed Mademoiselle Serafina in to choose a book to read.

It sounded innocent enough, but something about Mademoiselle Serafina in his library made him suspicious. It was ridiculous. People took books out of libraries to read all the time. That was what libraries were for. He had gone over and through his desk and seen that nothing was missing. Nothing looked touched.

And even if it had been touched, even if she did find the letter about Armand, what did it matter? She was a French émigré, just like him. She would certainly understand.

And yet… he did not trust her.

What if Rigby was right about the Italian?

"What book?"

"*Botany and Horticulture, Volume One*. Mrs. Eggers

told me you wanted a book but then had a headache and went to bed. You must have left it on my desk."

"I must have," she said, her eyes on the theater.

"I didn't know you had an interest in botany."

She glanced at him, and he tried not to notice those strawberry lips. "Oh, I love plants. At... home, we have a beautiful garden."

The images from the dream were coming back to him now, too fast to control. He pulled Serafina into his arms, molding her body tightly against his, pressing her breasts against his chest, and cupping the back of her neck, holding her firmly. Those strawberry lips parted in surprise, and he bent to claim them. He didn't sample, he took and took, parting that ripe flesh and delving inside.

She'd been sweet, so sweet and yielding, and he moved his hands up her sides, cupping those ripe breasts—

"Is there something wrong?"

Julien blinked, shifted uncomfortably. "No. You were telling me about your garden? What kind of plants do you have in it?"

Plants. That was good. He would not be aroused if they were talking of plants.

She proceeded to list some generic flowers and then to describe some of the more exotic flowers she would like to grow. Julien forced himself to think about plants—roses, violets, poppies, lilies.

"Why don't you grow more exotic flowers if you want?"

She blinked at him, as though the idea had never occurred to her. Then she nodded. "I hope to. One day when—"

She paused and stared at someone or something across the stage.

Julien glanced in that direction but saw nothing out of the ordinary.

"I need the…" She rose, looking about for her shawl. He stood, plucked it off the back of her chair, and handed it to her. "Thank you. I need the… ah, ladies' retiring room. I'll be back in just a moment."

"I'll be here." But Julien did not think she heard him.

He turned and scanned the theater again. What had she seen? Or rather, *whom* had she seen?

With a muffled curse, he went out after her.

Ten

"GOOD-BYE," SARAH TOLD THE WIDOW FIFTEEN minutes later, then rose from the seat she had occupied. She knew it was dangerous to be seen with the spy, but she paused before exiting anyway.

Part of her felt like fleeing the theater, fleeing London, and never coming back. The Widow had just reiterated all Sir Northrop had said at Lord Aldon's ball: Sarah was to find evidence, convince Valère to propose again, and she should have done it all yesterday.

She was not working fast enough, and Sir Northrop was becoming impatient. The Widow was impatient as well, but there was something more. Sarah glanced back at The Widow to confirm her suspicions. The woman was frightened. How else could Sarah account for her strange behavior? Moments ago, The Widow had suddenly clutched Sarah's hand tightly and hissed, "Be careful. Trust no one."

Sarah had frowned and tried to loosen the woman's grip on her hand. "I understand."

"No, you don't," The Widow said, still hissing. "Trust *no one*."

Sarah frowned, her heart beginning to pound in alarm. "What does that mean? What's happened?"

"I can't tell you here." She peered over her shoulder, checking once more that they were alone. "All I can say is I have reason to be suspicious of Sir Northrop." She said the name so quietly, Sarah had to lean forward to hear.

"Why? What's—"

"Shh!" The Widow clenched her hand so tightly Sarah winced. "Meet me tomorrow morning in the square outside the Valère town house. I'll find us a secluded spot to speak then."

"Very well."

"In the meantime, work quickly. Do not fail Sir Northrop. More than your position may depend upon it."

Sarah wanted to ask what else she had to lose, but The Widow released her and shooed her away with both hands. And now Sarah stood at the exit, wondering what had frightened The Widow so much. It was becoming more and more apparent that she could not fail at this mission. But how was she supposed to get the key to the secret drawer from Valère? She had tried to search his room, but his valet had shooed her away. No matter. She suspected he kept it on his person. Which meant...

Sarah closed her eyes.

She would have to find a way to steal it off his person.

Opening her eyes and taking a deep breath, Sarah stumbled out of The Widow's box just as the first strings of the orchestra whined. It took a moment for her eyes to adjust to the dark corridor as well as the sudden burst of sound, and then she was engulfed in what felt like warm steel. "What—"

"Shh."

She knew his scent. The smells of citrus and wood brought an image of Valère's library to mind. "Your Grace?" Her voice wavered slightly. She pulled back, and the lines of his face became clear.

"You looked unsteady," he said, but he did not release her.

"I'm fine." She was trembling from... anticipation? Arousal? She tried to make her body cease shaking and couldn't. His body, on the other hand, was perfectly still. He was solid, big, masculine. She realized suddenly that she had never been this close to a man before, and her trembling increased.

"I thought you might have gotten lost."

She knew that was not the case and suspected he had been watching her, following her. That was dangerous. *He* was dangerous.

He was still holding her pressed against him, and the feel of him made it difficult for her to think. She should push him away, should demand that he release her, but his arms felt so good around her waist. His hands on her back were soothing, and the whisper of his breath on her forehead was sweet and warm.

She wanted him to kiss her.

She realized it suddenly. Realized as well that she did not want to be soothed at the moment. She wanted him to push her against the wall, press his lips to hers, and kiss her until she forgot all about letters and keys and spies. She wanted his two days' growth of beard to scratch the sensitive skin of her neck, his large hands to pull her tight against his hard body. She needed something to numb her mind and arouse a feeling in her other than worry and fear.

Heat rushed through her, making her lightheaded. Surprised at the ferocity of her thoughts, she lifted her hands to push him away.

But something went amiss. Somehow when she brought her hands to his chest to push him away, she found herself clutching at him and drawing him nearer. His warm breath brushed against her cheek. *"Embrasse-moi,"* he whispered.

Kiss me.

She did not know how it happened, did not know how it was that suddenly she was flush against him, but before she could protest, his mouth was on hers.

Of course, truth be told, she was never going to protest. This was what she wanted. His lips felt exactly as she had imagined—cool and firm. Coaxing. They wanted more from her, and she wanted to give it. If only she knew how. Her head was spinning so fast that all she could think about was his lips slanting over hers, making her body feel heavy and warm.

Yes.

Could the duc de Valère really be kissing her? A plain governess? But she was not a governess at this moment; she was a spy. And he was a traitor. She had to be smart now. She could not succumb to the desires he aroused in her. Using the scant willpower she still possessed, Sarah pushed the duc away.

"You followed me," she said as soon as there were a few inches between them. She did not want to speak of this kiss, too afraid she might succumb once again.

"You're my responsibility," he said, voice husky. "A young attractive woman shouldn't be left unattended."

She melted for an instant, forgetting her good intentions. He thought she was attractive? He—the duc de Valère and one of the most handsome men she knew—thought *she* was attractive?

No, she told herself, fighting to reclaim control. He thought Serafina was attractive. He did not know Sarah. He would not care about Sarah.

That grounded her. All the swirling in her head slowed, and the heat zinging through her cooled and froze. She could think clearly again.

"Thank you, sir. That's very thoughtful. I was only visiting with a friend. Perfectly safe."

She moved forward, indicating she was ready to return to their box, and he held out his arm. She took it, forcing herself not to remember the feel of that arm around her, pulling her close, molding her body to his—

Drat!

"Who was your friend? She didn't look familiar."

Oh, no. She would *not* venture into this discussion with him. "Oh, no one you would know," she said vaguely.

To Sarah's relief, she saw they were nearing the Valère box. But just as she would have increased her pace, the duc slowed and turned to her. Sarah tried to keep walking, but he maneuvered her against the wall, blocking her escape. With dismay, Sarah saw that the corridor was quite deserted now. With increasing dismay, she realized she was in exactly the position that had caused her trouble mere moments before.

Valère leaned close, so close she could count his thick black eyelashes. "I don't know what to think about you, Serafina. May I call you Serafina?"

"I-I—" She swallowed. "No." She did not want him to kiss her again. She did *not* want him to kiss her.

He ignored her. "What I don't understand, Serafina, is why you would travel all the way from Italy only to reject my proposal of marriage. And yet, you don't seek out other suitors."

The rejoinder came to her quickly. "Not every woman's objective in life is marriage."

He gave her a rueful smile. "That's another thing. One moment you're nervous and shy. Another, bold and argumentative. Another—" He gestured back the way they had come, and she perfectly understood his meaning. A moment before she had been wantonly kissing him. "You have friends in England, yet you've never been here," he continued. "You have an interest in botany, but you've never been to the opera and obviously haven't studied under a dancing master."

Her heart was pounding now, and she did not know if it was arousal brought on by his nearness or fear that he would put the pieces together and realize she could not possibly be who she said.

"You're a mystery, *ma belle.*"

She took a shaky breath. "I'll take that as a compliment. Now, if you would please move aside—"

"You're trembling. Why?"

She gave a short laugh. "I'm not trembling." But she was. She was shaking like a wet cat.

"You are. Are you cold or could it be"—he lifted

a hand, pressed a finger against her lips—"something else?" He parted her mouth slightly, and Sarah's body exploded with white heat. If he didn't kiss her in a moment, she feared she would grab him again.

Then suddenly, he stepped back. His absence was like the tearing away of a warm blanket on a bitterly cold night. She stumbled toward him, and he caught her, turning her toward the Valère box.

"Here we are," he said as though the exchange a moment before had never happened.

Sarah nodded. Her wits were coming back to her. Yes, the Valère box was exactly where she wanted to be.

Valère pulled the curtain aside, and—a prayer answered—the duchesse had returned. She turned, opera glasses in hand. "*Très bien!* It is about to begin."

"*Merveilleux!*" Sarah said too enthusiastically. She took her seat on one side of the duchesse, grateful to ease her wobbly legs. Valère took his on the opposite side. Sarah was still shaking, but she turned to enjoy the opera. She focused intently, but it was not enough.

She could feel Valère watching her.

⁂

Sarah waited two hours in the park surrounded by the town houses of Berkeley Square. She examined every daffodil, every crocus, every violet—every blade of grass at least three times before she realized The Widow was not coming. Carriages came and went, but few slowed, and those who did disembarked at one of the town houses. These were the duc and duchesse's neighbors. Few gave the woman lingering in the square on a sunny day a second glance. Why should they? In her yellow sprigged morning dress, she looked as though she belonged.

She felt rather silly walking about the grass in a trained gown with a bright yellow ribbon about her waist. Serafina would have stayed on the path, avoiding the grass, but now that she was outside, Sarah realized she had missed the fresh air. The balls and operas were so stifling, and everyone wore too much cologne.

Well, not Valère. She did not think he wore any cologne, nor needed to. He smelled delicious enough without it. She blew out a sigh. She had not come out here to daydream about the duc. She could do that well enough inside. She glanced at the sky, measured the progress of the sun, and knew it was well after ten. Where was The Widow?

Sarah's stomach clenched. Something had happened. Something bad.

She knew it. There was no other explanation. The Widow had been afraid last night; she had wanted to tell Sarah something important about Sir Northrop. Something potentially urgent.

And now the woman failed to appear at their appointed rendezvous. Had Sir Northrop done something to her?

Sarah shook her head. She was allowing her imagination to run away with her. Why would Sir Northrop hurt The Widow? They both worked for the Foreign Office. They were allies.

Weren't they?

Sarah glanced about the park one last time, but The Widow did not appear. She lifted her skirts and trudged back to the Valère town house. She wished she could blot out her fears and anxieties, silence her brain, but it was churning now.

If The Widow and Sir Northrop were allies, why was she afraid of him? And why was The Widow afraid for Sarah? Was it simply because she was not working fast enough to expose Valère, or was there something else? Something more?

Perhaps Sir Northrop was not who he seemed...

Sarah shook her head and huffed out a breath. Now she was truly allowing her imagination to run away. Sir Northrop had been knighted by the King. He was a respected naval officer, had served the Crown faithfully for many years. His reputation and honor were sterling. Why was she questioning it?

That might not have been what The Widow wanted to discuss at all. As the Valère butler opened the door to admit Sarah, she gave one last glance at the park. The Widow was not there, and now Sarah feared she might never know what the woman had wanted to say.

What Sarah did know was that, no matter the cost, she did not want to disappoint Sir Northrop.

∽∾

"I can't dance with your Mademoiselle Serafina tonight," Rigby said, handing Julien a glass of champagne. "Miss Wimple is here."

"I'm sure Serafina will be heartbroken."

Rigby raised his auburn eyebrows. "Oh? So it's just *Serafina* now? Anything you want to tell me, old chap? You know I hate being the last to know."

Julien scowled. He had not meant to refer to her so familiarly, but she had become simply *Serafina* in his mind.

Which proved he was thinking of her far too often.

"Nothing to tell. Forget it."

"You want to tell Stover first, don't you?" Rigby complained.

Julien pointed across the room. "Why don't you go annoy Miss Wimple? She's over there with her friends, giggling and pointing."

Rigby sighed. "I suppose I had better claim the first dance. Will you and *Serafina* be joining our set?"

Julien shrugged. "Doubtful."

Rigby made the long trek across the ballroom, but Julien made no move toward Serafina. She was at his mother's side and doing just fine there. He had no intention of asking her to dance.

And after her poor showing at Lord Aldon's ball, most men with a care for their feet would not be lining up to ask either.

Which meant she would have to sit out the first dance.

Damn it.

He marched across the room, scowling at everyone he passed. When he reached her, she spun and blinked at him in surprise. He kept scowling. Why did she have to wear white? Not just white—white with small pink bows? She looked young and fresh and pretty. He felt as though he should put his arm around her and protect her from the evils of a world he knew far too well.

But he was not going to protect her. He was going

to France, and he would find Armand. He would dance with Serafina, and that would be the end of it.

"Dance?" It was as much a question as he could muster at the moment.

His mother frowned at him, probably disappointed in his poor manners. But Serafina did not seem to mind.

"Yes, thank you."

He jabbed his arm out, eliciting a huff from his mother, but Serafina took it graciously. He led her to Rigby's set, where the other couples made room for them at the top. His title might be French, but a duc was a duke. As such, he was the highest-ranked peer dancing.

But Julien did not want to lead the dance, did not want to put that much pressure on Serafina, so he led her to the middle of the set, taking his place beside Rigby. Serafina was next to Miss Wimple, who smiled at her kindly.

"Decided to dance after all, eh?" Rigby grinned knowingly at him. Julien opened his mouth, but Rigby waved a hand. "I know. Stubble it."

The music began, and Serafina watched the dancers at the top of the set, obviously trying to memorize the forms of the dance. Julien watched her. He could not figure out why he was so drawn to her. He knew women more charming, more attractive. He was not so shallow as to be simply drawn by her beauty, and there was more to her. She was intelligent and unafraid to stand up for herself. She was kind to his mother, and she had varied interests—botany among others, he assumed.

Their turn came, and he took her hand, spinning her.

"Sorry," she whispered when she stepped on his foot.

"My fault." He led her to the end of the set where they took their places again.

And then there were the negatives: she could not dance—which didn't matter a fig to him—and she had refused his marriage proposal.

Ah. There it was. *She* did not want him.

She might have kissed him at the opera last night—an impulse she was probably very sorry for now—but as much as he had enjoyed that all too brief exchange, it did not soften the blow of her refusal. She did not want him.

He watched her move diagonally to take Rigby's hand and turn; then he moved to do the same with Miss Wimple. Serafina was hardly a ballet dancer, but she was improving.

Julien shook his head. He was wasting his time at this ball. He should be making a greater effort to meet the smuggler Stover had told him about. He should be amassing the necessary papers and making preparations for a trip to France.

And he would. He was leaving after this dance.

He took Serafina's hand again, turned toward her, and noticed that she put her hand on his chest. His gaze flicked to hers quickly, but she was not looking at him. Rigby and Miss Wimple stepped forward, and he had to cross in front of Serafina to meet Miss Wimple. As he passed her, he could have sworn he felt her hand on his side.

What was she doing now? Feeling his chest?

He darted a glance at her again, but—again—she was not looking at him. Had it been an accident? Was it a sign?

He finished turning Miss Wimple and went back to his place beside Rigby. Serafina was looking past him, her cheeks flushed and pretty and her breathing quick enough that the swell of her breasts rose and fell above her modest bodice.

He watched the rise and fall of that swell, watched the pink ribbons that ruffled as she breathed.

Damn. He needed a drink.

The dance ended, and out of rote, he moved forward and took her arm, leading her around the dance floor. Neither spoke, though half a dozen times Julien considered telling her he was leaving. But the words would not come. Finally, he managed, "I'll fetch you a refreshment."

"Thank you."

She released his arm; he bowed then headed for one of the footmen carrying trays of champagne before he remembered she had said she did not care for champagne.

Well, she was going to drink it tonight. He snatched two glasses and almost ran into Lord Melbourne. He had attended school with Melbourne, and they belonged to the same club. They were on friendly terms, though Julien had never liked the man.

"So, Valère, when is the happy day?"

Julien frowned at Melbourne. "Good evening to you, too, Melbourne. What are you going on about?"

"Your engagement. Shall we wish you happy?" He motioned to his wife, a silly blond watching him beside several others of her ilk.

"Are you on a reconnaissance mission?"

"Perhaps."

Julien smiled tightly. "Sorry. No scandal broth for the gossips tonight." He waved to Lady Melbourne and turned back toward Serafina. But he took only one step before he paused.

Serafina was talking to the same man with whom he had seen her on the terrace at Lord Aldon's ball. The man was watching him now, and Julien intended to find out why.

Eleven

"HE'S COMING THIS WAY," SIR NORTHROP SAID, BUT Sarah forced herself not to turn and look. Truth be told, she wanted to run to Valère. The way Sir Northrop was looking at her terrified her. "I won't tolerate further failure," he growled. "Get that key. Tonight."

With a glare, he walked away, and Sarah stifled a sob. What had he done to The Widow? When she asked about her, Sir Northrop had said, "She is unavailable."

The vague answer only made Sarah worry more. But she could not show that to Valère. She had to acquire that key. She turned to him and smiled.

"Who was that?"

She tried to ignore his demanding tone and took one of the glasses of champagne. She did not care for the taste, but right now she wanted a drink. "I told you at Lord Aldon's ball." She tried to make her voice sound light. "That's Sir Northrop, a family friend."

He did not answer, just stared at her, his look dubious. *Oh, please believe me.* If Valère figured out who Sir Northrop was, and what her mission was now, she was doomed. Sir Northrop had just spent five minutes castigating her for her slow progress. She had apologized, tried to explain, but he would have none of it.

"Make progress tonight, or you'll be out on the streets tomorrow," he'd said. Sarah had wanted to grab his sleeve and plead with him to give her more time, but she knew it would do no good. And she feared losing her position was the least Sir Northrop would do to her.

So now here was Valère, and she had to get that key.

She took a large swallow of champagne and tried not to panic.

"Thirsty?"

She nodded. "I…" *Think!* She had to get that key. Her efforts to pick his pocket during the dance had been—not surprising—unsuccessful, which meant she needed him to remove his coat.

How was she going to do that?

Seduce him? The idea was laughable—and required another large swallow of champagne.

"Don't drink that too quickly," Valère cautioned. "You'll get sick."

She stared at him. That was it!

"Oh, dear." She felt ill as it was and did not think she would have to do too much more to look the part.

He narrowed his eyes. "What's wrong?"

"I think I need to sit down. I'm not feeling well at all."

Anxiety flitted over his face. "Do you need the ladies' retiring room?" He looked about frantically. "Or perhaps I could fetch a potted plant?"

She sighed. She had tossed up her accounts once. *Once!* Was he never going to forget that?

She put her hand on his arm. "I feel… dizzy. I need to sit down."

He looked relieved, and then he glanced down at her hand on his sleeve. Sarah thought his eyes would sear through her skin, and she fought the urge to break contact. After all, she was supposed to convince him to propose again.

Somehow she doubted her hand on his arm would be quite enough. But it was a start.

He pointed to a series of chairs at the side of the room. Most were occupied by wallflowers, but there were several available. "You can sit there, and I'll fetch my mother."

Among the wallflowers was exactly where she belonged, but it was not what she needed. He led her forward, but she stopped him, this time with a hand on his bicep.

Oh, my.

He glanced at her hand, then at her.

"Oh, Your Grace, I do so need to get away from some of these people. The ball is such a crush." This was not true. Compared to Lord Aldon's ball, the Vichou ball was empty. But she was going to ignore that point for the moment. "Do you think we could go somewhere more private?"

She had not meant it as a romantic invitation, and if he took it that way, she could not tell. His azure eyes betrayed nothing, but he nodded and escorted her out of the room. The vestibule was hardly private, but he soon led her toward another door. Trying the handle, he found it open, and then held her back as he peered inside. "It's empty," he said, holding it wider so she could enter.

She stepped inside, glanced around at the darkened parlor, where only a low-burning fire shed light. Behind her, the door clicked closed, and she gasped in a breath. She should not be here. She should not be alone with a man in a dark room. Reverend Collier, the minister who had come to preach at the Academy every Sunday, would be so disappointed in her.

But, she reminded herself, she was not here for illicit reasons. She just needed that key.

She turned toward Valère, who was still standing at the door, watching her. "Is this better?"

"Yes, thank you." She took a seat on the chaise longue and tried to think. The fire was warm. Perhaps if she could lure him close to it, he would remove his coat.

"I'll go fetch my mother," he said, pushing away from the door. "I'll return in a moment."

"*No!*" It was a yell, and she immediately lowered her voice. "I mean, just wait with me for one moment, please. I don't want to take your mother away from her friends."

"Alright." But he looked uncertain.

She closed her eyes and forced herself to speak. "Why don't you come sit beside me?" She indicated the section of the chaise longue closest to the fire.

Opening her eyes, she gauged his reaction, and panic stabbed through her. He was going to say no. She could see it. And why wouldn't he say no? After all, she had refused his proposal, refused him.

Then, to her shock, he crossed the room and sat

at the edge of the chaise longue. She smiled at him, but now she had no idea what to say. He looked somewhat uncomfortable, so she knew she had better say something. She had to keep him here until he was warm enough to remove his coat.

"So do you like being a duc?" It was stupid. She knew it the moment the words left her mouth, but she did not know what else to say to him.

He furrowed his brow, obviously surprised by the question. "I suppose. Of course, I wish my father were still alive. He was a far better duc than I'll ever be."

"And your father died in the revolution."

"Guillotined."

"I'm so sorry." She put a hand on his arm, truly horrified.

"So am I. I was only thirteen when he was murdered. I wish I'd known him better."

She nodded, understanding. All her life she had wished she knew something of her mother or father— known anything about them. At least a name.

Sarah realized she was leaning close to Valère, her hand still on his arm. And he was looking at her, his eyes darker and bluer than she could remember seeing them.

"Are you feeling warm?" she breathed.

"Yes." His voice was a murmur, his eyes intent on hers.

"Would you like to take off your coat?"

Surprise flashed over his face, and then he reached for the buttons. "Would you like me to take off my coat?"

Oh, Reverend Collier would definitely *not* approve of this.

But she needed that key.

"Yes."

He inclined his head and slowly unfastened the buttons. Then he stopped. "Perhaps you could help me."

"Oh?" She had been watching his hand undo the buttons, anticipating how he would look sliding the coat off his shoulders. Would she see the muscles of his chest flex under that stark white shirt? And what if she skimmed her hand over that shirt, loosened that cravat, slid her hand—

"Come closer," he said.

She could not seem to resist the lure of those eyes. She moved toward him.

Then her cold hand was in his warm one. She looked down at their joined hands then up and into his eyes. With a slight tug on her wrist, he brought her closer, so close she could see the flecks of indigo in his dark blue eyes, so close she feared he could hear her heart pounding.

"Put your hand here," he instructed, laying it on his shoulder. "And then pull."

She knew he meant for her to pull the fabric off his shoulder—it really was a tight-fitting coat—but instead of tugging on the fabric, she tugged him, bringing him a whisper from her lips.

His hand came up behind her, cupped her neck, and he closed the distance. *"Ma belle,"* he whispered. *My beauty*.

His lips were light and feathery on hers, making her mouth tingle. She had not expected that sensation. It was different from what she felt at the opera. Then she had felt warm and heavy; now she felt heady and breathless.

And she did not expect that she would want so much more. She wanted more of his mouth, more of his hands, more of his body. He seemed to sense her need, and the feel of his mouth on hers changed. The light, teasing pressure ended, and his lips became firmer, more insistent. Her whole body blazed alive at this new touch. Every sense was awakened. His citrus and wood scent engulfed her; the warmth of his hands on her neck and back fired her blood; the sound of her heart pounding in her ears drowned out everything but the feel of his lips, his body.

And the feel of him. She was wantonly clutching his shoulders, her hands caressing the tightly corded muscles there.

His mouth left her lips and drifted to her chin, then to her ear. She shivered, feeling the light whisper of his breath against that virgin flesh. Until him, she had never been kissed, never been held, never been wanted. All of this was simply too much, and yet she could not make herself release him.

"Open for me, *chérie*. I want to taste you."

Sarah did not know what he meant, but his words made her quiver. Then before she could speak, could protest, his lips were brushing against hers again. "Open for me, *mon ange*." He was speaking in French now, his words like thick warm cream.

"I-I don't know what you mean," she stammered in French.

He pulled back, looked at her with those azure eyes. They were dark, so dark. His thumb caressed her chin gently. "Are you that innocent?"

She looked down, embarrassed, but he lifted her chin with a finger. "Don't be ashamed, *chérie*. I wouldn't dream of ruining you. Let me kiss you. *Laisse-moi te toucher.*" *Let me touch you...*

Yes, this was what she wanted—his hands, his fingers, his lips... everywhere. He slanted his mouth over hers again and, with gentle, insistent pressure, he opened her lips and swept inside.

Sarah held on, gripping his back to keep from sinking. Her head spun, her heart slammed against her breast, and her body was a furnace. He explored her slowly, gently, but oh so thoroughly. He tasted of champagne and raspberries.

And then, suddenly, he drew back. She could not open her eyes for a long moment, and when she did, he was staring at her, looking out of breath as well.

"I shouldn't have done that," he murmured, now speaking in English. She wished he would go back to French. English seemed far too cold and rational a language for what she was feeling at the moment.

"Why?" she breathed.

"Because now I want to do it again."

She let out a short laugh that ended in a moan when he reached for her again. This kiss was just as penetrating, just as deep, and even more intoxicating.

When he pulled away this time, it was to remove his coat. "I'm too warm after all," he muttered, and the words were like ice poured down her back.

The key.

She had come in here to pilfer the key, not to be swept off her feet by Valère's skillful kisses. But she could not concentrate with his mouth on hers, could not think of anything but kissing him back.

And yet, if she stopped kissing him, he would put his coat back on and leave.

They should both leave. How long had they been missing from the ball?

He laid the coat on the chaise longue behind him and reached for her again. "Your Grace—" she began in a halfhearted effort to dissuade him.

"Julien."

He nuzzled her neck, and the hairs on her arms tingled. "Julien," she whispered.

"Yes."

And then his lips were on hers again, plundering her, robbing her of any thought except that she never wanted him to stop. She felt his hands stroke her back, her neck, curl in her hair. And then he broke the kiss again and dipped to kiss her neck. "Serafina," he whispered.

She jumped and pulled back.

"What's wrong?"

Now that she was out of his arms, she could see that his hair was tousled and his eyes were hazy with passion. She probably looked just as disheveled.

But her head was clear now. She was Serafina to him, not Sarah. He had been kissing Mademoiselle Serafina Artois, not Sarah Smith.

She wanted to hit herself for being such a fool. He would never want her if he knew who she really was. She needed to end this charade once and for all. But she couldn't do that without the key.

"Serafina, what's wrong?" he asked again.

"I-I just think we should pause for a moment. I mean, what are we doing?"

He smiled. "Would you like me to show you again?"

She did. Oh, how she wanted him to show her, but she needed to get that key.

"I think we should return to the ball." Perhaps she could help him put his coat on again and pilfer the key while his back was to her.

"Are you feeling better?"

"Much."

He gave her a half smile, then rose and offered his hand. She took it, and he pulled her up and into his arms.

This time the kiss was her fault. She did not know if she would ever feel this way again, if she would ever meet another man who wanted her this way. A man who wanted her as his wife, the mother of his children.

Desperate for one last taste of what she would never have, she kissed him with all the passion and ardor she had saved for almost twenty years.

And so she was firmly in his arms, his lips solidly on hers, when the door opened.

In the next moment, she was thrust behind him, away from the eyes of Lord Vichou and—

Sarah wanted to groan.

There was Sir Northrop.

"It appears we have interrupted something," Lord Vichou said, taking in the scene with one glance.

"It was only a kiss," Valère said stiffly. "The lady did not feel well and wanted to get away from the crush of the ball."

Sarah felt her cheeks heat and wanted to climb under the chaise longue. This was so humiliating. Who would believe they had only been in here kissing?

No one. And that was precisely what Sir Northrop wanted. She had no illusions their discovery had been an accident. Obviously the man would stop at nothing to get what he wanted. In this case, her engagement.

Well, she wanted out of this so-called mission. With Valère's back to her and him shielding her from view temporarily, she scooped up Valère's coat, patted it down, and pulled a small gold key out of an inside pocket.

Finally!

"And who is the lady in question?" Sir Northrop asked. Sarah wanted to disappear. She knew exactly what was coming next.

"That's none of your concern, Sir Northrop," Valère said, his voice stern. "If you'll give me a moment to retrieve my coat"—Sarah handed it to him—"I'll fetch my mother, and we'll be on our way."

"That looked like Mademoiselle Serafina Artois," Sir Northrop said. "If that's the case, I must insist you make some restitution for the harm you've done her."

Sarah felt Julien tense and chose that moment to step out from behind him. Oh, dear. The crowd at the door had grown considerably larger. "Sir Northrop, thank you for your kind concern," she said, her voice wavering. "But I assure you that what you witnessed was nothing more than an innocent kiss. I've been in no way harmed."

Sir Northrop's steely gaze met hers, and she willed him to walk away. *I have the key. Forget the engagement.*

Lord Vichou nodded. "Well, if the lady says no harm was done—"

"The lady's reputation is harmed," Sir Northrop growled. "As a friend of her family, I must insist His Grace do the honorable thing."

Sarah held up her hand. "My honor has not been compromised. There's no need—"

Valère stepped in front of her again. "I won't have anyone challenge my honor." His gaze locked and held with Sir Northrop's. Sarah saw the duchesse in the back of the crowd, her face pale and her eyes wide.

"I assure you, on my honor, that nothing improper happened here. But"—he locked eyes with several of the guests, including Sir Northrop—"for those of you who question that, I am prepared to marry Mademoiselle Serafina. It's been my intention all along."

He turned back to her, his blue eyes hard as cobalt. "Mademoiselle Serafina, will you consent to be my wife?"

She sighed, feeling as trapped as he probably did. Perhaps more so as her heart was now involved. Why could nothing be simple or easy?

"Yes, of course I'll marry you," she said and clutched the small gold key in the palm of her hand.

Twelve

HE WAS ENGAGED. JULIEN LAY IN HIS LARGE FOUR-poster bed and stared at the ceiling.

Engaged.

He could still hear the shouts of well-wishers at the ball, the clink of champagne glasses as toasts were made, and the waver in Serafina's voice as she accepted him.

She didn't want him. She had told him that once before and had tried to escape her fate tonight.

Perhaps he could win her over. Perhaps he could make some grand romantic gesture. He had no idea what that might be, but Rigby was probably the fellow to help him out there. Rigby was always popular with the ladies.

Julien was not so popular. Rigby said his scowls scared women away, but Julien had never been interested in those timid creatures anyway.

Serafina was not timid. Or at least not as timid as he had first thought. When she had kissed him tonight, he had to pour every ounce of self-control into resisting the urge to push her down on that chaise longue and take her right there.

But he had resisted. He had been truthful when he said nothing inappropriate had happened between them. Yes, he had kissed her, but neither his hands nor lips had strayed. There was no reason he should have to marry her.

And yet he was not sorry. He wanted to marry her, wanted her in his bed, wanted to allow his hands and lips to stray over every inch of that long, lithe body.

He groaned at the image, then turned over, pulled a pillow on top of his head, and tried to go to sleep. He lay there for what seemed an interminable length of time, debating the merits of persevering or giving up, going to his office and getting some work done.

His office.

Julien threw off the pillow and sat. Had he locked the door when he had come to bed? He had already dismissed Grimsby for the night, so the butler would not have undertaken the task.

Julien shook his head and lay back. It didn't matter if the office was locked. His papers about Armand were secure in the secret drawer in his desk. Still... he felt uneasy.

With a sigh, he climbed out of bed and pulled a robe on over his nakedness. He would just lock the door and then go back to bed.

The house was quiet as he padded downstairs. He carried a candle, and the flame cast long, flickering shadows. He hated shadows. When he had been younger, he had nightmares where the shadows in his room turned from gnarled trees into old women brandishing pitchforks. He would close his eyes, only to remember the gurgling sound his nanny had made when she had been murdered. Thank God the smoke had prevented him from seeing that horror.

But he was a man now. He was too old to jump at shadows.

He continued down the wide staircase, liking the feel of the cold marble on his bare feet. He had bought that marble. He had paid for it, and it was a reminder of his success. A reminder that though the peasants may have tried to kill him, he was far from dead.

Julien stopped at the bottom of the stairs, turned toward his office, and stopped.

His office door was ajar.

Not by much. But he could see a minuscule glimmer of light through the sliver of space between the door and the casement.

Julien blew out his candle and set it on one of the side tables. Silently, he moved toward the door, stopping outside and listening. He heard nothing. Perhaps no one was in there, and it was he who left the library this way.

But he knew it wasn't so. He would never leave a light burning in the library. He would have shut the door securely.

He reached out and pushed on the door with two fingers, gently easing it open. The hinges were well-oiled and silent as the widening gap revealed the room.

There at his desk, oblivious to his presence, sat Mademoiselle Serafina. She was writing furiously, and from the way she glanced from one document then back to her own paper, he surmised she was copying something.

She still wore her ball gown, but her hair was down about her shoulders. It gleamed in the light from her candle and pooled about her face, her expression stern with concentration. In that long moment, Julien noted something else—Mademoiselle Serafina was wearing spectacles.

Casually, he crossed his arms over his chest and leaned on the door jamb. "What are you doing?"

She started, her pen flying out of her hand as she jumped to her feet. "Your Grace!" She put a hand to her heart, and he could see the thoughts rush across her face. How long had he been there? What had he seen? How could she escape?

He took a step forward. "Answer the question."

"I-I was writing a letter to my mother."

He moved closer. "Why not do so in your bedroom?"

"It was more comfortable in here." She leaned toward his desk in an effort to cover the papers spread there, but he hurried forward and grabbed her hand. He held it tightly as he first lifted the letter about Armand and then the copy she had been making.

"What the hell is going on here?"

"Nothing. I was—"

He yanked her around the desk, adjusting his grip so he now held her wrist. "Do not lie to me." He moved around the desk so he could see his secret drawer. It was open, his small gold key glinting in the lock.

He looked up at her, anger like he had never felt before churning through him. He wanted to throttle her. "How did you get my key?" Before she could fabricate another lie, he yanked her close and stared directly into her eyes behind the spectacles. "And think long and hard before lying to me again."

She swallowed and looked away.

"Serafina, tell me."

She whipped her head back to stare at him. Angry. Defiant. "Fine. You want the truth? I'm not Serafina."

He frowned. "What?"

"I'm not Serafina Artois, daughter of the comte de Guyenne. There is no Serafina. She died as a child. The whole family was killed when they fell out of favor with the king."

He stared at her, trying to comprehend her words. "But there were letters—"

"Fabricated." She must have seen something in his eyes because she quickly raised her hand as a shield. "Not by me, Your Grace."

"Who are you, and what are you doing here?" A knot had formed in the pit of his stomach, and those shadows he had always feared as a child crept in again.

She shook her head. "I can't tell you more. I've told you too much already."

Fury surged in him, and he gripped both of her arms tightly, pushing her back against the desk. "You're going to tell me everything I ask, and if you don't I'll—" He didn't know what he'd do.

She shook her head. "Go ahead. I'm doomed now anyway. And so are you."

"What the hell does that mean?"

"They're on to you, Your Grace. Do what you want to me, but you're the one who'll be drawn and quartered."

He stared at her, completely confused. "What are you *talking* about?"

"Treason." She spat the word, contempt in her eyes.

"What are you talking about?" he repeated, shouting now.

"I can't tell——"

He shook her, causing her spectacles to tumble down to the floor and her hair to fall back over her shoulders. "Tell me now, or so help me God——"

"Fine!" she cried. "I'm Sarah Smith. I'm a governess."

He did not know what he had expected her to say, but that was not it. He almost released her. "Why are you pretending to be Mademoiselle Serafina?"

"Not by my choice, I assure you. I had to do it, or they said they'd throw me out on the streets."

"Who are *they*?" He squeezed her arms. "Tell me."

"The Foreign Office. They know about you."

"Know what? That I'm French?"

"That you're a——"

"Traitor." Realization glimmered even as he asked the last question. Those trips to France had not gone unnoticed. The English government thought he was a traitor, and they had sent a woman to spy on him.

And not a very good spy either, if tonight was any indication.

"You said you were a governess. Why are you spying for the Foreign Office?"

"I had no choice. The Widow was assigned this mission——"

"Who?"

"I don't know her real name. She's a spy and

wounded. They had no one else to send. Sir Northrop said I had to go."

"Sir Northrop? Your helper at the ball tonight? The protector of your honor?"

"He's my employer. I'm governess to his children, Anne and Edmund." He was beginning to see her predicament, but he would not allow his sympathies to be touched. "But now I suppose he'll make good on his threat and throw me out on the street."

"You'll be lucky if all I do is throw you out on the street, you little vixen. You lied to me."

"I *had* to," she shouted back. "And I'm not sorry. I hope they catch you and throw you in Newgate!"

He released her arms and pushed away from her. "I'm no traitor."

"How do I know that?"

"I'm not the liar here. You are."

"Everything I've told you tonight is the truth."

"How can I believe you? Maybe this story about Sarah Smith is just another falsehood. After all, you had no scruples when seducing me at the Vichou ball. Perhaps you even orchestrated our engagement."

She looked away, and he swore. "You *did* orchestrate it."

"No." She shook her head. "Sir Northrop did that. I had no idea."

He crossed his arms again. "Really? No idea."

"Well, I knew he wanted me to become engaged to you, but I didn't think he'd go that far."

Julien shook his head, his thoughts in a muddle. Everything was jumbling about in his head, new questions popping up before he could ask the last ones.

"Alright." He raked a hand through his hair, crossed the room, and closed the library door. "Let's take this step by step."

"I've already said too much. I think I should go to my room and begin packing."

"And go where?" He crossed to his bottle stand and poured three fingers of brandy into one of the cut crystal glasses there, swallowed it down, and poured three more. "Want one?" he said without looking at her.

"No. My head is pounding." She sounded so miserable that he poured her one anyway.

"Here." He handed it to her. "Drink this. You sound like you need it."

She took a small sip and made a face. If he had not been so angry, he would have smiled. He sat in his desk chair and pulled the key out of his secret drawer. Holding it up for her to see, he palmed it.

Her behavior at the ball made more sense to him now. She had wanted the key. That was why she ran her hands over him during the dance, why she lured him away from the ball, why she kissed him. He fought not to show his disgust. All of the passion she had shown during their kiss had been a pretense for stealing his key. Was anything about this woman, this Sarah, not a lie?

"Can we talk about this tomorrow when you're"—she swallowed—"dressed?"

He glanced down and remembered he'd simply thrown a robe on over his nakedness. It was belted closed, but the vee in front revealed his bare chest. He pulled the material closed. "You're not going anywhere until I have the answers I want."

She sighed and sat on the couch to his right. She balanced her brandy on her knee but did not drink any more. He clenched his jaw, working to control his anger. "You took this key while I was kissing you."

"No. It was when we were... interrupted. I took the coat and extracted the key then."

"When we were interrupted," he repeated. "You mean, when I was forced to propose to you. Again."

She nodded.

"It occurs to me, madam, that you had no need to orchestrate a second proposal from me. You already had one, and you turned me down."

"I know. That's because I didn't know I was supposed to accept."

"What?"

"I was given this assignment at the last minute." She took another small sip of brandy, made a face. "I didn't know everything I was supposed to do."

"And what exactly are you supposed to do?"

"Find evidence to prove you're a traitor, turn it over, and turn you in."

Julien leaned back, heard the first nail hammered into his coffin.

❦

When he leaned back, his robe gaped open again, and Sarah had to take another gulp of the brandy. It burned when it went down, but her throat was parched. Was he wearing *anything* under that robe?

She had a feeling he wasn't.

If he had been more fully dressed, she might have

resisted telling him so much, but his bare legs and bare chest flustered her.

She sighed. Who was she fooling? She was a horrible spy. He had merely scowled, and she had told him all.

Not that he wouldn't have figured it out anyway. She was well and truly caught. He was no fool.

She did not know what to do now. She supposed she would have to go back to Sir Northrop and confess that she had botched this whole operation. She could tell him about the letter she had been copying, but that didn't really prove Valère was a traitor. In fact, it seemed to give him a legitimate reason for returning to France.

She sipped her brandy again. Agh! Awful stuff.

She glanced at Valère. Perhaps all was not lost... Perhaps she could prove Valère innocent. *Was* he innocent?

He was swirling his brandy glass, looking morose. "Is Armand your brother?" she asked.

His gaze snapped to her face, his look dangerous. She had better be careful here.

"Are you looking for more information to build the case against me?"

"No. I'm trying to help you."

"Why help a traitor?"

"*Are* you a traitor?"

He set the glass down. "I thought that was a given."

"It is—was. I don't know what to think anymore. You don't behave like a traitor. And the papers you have locked up, none of them are about state secrets. They're letters about family."

"Perhaps it's a code I use. *Armand* could stand for munitions or troop levels."

"I don't think so. I think he's your brother, and he's still in France, and you want desperately to get him out."

He kept his gaze locked on hers. "You're not such a bad spy after all, Miss Smith."

She felt strangely pleased by the compliment.

"And if that were true—that my brother needs my help—*would* you help me?"

She swallowed and looked down. "I don't know."

"I see. Why don't you think about it and tell me tomorrow." He rose and cinched his robe again. "I think it's best if we go to bed." He walked to the door of the library, and not knowing what else to do, she followed.

"But shouldn't we discuss our situation more? Sir Northrop will want to know what my progress has been. I'll have to tell him I've been compromised."

One hand on the door, he glanced at her. "You don't have to tell him anything. Yet."

"But—"

"That's your choice, Miss Smith. Short of locking you up, what can I do? My fate is in your hands."

"But—"

He reached out and grasped her shoulders. "Go to bed before I do or say something I'll regret."

His hand was warm and strong on her. She nodded and tried to pull away. Strangely enough, she wanted him to kiss her again. Of course, he would never do it. Not now that he knew the truth, but she wanted him anyway.

"We'll talk again tomorrow," he said then released her.

She swayed, feeling the absence of his touch keenly. "When? Where?" she asked.

"I haven't decided yet. Damn it." He grasped her arm, and she could feel the fury racing through him. "You want to speak with me? How about your bath?"

She gasped. "Your Grace!"

"Too private?" He caressed her cheek, but his touch was not gentle. "You had no qualms about breaching my privacy."

She tried to speak, but the words caught in her throat as his finger slid over her skin and down to her mouth.

"Perhaps I'll come to you in your room, when you're in bed. What do you sleep in, Sarah?"

She swallowed. His touch was robbing her of thought. "Nothing."

His eyes went dark.

"No! That's not what I meant. I have a—a night rail."

He smiled. "White? With ruffles here?" He touched her neck, and she shivered. His hand dipped lower. "And laces here?" He brushed the tops of her breasts, and she jumped back. "Perhaps I'll strip it away. Leave you as few secrets as you've left me."

"Your Grace—"

"Go to bed, little governess. Now. Before I change my mind and—"

She didn't wait for him to finish.

Thirteen

SARAH DID NOT SLEEP. VALÈRE'S PROMISES—OR WERE they threats?—swirled about in her mind until she was feverish with worry and, though she would never admit it, desire. Every time she closed her eyes, she imagined him standing beside her bed, wearing only his robe. She imagined that robe falling open to reveal his bronze chest...

And then she would sit up and force herself to think of geography or Latin verbs. Reverend Collier would have had much to say to her if he knew her thoughts and behavior this past day. She decided it would be best if she went to church Sunday. As that was the next day, she would go that very morning. The duchesse had not mentioned attending services, which meant it was not something she regularly did. Hopefully, Sir Northrop would not be waiting for her in one of the pews.

"You want to go where?" the duchesse asked the next morning at breakfast.

Sarah, who upon entering the dining room and seeing Valère at the sideboard was too nervous to eat, sipped a weak cup of tea instead.

"Church. Is there one nearby?" She tried to keep her eyes on the duchesse, but she caught Valère's look anyway. He was smiling at her, one brow cocked in a knowing expression. She looked away.

"Oh, dear," the duchesse said. "I suppose that living in Italy all this time, you may not be aware that the English despise our kind. The best we can do is to ask a priest to come to the house."

Sarah stared at the duchesse for a long, confused moment then blinked in understanding. Of course! The Valères were Catholic, as was Serafina. There were laws against Catholics, and Sarah could not think of any Catholic churches. She supposed there might be some underground, but she hardly wanted to force the duchesse to sneak into Mass. Not to mention, she had been raised Anglican at the Academy.

"Julien, could you send one of the servants for the priest?" the duchesse was saying.

"No, wait—" Having a priest in the house would not accomplish her purposes: escaping Valère. "I don't mind attending an Anglican church."

"Really?" the duchesse raised a brow.

Sarah spread her hands. "I doubt God has any objections."

The duchesse looked as though she did not agree, but she said, "In that case, I suppose St. George's in Hanover Square is the closest. I wonder what time services begin?" She glanced at Valère, who had taken a seat across from Sarah and was cutting a piece of ham.

Sarah had already dressed—hastily, as she feared Valère would interrupt her at any moment—and was ready to depart. "I don't want to disrupt your plans for the day, Duch—Rowena." She peeked at Valère. What would he think of her using his mother's Christian name, now that he knew she was no daughter of a comte but a plain governess?

He did not look up from the ham.

"If I could just borrow the coach—or better yet, if you would have a footman fetch a hackney for me—then—"

Rowena set her tea cup on the table with a rattle. "I will do no such thing. A hackney, indeed. You will be my daughter before long, and no child of mine will ride in a hackney."

Sarah's cheeks heated, knowing Valère heard all. He certainly did not truly intend to make her his wife.

"If you give me a quarter hour," the duchesse continued, "I'll change and go in the coach with you myself. Only I had planned to write a letter this morning, but I can put that off—"

"I'll go with her," Valère said without looking up from his plate. "You stay here, ma mère."

Rowena looked relieved. "Would you, Julien? I have fifty things to do this morning."

He rose. "Of course. I'll call for the coach immediately."

Sarah had not foreseen this possibility, and she wished she could take back the whole idea. She had imagined herself going to church—a small church, not the large, fashionable one at Hanover Square—alone. She needed time to herself.

Instead, she would have to travel with Valère, and escaping time alone with him was one of the chief reasons she wanted to go to church! But there was no way around the situation now. She gathered her

spencer and reticule and waited in the vestibule for
Valère and the coach.

Perhaps Valère would take this time to speak with
her, to prove he was not a traitor after all. She wanted
to believe that. She already did believe him innocent.

And that bias was certainly a problem.

What if she was wrong, and he was a traitor? Did
she know better than the Foreign Office?

She could not trust Valère. Not yet.

And she certainly could not trust herself. Valère's
kisses at the ball had exposed her feelings for what they
were: she was half in love with him. No matter that he
had no idea who she really was. No matter that he might
very well be a traitor to her country and her king.

He was a man of honor and principle. He had
wasted no time offering her his hand in marriage
when even the slightest slur had been leveled against
her reputation. He had danced with her, even after
she had stepped on his feet half a dozen times. He had
acted as a chaperone, making certain no one, not even
his friend Rigby, took advantage of her.

And he had done all this after she flatly turned
down his first marriage proposal. That must have been
a hard blow for a man with pride. And yet, he put his
own discomfort aside and did his duty.

What woman could resist a man like that? Especially
if he was tall and strong and handsome?

A better woman than she.

Valère swept into the vestibule, looking even more
handsome than her imaginings. He wore a dark blue
double-breasted coat, buff pantaloons, and polished
black boots. His white linen shirt and cravat were

simple, ideal to set off the hard lines of his freshly shaved jaw. And that was not the only concession he had made to his appearance this morning.

His normally unruly black hair was pulled back into a queue, fastened at the base of his neck. She stared at him, wondering how he managed all of this in just a matter of minutes.

He grinned at her. "Ready?"

He escorted her to the carriage, helped her up, and climbed in after her. He sat across from her, facing backward, while she took the choicer seat. He had already given the coachman the direction, so they both settled back as the coach began to move.

"You didn't have to come with me," she said after a long moment of silence.

"Didn't I?" He was staring out the window, and he did not turn to look at her.

"No, you didn't. I wasn't aware that you were particularly religious."

His gaze met hers. "I wasn't aware that *you* were. You're obviously not Catholic."

"Reverend Collier came every week to the Academy, and I faithfully attended services."

"What's the Academy?"

"The Ladies Benevolent Society Academy for Young Girls. It was where I grew up and was trained to be a governess."

He sat back and stared at her. "God's blood. You really are a governess, aren't you?"

She frowned at him. "Should you really blaspheme when we're on our way to church?"

He grinned. "Sorry. I didn't realize you were

serious about this. I thought—" He waved a hand as though dismissing the thought.

"You thought?" she prompted.

He shrugged. "I thought this was a ploy to get out of the house, to meet with the Foreign Office."

"It's not. In fact, I pray that Sir Northrop isn't present. However, as we are alone at the moment, perhaps we could have that talk you promised me last night."

"Worried I'm going to surprise you in your bed?"

"No," she said indignantly.

"Did you sleep at all last night?"

"I slept very well, thank you."

He sat back and crossed his arms over his chest. "You're a horrible liar, Sarah Smith. Is that really your name?"

"Yes."

"And what do your parents think of your working for the Foreign Office? Do they know?"

She looked down at her gloved hands. She was twirling the handles of her reticule around and around her fingers. "I don't have parents. The Ladies Benevolent Society Academy for Young Girls is an orphanage."

He did not speak, and she chanced a quick peek at him. "I didn't think. I'm sorry."

"It's nothing." But she could feel her cheeks heating, could feel the sting of unshed tears behind her eyes. He had probably already surmised her story. Left on the Academy's doorstep. Unwanted. Unloved. The daughter of a loose woman or worse.

"We're here," Valère said a moment later. He jumped down when the coachman opened the door, then assisted her down the stairs. Services had not yet begun, but the bells were pealing, and the *ton* was making its way inside via the columned portico.

Sarah had thought the theater was a showplace, but apparently church was as much so. The simple muted lavender gown and white cap she had chosen made her severely underdressed in the wake of ruffles, flounces, plumes, and sparkling gems.

No wonder Valère had shaved and dressed. Not that he had taken any special care for the balls or theaters they attended.

She glanced at him curiously and found him watching her, his look unreadable. And then he took her arm, placed it in his, and led her into the church.

∽

Julien had rarely attended church. It wasn't because being a Catholic put him at a severe social and political disadvantage. The disadvantages were not such that he cared to convert. And it wasn't that he minded the fashion show put on by the beau monde. He was used to that.

But he did mind having to think too much about God. This God, whom the rector called compassionate and merciful, did not seem so to Julien. Where had God been when the peasants had attacked his chateau? Where had God been when his father had been dragged away, beaten, imprisoned, and then guillotined? He was an innocent man as were many who had been put to death by the mobs. Was God in the blood that ran through the streets of Paris?

Was God here now, in the church in London?

He looked at Sarah and thought perhaps He was. So far, Julien had seen no sign that she was attempting to communicate with anyone from the Foreign Office. She was simply singing and praying and now listening to the rector's sermon.

She had, apparently, actually wanted to come to worship. The more Julien thought about that and thought about her, the more confused he became.

He had not believed her story about being a governess. He had not believed that Sarah Smith was her real name. It was too common—the perfect name for someone who was concealing their own identity.

Or the name of an orphan.

But could he believe that story?

He was afraid he could, and that changed everything. After he had left her the night before, he planned to wait until this morning, tell his mother who Serafina really was, and order her out. He doubted her story about the Foreign Office. The government of England was inept, but not so inept as to engage someone like Sarah in a scheme like this one.

She had to be lying, which meant this was probably some elaborate dupe intended to take him for as much as possible. Sir Northrop and The Widow were most likely her accomplices. This sort of thing was far too common in England, though the perpetrators were bold indeed to attempt such a ruse on someone of his rank and with his resources.

But sitting beside Sarah at church, Julien could almost believe her orphan-to-governess-to-spy story. And if she was telling the truth, he was in serious jeopardy. The government did not need real proof to convict a traitor. They could fabricate it, and paying witnesses to testify at the Old Bailey was all too common.

As a duke, he should be exempt from such treatment, but he was not a peer of England. His title was French and had been obliterated by the revolution. He had few rights under English law, and none of those afforded the peerage.

Which meant he needed Sarah. He needed her to convince the Foreign Office he was not a spy.

They were going to have a long talk tonight.

The service ended, and Julien was forced to stay and speak with several of his acquaintances. He was not surprised that word of his engagement had spread quickly, and he was heartily congratulated all around.

Then, to his surprise, Marcus Stover was at his side. "Didn't expect to see you here."

Julien shrugged. "I'm full of surprises lately."

"I hear congratulations are in order." Stover clapped him on the back. "I'm happy for you." He glanced at the small groups surrounding the new couple and lowered his voice. "Can we speak in private a moment?"

Julien stole a glance at Sarah, who was nodding and listening faithfully to the Dowager Marchioness of Heathstone, then followed his friend into an alcove. "What is it?"

"Have you had any success contacting the person we spoke of?"

Julien knew immediately that Marcus was referring to the smuggler who might be willing to transport Julien to France. "Not yet. I've sent notes, but my messengers have been unable to locate him. Is he still in London?"

"He's in Town, and I know where he'll be tomorrow night."

Julien's blood was pumping now. Things were beginning to come together. "What time?"

"Meet me outside Covent Garden at ten."

Julien raised a brow. "We're going to the theater?"

"You may wish we were. Come armed."

"Your Grace?" Somehow Sarah had escaped the dowager and was coming toward him. "Mr. Stover." She smiled and came to stand beside Julien. Without thinking, he gave her his arm.

She took it, still smiling at Marcus. "How are you, sir?"

"Very well, my lady. Congratulations on your engagement. I'm sure you'll make Valère a happy man."

She gave Julien a rueful glance then said, "I hope so."

Julien escorted her back to the carriage and directed the coachman to take them home. Sarah was silent, and that suited him. He had much to do before departing for France, and he might need to be ready on a moment's notice.

"Your Grace?"

Julien looked away from the window. Sarah sat across from him, her gloved hands knotted in the lap of her muted purple gown. "What is it?"

"I was just thinking that now might be a good time for us to finish the discussion we began last night. We're alone, and no one can overhear."

"You did, did you?" She was probably right, but they were too close to home now to begin a discussion.

"It seemed appropriate."

He leaned back. "Don't worry, Sarah. We'll have our talk."

She clenched her hands again. "When?"

He grinned. "Leave that to me."

She sighed heavily and looked out the window. "That's what I was afraid of."

Fourteen

SARAH WAS NOT ASLEEP WHEN HER BEDROOM DOOR opened. She had been in bed for almost two hours, and she had not so much as closed her eyes. All day she waited for Valère to make an effort to pull her aside, speak to her alone. But he seemed content to work in his library, not even emerging for dinner.

Sarah had been immensely annoyed. If he were going to stay in his library all day, why not think of some pretense to call her in?

The duchesse must have sensed her annoyance, because she made excuse after excuse. "Julien has always worked far too hard, my dear. Perhaps when you are married, you will be able to encourage him to take more time for himself."

Sarah doubted it. She wouldn't be marrying Valère, and it taxed her already thin patience to pretend she was. But the duchesse was obviously overjoyed with the engagement. She was busy writing letters to Serafina's mother—letters Delphine Artois, long dead in her grave, would never receive—discussing the trousseau and attempting to determine the best date for the nuptials.

"We don't want it to be too soon," the duchesse said, consulting her calendar. "I need time to make all of the arrangements. Can you bear to wait four months?"

Sarah gaped at her. The prospect of spending four months pretending to be Serafina was like a prison sentence.

"Three months, then," the duchesse added quickly. "Can you bear it?"

"Of course," Sarah answered cheerfully. After all, she would not have to play this role much longer, no matter what the duchesse planned.

But as much as the preparations vexed Sarah, there was some joy in them as well. She would probably never have the opportunity to plan her own wedding, and the more time she spent with the duchesse, the more the woman became like a mother to her.

In Sarah's own phantom memories of her mother, her mother's shadowy face was at times replaced by Rowena's.

At eleven, Sarah finally decided that Valère was not going to deign to come out of his library, so she excused herself from the talk of wedding preparations and went to bed.

She told Katarina to lay out the most modest night shift she owned, but the girl had either not understood, or Serafina only owned one night shift, because the girl had put out the same one she always wore.

Sarah had dismissed the girl and then put it on. She wondered how Valère knew it had lace at the throat and laces down the front—laces that tapered into a vee at the valley of her breasts.

She laced the gown tightly, put her robe on over it, and climbed into bed. After about an hour, the robe was stifling her, but she kept it on for another thirty minutes. Finally, she decided Valère was not coming, discarded the robe at the foot of her bed, and tried to sleep.

She only succeeded in tossing and turning so much that the bed clothes were in hopeless disarray. She had her eyes open and was counting sheep—number three hundred and seventy-six—when the door opened and Valère entered.

At least she hoped it was Valère. Her eyes darted to the entry, and she watched the large form quietly close the door and then move toward the bed. Her heart was pounding in her chest, and she squeaked, "Your Grace?"

"Damn it," he muttered. "I told you to call me Julien."

She scrambled to a sitting position, pulling the bed clothes to her chin. "I don't think that's wise, Your Grace. Your presence here is already most inappropriate."

She thought she heard him chuckle; then a match near the fire flared, and the candle beside her bed flickered to life.

He was standing about two feet away, hands on his hips, wearing a linen shirt and buff breeches. He had removed the boots, probably so he could move about quietly, and she could see his white stockings. She could also see a good deal of his bronze chest. The buttons at his throat were open, and he was not wearing a cravat.

"Would you care to go to my room?" he asked casually. "Would that be more appropriate, *Miss Smith*?"

"Might we consider the library?"

"We might, but I'm already here."

She bit her lip, desperate to get him out of her room. She was lying in bed in nothing but her night rail. It was heavy and plain, to be sure, but she should not be in bed in his presence. "What will the servants think if they see you coming or going?"

His eyes glittered like sapphires. "I think you already know the answer to that question."

"Your Grace!"

"Julien." He took a seat at the foot of the bed, his weight causing her robe to slide off. Drat!

"The only servant I'm concerned about is your maid, but I have it on good authority that she has a closet on the upper floor."

"You asked?" Sarah hissed. "The servants will wonder why you asked."

Valère looked unconcerned. "I can be discreet, although apparently not discreet enough to keep my travels to France from the notice of the Foreign Office. Can you tell me when they began to suspect I was a traitor?"

"No. I don't know, and I wouldn't tell you if I did."

"Because you don't trust me."

She looked away, glad to look anywhere but at that bronze chest and his form sitting on her bed.

"What about all that talk last night of trying to help me?"

"I do want to help you, but I won't betray my country to do so."

"How can I make you trust me?" he asked, looking more serious now.

When she did not answer, he moved closer, his

hand reaching out to smooth a stray hair away from her cheek. Her breath hitched, and she leaned away from his touch.

He was quiet for a long minute, and then he began speaking in a low voice. "I was thirteen when the peasants came. I was thirteen and the oldest of three sons. My twin brothers, Bastien and Armand, were just eleven. We'd been in Paris for several months, and we didn't understand why my father suddenly wanted us to move back to the country. We'd heard about the riots, but there were always riots in Paris.

"That time we heard even more disturbing rumors. My parents would not discuss them with us, of course, but some of the servants would. Our nanny told us that the crowds were screaming, *Mort à l'aristocratie!*"

She looked at him now, moved by the sound in his voice when he spoke in French. But he was not looking at her. His eyes were far away, back in France, hearing his nanny tell him the stories.

"We heard terrible things," he continued, and Sarah did not think he realized he had reverted to speaking in French. "We heard things we couldn't believe—the Bastille stormed, innocent men and women killed in the streets, children murdered. We didn't believe it.

"The family protested when my father moved us to the country. Not I. I always did what was expected of me. But I sympathized when Bastien—it was always Bastien—complained. He loved Paris and found the country dull. Armand was happy anywhere he had books. He was so intelligent. He could talk his way out of any difficulty."

Sarah smiled, liking the image he painted of his

younger brothers. Bastien, the recalcitrant child, and Armand, the brains of the family. It was obvious Julien had been—as he was now—the leader. The perfect heir to the title. She could see him, even as a little boy, playing the man.

"And then one night I awoke and saw flickering on my ceiling." He looked at her candle, seemed to watch it flicker. "I don't know what woke me, probably the noise, and when I looked out the window, I saw our courtyard was overrun by peasants carrying crude weapons."

He met her gaze now, his eyes cold and hard. "We weren't cruel to them. I know some landowners were. They took the peasant women for their own purposes. They overworked children. They put a heavy tax burden on their workers. My father was a fair man and a good man. We thought our peasants loved us."

He swallowed.

"They didn't."

∽

How could he explain to her the sense of betrayal he had felt—that night and even more so later? Was there something he could have done to prevent the uprising? Something he did to provoke it?

He had never mentioned these feelings of guilt to his mother. He knew she would tell him he had done nothing wrong, and perhaps he hadn't. But he did not know how else to make sense of his shattered life.

Sarah was watching him as he told her about meeting his mother in the hall, rushing to the twins' rooms, and finally the sprint to safety. Her eyes were wide and so very brown in the candlelight. He didn't know if telling her his story, opening his past to her, would make her trust him, but it was the only thing he knew to do.

He had told this story only once before—to Marcus Stover. Rigby knew bits and pieces, but Marcus knew the whole. For some reason, it had been easier to tell Marcus.

"What did you do when you came to London?" she asked. "Did your mother's family take you in?"

"Yes. They were kind." He told her about living with his mother's people, the adjustment to life in England and schooling, and his relentless drive to restore his family fortune. *Ne quittez pas.*

"I made some good investments," he said, summing it up. "And now my mother never has to worry about money again."

She nodded, leaning forward. He thought she had probably forgotten they were in her bedroom and she was dressed in only her night shift. It was almost exactly as he had imagined it, though seeing her in it was not at all what he expected. The laces at her throat were tied tightly, but the more he talked, the more engrossed she became. The bedclothes had slipped down, and he could see the laces plunged between her breasts.

They were full, ripe breasts, if their shape under the linen was any indication. He could see the swell of one in the narrow gap between the laces. How his fingers itched to unfasten that knot and spread those laces apart. How he would enjoy slipping the gown off her shoulders and kissing every single part of her as he slowly exposed inch after inch of creamy flesh.

He swallowed. Such thoughts were out of the question. This was not some strumpet, and he would do best to remember that.

"I don't think that's the only reason you work so hard to make money," she said, and her voice snapped him out of his reverie.

"I suppose I like to be comfortable as well," he admitted.

"But that's not all. Your childhood security was splintered. You lost everything. It's only natural that you would want to make sure you could never lose everything again."

He shrugged. "Or perhaps I just enjoy business. I'm a duc without land, without an inheritance to oversee. I need something to keep myself occupied."

She nodded, looked thoughtful. "And you never knew what happened to your brothers? You think they're still alive?"

"I have no reason to believe otherwise." He could feel his defenses rising, but he tried to tamp them down.

"And your search for them is why you've traveled to France so frequently?"

"Yes."

"That's the only reason?"

He clenched his jaw. "Yes. I'm not selling state secrets. I just want answers."

"Have you found any?"

He gave her a long, hard look.

"Have your trips to France given you any reason to believe your brothers are still alive?"

When he still did not answer, she put a hand on his arm. "I'm not trying to disparage your search, but I need to give something to the Foreign Office. I need some proof that what you say is true."

He looked away from her and debated telling her about his plans to return to France. If he told her, would she alert the Foreign Office? Would she interfere with his plans?

"I have a letter," he began cautiously. "It's from one of the Valère servants. He says he has information that my brother Armand is alive."

She was nodding quickly now, excitedly. "That's the one I was copying in your library. But from what I understood, the servant won't tell you any particulars. He wants you to—" She glanced up at him, her eyes huge. "Oh, no."

He nodded. "I'm going back."

She shook her head. "You can't do that right now. The Foreign Office is watching you. They're watching *me* watch you." She threw off the bedclothes and knelt before him. "If you try to leave now, you'll be caught for certain."

"Not if you help me."

She shook her head. "How can I help you? I don't even know if I believe you."

Frustrated, he took her shoulders. "What else do I have to do? What do I have to say to make you believe me? You've heard my story; you've seen the letter. I have other documents you can see, correspondence, but nothing as convincing as the letter you have seen."

She was staring at him, her face close to his, her breathing rapid.

"I need you, Sarah. If the Foreign Office realizes I've left…"

"Alright," she snapped, jerking out of his arms. "I'll help you, but you have to be completely honest with me. I want no secrets."

He knew when his back was against the wall. "Fine. You've seen the letter. What else do you want to know?"

She thought for a moment, her head turned slightly away from him as she stared vacantly at a watercolor across the room. His eyes traced the curve of her chin and the sweep of her eyelashes. "How will you travel to France?" she said finally, turning back to him. "You can't exactly book passage."

He paused, his stomach knotting with uncertainty. If he told her the truth, she could ruin everything. But if he lied…

"Stover knows a privateer—a smuggler—who's still willing to make the passage. I haven't been able to contact the man yet, but that should change tomorrow night."

"What happens tomorrow night?"

"That doesn't concern you." He rose. "What I need—"

"—is my support," she finished for him. "You want me to vouch for you? Then you have to prove you speak the truth." She climbed out of bed, and he caught a flash of one ankle and calf.

"I will—when I arrive home with my brother."

She put her hands on her hips and shook her head. "And what am I to tell the Foreign Office in the meantime? What if they discover you've left England? I need some proof to hold them off until you return."

He clenched his fists. He had a pretty good idea what this proof she spoke of was going to be. "What proof?" he ground out.

"I want to go with you and Mr. Stover tomorrow night."

"No. Out of the question. It's not safe for a woman."

She glowered at him. "That's a risk I'm willing to take."

"Not I."

"Very well, then I'll tell Lord Northrop I've been compromised. He'll have to send in someone else or arrest you."

He stared at her, saw the determination in her eyes. Damn it! He couldn't be arrested. Not now. Not when he was so close to finding Armand. Even more of a concern was Sarah. What would happen to her if she admitted she had failed? Would this Sir Northrop really throw her out on the streets?

He could not allow that to happen. And he was angry that he cared so much, that he felt this need to protect her.

She had turned away from him and was climbing back into bed, but he grabbed her arm and spun her around. "You want to come tomorrow night?"

Eyes wide, she nodded.

"Petite sotte." Little fool. He took her by the shoulders and looked directly into her eyes. "Don't you care anything for your safety? This won't be a day at church. This could be dangerous."

"You'll take care of me."

He stared at her, shocked by her response. "Why the hell do you say that?"

"Because you see it as your duty."

He flinched, not wanting to admit she was correct. Devil take it! He did not want to take her into danger, but he could not leave her behind either. The woman was damn exasperating.

Damn attractive too. His mind might have been debating whether or not he could leave her behind, but his body was all too aware that they were alone, in her bedroom, and he was holding her in his arms.

She pulled back, eyeing him warily. "Why are you looking at me like that?"

He slid his hand behind her back, pulling her closer. "You're right that I'll have to protect you, *chérie*. I can't have my fiancée accosted."

She put her hands on his chest to hold him at a distance. "I'm not your fiancée. You're engaged to Serafina."

"*You're* Serafina."

"No, I'm not. I'm—"

He lowered his mouth to hers, cutting off her protest. At first she resisted, her hands pushing him back, but gradually she melted into him, her arms wrapping around his neck.

He liked the feel of her in his arms, liked the way her body trembled and her breath hitched. He slanted his mouth over hers, deepening the kiss, tangling his hands in her hair and cradling her head.

Gently breaking the kiss, he brushed lips against her cheek, her eyelids, her chin. He dipped to her neck, sorely tempted by that knotted fabric at her throat. One tug with his teeth, and he could loosen the laces, kiss her bare flesh, plunge a hand inside.

He looked up and saw that Sarah's eyes were closed, her cheeks flushed, her head fallen back.

She trusted him completely.

With a deep breath, he moved back and slowly released her. Her eyes fluttered open in surprise.

"Meet me in the library at nine tomorrow night. I'll come up with an excuse for my mother. You hold off the Foreign Office."

She nodded.

"Can you meet with them tomorrow?"

"I'll try."

"Good. I need time, and I need you to get it for me."

And then against his every bodily instinct, he turned and walked away from her.

Fifteen

SARAH WAS STARVING BY THE TIME NINE O' CLOCK arrived. She had been too edgy all day to even think of food, but at least her skills at lying were improving.

First, she had to lie to the duchesse. She told Rowena that she wanted to go shopping. The duchesse offered to go along, of course, and Sarah spent the entire morning walking along Bond Street, driving through Hyde Park, entertaining the duchesse and, at the same time, attempting to be seen and contacted by The Widow or Sir Northrop.

After four hours, the duchesse begged off, and Sarah took a footman to Gunther's on the pretense of buying a flavored ice.

She had just given up on meeting with the Foreign Office and ordered a strawberry ice, when she heard a familiar voice in her ear. "You had better have something for me."

Ice in hand, Sarah whirled to see Sir Northrop frowning at her. She took a deep breath. Each time she saw him, he seemed more impatient and angrier. She needed him to believe her lies.

Sir Northrop pulled her aside. Gunther's was not crowded, and it was easy to whisper in a corner without being overheard. "Did you acquire the key?"

"Yes." That was an easy question and required no lying whatsoever.

"Did you use it?"

"Yes." Another easy question. Buoyed by her success, Sarah ate a small spoonful of the ice. "I was able to open the hidden drawer in Valère's desk."

"What did you find?"

"A large cache of correspondence." This was not exactly true, but she had found that one letter. Her hand was cold, and she set the ice aside. "Unfortunately, I wasn't able to read much of it." Deep breath.

"Why not?"

"Valère came in."

Sir Northrop gripped her arm savagely. "Did he discover you?"

Sarah winced and tried to free her arm from his punishing grip. This lie was the most difficult. "No." She swallowed. "I managed to escape into the parlor without him realizing anything was amiss."

Sir Northrop frowned. The story was vague and implausible, and Sarah knew it. But she was too nervous to be able to remember any of the details she had fabricated while lying in bed last night.

If she had fabricated any details. It seemed she lay there thinking of Valère's kiss for most of the night.

"Did you manage to read anything?"

She nodded. "A little. Something about someone called Armand." She watched him closely now, wondering how much Sir Northrop already knew. If

Valère had lied about his brother, Sir Northrop might not know of him. If Valère told the truth, the Foreign Office—if they were any good at their work—should know something about this lost sibling.

"The duc's brother." Sir Northrop nodded, his eyes narrowing. "So he's still looking for him." Sir Northrop made the statement almost to himself, and Sarah felt her heart speed up. Valère had spoken the truth!

"Do you know where he is?" she asked.

Sir Northrop gave her a long look. "Somewhere Valère will never find him."

She thought that was all he would say, and her heart sank. But then he smiled, looked almost cocky. "Locked in the attic."

"Where?"

Sir Northrop waved away her question. "It need not concern you. Do you still have Valère's key?"

Sarah wavered for a moment, and then decided to tell the truth. "No. But I know I can get it," she added hastily. "Now that I'm Valère's fiancée, I have more freedom within the house."

"When will you have it again? I *need* those documents. My other sources are telling me that Valère is planning another trip to France. He's made inquiries. This time I intend to catch him."

Sarah blanched and gripped the back of a chair to steady herself. He knew about Valère's plans to return to Paris.

"When can you have the documents?"

When she did not answer, he twisted her arm, causing her to cry out in pain. "If you can't do this, say so now. I'm running out of time."

"I can do it," Sarah said through the pain. "But why are you in such a hurry? If I just had more time—"

"We're out of time! Do not fail me or—" He pressed his lips together, forming a razor-thin line.

Sarah swallowed. "You'll do to me what you did to The Widow?"

He grinned at her, slow and evil. "What do you know about our friend?"

"I know I have not seen her. I know she was frightened of you."

He nodded, satisfaction on his face. "You should be frightened too. My back is to the wall. I have nothing to lose by killing you."

Sarah inhaled sharply, fear stabbing through her. "Is that what happened to The Widow?"

"Worry about what might happen to you." Sarah's blood ran cold as he gave her a look that said he meant every word. "I'll look for you at Mrs. Southwick's musicale."

"Mrs. Southwick's musicale?" Sarah frowned. She had not realized she had anything but Valère's mysterious appointment on her calendar. They had told the duchesse they were going to Vauxhall Gardens.

"You had better be there."

"Of course."

"Eat your ice before it melts." He handed the treat back to Sarah, who took it. She dug in her spoon and pretended to eat, but when Sir Northrop was gone, she had to struggle not to gag.

Later that day, she was still lying. This time to Valère himself. She knocked on the library door at nine, hoping he would be so engrossed in his plans for the evening that he would not question her too closely about the meeting with the Foreign Office. If he knew how much danger she was in, he might turn himself in just to protect her. She could not allow him to do that. She could not allow him to fall into Sir Northrop's plan. There was more to this than a simple investigation by the Foreign Office, but whatever Sir Northrop had planned, until she acquired unquestionable proof that Valère was innocent, he was in danger.

"Enter," he called, and when she walked in, he looked up from his desk and said, "How did your meeting go? Did they find you?"

"Sir Northrop found me at Gunther's."

"And?" He rose, and she noted he was wearing all black except for his shirt and cravat—black breeches, black coat, and a black greatcoat draped over the couch. The greatcoat would certainly cover the white linen.

"And they're very anxious for progress," she told him. "They want documents. They know about the drawer in your desk"—he frowned at that—"and they want to know what's in it."

"But you held them off?"

"Of course." That wasn't exactly true, but she thought she sounded convincing.

"For how long? I may not be able to sail right away."

For a moment, she wondered if she should reveal what Sir Northrop had said about Armand. Then she decided to wait. It didn't make sense to her, and she might need the information later. "About your travel plans," she said, eager to leave the topic of how patient the Foreign Office was prepared to be, "they know you've made inquiries about leaving the country."

He stared at her, blue eyes blazing. "How the devil do they know that?"

"*I* didn't tell them."

He gave her a dubious look.

"They are spies, you know. They have ways of finding out these things."

"Right."

She frowned at him. "You're going to have to trust me at some point."

"Are you ready to go?" he asked, neatly evading her statement.

"I suppose."

"Is that what you're wearing?" He gestured to her crushed cranberry evening gown.

She looked down at it, surprised she felt almost natural wearing it. Amazing how, after mere days, she had grown accustomed to dressing in velvet and silk, draping herself in diamonds or rubies, such as she wore tonight. She almost looked forward to dressing in the morning. When she dressed as Serafina, she felt beautiful. It was easy to notch her chin up and look others in the eyes. She could almost look Valère in the eyes. "It's the only dark evening gown I have," she told him.

"What about that blue gown you wore the day you arrived?"

She raised a brow, surprised he remembered such a detail. "It's a day dress."

"Well, you can't go about in that." He walked past her, opened the library door, and called for his valet.

"Why not?"

"Shows too much flesh."

She glanced down again. Compared to the dresses

other women wore, it was quite modest. But she smiled slightly at his protectiveness.

The valet appeared at the door and bowed obsequiously. "Monsieur le Duc?"

"Fetch my cloak."

"I thought Monsieur le Duc was wearing the greatcoat."

"The cape isn't for me. It's for Mademoiselle Serafina."

The valet looked past him to her, then back at him again. "Oh, no, Monsieur le Duc. She is too short. The cape will drag on the ground."

Sarah covered her mouth to keep from laughing. Valère's valet was actually arguing with him, and she could tell the duc was annoyed.

"Luc, get the cape."

"But I worry. The hem will come back dirty and frayed. Doesn't the lady have a cloak of her own? I can have it fetched in just a mom—"

"Get. The. Cape. *Now.*"

Not in the least intimidated, the valet sighed heavily. "If that is what you wish."

Valère turned back to her, giving her a look that precluded any comments about his valet.

"Where are we going?" she asked instead.

"Covent Garden." He led her out into the vestibule, locking the library behind them.

"The theater?"

He did not answer, seeming impatient for his valet to return. The house was quiet. The duchesse had gone on to the musicale alone because she expected they would spend the evening at Vauxhall Gardens. His mother was more than happy to give the couple time alone, but Sarah worried about what would happen when Sir Northrop realized she was not coming to the musicale.

She had little time to dwell on it. Valère's valet returned with the cloak, and the duc dropped it over her shoulders. It was heavy and smelled like him. She shivered, remembering his hands on her the night before.

"Let's go."

Obviously Valère desired anonymity. Instead of a coach, the duc had a hackney waiting. Sarah was pleased to see that it was clean inside. The drive to Covent Garden was long as the traffic in London was considerable. The ride was made longer as Valère kept up a steady stream of rules and admonishments.

Sarah sighed. "I understand. I'm to stay with you at all times, say nothing, do nothing, and keep my face hidden."

"You forgot that you are not to say your name or give any indication of who you are."

She frowned at him, and thankfully the hackney slowed.

They alighted and were met by Marcus Stover. Sarah liked him. He was amiable and intelligent. He did not appear as gratified to see her. He gave Valère a questioning look, to which the duc replied, "Don't ask."

Stover didn't. Instead, he bowed and began to greet her, but Valère clapped him on the shoulder. "Don't give any indication that she's anyone important."

Stover nodded. "Good idea. Where we're going, it's best if everyone assumes she's just a doxy."

Sarah sighed. From governess to spy to prostitute. What was next?

Stover gestured to the hackney he had procured. "I had to pay a king's ransom, but the jarvey's agreed to take us into Seven Dials."

"Seven Dials!" Sarah blurted out.

"You've heard of it, my lady?" Stover asked.

"I—" She had forgotten she was supposed to be from Italy. "I thought I heard one of the gentlemen at a ball discussing it. He said it's a den of thieves and cutthroats, and few who go there come out alive."

"It's not as bad as all that," Valère said, and Sarah felt somewhat reassured. Stover opened the hackney's door, but Valère held her back for a moment. "Remember what I told you. Do *not* leave my side."

He took her hand, and Sarah closed her eyes, allowing herself to be handed up. She wished she had known those cucumber sandwiches would be her last meal. She would not have refused the slice of lemon cake.

If she made it through this night alive, she was eating as many ices at Gunther's tomorrow as she could stomach. Cake, pies, and tarts too.

The men climbed into the hackney after her, and Sarah could not help staring out the window. It was not long before the sundial marking the entrance to Seven Dials came into view. She blew out a breath. What she would not give for a piece of cake.

❧

Julien did not like taking Sarah into Seven Dials. He had seen her face go white at the mention of the place, and he didn't feel much better about it.

But he was not surprised. After all, smugglers

weren't exactly the type to hold soirees in their drawing rooms. Sarah would be fine, he reasoned, even as they drove past several rough-looking men. He saw Stover clench his walking stick a little more tightly and did the same. As long as Sarah did as he had instructed, she would be fine.

The hackney wound its way past the dregs of humanity. Children begged in the streets, some deformed and so thin Julien did not see how they could walk. Prostitutes plied their trade brazenly, and men and women gambled in every door. The sound of music and the clinking of glass and a baby's forlorn squalling filled the night.

In the hackney, Sarah clutched his hand tighter.

Stover rapped on the roof of the hackney, and the conveyance slowed. "I have it on good authority that our man can usually be found in The King George."

Julien half laughed at the name. He would bet a thousand pounds the King had never been within a mile of his namesake, nor ever would be.

The tavern had little in the way of royal accoutrements. The wooden sign outside was dirty and crooked, as were the patrons spilling out of it. Julien moved aside to allow the two men and one woman to pass, and then pushed through the people at the entrance.

Dark and crowded, the place smelled of rotted wood, dried ale, and unwashed bodies. Stover led them to a corner, which gave them a view of most of the room. He stood and observed for a few moments, then turned to Julien. "I have a pretty good description of the man, but I don't see anyone who matches it."

"Who are we looking for?"

"He goes by the name Captain Rex Stalwart."

Julien raised a brow. It was almost certainly an assumed name. "What does he look like?"

"Medium height. Black hair, long and curly, and a black mustache." Julien scanned the room without any luck. If it had been just he and Stover, he would have ordered a gin and sat at a table with Stover to wait. But he did not want Sarah here any longer than necessary.

"Wait here," he told her, putting her arm through Stover's. "Keep an eye on her," he admonished his friend.

A large, muscled man was behind the bar, and Julien had no trouble attracting his attention. "What can I get you, gov? I've got some good wine if you've the coin to pay for it. And if these old eyes don't deceive me"—he gave Julien's greatcoat a long look—"you do."

"What I need is information," Julien said, placing a crown on the scratched wood of the bar. The bartender eyed it and then Julien.

"Go on."

"I'm looking for Captain Rex Stalwart. Heard of him?"

The man covered the crown with his hand, sweeping it away. "I might have."

"Know where he is?"

"I might."

Julien laid another crown on the bar, and the man just stared at him. Clenching his teeth, he laid another crown beside the first.

"He has a room upstairs. Third door on the left."

He turned away, taking the crowns with him, and Julien went back to Stover and Sarah.

"He's upstairs. Let's go."

"I could wait in the hackney," Sarah offered.

Julien frowned. "Don't talk."

He barreled his way through the room and up the stairs with Sarah behind him and Stover directly behind her. At the appointed door, he gripped his walking stick tightly and knocked firmly.

"Are you certain this is the right door?" Sarah hissed. Julien gave her a silencing glare.

The voices behind the door ceased, and a moment later, it opened enough so Julien could see a large, shirtless dark-skinned man with two gold hoop earrings. "Who are you?"

"No one." Sarah stepped back, but Julien grabbed her before she could retreat.

"Julien Harcourt. I need to see Captain Stalwart."

"The captain ain't in."

Sarah pulled back again, but Julien ignored her, sticking his foot in the doorway before the pirate could shut him out.

"We can wait. I think the captain will be interested in seeing me."

"Why's that?"

"Because I have the money to make it interesting."

"Let him in, Oak," a voice from the other side of the door called. Oak, who was as big as a tree and thus aptly named, moved aside and opened the door.

Julien entered, keeping Sarah, as skittish as a new colt, behind him, and Stover on his right. The room was tastefully decorated. It was a sitting room with a door on one side that probably led to the bedroom. Captain Stalwart sat in a chair, and in his hands he held several documents. Julien also saw maps strewn about.

But for Oak, the captain was alone, and his eyebrows rose as the three of them entered. "A visit from the quality," he said, tone mocking. "To what do I owe this honor?"

"I understand you're a man who can acquire things—French silks, French wines."

"Is that what you need? Something pretty for your ladybird?"

"I need much more than that. I need passage to France."

Stalwart didn't blink. "I can't get you there."

Julien pulled out a sizeable stack of blunt. "That's not what I hear, and I'm prepared to pay."

Stalwart leaned back. "Julien Harcourt," he said lazily. "You wouldn't happen to be related to the duc de Valère?"

Julien did not answer.

"I've received several letters from this duc. But I haven't responded. Know why?"

Stalwart rose, not seeming to expect an answer. He stepped forward, rested his hands on the back of another chair. "Because I don't take passengers. You can take a packet across the Channel, if that's what you want."

"There aren't any at present."

He gave a look of mock despair. "Too bad."

"Yes, it is," Julien said, putting his money away. "Let's go," he said to Stover.

They turned to leave, but before they could reach the door, Sarah cried, "Wait!"

Julien clenched his jaw. How had he known she would not be able to do as he had told her?

Sixteen

"SERAFINA, LET'S GO," VALÈRE SAID FROM BEHIND HER. He took her arm firmly, but she shook him off. She knew she should shut up and go with Valère, but then what? If Valère did not succeed in traveling to France and recovering his brother, Sarah would have to admit to Sir Northrop that she had failed. She could not surrender Valère to Sir Northrop, especially now that she knew, almost without a shadow of a doubt, Valère was innocent.

This was her last chance, perhaps Valère's only chance. She could not walk away without a fight. "Captain Stalwart, you have to allow His Grace go with you."

Stalwart's eyes narrowed at her. His eyes were dark and his skin swarthy. He might have been a handsome man once, but now he was hard and weathered. "I don't *have* to do anything, madam."

"But you don't understand—"

"Serafina? Is that your name?"

She pursed her lips. "Yes."

"Well, Serafina, I decide who gets on and off my ships, and your duc isn't coming."

"But if you only knew why he needed to go—"

"I already know."

She paused. "You do?"

"*Serafina.*" Valère took her arm again. "We're leaving."

She shook him off again. "Not yet." Valère swore under his breath, but she focused on the captain. He was watching them, eyes glittering. "I don't think you do know why His Grace wants to go back to France."

"You're a feisty one, ain't you?" Stalwart said, sitting down again and raising his wine glass.

"Not usually," she muttered. Valère was going to kill her for this. She had broken just about every one of his rules.

"Your duc wants to go back to France to see if he can reclaim any of his fortune. I see a dozen of his kind in a year. They want to reclaim what's rightly theirs. Well"—he looked at Valère—"you're not going to get it, and in my opinion, you probably don't deserve it back anyway."

Valère stepped forward, but Oak jumped in front of him, blocking his access to the captain. "You don't know anything about my family, Stalwart."

The captain shrugged. "And I don't care. Good night."

Oak began to push Valère and Stover out the door, and Sarah figured she had exactly two more minutes before she was thrown out as well. "But you don't understand. Valère doesn't care about money or land he lost in France. He has far more wealth here in England. What he cares about is his brother Armand. He wants to rescue him."

Oak grabbed her arms and lifted her off the ground. She was too determined to stay to be frightened.

Struggle as she might, the big man moved inexorably toward the door. "Surely you can't refuse a man who just wants to save his brother! The boy was only eleven when he was left behind. Surely you can't hold a boy responsible"—she grabbed onto the door jamb, and Oak tried to pry her hands loose—"for the crimes of the aristocracy."

Her hands fell free, and she stumbled back into the hallway. The captain's door slammed shut in her face.

Valère caught her. "What the hell were you thinking?"

She looked down, feeling stupid and ineffective. "I'm sorry. I should have remained silent. I just wanted to help."

"Well, next time you can better help by not announcing my life story to complete strangers."

"Perhaps we should be on our way." Stover, who had been standing a few feet away to give them privacy, spoke up now. "I don't like to court trouble any longer than I have to."

"Right. Let's go." Valère took her arm and followed Stover down the stairs and back into the tavern. A few people glanced at them curiously, and Sarah quickly replaced the hood of the cape, covering her hair and face.

Once outside, they realized the hackney was gone. Stover swore, but all three knew they were not likely to find another. Valère began walking. "What will you do now?" Sarah asked as they made their way past a group playing dice.

"I'll find another way to get to France," Valère growled. "I'll never give up."

"Perhaps you should wait," Stover said.

Sarah did not like Stover's suggestion, but what other choice did they have? "Perhaps Mr. Stover is correct." She tried not to cough as they passed a woman stirring a pot containing a foul-smelling concoction. Oh, how she wished this night were over. "Right now you're being watched so closely—"

He stopped and whirled to face her in front of a bakery whose windows were darkened. "I'm not going to wait. That's the mistake my father made. He waited too long to get us out and then—"

He glanced up and saw that Stover was ahead of them. "Come on." He took her arm and would have pulled her along with him, but she yanked back and stood her ground.

"You are not your father," she said, looking directly into his eyes to see the impact of her statement.

He scowled, but she was less intimidated by that now. "I know that."

"Do you?"

He glanced at Stover, and Sarah followed his gaze. Stover was waiting for them, but his foot was tapping impatiently.

"He couldn't save your brothers, and now you feel that you have to."

"Of course I have to save them. It's my duty."

She grasped his arm. "No, Julien. It's not your duty. You've done all you could—more than most. If you don't stop now, you're going to find yourself on trial for treason. Right now they have nothing but a mention of a letter. We show them the letter and explain everything. Perhaps that will be the end."

But she knew that was a lie, knew that there was more to this than Sir Northrop had told her initially.

Stover approached now and said under his breath, "The hour is late. We should go before it gets dangerous."

Sarah nodded but did not take her eyes from Julien's. He shook his head at her. "Do you think they need evidence to convict me? The government pays men to lie on the witness stand all the time. If they want me, they'll have me."

His words were her worst fear, and her hopes sank. It seemed they were doomed no matter what course they took.

"At least I can save my brother first," he whispered.

"Don't look now," Stover murmured, "but our tree-like friend is approaching."

Sarah could scarce turn to look before Valère pushed her behind him, thrusting her against the rough wood of the bakery. But Stalwart's man was so large that she could see him around Valère. The inhabitants of Seven Dials made way as Oak lumbered toward them. Finally he stopped in the middle of the road, hands on his hips. "The captain would like to offer you the use of his carriage."

A sleek black carriage, as nice as any seen in Mayfair, stopped behind Oak, and the dark-skinned man turned and opened the door.

"I don't think—" Stover began.

"This is not a request," Oak said.

"That's what I was afraid of," Stover muttered. "Should we make a run for it?" he said over his shoulder. Those were Sarah's thoughts exactly.

"I think we'd better see what the captain wants."
Valère gave her a furious look, as if to say that he
would be halfway home if it weren't for her.

He took her hand and led her to the carriage,
keeping her close by his side. "Berkeley Square,"
he told the captain's coachman, then helped her up
the stairs. The three of them took the seat opposite
Captain Stalwart. Sarah was between the two men, but
the relative safety of her position did not stop her from
trembling when Oak shut the door and the carriage
started on its way.

"What is this about?" Valère was direct as usual.

"I'm not a sentimental man," the captain said. With
his hat pulled down and his collar high, only his eyes
were visible. They glittered in the darkened interior,
for he hadn't lit the carriage lamps. "But I find the
story your lady tells interests me. Is it true?"

Sarah's heart lifted. Could her words have made
some impact?

"Every word," Valère said.

"How is it you are here and this brother of yours
still languishes back in France?"

"What business is that of yours?"

Sarah flinched but refrained from apologizing for
him. Valère was going to get them all killed, but at
least she would be silent while he did it.

"Do you still want passage to France?"

"Yes, and I'm willing to pay for it."

"Oh, you will." The captain steepled his hands.
"We sail in five days. Five thousand pounds now, and
five thousand on the day we sail."

Sarah could not stop the gasp that rose up in her

throat. Ten thousand pounds! That was a ridiculous amount of money. Valère would never agree.

"Five thousand the day we sail, and seven thousand when you bring me and my brother safely home again. You see"—he spread his hands—"I don't intend for this voyage to be one-way."

Stalwart did not speak, and for a long while there was only the sound of the wheels clattering over the cobblestones. That and her heart beating. It was so loud, Sarah feared all could hear it. Finally, Stalwart said, "I'm not certain seven thousand is enough to account for the risks you expect me to take."

"You won't do any better. Twelve thousand is a lot of money."

Silently, Sarah agreed. Twelve thousand pounds was more money than she thought she would ever see in a lifetime.

Finally, the carriage slowed, but no one inside made any move to depart. Sarah sat completely still, feeling the darkness close in on her. She tried to ignore it and was thankful when the captain finally spoke.

"The *Racer* sails in five days from the east dock. Be on board by midnight, or we leave without you."

"Very good." Valère opened the door and climbed out, reaching in to assist Sarah.

"And Valère?" the captain said as Sarah climbed down the steps. "Bring the blunt, or you'll be food for the sharks."

Sarah looked back and shivered at the glint in his eye. The carriage door shut behind her, and then the captain was gone.

❧

"Well," Stover said, downing his second brandy, "that was a successful venture."

Julien poured him another and then refilled his own glass before taking his chair behind his desk. Sarah, who was sitting on the couch, had refused the brandy, though she looked like she needed it badly.

"Scary as the devil," Stover said, swirling his brandy, probably to cover up the shaking of his hands, "but successful."

"Do you think you can trust him—the captain?" Sarah asked.

"As much as I can trust any of his kind," Julien said, leaning back. "I don't see that I have much choice."

"I wish you didn't have to go."

Stover crossed the room to sit beside her. "Don't worry, Mademoiselle Serafina, His Grace always returns none the worse for wear. And think how much it would mean to have Valère's brother at your wedding."

She glanced at Julien, and he smiled tightly. There would not be a wedding, but Stover did not need to know that yet.

"A week doesn't give me much time," Julien said. "I have documents to acquire and money to withdraw—and all without making anyone in the government suspicious." He gave Sarah a pointed look, reminding her that her task was to keep the Foreign Office from suspecting any more than they already did.

"And I have calls to make tomorrow," she answered. "But I also want to do what I can to help you, Your Grace."

He frowned. In his opinion, she had seen more

than enough to prove to herself and to make a case for the Foreign Office that he was no spy. "I think you've done quite enough, my lady," he answered. "You have a wedding to prepare for."

"Oh, but I want to help," she retorted with a forced smile. "I don't want there to be any secrets between us."

Julien clenched his jaw to keep from reminding her exactly who had kept secrets in their relationship, and the moment was mercifully ended by tap on the library door.

"Pardon the interruption, Your Grace," Grimsby said, opening the door. "Mr. Rigby is here to see you."

Julien sighed and exchanged a look with Stover before Rigby breezed in. "Well, here you all are!" he exclaimed. "You'll never guess my news."

"In that case, just tell us," Julien said.

"I can't just tell you. We need champagne. Oh, *buona sera, signorina.*" He bowed and, ever the gentleman, took her hand and kissed it.

"Good evening, Mr. Rigby. You have news?"

"Grimsby?" Rigby turned to the door. "Where is that champagne?"

With a pained look, Grimsby bowed to Julien. "Would you like me to bring a bottle, Your Grace?"

"Go ahead." Julien had learned long ago that giving Rigby his way resulted in a more peaceful evening. The butler left to fetch the bottle, and Rigby turned and stared at them accusingly. "Where were all of you tonight? I thought everyone was to attend Mrs. Southwick's musicale. Valère?" He rounded on Julien. "Your mother says you were to go to Vauxhall Gardens. Did you take Stover with you?"

Julien didn't answer, and Rigby didn't require one.

"Because if you were going to take him, you should have asked me to go along. As it was, you missed the most exciting night of the Season. Everyone will be talking about it tomorrow."

Stover looked dubious. "Everyone will be talking about Mrs. Southwick's musicale? Doubtful."

"No," Rigby said. Grimsby returned with a tray, carrying the bottle of champagne and four glasses. Rigby took the bottle, popped it—spilling champagne on the carpet, Julien noticed—and poured it into the flutes. When everyone had a glass in hand, he announced, "I proposed to Miss Wimple!"

"Oh, how wonderful!" Sarah exclaimed.

Julien raised a brow. "Did she accept?"

Rigby glared at him. "Of course she accepted. She practically fainted with happiness."

"Happiness, eh?" Stover said.

Rigby set down his glass and crossed his arms. "Yes, happiness. The woman would have eaten her left arm if it would have made me propose sooner."

"Oh, dear," Sarah said.

Rigby turned to her. "Well, not literally—"

"And what precipitated this proposal?" Julien asked. "Just last week you couldn't get past her—what did he call them, Stover?"

"Horse teeth."

"Oh, no." Sarah shook her head.

"I never said that," Rigby protested. "Well, maybe once. But since those words were uttered, my opinion of Miss Wimple has changed."

"Why?" Stover asked.

"Does something need to happen to make it change? If so, I think it's called love."

Julien laughed. "More likely, it's called your father. What'd he threaten you with?"

"Hmpf." Rigby shook his head. "I don't respond to threats."

Julien did not speak, just waited, and finally Rigby broke. "All right! He promised me he'd buy me that new hunter I saw at Tatersall's the other week. You know he's going for fifty pounds."

"So you married her to acquire a horse?" Sarah looked incredulous.

"Not very romantic, is it?" Julien said, glad he wasn't the only one to fail in this area.

"But," Rigby interjected, "the proposal was quite romantic. I had rose petals strewn over the terrace, and during the intermission at Mrs. Southwick's program, I led Miss Wimple—Amelia—onto the terrace, got down on one knee, and proposed." He glanced down at his breeches. "I hope these rose petal stains come out of this fabric."

Julien rolled his eyes, and even Sarah was shaking her head. But she raised her glass anyway. "I think we should toast to your health and a long happy life together, Mr. Rigby."

"Thank you." Rigby lifted his glass, and Julien and Stover followed reluctantly.

They toasted Rigby's engagement, and Julien glanced at Sarah across the room. She was watching him, her expression thoughtful, and for the first time in this ordeal, he wondered what life would be like with her as his bride. He hadn't even wanted a wife, and now when he looked at her, it was difficult to imagine life without her.

Unfortunately, it was difficult to imagine life with her. She had spied on him, thought him a traitor. She was a governess, and he was a duc. A marriage between them would never work. After he returned from France, they would have to end this farce and go their separate ways. But he was beginning to wonder if he would be able to send her away.

Seventeen

THE NEXT FEW DAYS PASSED QUICKLY. SARAH WAS BUSY preparing for a wedding that would not take place and avoiding the Foreign Office. She would have liked to have been more involved in Valère's preparations, but he was skillful at evading her and stayed locked in his library. She knew she had angered him by not following his dictates with Captain Stalwart, but she sensed this was more than petty anger. He wanted distance between them. Perhaps that was for the best. She knew their separation was inevitable.

The benefit of Valère's locking himself in his library was that the family did not go out. Those circumstances made it simple for her to avoid Sir Northrop, and he finally resorted to sending her a letter, passed on by her maid, Katarina. As she sat in her room and read the note, she trembled. It was filled with veiled threats. Obviously, Sir Northrop's patience was at an end. Sarah wished she had someone else to go to—even The Widow, but she feared the worst had befallen the other spy. She had disappeared completely, and now Sarah worried the same might happen to her. And she knew what would happen to Valère if he was not able to find his brother.

Time was running out, and she could not wait for Valère to come to her. Sir Northrop would not be held at bay much longer. Tucking Sir Northrop's letter into her pocket, she put on a white muslin morning dress with a blue ribbon about the waist. The bodice was *en cœur* with delicate lace edging and short sleeves. A quick look in the mirror told her she should wear her hair tied simply at the nape of her neck, with only a blue ribbon to restrain the chestnut curls. Finally, she examined the full effect in the cheval glass.

She blinked at the picture she presented. When had she become so pretty? When had she begun to look as though she belonged in this room full of silk and satin? There were moments lately when she could almost forget she had been a governess. She could almost believe she was Serafina.

Sarah made her way down the curved marble stairs, hardly noticing them now, and was pleased to find the vestibule empty. The duchesse wanted to shop for bridal lace this afternoon, but Sarah had hoped to avoid the excursion. Now she planted herself outside Valère's library.

She paced back and forth for almost an hour, and finally the door opened, and a small, mustached man scooted out.

Before the door could close again, she slipped inside. Valère, seated at his desk, spoke without looking up. "Did you forget something Thompson?"

"No, but perhaps you have."

His head jerked up, and she had some satisfaction knowing she had surprised him. He rose. "Mademoiselle." He had told her he thought it best if, even in private, he addressed her as Mademoiselle Serafina. Consistency meant there was less chance he would make a mistake in front of the servants or his mother. "I didn't know you'd come in."

She raised a brow. "You mean you didn't *want* me to come in. You've been avoiding me."

He sighed and sat back in his chair. "I've been busy."

"I can see that." She eyed the stacks of papers on his desk but did not move away from the door. "Pray, who was that man Thompson?"

"No one who need concern you."

This was not the answer she wanted to hear, and it pushed her over the limit of her patience. "Then what does need concern me, Your Grace? Your hanging? Or perhaps your disembowelment, because that's what's going to happen if you're convicted of treason. You must tell me what progress you have made. The Foreign Office is becoming impatient!" She stood on the opposite side of his desk now and leaned both hands on it as she spoke.

He frowned at her. "Just hold them off a few more days."

She spread her arms. "With what? I promised them a cache of documents, and I have nothing. In the meantime, you have a parade of clerks and dour-faced business men in and out, and I don't know what to tell the Foreign Office about any of that either."

"Tell them I'm working, and you are taking every opportunity to spy on me." Valère sat back in his chair, crossed his arms over his chest.

"Very well, but then I must have something to show for my efforts. I've avoided Sir Northrop as long as I can. The next time I am out, shopping for lace or some such thing, he *will* find me."

"So stay in."

"How can I? I'm forced to spend hours a day preparing for our wedding. I feel as though I'm engaged to your mother."

His blue eyes swept over her, and she was glad she had taken care with her appearance. She did not mind his penetrating looks so much now.

"I see," he said, gaze lingering on her face. "You feel neglected."

She closed her eyes. Was Valère intentionally trying to exasperate her? "I don't feel neglected, but I must have something to show the Foreign Office before they give up entirely and just arrest you." And her with him.

"Then you'd certainly be feeling neglected."

She felt her face color now, knew he was teasing her and was not quite certain how to react. "That was not what I meant. I simply find it ridiculous that I spend six hours each day planning a wedding that will never occur."

"Why do you assume it will never occur?"

She gripped the edge of his desk, so surprised she could barely speak. "Wh-what do you mean?"

He shrugged. "What if I did marry you?"

Was the man mad? "You can't!"

"*Pourquoi?* Are you already married?"

"No, b-but I'm not"—she lowered her voice—"I'm not Mademoiselle Serafina." And no amount of wishing or looking in mirrors would make it so.

"Will that really matter once I return from France with my brother?"

She blinked at him. "Of course. Do you think your mother wants her son married to a governess? An orphan no one wanted and no one cares about?"

She had said too much. She realized her mistake immediately and clamped her mouth shut. He was staring at her, and she knew she should leave immediately. But her feet would not move.

"Is that how you see yourself?" He stood and came around the desk. Finally, she gained control of her feet and took two steps back. "You think no one cares about you? No one wants you?"

"Yes—no—I don't know."

He was coming closer. With each step she took back, he took one forward. "I don't want to talk about this. I just need you to give me something to hold off the Foreign Office." She bumped into the wall and looked for an escape, but he trapped her, placing one hand on either side of her shoulders.

"Sarah." He whispered the word, and she closed her eyes. Her name on his lips was more riveting than any book she had read and sweeter than any of Gunther's ices. "Do you know why I stay away from you?"

She shook her head, keeping her eyes closed.

"Because I *do* want you."

Of their own volition, her eyes opened, and she stared at him. She could not have heard him correctly.

"Do you know that every night I walk past your bedroom door, and it takes every ounce of willpower I have not to open it, not to go inside and—"

She should have been thankful he left the last to her imagination, except she had a very vivid imagination. She could remember his kisses, the heat of his body, the gentle pressure of his hands all too well. And she had spent her own restless hours, tossing and turning in the lonely bed, thinking of him.

She looked up and met his eyes, and that was her mistake.

"Tu es si belle." With a groan, he took her in his arms. Enveloped in his strength and warmth, she melted into him. His lips caressed hers so gently and tenderly that she moaned. She wanted more. She ached to feel wanted. Ached to feel beautiful—*Tu es si belle*. Did he really think her beautiful?

She raised her hands and wrapped them around his shoulders, gripping his hair in her hands, and pulling his mouth down hard on hers.

He did not hesitate but kissed her so thoroughly it took her breath away. His mouth was firm and yet gentle, and when he parted her lips and tasted her, she clung to him.

After a moment, he broke the kiss and dropped his head on her shoulder, breathing rapidly. "You don't know the effect you have on me. I'm afraid what might happen if you ever realized, ever tried to seduce me."

"I wouldn't know how to seduce you," she admitted.

He glanced up at her, his eyes so blue she felt she could drown in them. "Would you like me to show you?"

"No." She shook her head. "It's not proper—"

He put a finger over her lips. "Just a kiss." He lifted a finger, placed it on her lips. She did feel self-conscious then. She hated her lips. "Do you know I dream about your mouth?" he whispered.

Sarah felt heat rush to her face and looked away, but he drew her eyes back to his. She was certain he must be having nightmares.

"I think about its shape, color, how it feels pressed against mine."

She almost groaned but held herself in check with a single thought: "But my mouth is is horrible."

He frowned, his forehead creasing. "What do you mean?"

"It's too large. I–it doesn't fit my face. It—"

Surprising her, he leaned down and brushed his mouth over hers lightly. Once. Twice. "You're wrong, Sarah. It's perfect. It's the most perfect, most seductive mouth I've ever seen on a woman."

Sarah could not believe his words. He actually *liked* her mouth? He thought it was perfect? She had always seen it as such a flaw, as so glaringly unattractive. But Julien loved her mouth. Was it possible she was indeed beautiful in his eyes?

He pulled her closer. "If you want to seduce me, show me you want me with a kiss."

"I don't think—"

"*Embrasse-moi, chérie.*"

"And then we'll stop?" She sounded breathless.

He raised a brow. "Do you want to stop?"

She felt her cheeks heat. "No."

"Sarah." In that one word, he managed to sound pained and aroused all at once.

Feeling bold now, she leaned forward and brushed her lips against his. She made her touch feather-light, allowing him to feel the softness of her skin, and then pulling away.

He took a deep breath. *"Une fois de plus."* Once more.

Pleased at his response, even more pleased that she should be the cause, she leaned forward and caressed his lips again, this time lingering longer and kissing him gently.

His hands on her waist tightened. "You're killing me," he murmured into her ear. "Now really kiss me. Kiss me like I kissed you before."

She shook her head. "But I don't know how—"

"Don't think. *Embrasse-moi.*"

Her heart was pounding now, the blood so loud in her ears it sounded like a roar. She was embarrassed and thrilled and scared all at the same time. Part of her wanted to break free from the safety of his embrace, to resist falling even more in love with him than she already was. For she knew now, without any doubt, that she was more than just infatuated with him.

Infatuation was admiring how handsome he was, being awed by his title and wealth.

Love was missing him miserably the last few days, dwelling on all the little kindnesses he had ever shown her—from dancing with her at the Aldon's ball to shielding her from danger in Seven Dials. Love was not ever wanting to be outside his arms.

She pulled his mouth to hers and kissed him gently. He accepted it, returning the kiss but allowing her to take charge. The kiss was tender, but what she wanted was passion. She wanted him to feel the passion he flared in her.

As he had done, she used her tongue to part his

lips, delving inside tentatively, just to taste. He tasted sweet, like brandy and cinnamon. Feeling brash, she explored further, pressing her body to his, liking the feel of his hardness against her softness.

He kissed her back, his tongue twining with hers until she could not tell who was kissing whom. His hands were on her back, her waist, and then her ribcage. She could feel them inching upward. Her breasts felt heavy with need. She needed him to touch her there, ached for it.

And then his hands were on her, cupping her, stroking the tender peaks of her nipples through the thin material of her stays and gown. She allowed her head to fall back, and he pushed at the edges of lace at her throat, kissing her neck, his mouth and his hands stroking her until all she could think of was how much she wanted him.

"Julien?" There was a tap on the door. "Are you in there?"

The door opened, and he jumped away from her, but it was too late. Even had his mother not seen the two of them wrapped in each other's arms, Sarah knew that one look at her flushed face would tell all.

The duchesse blinked then nodded briskly. "Excuse me. I didn't realize."

She turned and walked out, the train of her light blue gown trailing after her.

ᴥ

"Damn," Julien swore again, then gave Sarah an apologetic look. "Sorry. I need to go after her."

"Of course." She was almost breathless, and her

face glowed with desire. Her lips, those lips that kept him awake at night, were swollen and red, and all he wanted to do was claim them again.

But he wouldn't.

Thank God his mother had entered when she had, because he had already gone too far, and nothing, short of a fire or flood would have induced him to stop. When he was touching Sarah, he could not get enough of her. Her body fit with his, and even now his hands ached to span her waist, dive into her thick hair, or cup those ample breasts.

He could not stop his eyes from straying to her bodice. The lace was so delicate he could easily tear it away. Then there would be mere inches of material between his mouth and that soft flesh.

He almost groaned aloud at the image and took another step back. "I'd better speak with my mother."

"Yes."

"You wait here," he said in case she thought to go with him.

She did not argue, just walked slowly to the couch and sank down on it.

He found his mother in the parlor. This was obviously where all the wedding preparations were being made, and the small rosewood desk she used for correspondence was covered with sheets of parchment. His mother was seated at that cluttered desk, scratching out another list of tasks to be completed before the wedding.

Julien stood in the doorway and cleared his throat. She glanced up and then down at her list again. "Yes, Julien?"

He was not used to coldness from her. "Am I interrupting?"

She did not look up. "No more than I interrupted you a moment ago."

"I know how that must have looked—"

"It was exactly how it looked," she said, dipping her quill in ink and continuing to write. "That's why I'm moving up the date of the wedding."

"That's not necessary."

She glanced at him, brows raised. "It looked necessary a moment ago."

"I know. I'm sorry. It won't happen again."

"I certainly hope it will happen again—just not until after the wedding vows." She set down the quill. "Do you know what surprises me the most, Julien?"

He shook his head.

"I didn't think you liked her."

He ran a hand through his hair and considered, took his time choosing the words. "She's not what I expected."

"Nor I. She's nothing like her mother. Delphine is lively and vivacious. Serafina is quiet and unassuming, and her beauty surpasses that of Delphine." She held up a hand before Julien could protest. "But her beauty would be nothing to me if I did not see the way she looks when she speaks of you. Then, well, she's absolutely stunning."

Julien froze and felt his heart clench. "What do you mean?"

"I mean, it's obvious she's completely smitten with you. Her face lights up when she mentions your name."

At her words, all the air in his lungs dried up. Could it be possible she felt something for him? That all of this was more than simply the work of a spy, that she truly cared for him? He did not know if he could trust her, but he knew he wanted to. Desperately.

"I wasn't certain about this match," his mother was saying, "but now that I see you return her passion, I think we had better proceed quickly. You'll need to get a special license."

"That's not possible right now." He took a seat in the small, curved-back chair opposite the desk. It was so dainty, he feared he would break it with his weight.

"It had better be possible, if we're going to have the wedding in two weeks."

"I may not be here."

He allowed the words to hang between them. He had made no mention to his mother of the letter he had received with news of Armand or his planned voyage to France. They had traveled this road before, and it only brought her great pain. She preferred to believe her youngest sons were dead. Believing them still alive was too painful. And even more painful was hoping Julien would find them, only to be disappointed again and again.

By implicit agreement, he had not mentioned his plans to travel to France, but he knew his mother was extremely astute. She knew what went on in her home, could guess why businessmen came in and out in a steady stream for the last several days.

"I was afraid of this," she said quietly.

"Perhaps it's best if we don't talk about it."

"We haven't talked about it for years, and that hasn't yet stopped you from pursuing this foolish quest."

Julien clenched his hands around the arms of the chair. "You wouldn't think it so foolish if you had access to the information I do."

"A letter from Gilbert, our former butler, saying he knows where Armand is? That information?"

Julien stared at her. "How did you—"

"He sent me a letter as well, probably hoping one of us would believe it."

"Why would he lie? He was always a loyal servant."

She stared at him, disbelief in her eyes. "Were you there that night, Julien? Do you remember our *loyal* servants hacking down our doors, assaulting us with candlesticks and brooms and"—she looked down at his foot, and he felt a twinge of pain at the memory—"pitchforks."

"That wasn't one of ours."

"Don't be deceived. Our servants wanted us dead and gone."

"Not all of them."

She ignored him. "And do you know what Gilbert will do once he has you in France? He'll send you to the guillotine, his revenge complete."

"Ma mère, I don't believe that."

"Fine, then he'll threaten to reveal your identity or turn you into the authorities unless you give him money. Or perhaps he hopes to blackmail you into bringing him to England. I don't know."

Julien rose and went to her, kneeling in front of her and taking her hands. "And what if, just possibly, Armand is alive?"

She shook her head. "I cannot believe that, Julien. I know he's dead."

"And if he's not? If there's even the slightest possibility, shouldn't I go and investigate it?"

"That's not your responsibility!"

"Then whose is it?" He rose and turned away from her, stalking across the room. "Who's going to save him if not me?"

Damn it! He had raised his voice and was fighting to keep his temper under control.

She came up behind him, and he felt her hand on his shoulder. "It's too late to save him, Julien. And it was never your responsibility. If it was anyone's, it was mine. *I* failed him and Bastien, not you."

"Father failed them." The words were out before he even knew what he was saying. Belatedly, he remembered Sarah's argument that he was not his father. Was she right? Was he trying to right his father's failures?

His mother turned him around, put her hands on his cheeks. "Your father gave his life to give us a chance, Julien. He fought with everything he had so I might escape, so I might save you boys. *I'm* the one who failed."

Julien sighed. "We're a family of failures." She smiled ruefully at the sarcasm. "It's none of our faults, ma mère. But I could never live with myself if I didn't respond to that letter. I have to go to France. I have to try once more to find Armand."

She shook her head sadly. "He's dead, Julien."

"How do you know?" He said it gently, seeing the tears in her eyes.

"I would have felt something if Armand or Bastien was still alive. I would have felt something, and I don't, Julien. I'm just dead inside."

"Ma mère." He took her in his arms, holding her as she wept silently.

A long time later, she parted from him, wiping her eyes with a handkerchief. "I don't want you to suffer the same fate I have, Julien. You don't have to die inside. Stay here, marry Serafina, start a family. Put this search for your brothers aside. It will only bring you grief. I know."

"I can't, ma mère."

"You can't marry Serafina or you can't forget your brothers?"

"Either. Both. I don't know. I just know that I leave for France in two days."

She closed her eyes, pain making her features stark. "What can I do, Julien? What can I do to help?"

He smiled. His mother had never let him down. He leaned down, kissed her on the cheek.

"Just pray."

Eighteen

SARAH SAT ON THE COUCH IN THE LIBRARY, STILL AND silent for a long time. Her mind went over and over the kiss she had shared with Valère—Julien. In her thoughts, at least she could call him Julien.

She could not believe she had been so wanton, that she had completely lost her reason and allowed him to touch her so intimately. But she knew why she had been carried away.

For the first time, she had actually believed he might want to marry her. For the first time, she dared to believe he wanted her, might feel something for her. Not as much as she felt for him. No, she did not think he was in love with her, but he said he wanted her.

Still, she could hardly believe that he, a duc, would marry her, a mere governess. Everyone knew the aristocracy did not marry for love. His two completely business-like proposals proved that well enough.

No, he would marry someone of his own station, someone who would bring him wealth or power or prestige. Sarah knew she could give him none of these things. She was not silly enough to believe love would win the day.

Which meant, she still had a job to do. She had to exonerate him. If she could not, and the Foreign Office learned she had helped him make travel preparations for France, she might be considered equally guilty of treason.

It was common knowledge that women convicted of this crime were not hanged, drawn, and quartered. Unfortunately, the prospect of being burned at the stake was no more appealing to her. She had once read a book describing the practice, and the punishment was gruesome indeed.

She wanted to go with him to France. She wanted to see firsthand his search for his brother, be able to prove without doubt that he was not selling secrets to the French.

And yes, she wanted to be with him. How could she stay here in London while he risked his life abroad? She would lose him soon enough when he returned.

And there was another concern as well. If she were here in London and it became known that Julien was away, Sir Northrop would not waste a moment in finding her. She shuddered to think what he would do to her. She was probably safer in France.

But if she wanted to go to France with Julien, she would need documents. She would need papers that gave her a false identity. Julien would need the same. Suddenly, she looked at his desk with new interest. There were several documents on top, most likely those Mr. Thompson, who had left just before her arrival, had brought.

She glanced at the library door. It was ajar, and no one was in the vestibule. She fumbled in her reticule until she found her spectacles, went to the desk, and keeping her eyes on the door, scanned the papers lying in front of her.

She gasped when she moved the top sheet. Underneath were French papers for a Monsieur Julien Harcourt. There was no mention of his title. In fact, his profession was given as *baker*. This was exactly what she needed. She would find this Mr. Thompson and persuade him to make her false documents. She would be Madame Harcourt, the baker's wife.

She glanced at the door again, making sure she was not seen as she rummaged through the papers, looking for Mr. Thompson's address. She found it quickly enough and made note that he was located on Fleet Street.

She would go tomorrow and then—

What?

Julien was not going to welcome her along on the voyage, and he might change his plans altogether if she told him her suspicions about Sir Northrop. She could not allow that. Finding his brother was the only way to ensure his safety. She would have to surprise him. She would have to find a way to make it impossible for him to refuse. Her life might depend on it.

She began to rearrange the documents so they looked undisturbed, but her hands stilled when she saw the list stuffed under the false identification papers. She stared at it for a long moment.

The attic. That was where Sir Northrop had said Julien's brother Armand was located. But could he have meant... She heard a sound and quickly restored the papers to their original order. Yes, she was definitely going to France, and right now she had packing to do.

∽

The remainder of Julien's preparations went smoothly. His mother looked worried each time he saw her, but she no longer tried to persuade him to stay in England.

Sarah was distant. There had been no repeat of the kiss they had shared in the library the day before. In fact, he had hardly seen her.

That evening he escorted her and his mother to the opera, and he pulled Sarah aside during the intermission. "Is everything well with you?"

They were in the privacy of his box, his mother having gone to speak to friends in their box, but that did not mean they had any real privacy. The *ton* was watching everything that went on.

Sarah smiled and waved her fan. "*Oui, bien sûr.* Why do you ask?"

"Where have you been lately?"

"Busy."

"With our friends?" He did not want to mention the Foreign Office. He was to sail for France tomorrow evening, and the last thing he needed was to slip up and have someone hear him reveal something he should not this close to his departure.

"Who else? I've promised them the moon, and I must give them something soon."

He nodded, though something about the way she would not meet his eyes made him question. But why would she lie to him? Who would she have gone to see if not Sir Northrop? "As we discussed, I'll leave you the letter to show them. It might not be enough to persuade them, but when I return with Armand, I should have no trouble convincing them."

She nodded and looked back at the stage.

"You will be all right while I am gone? There's no danger?"

She smiled, though it did not quite reach her eyes. "Of course not."

He was hardly reassured, but he had little other choice but to trust her. The Foreign Office would not hurt one of its own. And she would be safe in his home while he was away. He realized this might be their last chance to be alone together. "Sarah," he whispered.

She glanced at him, alarm in her eyes. He was a fool to use her real name, but he could not call her Serafina. She was Sarah to him now. "You will be here when I return?"

"Of course. Where would I go?"

He did not know, but he had the feeling he might never see her again. "I'd like my brother to meet you."

"And I would like to meet him. Having him in London will make proving your story to the Foreign Office a good deal easier."

He frowned. That was not what he had meant at all. He wanted the people who mattered to him to know her, but before he could say that, the orchestra began to tune, and they returned to their seats.

Perhaps it was best that their conversation had ended. It was clear she had no expectation he would marry her. Perhaps she did not want him in any case. And then again, did *he* really intend to marry her?

What did he know about her other than the fact that she was a governess and a poor spy? She had no family, no connections, no money.

And did he really care about any of that?

What he did care about was duty. It was his duty to marry and continue the line. His mother had never said he should marry a fellow aristocrat, but he had always understood it to be an obligation.

And what of his own desire to exact retribution on those who had tried to extinguish his family? News of his marriage to another threatened French aristocratic family would probably never reach the peasants who had killed his father, but it was a victory all the same.

The opera began, and Julien pushed all thoughts of marriage out of his mind. He would think about that later, when he returned from France and had Armand safely in England. He would think on it after the threat of a charge of treason was eliminated. Right now, he simply had to survive this opera.

❦

The following evening, he was at the east dock three-quarters of an hour before midnight. The docks smelled of decaying fish and unwashed bodies, and they were never completely deserted. Cargo was loaded and unloaded, and sailors came ashore looking for a pint or a willing woman. Tonight there was a smattering of noise from the patrons of nearby taverns, but at the *Racer*'s dock, all was deserted. No crew members walked about loading cargo, no one was preparing the sails or rigging for a voyage, and Julien had not seen Captain Stalwart.

The *Racer* was moored under a crescent moon, and the fog rolled in thick off the waters of the Thames. The masts, furled tightly with white sails, shot high into the cloudy sky. All in all, Julien judged it to be a good ship. It was small and likely fast—a racer indeed.

But with so little time before departure, where was the ship's crew? The vessel sat low, which meant the cargo might already have been loaded, but surely someone was about. As he stood in the shadows of a nearby alleyway, Julien felt a prickle on the back of his neck. Was this a trap? Had Sarah betrayed him?

And then he heard the sound of a carriage approaching. He ducked back farther into the shadows and watched as Stalwart's conveyance appeared, halted, and the man himself departed, followed by the large, black man Julien knew as Oak.

The captain stood, hands on hips, surveying his ship, and Oak put his fingers to his lips and whistled. A moment later, the dock was swarming with crew members. They had appeared silently and went about their work. Their first task was to lower the gangplank. Stalwart started toward it, and Julien moved out of the shadows. It was now or never.

"Captain," Julien called. "A word."

Stalwart paused, turned, and waited for Julien to approach. "Did you bring the blunt?" Stalwart asked.

Julien gestured to a satchel he carried. "Perhaps you'd like to see it in the privacy of your cabin?"

"That I would." He started up the gangplank again, then called over his shoulder, "Oak, bring our other guest to my cabin as well."

Julien frowned. "What other guest? We never discussed another passenger."

"This is my ship. I don't feel the need to discuss what I do aboard it with you."

That was true, but it did not mean Julien had to like the arrangement. What if this guest knew him, could identify him? Julien did not like the added risk. But what choice did he have? He could go along or go home.

Blowing out a sigh, he followed Stalwart across the deck, went into a hatch, and down a short flight of steps.

At the end of a narrow corridor, Stalwart paused and held open the door to his cabin. The room was small which, considering the ship was compact and built for speed, was expected. The sleek cabin had a berth, a trunk, a small desk, and a table littered with maps and charts. The furniture was bolted to the floor, and a weak lamp burned above the desk.

Stalwart motioned Julien inside, and ducking his head, Julien entered the cabin. He set the heavy satchel on the table. It was filled with five thousand pounds, and Julien hated to release it, but it was the price for Armand. He had to remember that. The rest of the money he had given to Stover, with orders to bring it as soon as Julien sent for it.

Of course, he had plenty of money on him—sewn into his coat. But that was in francs. He would be prepared if all did not go well in France.

"You'll get the rest when I return safely. I have it with a friend."

Stalwart shook his head. "I should never have

agreed to this. You'll cause me more trouble than five thousand pounds. You already have."

A knock sounded on the door.

"Come," Stalwart said, his eyes on Julien. The door swung open, and outside stood Oak with Sarah right beside him.

"What the hell?" Julien started forward.

She gave him a sheepish look and allowed the large man to push her into the cabin. The door closed behind her, leaving the captain, Julien, and Sarah alone.

"I can explain," Sarah began.

"What are you doing here?" Julien said at the same time.

"I knew this would be amusing," Stalwart drawled, taking a seat at his desk.

Julien rounded on him. "We need a moment alone."

The captain raised his brows. "Well, you won't get it in my cabin. I've been anticipating this all evening."

Julien turned back to Sarah. "What's going on? Is this some sort of trap?"

"No, this isn't a trap." She reached out to touch him, reassure him, but he moved away. "I-I'm going with you."

"The hell you say! You'll do no such thing."

Behind him, Stalwart chuckled, and Julien had the urge to throttle the man.

"Julien, just listen to reason. I need to come because—"

"I don't give a damn what you need. You're to go home this very instant. Stalwart?" He turned back to the captain. "May she use your carriage?"

Stalwart shook his head. "Of course. How do you think she arrived here?"

Fuming, Julien turned back to her. "What is going on?"

"If you'll just give me a moment to explain—"

"There's no time." Julien pulled out his pocket watch and examined the face. "The ship sails in ten minutes. You have to get off."

"I'm afraid I can't do that."

"Then I'll carry you off." He advanced on her with every intent of lifting her, throwing her over his shoulder, and bodily removing her from the vessel.

"Captain!" she cried, skirting around the table. "Tell him!"

"She's coming with us, Valère," Stalwart answered. "It's both of you or neither. That's the agreement."

⁂

Sarah had known Julien would not react well to this. She did not blame him, but she had no other choice—at least that was what she told herself when she left the house tonight.

As was expected of her, she had smiled through dinner and, alongside the duchesse, bid Julien farewell. They pretended he was only going to his club for the evening, not wanting to alert the servants to the truth.

As soon as Julien was away, the duchesse retreated to her room. Sarah pretended to do the same then sneaked out a back door, clothes and papers tied in a pillow case and thrown over her back. She had been trembling like a leaf as she left, terrified something would go wrong.

But fortunately, she had been able to hail a hackney quickly, and the jarvey had agreed to take her to Captain Stalwart. She knew she would need his support. Walking through The King George had been a daunting task with Stover and Julien and had seemed almost impossible on her own. But she had done it, and it was with a small sense of accomplishment that she knocked on Stalwart's door. Though obviously surprised to see her, he admitted her to his suite right away and, after the initial pleasantries, she told him she planned to sail with him.

He raised a brow. "Your duc's fee pays only for his passage." He was sitting in an armchair, sipping brandy while the large man he called Oak gathered the personal effects from the room and packed them in a trunk.

Sarah took the seat opposite him. She was resolved now. She had come this far and would not turn back. "There will be no passage at all if I'm not allowed to come along."

The captain set his brandy glass down on the table between them and steepled his fingers. "That's a serious threat. I hope you're prepared to back it up."

"I am. I'm an operative for the Foreign Office. I think they would be very interested to know about your recent excursions to France."

Stalwart did not blink. "They might, but do you really think I'd allow you to leave and tell them?"

He reached into his coat and pulled out a small knife. Casually, he began to groom his nails with the tip. Sarah swallowed, feeling the bile rise in her throat. She was no idiot. Captain Stalwart was threatening to kill her!

But she had thought her plan through, had tried to anticipate every detail. She smiled. "If I don't leave safely or give a signal within the next five minutes," she said, glancing at the clock on the mantel, "you won't be going anywhere but Newgate tonight."

He worked the knife on his nails and studied her. Sarah could tell he was trying to decide whether or not to believe her. She raised a brow, hoping she looked a good deal more confident than she felt.

"Why do you want to accompany Valère?" the captain finally asked. "Is the Foreign Office watching him?"

"That doesn't concern you, nor will it. Suffice it to say that Valère needs me."

The captain let out a loud bark of a laugh that made her jump. "He does, does he?" He shook his head, and for a moment she did not think he believed a word she said. Then he shrugged. "Very well. Come along. If nothing else, this will be amusing. And it's been some time since we've had a woman on board." He grinned. "Don't expect me to protect your virtue."

Sarah had considered that problem, and she knew with Julien beside her, she had little to fear. He would watch over her, protect her. But she wanted more than Stalwart's nonchalant acceptance. Valère would not give in so easily.

The captain had risen and was gathering his greatcoat, but Sarah stood in front of him. "One more thing."

He raised a brow.

"Valère will argue," Sarah said quickly. "He'll do everything in his power to have me thrown off your ship. I need you to agree now that it's either both of us or neither. If I'm thrown off, the Foreign Office will be waiting when you return."

He narrowed his eyes. "I don't care whether you two stay on the docks or get tossed to the sharks. I care about the blunt."

"Then you agree?"

"I agree."

"And—" She had scarce opened her mouth before he stepped forward and held a finger in front of her lips.

"Don't push your luck."

Sarah closed her mouth and waited while Oak and the captain made their last preparations. Finally Stalwart turned to her. "Don't you need to signal your friends?"

Drat! She had forgotten! "I'll do that right now," she said, trying to sound as if this was the way she had intended it all along. She went to the window, pushed it open, and leaned out. No one passing below paid any attention to her, but she felt like an idiot anyway. She waved her hands and made several impromptu gestures. She hoped they looked like some sort of code.

She closed the door and turned back to the captain. He had a bemused smile on his lips, but he bowed and gestured for her to precede him out the door.

And now she was standing in front of a seething Valère. At least the captain had kept his end of the bargain. She could see Julien taking in the situation, debating his options.

As she saw it, they could either both get off the ship or both travel to France. She did not know what options he was considering. She prayed there were not any loopholes in her plan, but her stomach plummeted when Valère's scowl faded, and he gave her a knowing smile.

Nineteen

JULIEN DID NOT KNOW WHAT HAD POSSESSED SARAH TO come to the ship and attempt to go with him, but no matter the reason, he was not taking her. Apparently, she had made some deal with Stalwart, but he saw a way out of that.

Smiling, he crossed his arms. "You can't come."

She met his smile with a defiant glare. If he was not mistaken, she was growing braver day by day. What had happened to the pale-faced girl who had barely been able to speak when he walked into the room?

"I can, and I will."

"How will you travel once we reach France? You don't have any papers." There. That was the end of this inane scheme. Now he just had to find a way to get her home before—

"I have papers."

"What?"

She nodded and reached into her makeshift knapsack—it looked suspiciously like a pillow case—producing a thick stack of documents. Before she could hand them over, Julien snatched them from her hands.

He perused them quickly and then more thoroughly. How could this be? These papers were as good as his! They were for a Serafina Harcourt, wife of a baker.

His alias was that of a baker.

He met her gaze, and she gave him a sheepish smile. "How did you—"

"Enough of this," Stalwart interrupted. "Are you going or staying? Either way, I'm taking the money." The captain had already claimed the satchel with the five thousand pounds.

Julien clenched his fists and blew out a breath. He leveled a glance at her. "I don't care the price. I'm not willing to put you in danger." He grit his teeth and tried not think about Armand. "We're staying," he bit out and turned to leave. But she grabbed his arm and leaned in close.

"Why are you so certain I'm safer here than in France?" She raised a brow, looking him directly in the eye. "What do you think will happen to me if it becomes known—as it surely will—that you are away and I have failed in my mission?"

Julien shrugged. "Why should anything happen? You can go back to your"—he glanced at Stalwart—"previous position."

"Or perhaps I'm expendable. Perhaps I know too much. Others have disappeared. I fear I'm next." She lowered her voice, whispering in his ear. "I fear Sir Northrop, Julien. He's desperate to capture you and will stop at nothing. If I stay—" She caught her breath on a shudder and met his gaze.

"Damn it," Julien swore and ran a hand through his hair. He could see real fear in her eyes. They were cornered—danger on every side. "Then I'll stay here and protect you. I don't even know if I'll be able to find Armand."

"You will. I have information that can help you."

He frowned at her. "What are you talking about? What information?"

"You need me, Julien. Armand needs us both. I can help you find him. Without him, I fear we are both doomed."

He gave her a long, hard stare. Did she really have information, or was this just a ploy to stay on board? Either way, he could not leave her behind, and with the Foreign Office watching him, this might be his last chance to find his brother, Julien's only chance to prove he was not a traitor. He closed his eyes briefly and heard himself tell Stalwart, "We're going." He was probably going to regret this, but he saw the captain nod and knew the decision was made now.

Stalwart opened the cabin door. Immediately, Oak, who had been standing guard, came to attention. "Take these two to the guest quarters," Stalwart ordered.

∽◈∾

Sarah had not realized how small the ship would be, had not realized she would be sharing quarters with Julien. And even if she had, it would not have changed her mind. She would rather die in France, attempting to help Julien rescue his brother, than perish in Sir Northrop's clutches in London.

As she stepped into the cabin, she felt the ship begin to rock. The tide had come in, and the crew was moving the ship into the river. Soon they would be well on their way.

The door closed behind her, shutting her in.

Just her and Julien.

In the darkness.

She had caught a brief glimpse of the cabin: it had only one small berth.

She heard Julien blow out a breath. "Happy now?"

"No, but what I told you was the truth. The last time I met with The Widow she told me she was afraid of Sir Northrop. She arranged a private meeting, and she never arrived. I have not seen her since." The boards under them creaked and shifted.

"And you think Sir Northrop killed her? Perhaps she was simply given another assignment."

"Perhaps." Sarah had considered that, had wanted to believe it, but she could not. "But I fear the worst. The last time I saw Sir Northrop, he was like a caged animal. He all but admitted to killing her, and he threatened me as well."

"Sarah, what would killing you or the operatives benefit him?"

She shook her head, even though she suspected he could not see. "I don't know. He's desperate, hurried… afraid of… something. He wants you labeled a traitor, and I don't think he even cares whether you are innocent or guilty."

The room was silent for a long moment, and then Julien said, "Alright. We'll deal with him when we return. *If* we return. Tell me this information you have. What do you know about Armand?"

She was not quite ready to reveal all. As long as she

had information he wanted, he would keep her with him. Not that he would ever abandon her, but he might be tempted to find a safe place to stash her until the danger was past. "Something Sir Northrop told me."

He scowled. "That's all? I hardly think—"

"There's more. But I'm not going to tell you. Yet."

"Bloody hell, but you're difficult."

She heard him move past her, and then a stream of moonlight showed through the porthole. He had pulled back the curtain shrouding the cabin and now stood before the single berth, legs braced, face in his habitual scowl. It was difficult to ignore that small, lonely bed behind him.

"Do you think they have another room where I can sleep?" she said, trying not to sound nervous.

"No. This is probably the first mate's cabin. We're lucky to have it at all. I'd expected to sleep with the men in the crew quarters. Obviously, you can't do that."

"No." She shook her head.

"And now neither can I."

Lord, he looked handsome, standing there with the moonlight behind him. But her gaze drifted involuntarily to the lone berth behind him. It was incredibly small. There was certainly no way she could sleep beside him without being pressed flush against him. She did not think Reverend Collier would approve of that.

"Why not?" she asked. "The berth is—ah, rather small."

"Oh, you noticed that?"

She frowned. "There's no call for sarcasm."

"No? You'll have to forgive me. Now, not only do I have to worry about getting safely in and out of France, finding my family's servant, finding my brother, overcoming whatever obstacles there are to free him, and returning to England without being arrested by the Foreign Office—"

She looked down. It was a rather long list of concerns, and she could see where he was going with it.

"Now I have to watch over you as well. And not just in France. Do you think I can trust these sailors to keep their hands off you? I'll have to stay with you night and day."

She swallowed. "The voyage isn't that long."

"Three days in good weather. Much longer if the weather is bad, the wind is unfavorable, or we have trouble with the French or the English fleets. We could be on this ship for weeks!"

"I didn't realize—"

He held up a hand. "That's obvious."

"Don't you realize I had no choice?" she said, dropping her knapsack. It suddenly felt unduly heavy.

"You could have told me your fears. You might have confided in me."

"No." She shook her head. "No. Then you would have turned yourself in, or something foolish like that—"

"It's not foolish if it saves your life."

"But it won't save yours! Only finding Armand can do that now. We must have irrevocable proof that your visits to France have been undertaken with the best of intentions. If we find your brother—"

He made a sound of protest, crossed the cabin in two steps, and took hold of her shoulders. "I *will* find him."

"*We'll* find him," she said, looking up and into his

eyes. He met her gaze, and she could feel the tension between them. It was so thick she felt as though she could reach out and slice through it.

Abruptly, he released her. "We're getting married."

"What?" She blinked, thinking she must have heard him incorrectly.

"We're getting married." He reached for the door and opened it. "I'm going to find the captain. While I'm gone, don't move, don't speak, and don't open the door for anyone but me."

"But, Julien!"

He closed the door on her protests, then opened it again and stuck his head in. "You might want to change into your bridal attire." The door slammed closed.

Sarah stood staring at the door. He could not mean it. Could he?

Oh, Lord. She knew him better than that by now. Of course, he meant it. He was going to have the ship's captain marry them.

She should be ecstatic. She was going to be Julien's wife. She had been in love with him practically since the moment she first saw him, and certainly since their first kiss. Now she would be with him always.

There might be children, and she would finally have the family she had always yearned for.

Except...

Julien did not want to marry her. Julien was not doing this because he wanted her to be his wife or because he was in love with her. He was doing this because it was his duty to protect her.

Sarah did not know if she wanted to be married under those conditions. She had not daydreamed about her wedding very often. She never really believed she would actually marry, but on the few occasions she had allowed herself to indulge in wistful fantasies, being married on a smuggler's ship to a man who felt obligated to take her had never once entered her imaginings.

What was she going to do?

She heard footsteps outside the door and glanced down at her clothing. No wonder Julien had suggested she change into her bridal attire. She did not want to marry in this plain gray gown and spencer. She had borrowed them—was it really borrowing if she did not ask first?—from her maid. Sarah had wanted something that would not attract notice or announce her as a person with any wealth.

The drab gown accomplished that but did little else for her appearance. Quickly, she shrugged off the spencer and the bonnet she wore. There was no mirror in the cabin, but she smoothed her hair as best she could and tried to shake wrinkles out of the gown. She wished she had thought to bring another gown, but there was not room in her makeshift knapsack.

The footsteps passed her cabin, and she blew out a breath. Where was Julien? Had the captain refused his request?

She clenched and unclenched her hands, wishing she had something to do. Finally, out of desperation, she folded her spencer and put it in a cupboard, then placed her knapsack on the bed, where it would be out of the way.

As soon as she touched the bed, her knees went weak. If Julien had his way, she would be his wife tonight, and this would be their wedding bed. He would have every right to kiss her and touch her and—

She closed her eyes. As much as she enjoyed his kisses and caresses, she had not allowed herself to think much beyond that. In fact, she knew very little about lovemaking. She had grown up surrounded by young girls and spinsters. Oh, they had whispered about this handsome porter or that fine-looking shopkeeper, but they were really quite sheltered.

Even Pippa's story of the employer chasing her about the library had not alluded to what would have happened if she had been caught.

And the books Sarah had read—romantic stories of knights and their ladies—had given scant detail about what happened after the happy couple rode off into the sunset.

She swallowed and tried to breathe. Perhaps Julien would not want to consummate the marriage. Perhaps he was only taking her as a bride in order to protect her with his name. It would certainly be improper for them to be alone together without being married.

Sarah closed her eyes and shook her head. Who was she trying to fool? Of course Julien would want to consummate the marriage. Had he not made it clear the last time they had kissed that he wanted her?

And, come what may, she must marry him. Not only because she needed his protection but because she loved him, and this was her last chance at happiness.

She heard footsteps again and took a deep breath. *Chin up*, she reminded herself.

⤝⤞

When Julien opened the door, Sarah was not in the cabin. He paused, frowning, while behind him, the captain shifted impatiently. "I don't have all day, Valère."

"She's not here."

"I'm here," a small voice squeaked. Julien moved inside the room and squinted. Yes, there, wedged in the corner beside the bed and the wall, was Sarah.

"Why are you hiding?"

She took a tiny step forward. "I'm not hiding."

"Good, then let's go. The ceremony will be in Stalwart's cabin."

"That is," the captain said, stepping into the already crowded cabin, "if the lady agrees. I'm not marrying her against her will."

Julien frowned at him. "Oh, now you have scruples?"

"I'm willing," Sarah said then looked at Julien. "That is, if you're willing?"

"I'm willing." He took her hand and pulled her in his wake. He did not know why he was in such a hurry to get this done. It wasn't as though she could run away. Perhaps he feared she would change her mind.

They reached Stalwart's cabin, where the first mate, a young man of perhaps one-and-twenty was waiting with a Bible and a Book of Common Prayer. Stalwart took the Book of Common Prayer and asked for their full names.

Julien gave his, but when it was Sarah's turn, she said, "Have you ever performed a marriage at sea, Captain Stalwart?"

He considered for too long a moment. "Can't say that I have, though I've been present at one or two. Of course, technically we're not yet at sea. We're still in the Thames."

Sarah, wide-eyed, turned to look at Julien. "Do you think this is even legal?" She turned back to Stalwart. "Are you even ordained?"

He laughed at that, and Julien took her shoulders and pulled her aside. "You're right. This marriage may not stand up in a court of law. But I'm not going to challenge it, are you?"

"No, but—"

"We'll marry again once we return. I'll get a special license."

"But—"

Exasperated, he cut her off. "This is the best I can do right now, Sarah. *Will* you marry me?"

For the space of three heartbeats, she did not answer. It was his third proposal to her, and the first one he truly meant. His heart pounded in his throat, fear gripping and paralyzing him. What if she said no?

She stood looking at him, staring into his eyes for an eternity. In her eyes, he saw uncertainty, distrust, and something else—affection? Something more?

"I'll marry you," she finally whispered.

"Good." Relief coursed through him and also, unexpectedly, guilt. He knew she wanted romance. She had made that plain the first time she had refused him. And now he had proposed three times and arranged a hasty wedding ceremony, none of it romantic in the least.

But he would make it up to her. When they returned to London, when he had his brother home safe, he would get the special license and give her the most lavish, most romantic wedding the *ton* had ever seen.

She deserved it. In another moment, she would be his, and he would do anything for her—anything to please her.

As Julien expected, the ceremony was brief, Spartan, and unromantic. Julien was vaguely aware of promising to have Sarah for better or worse, richer or poorer, and in sickness and in health.

Then it was Sarah's turn. Her voice was shaky as she repeated the vows. "I, Sarah, take thee, Julien, to be my wedded husband." She swallowed and looked up at him, and he gave her a reassuring smile.

The captain read the next line, and she repeated: "To have and to hold from this day forward, for better for worse, for richer for poorer, in sickness and in health, to love, cherish, and to obey, till death do us part."

She took a deep breath, and Julien, who was already holding her hand, squeezed it. Finally, she repeated the last. "According to God's holy ordinance; and thereto I give thee my troth."

Julien smiled again. It was almost done. She was almost his.

But after a moment, he realized Stalwart was not going on. The captain cleared his throat. "Do you have a ring?"

Damn! Julien shook his head. "No, I didn't think of that." He did not wear jewelry, so he didn't even have a signet ring to give her. One more thing to add to the wildly romantic wedding he would give her when they returned.

"The next section is about a ring," the young first mate said. "You have to give her something."

"It's alright," Sarah said, reassuring him. "We can just pretend."

"No." Suddenly Julien reached back and loosed the ribbon he used to keep his hair back in a queue. It was made of a plain black material, but he could tie it around her finger. "We'll use this."

"Tie it on then."

Sarah offered her hand, and Julien took it. Why had he never noticed before that her hand was so small and white? He tied the ribbon on her fourth finger, noticing how stark it looked there.

"Repeat after me," the captain said.

Julien did. "With this ring I thee wed, with my body I thee worship, and with all my worldly goods I thee endow."

He was staring into her eyes, and he saw a single tear cascade down her cheek. Gently, he wiped it away.

"There's more here," Stalwart said, "but I need to go topside, so I think I'll just end it by saying: Those whom God hath joined together let no man put asunder." With a bang, he closed the book and tossed it on his desk.

"Thank you," Julien said, releasing Sarah's hand for the moment and shaking the captain's.

"I hope you don't think I did it for free," Stalwart muttered.

Julien shook his head. "I'll throw in a bonus when we return."

"See that you do." And then he and the first mate were gone.

Julien turned back to Sarah, who was fidgeting with the ribbon he had tied on her finger and avoiding his eyes.

"Do you want to go back to our cabin?"

Twenty

SARAH'S HEAD SPUN, AND SHE LOOKED DESPERATELY about for something to cling to—something besides Julien. Her stomach was jumping as though there were a dozen butterflies trapped inside. She felt nervous and excited, tense and eager all at once. Sarah clutched the back of the chair and breathed deeply. When the dizziness passed, she closed her eyes and covered her face with her hands.

How mortifying it would have been if the first thing she did as Valère's wife was to fall over in a heap on the floor. He would probably begin planning the annulment.

She felt him move forward, and his hand was on her back. "Something I said?"

She frowned. Was that humor in his tone?

She glanced back and saw he did have a trace of a smile on his lips. "I can see you're anticipating the wedding night."

She swallowed. "Not at all. I think it must be the rocking on the boat." But it was no such thing, and they both knew it.

He reached forward and smoothed a strand of hair away from her face. "It's alright to be nervous."

"I'm not nervous," she lied.

He leaned forward and whispered in her ear, "I am."

She shivered at the feel of his warm breath on her skin and felt some of her fear melt away. This was Julien. She had nothing to fear. Of course, her stomach still twisted and jumped, and her body still quivered, but she no longer felt like falling over.

"Allow me to escort you back to our cabin," he whispered. She could not stop herself from tensing, but now he pulled back and looked her in the eye. "I just want you to be comfortable and safe while I go on deck. That's all."

She nodded. He was not going to ravish her in the cabin. He just wanted to have her settled. They would walk back to the cabin, and he would leave her alone.

For a little while.

Hands clenched, she followed Julien back to their cabin. Once again, he gave her strict instructions not to answer the door for anyone but him. She could tell he did not trust the sailors or the captain, and she found his protectiveness sweet.

Sarah did not know how long Julien would be gone, and she had nothing to do in the cabin. She was tired but resisted lying on the berth for as long as she could. Finally weariness set in, and she decided she would lie down for just a moment.

As soon as she lay on the berth, she noticed how small it was. She really could not think how Julien would fit in here with her. They would be sleeping on top of each other.

Sarah sucked in a breath at that idea and pushed it firmly from her mind.

Despite the berth's small size, it was comfortable, and she closed her eyes for a moment and drifted with the gentle rocking of the boat.

Something was stroking her cheek. It was gentle but persistent.

"Sarah?"

She heard someone calling from far away.

"Sarah, wake up."

But she was not sleeping. She was floating, floating, float—

Her eyes snapped open, and she scrambled to rise. Julien was sitting at the edge of the berth, looking down at her, but it was too dark in the cabin to discern the expression on his face.

"No, it's alright. You don't need to rise."

"I–I think I must have fallen asleep."

"I don't blame you. It's late. Move over so I can slide in."

She did as he asked without even considering what it meant, and a moment later his body, warm and solid, was beside hers. She was forced to turn on her side and back all the way against the wall in order to accommodate him. And then she was still cramped and uncomfortable.

It was impossible not to touch him, try as she might, and she realized after a moment that he had removed his coat, cravat, and shirt. The bare flesh of his arm touched hers, and she froze.

Her skirts were wrapped about her legs so she could not feel if his legs were bare or not. As he tried to settle in, she prayed fervently that he had kept some shred of clothing on.

"This still isn't working," he said after a moment of trying to get comfortable. "Here." He raised one arm and indicated his chest.

His bare chest. She could see the smooth bronze skin and the smattering of dark brown hair in the moonlight. Oh, my. She had never been this close to a man's bare chest before, and the blood thrummed in her veins.

"Put your head here."

She stared at his chest, then at his face. She did not see how she could lie there and avoid touching him. She did not mind touching him with her head, but in that position, her whole body would be pressed against his.

She hesitated, but he was lying there, looking at her, and she could hardly refuse him. Finally, she laid her head on his shoulder. Immediately, his arm went around her, and she was hauled against him, her body flush with his.

His skin was cool and the muscles of his shoulder firm. It felt strange to put her bare cheek against his skin so intimately. She could smell him, that tangy citrus smell mingled with a smoky, woodsy smell. She wondered idly if his skin would taste as good as it smelled.

"Comfortable?" he murmured. His voice rumbled through her, the sound low and strangely comforting.

"Mmm-hmm," she managed.

She counted three of his slow, steady heartbeats, and then he said, "You'll faint if you don't breathe."

He was right. She was holding her breath. She forced herself to inhale slowly, his masculine scent enveloping her. She felt quite suddenly even more lightheaded than she had before she had forced herself to take a breath.

"Better?" he asked.

"Yes," she lied.

They lay in silence for several minutes, what seemed to Sarah an eternity. Julien's breathing was regular and even, and he began to stroke her arm with smooth, light caresses. Gradually, she began to relax. She did not have to tell herself to breathe, and she even allowed some of the tension to ease out of her body.

She closed her eyes and relaxed enough to ask the question—well, one of them—that had been plaguing her all evening. "Are you still angry with me?"

He continued to stroke her arm, but he did not answer right away. After a few minutes, she opened her eyes and glanced up at him. Her nose was level with his chin, her eyes even with his cheek. His eyes were open, and he was staring at the ceiling.

Finally, he looked down at her. "No, I'm not angry. I'm worried, not angry. What am I supposed to do with you while I search for Armand?"

"I told you. I have information you need. And I can blend in. I speak fluent French."

He looked back up at the ceiling, and she lay quietly beside him, feeling the ship rock back and forth, listening to the sound of the crew calling orders, and feeling his heartbeat under her hand on his chest. "I didn't mean to force you to marry me," she said finally. "You have to believe that was never my intention—"

"Shh." He gripped her shoulder and squeezed it reassuringly. "You didn't force me to do anything."

"But—"

"You just gave me the opportunity to do what I've been wanting to do anyway."

She allowed the words to penetrate, played them over and over in her mind. "You *wanted* to marry me?"

"That's what I said."

"Why?"

He looked down at her again. "So I could do this."

He easily closed the distance between them, his mouth meeting hers in a kiss that was gentle and restrained yet promising a passion she could hardly fathom. As much as she welcomed the kiss, she trembled in his arms, uncertainty and self-consciousness making her quake.

And then Julien shifted, lowering her onto the berth and rising up on his elbows so he was over her, his arms about her. He deepened the kiss, slanting his mouth over hers, urging her to kiss him back, to follow him into the passion swirling around them.

Almost without thinking, she put her shaking arms about his shoulders and kissed him back, wanting to possess him as eagerly as he sought to possess her.

This was her husband, she realized. This man belonged to her and no other.

"Je t'adore," he murmured. His mouth moved to her throat, and the touch of his lips sent heat shooting into her belly. Now her trembling was not from uncertainty.

Her hands moved over his back, her fingers tracing the corded muscles that bunched and strained with the force of his own restraint. She could feel him shaking, trying to control his desire for her. For some reason that made her want him even more. Her breathing began to come more quickly, quickening even more when the hands around her waist skimmed up to her breasts and cupped them.

She moaned aloud, and then clamped her lips shut: mortified.

He met her gaze and chuckled. "So you like that, do you?"

"Um—" She did not know how to answer, did not want to sound wanton.

"Let's see how you like this."

He must have loosened the fastenings on the back of her gown at some point as they lay beside one another, because he easily slipped the material down off her shoulders. It was a simple matter then to pull the garment down farther until he exposed her stays.

She had worn a pair of stays that tied in the front so she could dress herself and not have to explain to Katarina why she needed that maid's gown. Now it served Julien's advantage.

With a deft flick of two fingers, he loosened the stays and pushed them aside. Now only her plain, white shift covered her breasts. The material was thin and fine, little protection. If the room had not been so dark, he would have been able to see right through it.

Slowly, his eyes still on her face, he ran a hand over her breasts, allowing his fingers to dip into the ruffled edge of the shift.

Under the material, her skin burned as his hands touched her. Where his fingers met exposed skin, she was scorched.

Another moan escaped, and she gasped in horror. "I'm sorry," she whispered.

"I like it, *chérie*. I want to know what you like."

"But the men on the ship—they'll hear."

"Then we'll be very quiet," he whispered against her neck, then stroked a thumb over the curve of her breast. "Tell me what you like."

She took a deep breath. "I-I like this."

"What if I pull this chemise down and kiss you— here?" His finger circled one erect nipple, making it peak and strain. "Do you think you'd like that, *ma belle*?"

"Oh, yes," she breathed, already aching.

Slowly, far too slowly, he eased the material over her breasts. She could feel the cool air brush her skin, and she had never felt such reckless abandonment.

And then he lowered his mouth. His tongue raked over the sensitive skin, teasing one nipple while his finger tantalized the other. Heat rushed to her belly and pooled lower, and she writhed, aching for... something. She did not know what she wanted.

"More." She did not realize she had actually spoken aloud until she heard him chuckle, his warm breath teasing her already sensitive skin.

"I'd like to do more," he said, looking into her eyes. She loved it when he looked at her. His gaze was so full of desire.

And that desire was all for her. She could hardly believe it.

"But you'll have to take off this gown first."

❧

Julien thought she might rebel at that suggestion. A look of pure panic streaked across her face. He had tried to move slowly, to make her want him as much as he wanted her, but he obviously had not moved slowly enough.

Damn it! He should have been more patient. The problem was that he was as hard as granite and aching to be inside her. Those little moans she kept making were driving him insane with need.

But whatever happened tonight—even if it was nothing more than this—he refused to toss up her skirts and take her that way. He wanted this to be intimate and memorable—their first time as husband and wife.

"Sarah?"

Silence. She was looking up at him, and he could see that a hundred thoughts flitted through her mind each second.

"Why don't you allow me to help you take off that gown?"

"But what about the sailors?"

"What about them? They're outside."

"They might hear."

"I told you," he whispered, standing then pulling her beside him. "We'll be very quiet."

To his disappointment, when she stood, she tugged her shift up over her breasts. She was supposed to be taking clothes off, not putting them back on. He should not have paused, allowed her to remember modesty. It was a good thing he had not asked Stalwart for a lamp. She would only feel more self-conscious in the light.

But, oh, how he ached to see her—truly see her.

She turned now so her back was to him, and he realized her hair had come undone. The dark tresses fell over the back of her gown like a river of chocolate. He reached out, took the hair in his hand and ran it through his fingers. He pushed it over one shoulder, then leaned forward and kissed her neck, inhaling her scent. He did not know what it was, something light and delicious. She was apples and cinnamon.

Intoxicating.

His hands made quick work of her laces, and the gown slid over her hips and puddled on the floor. He reached around and gently finished unlacing her stays so they too fell in a heap on the floor.

It was only then he realized she was shaking.

"Are you cold?" he asked.

"No," she answered, not looking at him.

He turned her to face him and winced at the fear he saw in her face. She was terrified of him. Or perhaps not him, but of the act itself. Disappointment shot through him. He could not make love to her this way, not when she was in this state.

He supposed it was understandable. Most brides had months to contemplate and prepare for the wedding night. She had mere hours.

"Come here," he said, taking her into his arms. She obeyed, but he felt her trembling grow worse. "Shh." He smoothed her hair and tried not to notice how soft her body was or how well it fit with his. "I'm just going to hold you."

"I-I'm sorry," she stuttered through chattering teeth. "I just need a moment."

"Take all the time you want." In fact, that was an idea with merit. Why not have her come to him? Why not tease and tantalize until she ached for him as much as he did her? He smiled and said, "I'm tired. Why don't we just go to sleep?"

She glanced up at him sharply. Was that disappointment in her face? "But I thought you wanted to—"

He waited, wondering what phrase she would use, but she only gestured helplessly at the berth.

"I do." He cupped her cheeks. "Sarah, I *really* do. But we're moving too fast for you." It was an effort not to smile. His little wife wanted him more than she was ready to admit.

"I'll be alright—"

"*Bien sûr*, but not tonight. We have the rest of our lives. I want you to want me as much as I want you."

"I *do* want you. I–I just don't know what that means."

He grinned. "I'll be happy to give you a lesson, little governess, but only when you're ready."

"I'm ready." She sounded eager, which he liked. He liked it so much that he almost abandoned his plan all together.

But he had willpower—at least he hoped he did. He could wait. Especially if waiting would enhance the pleasure. "Are you?" He brushed his fingers through her hair. "French lovemaking is very different from English lovemaking, *chérie*. In France, we move very"—he traced her cheek, her lips— "very"—he parted her lips and inserted his thumb gently—"slowly."

Her eyes were huge with desire, and he knew he could have had her now, if that was what he wanted.

But he rather liked this game, rather wanted her to pursue him. *"Comprenez-vous?"*

"Oui, but—"

"Bonne nuit, chérie. Until tomorrow." He brushed a delicate kiss on her forehead, over the wrinkles formed when she frowned, then gestured to the berth.

With slumped shoulders and a reluctant sigh, she climbed into the berth, scooted up against the wall, and then he climbed in, once again raising his arm and offering his shoulder. This time she moved to lie against him eagerly. He smiled—already he had made progress.

Of course, now that she wore only her chemise, he could feel all the soft curves of her body distinctly. He could imagine the weight of her breasts in his hands, the taste of her creamy skin in his mouth.

He bit back a groan and focused his gaze on the ceiling. He was tired and knew sleep would come.

Eventually.

Sleep, he welcomed. It was the dreams—dreams of her moans of pleasure and her body's response to him—he dreaded.

He closed his eyes and forced himself to count ugly sheep.

Twenty-one

SARAH ENDURED THE TORMENT FOR TWO DAYS AND two nights. At first she had liked the idea of waiting to consummate the marriage. She was nervous and told herself she needed time to prepare. But after sleeping beside Julien all night, feeling his body hot and solid against hers, she was ready to proceed.

But Julien was intent on moving slowly, and the man had the patience of a hunting lion. He would bring her just to the point of exquisite pleasure and then back away. By the third day, her body was in a constant state of yearning, and she was determined to satisfy that yearning—one way or another. It did not matter that it was broad daylight or the crew members might hear them. She wanted Julien.

By that time, their days had begun to take on a routine. Sarah, who had never slept past dawn in all her life, dozed until late morning and actually enjoyed the rest. Julien woke up early and went on deck. He would return, take her for a stroll about the ship, and then they would have a light lunch, usually with Captain Stalwart and his first mate.

In the afternoons, if Julien went on deck again, Sarah read something from Stalwart's library—he had a good collection—or joined Julien. If the weather was poor, they would stay in their cabin and play cards or tell stories.

But this afternoon would be different, she vowed, and after lunch, she took Julien's hand and pulled him to their cabin. She had not been able to eat a bite of the fare Captain Stalwart provided. Her stomach was twisted in knots of anticipation, and she could hardly believe she was being so bold. But this seemed the only way. And, she suspected this was what Julien wanted.

He raised a brow at her brazenness but did not argue. Once she closed their cabin door behind him, he said, "What's this?"

"I'm tired of walking about on the deck." She stepped forward, took his coat in both hands and tugged it off his shoulders. He watched her lazily, his eyes turning that dark shade of blue she loved.

"I suppose we could play a game of cards," he drawled.

"Oh, no." She flicked his cravat loose then undid the fastenings at his throat. "I have a different game in mind."

"What's that?" His voice was husky now, heavy with need. She liked that, and she knew she could provoke him further. She skimmed her hands beneath his waistband and tugged his shirt free, pulling it over his head in one motion.

She almost lost her breath then. Seeing Julien without his shirt was enough to leave her mouth dry and her hands shaky. She ran a hand over his chest then turned her back to him. She wanted to touch him with more than just the skin of her hands. She wanted to feel his heat over every inch of her.

"Unfasten me," she said, glancing at him over her shoulder. "I want to touch you. Skin on skin."

She caught his sudden intake of breath and felt the tremor in his hands as he slowly unfastened her gown. When it was loose, she shrugged it off and stepped out of it. Now she stood in only her shift and her stays, and she took pleasure in raising a hand to her breasts then deftly flicking the stays open.

Julien's eyes followed her every movement, growing darker blue as the stays fell away and revealed the shape of her breasts under the thin shift. She was shaking now, nervous from this last gesture. She reached for the material, raised it slowly, intending to pull it over her head so she was naked before him, but he grasped her hands and pulled her into a warm embrace.

"Remember what I told you, *chérie*." He kissed her neck, ran his hands leisurely down her back, cupped her buttocks. "Take it slowly. *Lentement*."

"I can't take it any slower," she moaned, kissing his neck and allowing her own hands to roam over his back and shoulders. "I *need* you."

He groaned, and his lips met hers in a barely controlled kiss. The contact between them now was primal, almost savage, and she could hear her breath growing ragged and the small mewing sounds escaping. She pushed against him, knowing she wanted more, needing to feel more.

His lips claimed hers, and then the world around them exploded.

She was on the cabin floor before she even knew

what had happened. The ship had been rocked hard, and she slammed into the wood planks. She tried to rise, but Julien was above her, shielding her with his body.

"What—"

"Stay down," Julien demanded. He was warm and solid above her, and she had little choice but to obey. Above, she could hear the crew yelling and scrambling into position.

"What is it?" she asked after a long moment punctuated by the sound of her heart pounding in her ears.

"It sounded like a shot from a cannon." He rose slowly, gave her a quick assessing glance, and helped her to sit. "Stay there." He strode to the porthole and peered out. "Damn it."

She jumped up to join him, and he frowned then moved aside so she could see. At first she saw nothing but black smoke dissipating, and then she saw the ship. It was larger than they, and its sails were tight with the wind. It was coming for them, coming at them fast and hard.

"They're flying French colors," Julien told her. "That was a warning shot. If Stalwart tries to run, they'll blow us out of the water."

Sarah gaped at him. "But I thought he was a smuggler. I thought he was supposed to be able to evade the authorities."

Julien gave a bitter laugh, his eyes still on the approaching ship. "Who said these are the authorities? It looks like the Navy, but that might be a ruse."

"What do they want? Are they going to attack us?" Worse yet, would they board? And if they did, what would become of Julien and herself? She could not imagine the French Navy would welcome them.

"I don't know," Julien said. "But whatever happens, I want you to stay close—"

Footsteps clumped rapidly in the passage outside the cabin before the door rattled and swung open. "Valère!" The first mate stuck his head inside, his voice calm but his manner brusque and hurried. Sarah jumped behind Julien to hide her state of undress, but the man did not even glance at her. "Valère, come with me."

"What the hell is going on?" Julien demanded. He seemed unconcerned about his bare chest or the pile of clothing on the floor at the door.

"We're about to be boarded by the French Navy. The captain can probably bribe his way out of this, but not if a French aristocrat is found on board. Captain's orders are that you hide in the cargo hold." The first mate pulled out a pistol and leveled it at them. "I'm to escort you."

Sarah clutched Julien's arm and stared at the pistol. But if Julien had any fear, he didn't show it. "Won't they search the cargo holds?" he asked.

"Not this one," the man said with a grin. "Now let's go." He motioned with the pistol.

Far too slowly for her tastes, Julien took her hand and moved forward. Once in the passageway, he pushed her before him so the pistol was aimed directly at him. For the first few minutes, Sarah forgot to pay attention to where she was going. The first mate called out "right" or "left," and she did as she was bade. At one point, a dozen crewman ran past them, their faces stoic and stony. She hugged the wall, trying to stay out of their way.

She was completely lost now. Despite the ship's small size, she had not seen much of it, and when they came to a dark passage that dead-ended, she turned to the first mate, certain he had taken a wrong turn. But he held up a lantern and gestured them forward.

"The captain has a hold for special cargo." When she reached the end of the passageway, the first mate stepped in front of her and pushed at a section of wall. Silently, a door slid open. Sarah stared at it, amazed at how perfectly it had blended in with the wood surrounding it.

"In there." The first mate pointed. "Climb down the ladder." He lifted his lantern, shining light into the void. Sarah peered down and down. She could barely make out the ghostly shadows of barrels and crates below. But the space was filled and would be cramped.

"I'll go first with the lantern," Julien told her.

"Hurry up," the first mate ordered. "They'll be coming alongside us in a few moments."

Julien nodded, took the lantern, and began the descent. Sarah watched, frightened he would lose his one-handed grip on the rope ladder, but he held on. Before he had even reached the bottom, the first mate was waving for her to follow. Hands shaking and knees wobbling, she did so. She knew Julien would catch her if she faltered. As she climbed, she shuddered, thinking of all the spiders and rats and who knew what else waiting below. But Julien was there as well. She did not want to be anywhere he was not.

When she reached the last rung, Julien caught her and pulled her into his arms. Together they looked up at the door and the first mate. Without a word, he shut the door. She heard it slide back into place, and then all went silent.

Julien held up the lantern, shedding scant light upon the barrels and crates. They were unmarked and stacked high. Finally, he gestured to a spot on the floor between two crates where they could sit and would be hidden from view should the door open. "This is probably Stalwart's most valuable cargo," he told her. "He'll make certain this isn't confiscated. We should be safe."

Sarah was not so certain, but the rapid pounding of her heart slowed as Julien pulled her into his arms. "You're going to be all right." He stroked her hair, and gradually she began to relax. After a few moments, he sat down on the wooden planks, and she sat beside him, wrapped in his arms. He held her tightly and covered her mouth when she felt the two ships scrape together and the sound of boots as the Navy officers boarded the smaller vessel.

"Don't make a sound," he whispered in her ear.

She could hear the men moving around, hear the faraway lilt of their French. But she could not understand them. Then all grew quiet, and Sarah held her breath. They were searching the ship, and she knew they would find her.

Julien pulled the lantern close to hide the light. Sarah wanted to tell him to blow it out, but she was too afraid to be trapped there in the dark. Finally, except for the occasional voice or jostle of the two vessels, all was still. She sat encased in Julien's arms and prayed. When she opened her eyes, she stared at Julien's face, memorizing it. His look was grim but confident.

The hours wore on. At some point she must have fallen asleep, because he was gently shaking her. She sat bolt upright, a scream trapped in her throat.

"Shh." He pulled her close to him again. "The Navy is leaving," he whispered.

Her heart lifted. "How do you know?"

"I heard the boots. Wait… do you feel our ship moving away?"

She nodded. "Yes!" Oh, thank God. They had not been discovered. She sat anxiously waiting for the door above to open. Julien's eyes were on the ceiling as well, but an hour passed, and no one came to free them.

"Do you think they forgot about us?" she asked.

He did not answer, and she knew he feared the captain would leave them there. After all, they could be valuable cargo. He might fetch a good price for them. Oh, why had she not thought of this before?

"Not exactly what you had in mind for this afternoon, was it?" Julien said finally. Lord, how could he sound so nonchalant? But then, what good was worrying going to do them? And if this was the last of their time together, she did not want to spend it fretting.

She took his hand, held it to her cheek. "I'm beginning to wonder if we'll ever be together."

He chuckled, and the sound rumbled through her. "Feeling impatient?"

"Very impatient."

He pulled her closer, put his lips by her ear. "Just wait until I get you back to the cabin, *chérie*. I don't think either of us wants to wait any longer." She kissed him gently, letting him know she agreed. Fervently, she prayed they would once again reach the cabin. After a long silence, Julien began to speak. He spoke slowly at first and of things of no consequence, but gradually he began to speak of his family, and his voice warmed. Sarah was glad for the comfort of his voice, glad for the steadiness she heard there.

She learned all about the Valère family. Julien's stories revealed how much he revered his father, who had been nothing short of a hero to his son. He told of how brave his mother had been during their flight from France and how she had tried to be both mother and father to him in those first years. He regaled her with dozens of stories about Armand and Bastien. She felt she almost knew them.

After he had spoken for some time, he asked her for stories as well, and she told him about life at the Academy and the friends she had made there. But she had nothing to rival his tales of mischief and camaraderie with his brothers.

Hearing so much about Julien's family, Sarah longed for a family of her own even more fervently. The phantom memories that had plagued her all her life—memories of a laughing mother and the warm, safe arms of a father—came back to her stronger than ever. She told Julien about the memories and her belief that they stemmed from a deep longing for her own family.

By now the lantern had almost burned down, and they were both weary. Julien was lying on his back, staring at the ceiling. She was flush against him, her head on his shoulder. He had one arm about her and the other under his head.

With no time to dress again, he wore his breeches and nothing else. She was still in her shift. She would have been cold had he not kept her close beside him. Her eyes were almost closed as she told him she yearned for a family of her own. She stroked his bare chest, letting her fingers swirl in and out of the smattering of hair there. When he sat and looked directly at her, she sat as well, unconcerned that the sleeve of her shift fell down, exposing her bare shoulder.

His eyes flicked in the direction of that naked flesh, and the feel of his gaze on her aroused her. Oh, why had the Navy had to interrupt everything?

"What is it?" she asked when he did not speak.

"It's just that I never realized how alike we are."

She raised her brows. "Alike? We're nothing alike. You're a duc. I'm a governess. You're rich. I'm poor. You're French, and I'm English."

"Yes, on the surface we seem to have little in common, but in here"—he put his hand just above her breast, over her heart—"in here we have the same wants, the same desires."

As always, the feel of his hands on her made her breathless. "How so?" she whispered.

"We both want a family. I've been searching for mine since I was thirteen. You—I suppose you've always been searching for yours."

She swallowed. "But I'll never find mine. I'll never know who my mother or father were."

"No, but I'd say you found a family anyway. Mine."

She felt tears prick her eyes, but she could not look away.

"We'll have our own family, Sarah. And we'll create our own memories."

She looked down, the doubts that had plagued her since they began this voyage creeping to the surface once again. This time she could not seem to contain them. This time she *needed* the words he spoke to be real and true.

"What's wrong?" he asked.

"What if, when we return to London, we realize this marriage isn't valid?"

"I told you. I'll get a special license, and we'll marry again."

"But"—she gathered the hem of her shift and twisted it—"what if when your mother learns who I really am, she doesn't want me for a daughter-in-law? What if all of Society laughs at you for choosing to marry a governess?"

He chuckled, and she glanced up at him sharply. *"Mon coeur,"* he murmured and pulled her against him again. "Do you think I care what Society says? If I never have to attend another ball, I'll be ecstatic."

"Oh, me too. I hate dancing."

"See, I told you we had much in common."

She smiled, listening to the soft thump of his heart under her ear. "But, Julien, what about your mother?"

"My mother wants me to be happy, Sarah. If you're what makes me happy, then she'll welcome you with open arms."

Sarah sat up and stared at him. *"Do* I make you happy?"

"Excessively—though I couldn't tell you why, since you also cause me enormous trouble."

"Maybe you needed some trouble in your life."

He grinned and pulled her into his arms. "Maybe I did." Even as the lantern began to flicker and die, she could see his blue eyes darken.

She looked at his mouth, touched it with one finger, and then met his gaze. It was already on her, filled with passion and longing—all the things she felt. *"Embrasse-moi."* His voice was husky, and it sent a shiver through her. She wrapped her arms around him and kissed him with all the desire she felt, wanting him to feel it as well.

He kissed her back, meeting her passion with his own. She welcomed his desire, matched it. She knew the pleasure his hands and lips could bring, and she offered herself to him completely. When his hands caressed her breasts, she arched to give him better access. When his lips brushed over the sensitive spot in the hollow of her throat, she moaned and pulled him against her.

With the hard floor beneath him, he pulled her on top of him, and she enjoyed kissing his chest and neck, running her hands over his abdomen, down to his waistband, where she paused, excited and uncertain.

Her fingers trembled as they grazed the edge of his breeches, and she looked up to find him watching her. "Perhaps we should stop," he said, his voice ragged.

She shook her head. "I don't want to stop. I want to be your wife in truth." It was as bold a statement as she had ever made. Bolder, because they might be interrupted at any moment. But she did not care. She glanced at Julien to gauge his response.

He closed his eyes briefly, then opened them and met her gaze. "Are you sure?"

"More than I've ever been. I want this. I want you."

He groaned, pulling her into his arms and holding her tightly. "I want you so much I'm afraid at some point I won't be able to stop."

"I don't want you to stop," she said into his chest. When he did not answer, she whispered, "Julien, please."

That was all it took. The next thing she knew, she was on her back, his arm beneath her to cushion her. He was over her, covering her with his body, kissing her with his mouth, stroking her with his hands. Sensation overwhelmed her. She savored the hardness of his body and the heat of his flesh.

When he rose up in the flickering lantern light, she marveled at how beautiful he was—until he stood and stripped off his breeches. Then she was afraid to do any more than focus on his eyes.

"Nervous, *chérie*?" he asked, tone light. "We can still stop."

She sucked in a breath. "No. I don't want to stop."

"You can look at me."

She nodded. How could the man stand there so comfortable in his own nakedness? She still wore her shift from neck to knee, and she felt utterly exposed.

"Aren't you even curious?"

She was. She had seen paintings of nude men, but even then she had tried not to focus on *that* part of the artist's work. Now she had a real man before her. And this was her husband. She had every right to look. Slowly, she slid her eyes down past his neck, his chest, his waist, his hips…

Oh my.

She tried to breathe and found it difficult. He was like the paintings and yet so very different.

He was watching her. "We can still stop."

She shook her head. "I don't want to stop."

"In that case, you'd better follow my example."

She felt her face flush, but part of her was also excited, aroused. She wanted his eyes on her, wanted to see the approbation she knew was waiting. He took her hand, pulled her to her feet. And when she was standing before him, she reached for the hem of her shift, prepared to lift it, to strip it off. But he caught her hand and placed it on his chest. "Allow me."

She did not know what she expected. Perhaps that he would grasp the material and rip it from her body. Perhaps that he would slowly draw it up and over her. But he did neither. Instead, he kissed her.

He pulled her close, wrapping her in his arms, twining his tongue with hers, grasping her hair in his hands. When she was breathless and wanting more, he gently drew the straps of the shift off her shoulders, kissing her there. His lips moved inexorably lower until she practically pushed the linen away from her breasts herself so he might take them in his mouth and tease them with his tongue.

She was vaguely conscious of the material falling away from her body. In the back of her mind, she realized she could feel the cool air on her buttocks and legs—where she had not felt it before. But he was kissing her belly and stroking her thighs, and she could not spare a thought to feel embarrassed at her nudity.

And then, to her surprise and shock, he lifted her into his arms and deposited her gently on the floor.

∽◈∾

Julien looked down at his wife and felt his mouth go dry. She was so beautiful. The way the last flickers of the lantern light limned her creamy skin, the shape of her body, the way she looked at him with absolute trust in her eyes. *"Tu es si belle,"* he whispered. God, she was beautiful.

He wanted to give her pleasure. He wanted her to remember this night forever.

He knelt then lay down beside her, relishing the friction of her skin against his. He had been desperate to feel that for days now. Desperate to touch her everywhere, desperate to sink himself into her.

But that would have to wait. He had to go slowly, be gentle.

He kissed her again, loving the way her mouth opened for him. He kissed her until she moaned and pressed her hips against him. The gesture was probably unintentional, but her body knew what she wanted, even if her mind did not. His hands roved over her soft skin, exploring, teasing, allowing her to become comfortable with his touch in one spot before he moved to another.

What seemed like hours later, she was breathing heavily and clutching him tightly. "Julien, please," she begged, looking up at him. This was what he had wanted, what he had waited for. He was leaning over her now, and it took only a slight movement before he was inside of her.

She moaned and arched, but he refused to drive into her as his body demanded. Instead, he continued to kiss and stroke her, bringing her with him, allowing her pleasure to mount as his own did.

They moved together, all semblance of time and space draining away. It was only the two of them. Together. Reaching.

He moved, stroked, kissed, and finally she cried out and clutched at him. Only then did he allow himself to shatter.

Some time later, he lay with eyes closed. He was vaguely aware he was on a ship and he held Sarah in his arms. But he couldn't think of anything else—did not want to.

He especially did not want to think about the experience he had just shared with his new wife. It had moved him profoundly. He felt as though someone had taken a knife and sliced open his chest, leaving his heart exposed.

He did not like vulnerability. He had learned early that those he loved could be taken away from him. It was better not to get attached. Sarah had not been far off when she had called his first marriage proposal a business arrangement. He had intended his marriage to be like a business partnership. He was most successful in business when he acted unemotionally. He had not seen why marriage should be any different.

Now he realized that, without intending it, he had feelings for his wife. Love? No, he was not prepared to admit to loving her, to allow that vulnerability. But how long before he could no longer deny it?

She stirred beside him, leaned on her elbow, and looked up at him. He imagined her hair tousled and her cheeks flushed. He could picture her lush mouth, which he had dreamed of so often, and which had not disappointed, smiling at him shyly. "I'm cold."

"Sorry." He was lying on her shift, and now he handed it to her, helped her to pull it over her head. Then he donned his own breeches and sat beside her, taking her into his arms.

He had almost dozed off when he heard the thump of boots above. The lantern was cold now, and they both sat forward, their blind eyes looking up. The door slid open, and a beam of light shot into the darkness.

"Are you still down there?" Stalwart called.

"Bloody hell, Stalwart," Julien swore. "What took you so long?"

He chuckled. "Would you rather talk down there or up here?"

Julien made Sarah go before him, and a few moments later, he was before Stalwart. The man was smiling, but his eyes were shadowed.

"What did the Navy want?"

Stalwart shrugged. "To search the ship for contraband. They didn't look too hard. Your blunt gave them some incentive to leave."

"Why are you letting us out?" he asked. "You could sell us for a pretty profit, I'm sure."

Stalwart grinned. "I thought of that, but I don't think I'd get seven thousand. So instead, I'll take you to France. But Valère, when we return to England, I had better get my money."

"Oh, you'll get it." Without another word, he took Sarah's hand and led her past Stalwart. He didn't speak a word, just pulled her back to their cabin, opened the door, yanked her inside, and slammed it shut. "That bastard. I know he's just toying with us, but I'd like to knock him senseless."

He paced back and forth, running his hands through his hair. The cabin had not been touched, and it was dark now. Through the porthole, the moon was visible, a low sliver over the dark churning waters.

He turned to Sarah and tried to tamp down his fear. What if Stalwart had sold them out? What if another ship attacked? What if he lost her in France? He might have no more than this night with her, and he was not going to spend it angry or anxious.

"Come here." He pulled her into his arms, stripped the chemise off of her, and tugged her toward the berth. He might not be able to make love to her again tonight, but he could hold her warm body against his. She moved self-consciously, aware he was watching her.

But how could he keep from watching her? He knew her body now, knew where she liked to be touched, the slopes and valleys where his lips could bring her the most pleasure. But he wanted to know more. He had not kissed the back of her knee. How would she react? He didn't know if she was ticklish. If he stroked her feet, would she laugh?

He wanted her again. He could not understand it. He had been well pleased by her, and yet he felt as though he had barely touched her. His need for her was as great as it had ever been.

But, no. He would have to wait. She had been a virgin, and there was no possibility she would be ready for him again tonight.

She climbed back into the berth, and he followed.

He would have to wait until tomorrow night, when they could be alone again.

She snuggled against him, and his arm went about her, drawing her close.

It was going to be a long, agonizing twenty-four hours.

Twenty-two

SARAH WOKE THE NEXT MORNING, NAKED AND WRAPPED in Julien's arms. She had never felt so secure, so warm, so… aroused. Images from their lovemaking the day before flooded her memory, but instead of feeling embarrassed at her boldness, she found she wanted more. She wanted Julien again, wanted to see his eyes darken with desire, hear his breath hitch in pleasure, feel his hands on her.

His eyes were closed, his eyelashes making a dark sweep across his cheek, and she reached up and stroked the strong plane of that cheek. She touched his aristocratic nose, the sensuous lips, and allowed her fingers to trail down to his bare chest.

"You'd better stop now." His voice was low and husky. His eyes were closed, but he had a playful smile on his lips.

"Or what will happen?" she murmured, sliding her fingers lower so they grazed his hard, muscled abdomen.

"I might not be able to control myself."

She smiled. "I like the sound of that." The sheet was anchored at his slim hips, and she toyed with the edges for a moment, trying to decide if she should delve underneath. She glanced up at his face and saw he was watching her now. *"Touche-moi, mon amour."* His voice was hoarse with need, and yet she paused. Was she really his love, or was that something he said in the heat of passion?

His fingers reached out and cupped her breast, sending a flood of heat between her legs. One hand fingered her nipple, making it rise to a sensitive peak.

"Touch me," he whispered again.

Slowly, she drew the sheet down and saw he was already hard, already ready for her. She wrapped her hand around him, liking how the velvet texture contrasted with the steel of his hardness. He jumped in her hand, and she glanced up at him again. His eyes were so blue they were almost black.

"Do you like that?" she whispered.

"N'arrête pas." Don't stop.

She smiled and ran her hand up and down the length of him. He groaned, and she felt the dampness between her own legs. His hand had found her other breast now and was kneading the stiff peak of the nipple. She ached to feel his hands on her belly, between her legs.

"Julien—" She could hear the need in her voice.

"Climb on top of me," he whispered.

She frowned at him but made to comply, and when he settled her over that hardness, she understood.

"Slide down, *chérie.*"

She did so, feeling him penetrate her, moving slowly, so slowly she could see his reaction.

"Yes. *Lentement.*" She began to move over him, and he groaned. At first she was absorbed in his response—the way his hands gripped her hips, the way he rose to meet her. They moved in unison, their bodies seeming to sense what each other's needed. Their rhythms were slow-paced, exquisite agony. But then she felt her own pleasure building, and she raced to meet it. The white-hot heat building inside her urged her to a frenzy. She arched back, heard Julien whisper, *"Tu es si belle."* For that moment, she believed she was beautiful.

And then he arched with her, drove into her, and the pleasure exploded inside her.

❧

They were off the coast of France the next afternoon. Stalwart had hoped to arrive at night, and this timing was unfortunate. They would have to wait for cover of darkness before approaching shore and attempting a landing. That meant they had to sail up and down the coast, hoping none of the French warships caught sight of them.

Everyone was tense, including Julien, who worried not only about the landing but about getting Sarah and himself deeper into the countryside. Stalwart still refused to say where they would land, though he had offered to escort them on the first leg of their journey.

Julien knew if Stalwart wanted to be rid of them, now would be his opportunity. The captain could easily turn them over to the French authorities or sail without them.

Of course, it would have been easier to simply throw them overboard, and Stalwart had not done that, so perhaps the man would be true to his word and wait for them to return. It would take him several days to contact his suppliers and load French luxury goods into his cargo hold.

When darkness finally fell, Julien went below deck to the cabin he shared with Sarah. He opened the door, and she was beside him in an instant. Her face was pale and drawn. "Are we going to land soon? Is it safe?"

He could not offer her any real assurances, so he took her in his arms and held her. He felt a moment of regret that they would not be sharing the cabin tonight. In the past two days, he had found her an eager and responsive pupil. But his ever-increasing desire for her would just have to wait to be slaked.

"Stalwart wants to anchor at midnight. We'll row ashore with a few other members of the crew."

"Where are we landing?"

"Stalwart won't say. He promised to escort us on the first leg—not that I know where we should begin."

"Paris," she said decidedly.

He raised a brow. "You sound very sure."

"I am. Your brother is in Paris."

"And you know this because…?"

She looked away, indicating that was all she would say for now. He had intended to start his search in Paris at any rate. He knew his old butler, Gilbert Pierpont, still lived there, but Armand could be anywhere in France—if he was alive at all. "You should try to rest," he told her. "We might be traveling all night."

She pulled away. "Do you trust him—Stalwart?"

Julien looked away, debating his answer. She obviously had the same questions and doubts he did.

Finally, he met her gaze. "I don't see that we have any choice."

At half past midnight, Julien and Sarah stood on deck, staring at the dark shore. They had anchored in a cove that was well-sheltered from the open water. A French warship would have to come quite close in order to spot them. Julien figured this location had been used by Stalwart before and possibly by other smugglers.

"Are you ready?" Stalwart asked, indicating the long boats already bobbing in the black water below the vessel.

"Ready."

Julien climbed over the side of the ship and began to negotiate his way down the rope ladder. Sarah followed, with Julien helping her navigate the precarious descent.

An hour later Julien, Sarah, and Captain Stalwart were in a carriage speeding toward Paris. The captain had insisted Julien and Sarah make the first part of the trip blindfolded so that, no matter what, they would not be able to share his secret landing spot. Julien had argued that they would not be able to find their way back to the ship if they did not know where it was anchored, but Stalwart was taking no chances.

"I'll meet you in Paris in three nights," he said, finally removing the blindfolds. "A place called La Petite Coeur. It's in the Latin Quarter, near the river."

Julien nodded. "Three nights isn't much time."

"Take all the time you need, monsieur," Stalwart said, knocking on the roof of the carriage. "But if I don't see you in three nights, you'll have to find another way home."

The carriage slowed and stopped, and Stalwart threw the door open. "Good night."

Julien peered out the door. "There's nothing here but woods. Take us to a posting house where I can hire horses."

"I'd love to, monsieur, but I have other business tonight. Get out."

Julien sat forward. "Listen, Stalwart—"

The captain reached beneath his cloak, and Julien saw the glint of the pistol. "Get out," Stalwart ordered again.

With a scowl, Julien climbed out of the carriage and reached back to assist Sarah. He pulled her down beside him then retrieved their luggage—her knapsack and his satchel. "La Petite Coeur in three nights," Julien said. "You had better be there."

"Good night." Stalwart closed the door, and the carriage drove away.

⁓

Sarah stood in the darkness, wishing she could see the moon through the trees. She had lived in London so long and had been in the country so infrequently that she had forgotten how dark it could be at night. She had forgotten the sounds as well. All around them, the wind rustled the trees, leaves crunched underfoot, birds chirped, and insects buzzed. She shivered.

"What now?" she asked.

"Speak only in French," he answered, taking her hand and leading her forward, God knew where. They walked for several minutes, and Sarah saw no sign of habitation. For all they knew, Stalwart could have left them stranded in Belgium. Was this even the road to Paris?

"Are we even traveling the right way?" she asked after stumbling over a tree branch lying on the side of the road.

"We'll find out soon enough." His tone was dark, and she decided she had better not ask any additional questions. She could tell by the firm set of his mouth that he was angry, and she did not want to provoke him further.

It seemed to Sarah that they walked for hours, stumbling in the darkness. In reality, it was probably only three-quarters of an hour before they came upon a small farm. The farmhouse was dark, the inhabitants all asleep. But Julien made her duck behind a tree and pointed to an old cart standing near the barn. "We're taking that," he whispered.

She gaped at him. "We're stealing it?"

He gave her a sidelong look. "Borrowing it. And a horse."

"Do you *want* to be put in prison?" she hissed. "We can't steal other people's property!"

"Do *you* want to walk to Paris? It could be miles."

She frowned and stared at the cart. Reverend Collier would not approve of stealing, and the very idea made her stomach churn.

"Besides," Julien said, peering around the tree to get another look at the cart. "We need an excuse for having been out of the city. We'll say we went to visit your sister in Orléans. We'd need a cart to travel that far."

"I don't like it," she said, pressing a fist into her stomach. "I think we should walk."

He nodded. "Alright. You walk. I'll drive the cart."

In the end, she helped him steal it. She figured she was probably going to hell for all the lies she had told, so what did it matter if she added stealing as well? She did make Julien promise to return the cart. God might look favorably on that action.

By the time the sun was coming up, Sarah knew they were indeed on the road to Paris. She had never been to Paris, but she could not imagine anywhere else so many of the peasants from the country would be traveling. Most were laden with fruits and vegetables from their farms, and Julien bought some grain and vegetables to pile in the back of their cart.

Though he spoke the language perfectly, the peasants eyed him with suspicion. His clothes and manners were simple and plain, but there was something of the aristocrat in him he could not hide.

Nobility was in his accent, in his bearing, in the structure of his bones. For the first time, Sarah realized the danger they were in. If Julien was discovered to be an imposter, they would probably die here. Napoleon might not have continued the policies of the peasants during the Reign of Terror, but his government would not look kindly on their visit. Like the English government, the officials would assume the worst.

By the time they reached the gates to Paris, Sarah's head was pounding, and her stomach was tied in knots. It might have been hunger, but more likely, she was terrified of discovery. *Chin up*, she reminded herself as they waited in the line of carriages while soldiers checked the papers of all who wanted to enter. Sarah could not image London ever being so closely guarded, but then France was still recovering from its recent revolution.

Not to mention it was at war with almost the whole of the European continent.

But the soldiers seemed less worried about an invasion from the English than missing an opportunity to flirt with the pretty farm girls. Thus, when it was Julien's turn to pass, a young soldier took their papers and barely glanced at them, all the while smiling and carrying on a rapid conversation with a plump brunette dressed in peasant clothing.

They drove into the city, and Sarah breathed a sigh of relief.

"We need to find Gilbert," Julien said when they were well away from the gates.

"Who's that?"

"Our former butler and the man who can help us find Armand."

"Did you write and arrange to meet him?"

Julien shook his head. "Too dangerous."

"Then how shall we ever find him? Paris is huge and crowded."

"I have an idea. We'll find him."

She wondered if this Gilbert would corroborate Sir Northrop's information about Armand, if the former butler would know of the attic, would know of Le Grenier.

As they continued through the city, Sarah took in the sights and sounds of Paris. It was difficult to believe she truly was in Paris. She was in France—England's mortal enemy! She knew she was in danger every moment she spent in this city. Her French was flawless—the accent that of a native. But what if she accidentally reverted to English? There were a myriad of tiny mistakes that could give her away.

She watched Julien navigate the stolen cart through the city. He appeared confident and unperturbed, despite the fact that he was in more danger even than she. How had he done this before? How had he mustered the courage to return to a place whose people had murdered his family?

He had more courage and more honor than anyone she had ever met.

And he was her husband. She looked down at the ribbon she still wore about her finger, touched it briefly.

She wondered where they would sleep tonight and almost blushed remembering the last time they had been in bed together. She had never imagined lovemaking could be like that. She did not realize she could feel such heightened awareness, such agonizing anticipation, or such sweet pleasure.

No man but Julien could have made her feel that way. Of that she was certain.

And of course now she was even more in love with him. How could any woman who had been touched and stroked and cherished the way she had been fail to fall in love with Julien?

But was he in love with her? He had not said he was. He had called her *mon amour*, but had he meant the words, or were they just a meaningless endearment?

She glanced at him again, noting his strong jaw, his bronze skin, and the way a section of hair had come free from his queue. Except for that aristocratic nose and the hauteur that could creep into his eyes, he looked very much the rugged laborer. She would not have minded buying her bread from him. She saw some of the ladies they passed eyed him with admiration as well. He had garnered a fair share of smiles from the opposite sex.

Why would he love her? She was no one. A poor governess. Was she expecting too much to hope he might fall in love with her as she had with him?

Suddenly he glanced at her and flashed her a smile. "It's still here."

She followed his gaze to the street sign that read *Rue du Valère*.

Her eyes widened. "You have a street named after you?"

He shrugged. "My grandfather, really. He built a grand home here when there had been nothing but a field before."

"Is it still standing?"

Julien shook his head slightly. "This is the first time I've been back to this place, but we'll soon see."

The horse turned the corner, and the cart began down a small, tree-lined street that looked mainly residential. The houses were in various states of disrepair, but when Sarah saw the charred gray remains of a large structure, she knew Julien's town house had not survived.

She reached over and squeezed his arm, but he didn't respond. His look was stoic and grim. Sarah wondered what was next, as it was obvious Gilbert was not living in the Valère residence, but she did not speak, merely sat with her hands in her lap as Julien slowed the horse and climbed out of the wagon in front of the house.

She was aware that this was dangerous. If anyone walked by and saw them, their presence could elicit suspicion. But she had to give Julien a few minutes to make peace with this part of his past. He stood in front of the rubble, hands on his hips, face unreadable. His shoulders were back, his head high, but she could feel the pain within him. She wished she could take it away.

Wanting to give him privacy, she looked away, studying the nearby houses that were still standing. A curtain rustled in the small ramshackle home across the street. She could tell it had once been a fine building, but it was sorely neglected now.

The curtains parted again and then snapped shut.

She narrowed her eyes. "Julien."

He turned to look at her, and for a brief second, she glimpsed the agony that must have been devouring him inside. Then his face went blank.

She nodded to the house across the street. "I saw the curtains part. Someone is watching us."

"Well, let's see who it is." And he marched across the street. Sarah jumped down off the cart with an "oopmf" and ran to catch up.

"I don't think that's such a good idea," she hissed in French. "We don't know who it might be."

But Julien ignored her, stopped in front of the door, and knocked loudly.

Inside the house was a scraping sound and then silence. She tugged on his arm. "Let's go."

But Julien reached up and knocked again. There was a long silence, then the sound of a key turning in the lock. Finally, the door swung open, revealing a small, gray-haired man impeccably dressed but far too thin and haggard. His skin was sallow, his wrinkles deep.

He looked first at her then at Julien, his eyes widening. "Monsieur le Duc," he said, blinking as though to clear his eyes. "Is it really you?"

"May I come inside, Gilbert? I don't think it's safe to stand about talking on the streets."

Gilbert nodded furiously and swung the door wide. Beyond him gaped dark, shrouded rooms.

"I shall stable your horse and… carriage, Monsieur le Duc."

Sarah was instantly alarmed. How could they expect this frail old man to work for them? She would do it herself before she allowed that to happen.

"No," Julien said, obviously of her same mind. "We've traveled a long way. Please take my wife inside, and I'll join you in a moment."

"As you wish, Monsieur le Duc. Madame, this way, I beg you."

With a backward glance at Julien, who had already started back across the street, Sarah stepped into the dark home.

It was well-ordered and clean, but the windows were covered with heavy draperies, blocking out all of the light. It was nigh noon, but despite several candles burning, the parlor was gloomy and dim.

"Please sit, madame." He offered her the best chair. Indeed there were only two, and this looked the most comfortable. Sarah did not want to take it, but she did not see how she could refuse. She sat and smiled at him, hoping he would take the other chair. Instead, he remained standing, looking ready to serve her. "May I fetch you a light repast, madame? I'm certain you must be hungry after your journey."

She was starving, but she did not want to eat this man's food. "No, thank you. I'm fine."

"Some wine then. Surely your throat is dry." He looked so eager to be of service that she finally agreed. He disappeared into another room for several minutes and returned with a tray holding a bottle and two glasses. He filled one with the red liquid and then nodded for her to taste it.

She was no wine connoisseur, but the wine was sweet and refreshing, and she smiled her approval. "Won't you join me, sir?"

He looked horrified at the suggestion. "Oh, no, madame! This glass is for Monsieur le Duc."

"You'd better stop calling me that," Julien said, striding into the room. She had not heard him enter the house. "Or we'll all be thrown in prison by the end of the day."

"Of course, Monsieur le Duc." Gilbert poured Julien the second glass of wine and handed it to him eagerly. Sarah doubted he even realized his mistake.

"Call me 'Monsieur Harcourt,'" Julien instructed then sipped the wine. "Very good." He nodded his approval and then sat in the vacant seat. "And I shall call you Monsieur Pierpont."

"As you wish, monsieur." But she could hear in his voice that he wanted to add Julien's title. Sarah wondered if he would remember to omit it.

"How have you been, monsieur?" Julien asked. "I see you have kept a faithful watch on our home."

"Yes, Monsieur le... monsieur. I am only sorry it

is in such a sad state. I would give anything to have it back the way it was."

"As would I," Julien said quietly. "What happened?"

"I stayed in town when the family went to the country. Your father, God rest his soul"—he made the sign of the cross—"asked me to guard it with my life. But one morning, we received the news that all of you had been murdered, and that night the peasants"—he scrunched up his face in obvious distaste—"came and burned the lovely home." He paused and rubbed his eyes. "I would have rescued as many of the valuables as I could Monsieur le Duc."

Sarah saw Julien frown, but he did not correct his former servant.

"But I was fortunate to escape with my life."

"Of course." Julien nodded. "You did right. But if you thought we were all dead, then why did you watch over the house?"

"Because I heard that your father would be guillotined. I wanted to go visit him in prison, but it was too dangerous. I might have been labeled a sympathizer. But I went out on the streets the day he was to be…" He paused and swallowed. "On the appointed day, when I saw they had only him, I knew some of you must have escaped. If they had you and your brothers, the peasants would have killed them. They loved nothing more than a show."

Julien nodded. "So you saw it?" he asked, looking at a spot on the wall. "You saw my father's death?"

Gilbert nodded. "I did. He went honorably, Monsieur le Duc. He did not cry or fight. Kept his head high and walked on his own to the guillotine."

Julien nodded curtly. "How did you know where to find me?"

"I have been looking for you for years, and finally word came to me that you were making inquiries about your brothers. Do not ask me how I gained this knowledge, Monsieur le Duc. I cannot tell you. But I was able to learn that you and the duchesse made it safely to England."

"I'm sure all of this must have come at great risk to your personal safety," Julien remarked. "I hope you know you'll be adequately compensated."

"I want nothing but to leave this godforsaken country," the servant said, his eyes lit with fire now. "As I said in my letter, life here has become dangerous for me."

"Very well." Julien leaned forward. "Then let's get to the point. You know why I've come. Where is my brother Armand?"

Twenty-three

"ARMAND?"

Julien held his breath and watched Gilbert Pierpont's eyes flick to the floor. When he looked up again, the former butler looked anguished. "Oh, monsieur, I do not like to tell you this."

Julien's heart clenched, the vise of fear locking in. "I'm too late, aren't I?" Julien said, careful to keep his voice level. "He's gone." Damn it! He should have left as soon as he received the letter. He could have sailed one of his own ships across the Channel and to hell with the consequences.

Bur Gilbert was shaking his head. "No, monsieur. Where would Monsieur le Comte go? Your brother is in prison."

Julien stood. "Prison?" Thank God. Prison was not death, but it did pose problems. "What are the charges?"

"I do not know, monsieur. I fear he has been there a long time. Years, monsieur."

Julien did not like the ominous tone in Gilbert's voice. "Has there been a trial? What sentence is he serving?"

"Again, monsieur, I do not know. I might have asked questions, but I thought it best not to. It appears—" He glanced at the windows and doors as though afraid they were being watched. "It appears"—he lowered his voice to a raspy whisper—"Monsieur le Comte has been forgotten."

Sarah made a small sound of distress, but when Julien looked at her, she did not seem surprised at Gilbert's words. Julien himself had to exert all of his control not to react to the horror he felt. "For how long?" he asked, voice steady.

Gilbert shook his head. The man knew, but he did not want to say. Perhaps Julien did not really want to hear anyway.

"What prison, Gilbert? Can I see him?"

"Le Grenier," Sarah answered for him. "The Attic."

Julien glanced at her in surprise. So this was the information she'd held on to. How long had she known Armand's whereabouts? All along?

He looked back at Gilbert. "Can I see Armand?" Julien repeated.

Gilbert shook his head. "That would be very dangerous. He might recognize you and inadvertently give you away. I have seen him, and I assure you that the man I saw is your brother."

Julien reached behind him, fumbled for the chair, and sat. Gilbert had said the words he had hungered to hear for twelve long years.

Armand was alive. His brother was alive.

"I have to get him out," Julien said. "I'm taking him home to England."

Gilbert nodded, as though he had expected this, but

Sarah gaped at him. "Julien, he's in prison. You can't just get him out."

He scowled at her, dismissing her protests. "I'm not going to let him rot there. Tomorrow we'll go the prison," he said, addressing Gilbert, "and I'll take a look. We'll come up with a plan to get Armand out." His mind was working quickly now, plotting how he could steal the guard's clothing, when the best time to go inside would be. He did not dare picture his reunion with Armand. He could not allow himself to think of that yet.

"I'll take you tomorrow, monsieur, but you cannot rely on your brother to be of any assistance. He's... changed."

Julien's body went cold and numb. "What does that mean?"

Gilbert sighed. "Perhaps you will see tomorrow, monsieur. They allow him out in the courtyard once a week. I do not think it a fixed schedule, and some weeks I have not seen him at all. Perhaps tomorrow you will see him."

"And what will I see?"

Gilbert spread his arms. "He has changed, monsieur. Prison will do that to a man."

Julien clenched his fists but asked no more questions. There was something very wrong, something Gilbert did not want to talk about. Julien would rather see it with his own eyes anyway. He would form his own opinion.

He did not want to impose any further on Gilbert, so he rose and went to Sarah, assisting her to her feet. "What time should we call in the morning, Monsieur Pierpont?"

Gilbert's eyebrows shot up. "Oh, no, Monsieur le Duc! You must not go out into the streets again tonight. There are those who remember you and your family. You look too much like your father, monsieur. I beg you to stay here tonight. I know my abode is humble, but I will give you and madame the bedroom. I will sleep in the parlor."

"Thank you. Can we give you money to go and buy dinner?"

"No, monsieur. I have food in the kitchen. If you will just give me leave to prepare it?"

Julien nodded. "Thank you, Gilbert."

As soon as the old butler disappeared into the kitchen, Sarah smacked his sleeve. He gave her a disgruntled look, but she was frowning at him fiercely. "How could you agree to that arrangement? We are not taking an old man's bed."

"We'd insult him to refuse."

"Ha!" She swiped at him again. "You, Valère, have never been a servant. I assure you we are not offended when we get to sleep in our own beds."

"What is this *we*?" he said blandly. "You're a duchesse now, or have you forgotten?"

Her answering look was skeptical, enough that he wondered if she harbored doubts about their marriage. Did she think he was the kind of man to break a vow? He was her husband until death parted them. He had not taken those words lightly.

Had she?

For the first time, he wondered if all of this might be an elaborate ruse by the Foreign Office to collect evidence against him. But, no, he could not believe even the Foreign Office would go so far as to send in an operative to marry him.

"You knew about the prison," he said to Sarah. "You knew Armand was a prisoner and did not tell me."

She nodded, her eyes filled with pain he did not think she could have manufactured. "I realized only a few days ago. Sir Northrop said something to me once, something about your brother being hidden where you would never find him—in the attic. Later, I saw a list of prisons on your desk. When I read the name Le Grenier, The Attic, I knew that had to be where he was held. Now, after hearing what Monsieur Pierpont says, I am certain."

There was more, something else she was not telling him, but for the moment this was all he could take in. They were silent for a long moment, and then she gave him a direct look. "Your old servant risks much by taking us in and agreeing to help you, and you repay him by taking his bed."

He shook his head. Did she realize she was in just as much danger as Gilbert, if not more? "I plan to take Gilbert back to England with us and repay him handsomely for his kindness. Will that make his one night in a chair worthwhile?"

She still had a stubborn look on her face, but he could see that inside she had softened. "Perhaps" was all she would allow. She was looking away from him, the thrust of her jaw stubborn. If they had been alone, he would have taken her in his arms and kissed that stubbornness away. He liked that she was not afraid to challenge him. He liked that she worried about an old servant like Gilbert.

And more than any of that, he would have liked to strip off her clothes and kiss her until they were both shaking with need.

But Gilbert was just a few feet away.

Julien did not sleep that night. Gilbert's bed was small and uncomfortable, but no more so than the ship's berth. Sarah was asleep even before he pulled the bedclothes over her. He could tell she was exhausted. Their tenuous circumstances had given her faint blue smudges under her eyes and lines of strain on her forehead.

She had put on a brave face at dinner, had smiled and conversed with the grace and aplomb of any duchesse, but all he had been able to think of was putting her to bed.

Not for his own purposes.

As much as he would have enjoyed making love to her, this was not the place nor the time. He wished their honeymoon could have been somewhere romantic and peaceful. He wished he could spend hours and days exploring her body, giving her pleasure and taking it as well. He prayed there would be time for that in the future. The most he could do now was to protect her. He would not bring her with him to the prison.

Prison. Julien rolled over then finally gave up, rose, and went to Gilbert's small bedroom window. Parting the curtains, he looked out on a small moonlit courtyard.

Armand in prison.

The very idea made Julien shake with rage. Of all the members of the Valère family, Armand was the least deserving of such a punishment. He had been an obedient boy and an intelligent one. Sweet-natured, Armand had rarely misbehaved and then usually only at Bastien's urging.

Bastien was the bad influence. If Gilbert had said Bastien was in prison, Julien would not have blinked. But Armand...

Gilbert's words came back to haunt him in the darkness.

Monsieur Armand has been forgotten.

He has changed.

Julien could find no comfort in those words or the cold uneasiness that formed a hard lump in his gut and stayed there, making him feel slightly ill.

He clenched his fists, fighting to replace that uneasiness with determination. He *would* find Armand, and he *would* free his brother.

Ne quittez pas. He would succeed or die trying.

∽

They were gone by the time Sarah awoke. She wakened suddenly, sitting up and staring about the unfamiliar room in confusion. Slowly, chunks from the past few days began to fall into place.

She was married to Julien. She was a duchesse.

But before she could savor the improbability of that turn of events, she remembered she was in Paris—the country with whom England was at war—to search for Armand Harcourt, comte de Valère. But Armand was in prison, and Julien—

Where was Julien?

She stilled, cocking her head to listen for any signs of life in the small house. She heard none. Pushing the bedclothes back, she jumped up and rushed from the bedroom. Within moments, she had searched the house.

Gilbert and Julien were gone.

She did not know why she should be surprised. Of course Julien did not want to take her with him. She had intended to go anyway, which was most likely the reason he had been careful not to wake her when he left.

She went back to the bedroom and sat on the bed. Now what was she supposed to do all day? She would drive herself mad if she had nothing to occupy her thoughts but worries about Julien's safety. She supposed men never thought of that. They just went off on one adventure after another and never considered how worried those who loved them might be.

And she did love Julien. Every day in his presence meant her love for him grew. He was everything she could have ever hoped for in a man—handsome, loyal, intelligent, successful.

But there was one thing missing: he had not told her he loved her.

Sarah had never thought she would marry. She had barely allowed herself to dream that one day she would have a family of her own, children of her own. She always wanted to be a mother, not just a governess.

And suddenly all of that seemed possible. Only... what did a marriage and a family mean without the love of her husband?

Oh, she knew Julien cared for her. Amazingly enough, he desired her. But how long would lust last without love to support it?

She knew how the aristocracy lived. Men married, begat heirs, and then both partners went on to other pursuits. For men, this usually meant a series of mistresses. The wife found her own lovers or else suffered in silence.

Sarah had never thought she would be a part of such a pattern. She had never dreamed she would marry a peer—much less a duc! But here she was, and already the cold prick of dread jabbed at her heart. How could she make Julien fall in love with her?

And if she failed, would their marriage last? Anyone who knew Julien knew he honored his word. He had married her, and he would do whatever was necessary to ensure that marriage was valid once they returned to England.

But what if he bowed to pressure from his mother or his friends? He was a man driven by duty, but what duty reigned supreme? His duty to her, or his duty to his station, and thus, his family?

Sarah sighed and began to dress. She feared she would soon find out.

⧡

Le Grenier was not at all what Julien had expected. It was small and ugly and tucked away. No wonder the peasants of Paris had chosen to storm the Bastille. If they had stormed Le Grenier, the historians would have yawned.

"You should not scoff, monsieur," Gilbert said. They were seated side by side on the cart Julien had stolen. Julien had stopped across from the prison in the shade of several trees. In a moment, he would climb down and pretend to tend to his horse.

Not that such subterfuge would be necessary. The lone guard at the prison gate looked bored and sleepy. Every few moments, he hefted his bayonet from one arm to the next as though its weight was too much to bear.

"I'm not scoffing," Julien said, well aware that he was indeed scoffing. "How many soldiers are present?"

"The garrison is said to be about fifty soldiers, but I think it is perhaps half that."

Julien nodded. Twenty-five men was nothing to scoff at, but surely all would not be on duty at the same time. He would strike at night, when the men were tired and dozed in complacency.

He climbed down from the wagon and lifted the horse's hoof, but he did not examine the shoe. Instead, he studied the prison's façade. It was made of old stone, yellow with age. Past the gate stood a wide turret, easily three stories, with a heavy wooden door. Behind the turret was a rectangular building with few windows and no adornment. Julien imagined it housed the cells and perhaps quarters for the prison guards.

"Where is the exercise yard?" Julien asked, now glancing at the horse's hoof.

"In the back." Gilbert gestured toward a large gate with another guard just inside. "Through that gate."

"How can we get a look?"

Gilbert frowned. "Short of scaling the wall, I do not think we can, monsieur."

"Then how is it that you saw my brother?" Julien asked, careful not to say Armand's name. He climbed back into the cart, conscious that they would have to move on soon, or even the apathetic guard would take notice.

"There is but one entrance and one exit to the prison as well as the yard. You see it there. The prisoners exit through that gate and cross into the second gate. They are visible for a few moments but escorted and heavily shackled."

"How many prisoners go at one time?"

"Your brother went alone, but I have seen up to five men on other occasions."

Julien glanced at his pocket watch. It was almost eleven, the time Gilbert had said prisoners were led out for an hour of exercise. Unfortunately, there was no guarantee any prisoners would be allowed outside today. Gilbert had said there were days when he saw no one, even after hours of waiting.

Though he had already asked the question, Julien asked it again. "How many times have you seen my brother?"

"Twice, monsieur," Gilbert answered dutifully.

Twice. Only twice, and Julien knew his former servant had sat and kept watch dozens of times. It was highly unlikely he would see Armand. And as the minutes ticked by, highly unlikely he would see any prisoners. Why did they not appear?

"Monsieur…" Gilbert's voice was gentle, but the underlying tone was chiding.

They had waited too long. Julien knew he should drive away. He lifted the reins, but his hands felt numb and heavy. Armand was inside, and once more, Julien was leaving him.

Images from the night the chateau burned flashed in his mind, and the ghost of pain from his foot injury shot through his flesh.

, He had left Armand once and had not seen him again for twelve years. How could he leave him again?

"Monsieur." Gilbert's voice was gentle and soothing. "Let me take the reins, monsieur. I will drive us back."

Julien glanced at the man with a look of relief. He would have rather sat there all day than explain the paralysis that infected him. Gilbert took the reins, and they started away from the prison.

Julien did not look back.

He was going to Sarah now. Beautiful Sarah. He needed her, needed to see her, to remember who he was. He was no terrified child being chased by a white-haired witch wielding a pitchfork. He was a man, a powerful man. He was the duc de Valère, and no one, whether they wielded a pitchfork or a bayonet, would stop him now.

⤳

"Are you mad?" Sarah said shortly after they returned. She looked pretty with her long dark hair pulled into a simple ribbon at the nape of her neck and her cheeks flushed with indignation. "You'll end up at Le Grenier yourself. Or worse."

"It's a risk I'm willing to take," Julien said, glancing across the room to gauge Gilbert's reaction. The three of them were sitting in the old servant's parlor. Though it was bright and sunny outside, the drapes were shut, and the room was shrouded in gloom. Sarah sat in an armchair, Gilbert in the other, and Julien—too anxious to sit—stood at the fireplace.

He had just explained his plan to break into the prison and free Armand, and Sarah's reaction had not been completely unexpected.

"It's a bit vague in parts," he conceded.

"A bit?" Sarah said, rising. In the short time he had known her, she had gone from a woman who looked as though she would faint if he glanced at her askance to a woman unafraid to stand and debate him.

He would not have thought such a dramatic change possible.

"You don't know where your brother is being kept. You don't know how you will fetch the keys. You don't even know what your brother looks like. What if you free the wrong man?"

She had a valid point. Julien had not been inside the prison, and he did not know where Armand was kept. But dressed as one of the guards, he would have the opportunity to search the prison, find Armand, and get him out. Outside, Gilbert and Sarah would be waiting with the cart.

They would hide Armand under a blanket in the back, cover him with luggage and loaves of bread, and together they would escape the prison, drive to the rendezvous with Captain Stalwart, and flee Paris. They would tell the guards at the Paris gate, if they were even quizzed, that they were going to visit Sarah's mother in the country.

They would act tomorrow night.

Julien would have preferred to act tonight, but they needed time to gather the supplies that would hide Armand in the cart. Plus, Stalwart would not meet them until tomorrow night. Once Julien had his brother, he could not afford to stay in Paris. The whole of the city would be searching for him.

"Julien," Sarah was saying, "there must be another way. You said yourself that the turret could create a problem. There is but one way in and out of the prison, and that small entrance would be easy to cut off."

"It does create a bottleneck," Julien admitted. "But that would be more of a problem if we intended to storm the prison with a large group. It should be easy enough for two of us to slip out unobtrusively."

"Then you are set on this plan?" she asked, anger and something like disbelief in her tone.

"I cannot think of a better. Can you?"

"No." She shook her head. "It's madness, but I suppose if you won't listen to reason, I had better help you." But before Julien could ask what she meant, she had disappeared into Gilbert's room and returned with her knapsack. She reached inside and pulled out the sheaf of papers he had seen on Stalwart's ship.

"Your false identity papers won't be necessary."

She glanced up at him then back down at the papers. "That is not all Thompson provided me. The man is really rather resourceful, if you pay him enough." She pulled the documents she wanted from the stack and held them out. "You owe him three hundred pounds for this."

Frowning at her, he took the papers and stared at them uncomprehendingly. Then slowly, he stood, his heart thumping wildly in his chest. "How did you get these?"

"I told you, Thompson did. After I saw that list of prisons and put the few facts I had together, I asked Thompson to acquire these blueprints for me. I don't know how he got them, but I thought they might be useful if you decided to do something rash. Which, of course, you have."

The map to Le Grenier—that's what she had handed him. He had no idea how accurate it was, but the design of the prison was now laid out before him.

"You still don't know where your brother is housed," she said as he studied the layout intently. "But I did notice this area." She pointed to a small room depicted by a box. "It's called The Garrett here."

He glanced up at her.

"Garrett, attic. The words are not so different. If I were you, I would begin my search for Armand there."

She was right. If Sir Northrop's words to her had been true, and if Gilbert was correct in saying that Armand was forgotten, this small cell away from the others would be the likely place to house Armand.

Gilbert stood beside him and studied the blueprints as well. He had not yet commented. "Monsieur Pierpont, what is your opinion?"

Gilbert pursed his lips. "It is a good plan, monsieur," the old butler agreed. "And this map will make your task easier."

Julien nodded and returned to studying the map.

"But I think there is one variable you have not considered, monsieur."

Julien frowned. "What is that? The keys? I'll snatch them from one of the guards or find where they are kept."

"No monsieur, that is not it. I think you have failed to consider your brother. As I said before, prison changes a man."

Julien folded his arms. "How? How has my brother changed? Has he changed so much he will want to stay in prison? Has he changed so much he would alert the guards to my presence?"

"I do not know, monsieur. I know only what I saw."

Julien leaned down, looked Gilbert directly in the eyes. "And what did you see? I think it's time you told me, Gilbert." He hoped he was ready to hear it.

Gilbert opened his mouth then closed it again. "I can say only that your brother has changed. I do not know how to describe it."

"Try." Julien was angry now, and even knowing his anger masked his fear, he could not suppress it. "Tell me what you're hiding."

"The light," Gilbert said, his voice raspy and low. Julien had to lean closer to hear. "I know only that the light had gone out of his eyes, and with it, life. He has no life in him, monsieur."

Julien sighed and leaned back again. Time in prison could indeed dull hope and faith, but that hope could be restored. He would restore it for Armand.

"Then tomorrow we bring back that life," he said, glancing about the room. Gilbert nodded, but Sarah only watched Julien, her eyes filled with worry.

Twenty-four

THE HOUSE WAS DARK AND STILL, THE ONLY SOUND that of Julien's breathing and what might have been a mouse scurrying hither and yon, searching for food.

Sarah lay in the small bed Gilbert had once again offered them and stared at the shadows on the ceiling. Over time, the shapes shifted and changed, turning into open mouths with jagged teeth or the leering faces of prison guards.

Sarah looked away, turning to study her husband. His back was to her, his breathing regular, but she doubted he slept. This might be the last night she lay beside Julien. Tomorrow night they could both be dead.

She prayed they would succeed, but there were so many variables that could go wrong.

She heard Julien sigh, and he turned toward her. "I can hear you worrying," he murmured. "Come here." He opened his arms to her, and she went gratefully into his embrace. His warmth, his scent, his presence alone eased her anxiety. It did not remove it. She would not be able to take a deep breath until they were back in England, but being with Julien made her feel safe.

Julien rubbed her back in gradually expanding circles. "You should try and sleep."

"I know, but every time I close my eyes, I begin to imagine the worst."

"Sarah—"

"And don't tell me everything will be fine," she interrupted before he could repeat the platitude. "You can't know that."

"You're right," he said finally. He leaned over and kissed her forehead. "You're right, and if anything should happen, I want you and Gilbert to leave without me."

"No!" She pulled out of his arms and sat. "I'm not going to leave you. You would never leave me."

"And you wouldn't be here if not for me. Sarah, I could never live with myself if I knew you were hurt or imprisoned because of my quest." He pulled her back down into the comfort of his arms. "Promise me that no matter what happens, you'll meet Stalwart at La Petit Coeur. I'll leave you some francs just in case we're separated. Gilbert will see you safely to Stalwart and home to England. Once there, my mother will find a place for him. As for the Foreign Office, let them believe what they will. Let them implicate me in any crime they want."

Sarah clutched Julien's bare shoulders. "Don't talk like this. Don't act as though our separation is a fore-gone conclusion. Julien, I—"

She paused and swallowed. She had been about to tell him she loved him. Was now the right time? What if he could not say the same back? What if he said nothing at all?

And what if she lost him tomorrow and never had the chance to tell him?

She looked into his eyes. The room was dark, but she could see the shape of his face, make out his glittering eyes. "Julien, if anything does happen, I want you to know that I love you." She felt his body stiffen beside hers, and she hurriedly covered his mouth. "Don't say anything back. You don't have to. I just wanted you to know in case…" She trailed off, not wanting to tempt fate any more than they already had.

Julien reached up and took her hand, pulling it away from his mouth, and kissing her palm lightly. "I wish I could make love to you right now," he whispered.

She felt the same way and knew they were alone. The walls in the house were thin, and she had heard Gilbert go out earlier to fetch supplies.

"I wish I could show you how much I need you." He stroked her hair and pulled her close.

"Then show me," Sarah said, touching her lips to his neck. "Show me."

His arms around her tightened possessively, and she was drawn against the hardness of his chest and the solidity of his arms. She tilted up her face, and his mouth met hers, greedy and searching. She was greedy as well. She needed this, needed as much of him as he could give.

She rose above him, straddling him, and ran her hands down the flat planes of his bare chest. She liked the feel of his cool flesh against her own. Slowly, she lifted the hem of her chemise and dragged it over her body then tossed it aside.

Even in the dim light, she could see Julien's eyes go dark with desire. And when she leaned down to kiss him, his mouth took hers feverishly. She could feel the blood rushing through her body, and she was already moving against him, sliding his hard length inside her.

He groaned, and she arched up to take more of him. His hands were on her breasts, on her hips, on that sensitive spot at the juncture of her thighs. She could feel the pressure building, the pleasure taking over… and then he rolled her beneath him.

"What are you doing?" She had been so close.

"In a hurry, *chérie*?" She could hear the laughter in his voice. "I told you, the French way of lovemaking is not like the English. We move very—" He dipped his mouth and took one nipple inside, suckled until she bucked her hips with need. She could feel him inside her, feel him pressing against her. She needed him to move, just a little pressure…"Very—" He released her nipple and rose above her. "Slowly."

He drew out of her, then with a measured, unhurried movement, slid back inside. Her breath hitched, and her hips bucked to meet him. "Julien, please," she begged. She was at the edge of pleasure. One hard thrust…

He slid in and out again, but as she watched his face, she noted he was no longer smiling. His jaw was tight, his teeth gritted to exert control. She wanted that control to break, and she lifted her hips to take more of him, moved against him.

"Sarah." His voice was husky with need.

She pulled him close, kissed him then whispered, "Let go."

She arched one more time, and they both let go.

Afterward in his arms, Sarah tried to memorize everything about him—the way the scent of citrus and wood clung to him, the solid feel of his arms about her, the rhythm of his breathing. She tried to pretend this moment would last forever, that morning would never come, that they would never have to return to England. She wished there was only now.

But gradually the moment ended. Julien's breathing slowed and deepened, and her own eyes refused to stay open. She would sleep, the morning would come, and with it their fates.

∽∾

Julien crouched in the shadows of Le Grenier and waited for the moment to feel right. Gilbert had told him the guards changed at eleven. Julien hoped the guards on duty would be tired and inattentive an hour before they were relieved. He also hoped the changing of the guards would provide enough of a distraction to allow him and Armand to escape.

He had checked his watch when he left Gilbert and Sarah in the cart just down the street. That had been perhaps twenty minutes ago, at three-quarters past nine. It was surely after ten now. He had less than an hour and had to move.

He shuffled closer to the prison, moving as silently as possible, pausing when he reached the edge of the shadows and the last of his cover. As was the case yesterday, a guard stood at the entrance, his bayonet beside him. He did not look particularly alert, but Julien was taking no chances.

He fingered the small stone in his hand. It was warm

and familiar. Taking a deep breath, he hurled the stone past the guard and into the shadows beyond.

"Who's that?" the guard barked, straightening immediately and staring in the direction of the clatter the stone had made. "Show yourself."

Julien waited, counting to ten before the guard hefted his bayonet and moved cautiously in the direction of the noise.

With the guard's back to him, Julien leaped. He tackled the guard, pushing him to the ground and kicking the bayonet out of reach. The guard tried to call out, but Julien kicked him in the gut, rendering him breathless. Then he wrapped an arm about the man's neck and dragged him into the shadows.

Five minutes later, Julien stepped out, adjusting the too-small coat and leaning down to retrieve the forgotten bayonet. He prayed he had hit the guard hard enough to keep him unconscious for the rest of the night.

Straightening his coat again, he stepped through the prison gate.

᷒

"What are you doing here?"

Sarah jumped as the man's voice shattered the silence of the night. She glanced behind her and saw a constable approaching. Gilbert gave her a worried look, and Sarah knew this was not good. How were they going to explain why they were sitting in a cart on a residential street in the middle of the night?

If she were a constable, she would assume they were up to mischief. Which, of course, they were.

Gilbert put a finger over his lips, reminding her that she was to leave the explanation to him.

"Good evening, sir," Gilbert said in French.

Sarah did not dare turn and look. Her stomach clenched, and she swallowed the bile that rose in her throat. It had been a busy day, full of last-minute preparations and purchases. Sarah had not eaten until well after noon, and then she wolfed down a hunk of bread, cheese, and wine. If she had not been so hungry, she would have refused the food. She knew her stomach revolted when she was nervous.

And now she was about to cast up her accounts and be hauled off to a French prison. She wondered if the French penalty for treason was the same as the English: drawing and quartering. Since drawing and quartering was done publicly and required the victim to be all but nude, it was considered too immodest to draw and quarter a woman.

Women were burned at the stake. Alive.

Sarah shivered and kept her head down as the constable approached.

"I asked what you are doing here." The constable stood before them, his gaze roving over the cart and the two of them. His eyes were focused, and he seemed to miss little. Her stomach bucked, and she closed her arms over it.

"Good evening, monsieur," Gilbert said, his voice smooth and unwavering. "We are traveling to the country tomorrow and have been gathering our supplies."

The guard frowned, clearly skeptical. "It's late to be out shopping. What do you have here?" He began to rummage through the items in the back of the cart, none of which would have given them away. Gilbert had loaded the back with luggage and food and blankets.

"Where are you traveling?" the constable asked after pawing through everything. He returned to stand beside the cart, and his sharp gaze was on Sarah. Her stomach heaved violently, but she forced down the nausea.

"We're going—"

The constable held up a hand. "Let her answer."

Sarah's head jerked up, and she darted a scared glance at Gilbert. The constable was watching her, smiling slightly, as though he knew he had them.

Gilbert nodded, his look resigned, and Sarah opened her mouth and was sick all over the constable.

∽

Julien stood in the stone turret and listened. To his right was a door, slightly ajar. Inside he could hear at least two of the guards playing a card game. To his left was a long gun rack, and several weapons were leaning upon it. He did not see any keys, but there was another door a few feet ahead on the opposite side. Beyond it was the gate that led into the prison proper. The gate was closed and locked.

Damn. He had not considered the possibility of an inner gate.

Julien focused on that door again. The keys could be inside—along with more guards. He would need the keys to open the gate; then he had to slip inside the prison, all without the two men playing cards hearing him. And without being spotted by any other guards.

Impossible.

He needed a new plan.

Fast.

He had an idea, but the likelihood it would work was slim. Still, he had come this far. He was not going to turn back now. High up in the garret of this prison was Armand.

Reluctant to waste any more time in thought, he moved forward and rapped loudly on the open door. The two men started, swiveling around, weapons in their hands.

"Good evening, Corporal," Julien said, speaking to the highest-ranking guard.

The man stood and scowled. He had a short mustache and a long nose, and Julien guessed he was probably forty.

Forty and only a corporal. That did not speak well for his career.

"I've been sent by the lieutenant," he continued, "in order to treat one of your prisoners. I'm a trained doctor."

The corporal stared at him, and Julien held his breath. If the man did not believe him, he'd have to get out. Fast. He resisted the urge to turn and gauge the distance to the outer gate.

"Which prisoner?" the corporal asked slowly. His eyes never left Julien's.

Julien considered. How much did these men know about Armand? Did they know he was the son of a duke? An aristocrat? He would go the safest route.

"I was given the name Armand and the garret cell. That is all."

The corporal nodded and lowered his shoulders, relaxing. "If any prisoner needs your help, Doctor, it is that one. I, Jean Moreau, will take you to him."

"Thank you, Corporal Moreau."

Julien stepped back into the entryway, trying to block the gate with his body. He did not want the corporal to notice the absence of the guard.

But the corporal did not spare a glance for the prison's entrance. He hurried toward the inner gate, extracting a set of keys from inside his coat. He found the one he wanted, slid it into the lock, and turned. There was a loud snick followed by a piercing creak as the gate swung open. Julien thanked God he had not tried to open the gate without alerting anyone. The noise would have wakened half of Paris.

The guard stepped inside and waited for Julien to do the same. Then, to Julien's dismay, the corporal locked the gate again. He was inside, and it had been easy. But no one ever had difficulty getting into a prison. It was getting out Julien had to worry about.

"This way, Doctor," the corporal said, indicating a stairway carved into the stone. It was steep, winding, and dark as sin. "I'll take you to him."

⤶

The constable jumped back and swore loudly. Mortified, and now certain that they would be dragged off to prison, Sarah covered her mouth and stared. Gilbert stared as well but recovered himself quickly

"Monsieur, I am so sorry. My daughter is ill. The motion of the cart made her queasy. That is why we had stopped."

"Idiots!" the constable snapped, staring at his clothing. "You have ruined my coat!"

"A thousand apologies, monsieur. I would pay for another, but we are just poor bakers. We have no—"

"Get out of my sight!" the constable barked. "Move along. I don't want to see either of you again tonight."

"Yes, monsieur." Gilbert slapped the reins and urged the horse forward.

Neither of them spoke for several minutes; then Sarah broke the silence. "What should we do? Julien won't know how to find us."

"We will circle the prison and hope we are close by when Monsieur Julien needs us."

Sarah nodded, but her stomach threatened another revolt. How long could they circle the prison without attracting the notice of another constable? What if the constable they had escaped spotted them again? What if Julien needed them and they were blocks away?

As Gilbert drove past the dark houses and shops, Sarah closed her eyes and prayed. Their circle took about fifteen minutes, and when they approached the prison again, Sarah hardly dared glance at it for fear she would give Julien away. But she could not control her eyes, and her gaze slid traitorously toward Le Grenier.

She gasped when she saw the front gate. No one was guarding it. Did that mean Julien had disabled the guard and gone inside? Had the guard caught Julien and put him under lock and key? How long before someone else noticed the front gate was unguarded and reported it?

And then they were past the prison and moving away again. Once again, Sarah clasped her hands and closed her eyes.

∾

Above all, Julien was conscious of the stench. The noise was unsettling—men groaning, raving, crying out in anguish. The darkness was thick as a blanket. Julien was thankful for the corporal's dim lantern, which cut a swath of meager light through the blackness. But the odor was unbearable. It was the smell of the unwashed mingled with the scent of death and decay. Rotting flesh, excrement, sweat, and desperation choked the breath from his lungs. He put up an arm to ward it off.

"You learn to tolerate it after a while," the corporal told him. "You never get used to it, but you learn to tolerate it."

"How much farther?" Julien asked. They had been climbing the narrow stairs for several minutes.

"Almost there. The one you want is on the top floor. He's been up there for years. Thought everyone had forgotten about him by now."

Julien's hands clenched, and he bit his tongue to keep the angry words from spilling forth. No, he had not forgotten about his brother. But, dear God, how long had Armand been here?

"Here we are." The corporal paused at the top of the stairs and motioned down a short corridor. "His cell is through that door." He shooed Julien forward, but Julien hesitated.

"Don't I need a key?"

"Key?" The corporal smiled. "Oh, not with that one. He won't try to escape. I'll wait for you at the bottom of the stairs."

"A light?" Julien asked before the corporal could descend.

"Ah, right. So rare to have a visitor." He reached up and took a cobweb-covered torch from the wall. Opening his lantern, he lit the torch with the flame and handed it to Julien. "You tell the lieutenant we're doing our best here."

Julien nodded. "I'll specifically mention your name."

The corporal smiled and turned to go, probably already dreaming of a better post.

Not if Julien had his way.

He shuffled forward, his heart pounding, his body as tense as the strings in a pianoforte. Outside the door to the garret, Julien had to pause. If it was truly unlocked, why had Armand not escaped before now? His hand shook as he reached for the knob. He didn't want to know what he would find behind the door, and yet he could not go away without having done so.

He turned the knob, and the door creaked open. The room was dark, so dark that Julien immediately lifted the torch high. He was met with a hiss and caught a flash of movement as a figure on the far side of the room raised a hand to ward off the light.

Julien stepped forward, shedding more light in the room and the thing—the man, if the creature could accurately be described as such—crouched, drew back his lips, and prepared to attack.

Twenty-five

"ARMAND?" JULIEN CLOSED THE DOOR BEHIND HIM AND lowered the torch into a sconce on the wall. "Armand, it's me, Julien."

The man hissed and brought up his hand to shield his eyes from the light, but he remained ready to fight.

Julien moved closer, taking in the state of the room. It was barren—devoid of windows or comfort of any kind. A mat of old straw was lumped in the corner, and on this the prisoner crouched. In one corner was a fireplace, but it was cold and dark, and Julien wondered if it had ever been used. Beside the fireplace was a metal plate and a cup, probably left from the day's meal.

The prisoner himself was dressed in tattered rags. His gray breeches were frayed at the knee, and he wore no stockings. His yellowed shirt had boasted lace at one time, but now that hung in ruins. The man had no shoes.

Julien crouched beside the pile of old straw, so old it stank, and stared at the man. Could this really be his brother? The man looked back at him, eyes wary and suspicious. His dingy brown hair was matted, shaggy, and covered his face where the long, dirty beard did not.

The man was Armand. He remembered those brown eyes, those long lashes, the straight Roman nose. Years of imprisonment could not wipe away what had once been fine aristocratic features.

"Good God," Julien whispered. "It's really you."

The man did not answer, just continued to stare at him.

Julien reached out to touch Armand, but he hissed and raised a hand in defense. "Armand," Julien said, lowering his hand. "It's your brother Julien. I've come for you."

What had his brother done to deserve this? From all appearances, he had been locked up and all but forgotten. But by whom? The revolutionaries would have killed him had they known who he was. But it appeared even the guards did not know.

Julien clenched his fists.

He would find out who had hurt his brother.

Armand began to back away, posture still defensive, and Julien struggled for a way to reach his brother. Time was running out. He needed to free Armand before the changing of the guard.

"Armand. It's Julien. Your brother. Don't you remember me?"

Nothing. Armand stared at him, fists balled at his sides, ready to strike at the smallest provocation.

Julien sat back on his heels and attempted to think of something he could say, something he could do that would remind Armand who he was. When the fear that Armand might never again know who he was began to bubble to the surface, Julien pushed it down.

Had there been any games, any songs, any—

He lifted his head, the faintest memory of a song dancing across his brain. It was a bedtime tune their nanny had sung to them. Julien could not remember the words—not many of them—but he remembered the tune.

Quietly, Julien began to hum it, inserting the words wherever he could think of them. His rendition was tentative at first but grew more confident as he went along.

Au clair de la lune
Mon ami Pierrot
Prête-moi ta lume…

He continued to hum, gradually realizing Armand was watching him and had moved closer. There was still nothing akin to recognition in his brother's eyes, but there was something else: trust.

Julien prayed Armand would trust him enough to follow him. "Armand," he said quietly. "I'm taking you out of here. I'm taking you home to ma mère. But you have to come quietly. You have to do exactly as I say. Can you do that?"

Armand made no sign he heard, but he continued to stare at Julien. Julien stood, took Armand by the shoulders, and pulled him up.

He had expected some resistance, but other than a hiss when Julien touched him, Armand complied. He stood in the center of the room, his hair in his face, his clothes soiled, his back hunched. Julien had cried very few times in his life, and all of those instances were before the age of fourteen. But he felt like crying now.

"Come," Julien said. He lifted the torch from the wall and opened the door.

Armand shuffled forward, pausing at the doorway. He glanced back into the room, and Julien understood that, like a long-caged animal, Armand felt safe only in his prison.

Julien began to hum the lullaby again, and Armand glanced at him sharply. Julien backed up, motioning for Armand to follow.

Once in the corridor, Armand seemed to know what was expected of him. He lowered his head and shuffled forward. Julien stared ahead of him, lighting their way down the steps. He was well aware the corporal would be waiting at the bottom, and he had no idea how he would get Armand past the guards or get back out the locked gate.

But whatever happened now, he would escape or die trying. He would rather both of them were killed than leave Armand in that cell for one more minute.

⤞⤝

Sarah watched Le Grenier with a feeling that could only be described as terror. This was the second time they had passed the prison, and nothing looked to have changed. At least nothing they could see.

She checked the watch Julien had given her and saw it was twenty-five minutes to eleven. Julien had been gone over an hour. He had told them to leave without him if he did not appear by eleven.

But what if he had escaped and they had not seen him?

The cart moved forward, and Sarah craned her neck to watch the prison disappear. As she was not looking forward, she did not see when the man stepped out into the street in front of them.

∽

"Corporal," Julien said as he reached the bottom of the stairwell.

"Doctor," the corporal said, but his eyes widened as he saw Armand behind him. "What is this?"

Good question.

"Yes, what is this?" Julien demanded. His tone slipped automatically into one of authority, one who expected to be obeyed. "I find the state of this prisoner appalling, and I am taking this prisoner to the hospital with me."

The noise had attracted several other guards, and one younger one rushed up. He saluted. "Corporal, do you need any assistance?"

"Yes, we do," Julien answered before the corporal had a chance. "Unlock that door for me. Now."

The younger guard rushed toward the gate. "Do not open that gate, soldier!" the corporal commanded, and the soldier skidded to a stop.

Damn! Julien could see Armand beginning to shift nervously back and forth. He had to get him out of here.

"Soldier." Julien fixed the man with a look that had never failed to intimidate the competition in business dealings. "I am personal friends with your lieutenant, and I assure you that if I have to seek him at his mistress's home, pull him out of bed with her, and drag him here so I may do my job, you, soldier, and you, Corporal, will be mightily sorry."

Both men blanched, the young soldier more than Corporal Moreau. The corporal was still nervous, reluctant to agree. But Julien was out of time. The next set of guards would arrive any moment, and his chance would be lost.

"Open the gate," Julien demanded.

The soldier looked at the corporal, and Moreau finally nodded. Trying not to show his relief, Julien pushed Armand in front of him and started for the gate.

The soldier inserted the key and turned the lock.

Almost there. Almost there.

The gate swung open, and the soldier stepped out of the way just as another soldier rushed into the turret. "I found Christophe in the bushes. He's naked and unconscious."

Julien paused inside the gate as all eyes turned on him. "Oh, hell."

❦

It was the constable again, Sarah realized, and he was holding up a hand, indicating they should stop.

"What should we do?" she hissed, but Gilbert was already slowing.

"Good evening, monsieur," he called cheerfully. Sarah wanted to close her eyes and disappear. The constable looked anything but cheerful.

The man stepped up and grabbed the horse's reins. "I thought I told you I didn't want to see you again."

"We are on our way home right now, monsieur."

"No, you're not," the constable said. "You're coming with me."

Sarah's breath caught in her throat, and she clenched Gilbert's arm. His arm was thin and bony, and she felt as though she should protect him.

"Get down, madame," the constable ordered. "And don't get too close. I just cleaned up."

Sarah looked at Gilbert again, and he nodded. But his eyes flicked down briefly toward the blanket on the seat between them. Sarah swallowed the lump in her throat, released his arm, and inched over on the seat.

"Hurry up! You too, old man," the constable ordered.

Sarah stepped down, and the constable motioned her closer. "What's your name?"

She smiled and moved slowly, trying to give Gilbert more time.

"What's your name?" he demanded.

The sound of a pistol being cocked rang out in the night air. The constable whirled to face Gilbert, who held the old blunderbuss level. "Get back into the cart, madame," Gilbert ordered.

Sarah nodded and stepped toward the cart, but the constable lunged and grabbed her by the hair. He wrapped a solid arm about her neck and pulled her in front of him.

"She's not going anywhere," the constable yelled, "and neither are you. Put the pistol away!"

Gilbert's arm wavered, and Sarah closed her eyes, all too aware of what would come next.

Questioning. Imprisonment. Death.

And then suddenly the quiet night was shattered by

the sound of gunfire. Sarah opened her eyes and stared at Gilbert, but he was looking at the prison.

Shots echoed from Le Grenier.

⚜

Julien lowered the musket he had taken from the guard— apparently the man's name was Christophe—and pointed the bayonet at the man who had just delivered the news that poor Christophe was incapacitated.

He had the man's full attention.

"Step aside, and let us pass." That was if Armand would still walk. He was crouched and looking from side to side as if searching for an escape from the sound of the gunfire.

Julien hauled him up and moved into the turret. Fifty steps to the exit. Forty-nine.

He waved the bayonet at the guard, who was now holding his own weapon. "Move!" The man jumped aside, and Julien ran for freedom, pulling Armand with him.

About thirty steps to the exit, another guard jumped into his path, and this one had his musket. Julien leveled the point of the bayonet and caught the man's shoulder as he passed. With a cry of pain, the guard skittered aside, and Julien kept on going.

Twenty-five steps. Twenty-three.

Behind him, he heard the corporal yelling orders. Heard the men coming after him.

Twenty steps. Nineteen.

"Ready!" the corporal yelled.

"Devil take it!" Julien glanced over his shoulder and too late remembered Lot's wife.

Three prison guards were lined up inside the gate, their muskets primed.

"Aim!"

The weapons lowered in unison.

Julien glanced ahead. Eleven steps. Ten. Too many!

"Fire!"

Julien pushed Armand down and dove after him as the hot rain of bullets flew over them. He could hear the whine as they arced above him, knew they had barely missed him. Knew he had mere seconds before the guards reloaded and fired again.

He dragged Armand to his feet and hauled him the last few inches and out into the night air.

"Gilbert!" he yelled, still moving. "Sarah!"

But they were gone.

∾

The sounds of melee in the prison rose, and when the constable's grip on Sarah's throat relaxed slightly as he craned his neck to see what was afoot, Sarah jabbed him hard in the abdomen with her elbow.

His breath whooshed out, and she leaped forward. Before he could right himself, she kicked him between the legs. He stumbled, fell, but his hand snaked out to grasp her ankle.

"Sarah!"

Her head went up at the sound of her name. Julien was calling for her.

"Julien!" she cried and tried to move toward his voice, but the constable held fast. She tried to shake him off, but he was already rising to his knees, his eyes fierce and lethal.

"Release her!" Gilbert ordered. "Or I'll shoot."

Sarah gave him a panicked look. She could see the blunderbuss he held shaking from side to side. She did not want to be anywhere near its target when it went off.

But the constable did not release her, and when she glanced at the prison to try and make out Julien, she saw several figures rushing toward them. She had to free herself and rescue Julien.

The horse reared, and Sarah ducked to avoid his hooves. Just as she did, Gilbert fired, the noise deafening her.

The constable cried out in pain, and his fingers opened. Sarah, not completely certain she was not injured as well—her head was throbbing—picked up her skirts and rushed for the cart. She climbed in just as Gilbert urged the horse on.

They were driving in the wrong direction, but Gilbert quickly turned the animal about, narrowly missing the fallen constable, who was clutching his knee.

"Julien!" Sarah cried when she saw him dressed as a guard and practically carrying a prisoner on his back. Not far behind was a group of soldiers. "Julien, hurry!"

Gilbert slowed the cart, and Julien ran to the back, hoisting the prisoner, who must be his brother, into the back. But Armand moved slowly, and the guards were catching up.

"Go! Go!" Julien yelled to Gilbert, who followed orders. The cart horse, ears back and dancing with nervousness, shot off as soon as the whip was applied.

Sarah screamed when she saw Julien was being left behind. He ran after them, reaching for the edge of the cart. His hands stretched out, slipped, and he fell back.

"Julien!" Sarah cried as he reached again. His hands were so close. She stretched, reached, and grasped one of them. She would not let go. She would not leave him behind.

"Sarah, let go!" he ordered. "Save yourself."

"No." She tightened her grip and pulled with all of her strength. Seeming to sense her determination, Julien flung himself toward the cart. His chest was on the edge, but he was slipping back. She grasped him with both hands now and pulled until her arms burned as though set on fire. But she ignored the pain and focused on Julien's face. He looked into her eyes, and with a cry of anguish, she dragged him onto the cart.

He hoisted his legs beneath him and almost fell again. Sarah cried out, her strength gone, but then the ragged man beside her reached out and took Julien's other arm. Together, Sarah and Armand pulled Julien to safety.

The soldiers stopped, aimed, and fired, but the cart turned a corner and hurdled across the dark Paris night.

Twenty-six

FROM THE SUNNY DECK OF THE *RACER*, JULIEN WATCHED Armand. After all the years of searching, he could hardly believe he had found his brother. And yet this was not his brother at all. It had been almost two days since the rescue, and still Armand had not spoken. Julien was beginning to wonder if the man could speak. Clearly he understood some of what they said, because he would respond with a nod or a hand gesture. But, more often than not, Armand ignored them and stared at the open sea.

That was another thing. Armand refused to go below deck. He insisted upon staying in the open, no matter how inclement the weather. Obviously, he did not want to be figuratively imprisoned again, even if it meant a few hours' sleep in one of the cabins.

"When you told me you were going to France to find your brother," Stalwart said from behind Julien, "I didn't think that meant breaking into a prison and sending all of Paris into a frenzy."

Julien looked at the man, shrugged. "You'll be compensated."

Stalwart raised his dark eyebrows. "We almost didn't get away." His gaze drifted to Armand, who stood alone at the ship's rail, staring at the churning waves. "Is he going to be alright?"

It was a question Julien had asked himself many times. "Yes," he said with conviction. "He's going to be fine once we get back to London."

"*If* we get back to London." Stalwart pulled out a cheroot, lit it, and took a long drag. "I heard rumors that Captain Cutlass has been seen in these waters."

Something about the name sent a chill up Julien's spine. He turned sharply to Stalwart. "Who?"

"Captain Cutlass. You've heard of him?"

"No." But that was a lie. Julien had heard the name before. Like an object seen through the murky water of a pond, Julien could vaguely remember a game he and Bastien used to play. They were pirates, and Bastien had always been Captain Cutlass. What had his own name been? Julien could not even remember, perhaps because his younger brother had always been better at the game than he.

"I'm not surprised," Stalwart was saying. "He's a sneaky devil. Some say his ship's a ghost ship. One minute he's there, and the next he's gone. The Navy can't catch him."

Julien was almost afraid to ask. "Is he a… pirate?"

Stalwart nodded. "So you have heard of him." He shook his head. "Pirates in the Channel. As if we don't have enough to worry about." He stalked off, and Julien turned back to watching Armand. Could this Captain Cutlass be…

Armand looked over his shoulder, almost as though

he knew he was being watched. His eyes were hollow, his face drawn and pale. Julien went to stand beside him and offer what support he could, knowing Captain Cutlass would have to wait.

For now.

⤳⤳

Sarah did not want to be in London. As the hackney Julien flagged down drew the four of them closer and closer to Berkeley Square, her sense of dread grew. She knew she was the only one who felt this way. One look at Julien, and she could see he wanted nothing more than to reunite his mother and brother. The old butler, Gilbert, had not stopped smiling since they'd disembarked from the *Racer*. Of course, he had been ill the entire voyage, so it might have just been relief that his seasickness was over.

And Armand... Sarah could not tell what Armand felt. His emotions were hidden behind an impenetrable wall. He sat across from her, radiating danger. It had been a struggle to force him into the closed carriage, and he bore the confinement with locked jaw, clenched fists, and narrowed eyes. She was not afraid of him, but she sensed her husband's brother could be just as formidable, just as strong and powerful as Julien.

She glanced at Julien again and wished they could have stayed on the ship forever—not that she was overly fond of Captain Stalwart or sea travel, but the ship was safer than London. Sir Northrop could not reach her on the *Racer*. And for the most part, she'd had Julien all to herself. It seemed they could not be alone together for five minutes without him stripping her bare and finding some new, inventive way to bring her pleasure.

She blushed when she thought of all the ways he had made love to her, all the skillful ways his hands and mouth found to please her. And she knew she pleased him as well. Even now when he looked at her, she could see his desire for her smoldering behind those dark lashes.

But desire was not the same as love. He had still not said he loved her.

Did he? Would he ever?

It seemed inconceivable that a wealthy, handsome duc could love her—a plain governess. She was an outsider in his world and always would be. As if to punctuate her thoughts, the hackney slowed in front of the Valère home. It was as magnificent as ever and not at all like coming home. Even though Julien took her hand and led her to the door, she did not feel as though she belonged.

They had just reached the front door when Grimsby pulled it open. Sarah barely had a moment to nod to the servant when the duchesse sprang forward to pull them inside. "Julien! Serafina! You're home! You're safe. You don't know how worried we were. And—" She stared at Gilbert as though trying to place him, and then her arms went about him as well. "Gilbert!"

"*Duchesse, merci.*" Gilbert said.

She broke into a stream of rapid French, welcoming Gilbert and offering him shelter, and the old servant nodded and wiped his eyes.

And then Sarah saw the duchesse's gaze fall on

Armand. They had cleaned him up as best they could. His clothes had been paper-thin rags and his hair an unkempt mat, so Gilbert had found him new garments, washed him, and trimmed his brown hair so it swept back from his aristocratic forehead and fell in waves over his neck and shoulders. Armand had reluctantly consented to being shaved, and looking at him now, there was no doubt this man was related to Julien. The nose was the same; the eyes, while not the same color, had the same slant. And though Armand was taller, he held himself in the same regal way.

The duchesse took a tentative step toward Armand and held out her arms. Armand did not respond. He stared fixedly at his mother, his cobalt blue eyes focused and sharp. Sarah could tell he wanted to go to her, but after years without kindness, without touch, he could not or would not embrace her. Finally, she went to him, taking him in her arms in a fierce hug. Sarah watched as he raised his arms and awkwardly patted her shoulders. It would take something or someone very special to thaw the ice around Armand's heart, to heal his tortured soul.

The duchesse held her lost son and looked at Julien. "You found him," she sobbed. "I didn't believe in you, didn't believe he was still alive. But you found him." She opened her arms to him, and Julien embraced her. Sarah watched as the duchesse held both sons, her family all but reunited once again.

But how long would that last? How long would Julien be safe and free while Sir Northrop and the Foreign Office were determined to charge him with treason?

Not long. And it was up to her to ensure that this

family was never separated again. She might never truly belong to this family, but she could at least be certain she did all in her power to protect them.

Julien reached out for her, took her hand, and pulled her close. "Ma mère, we have other news as well. Sarah and I are married. We married on the ship."

The duchesse looked surprised, and Sarah tried to smile.

"Oh, but this is good news!" the duchesse exclaimed. "Serafina, not only have I found a son, I've gained a daughter."

Sarah but her lip. "Actually, there's a little more to the story. My name isn't Serafina..."

A few hours later, Sarah lay in Julien's arms as he stroked her bare shoulder. They had made love in his bed, and even though she was his wife, she felt as though she would be caught any moment.

"Relax," he whispered.

She tried, but she had too much on her mind. How long would it take Sir Northrop to realize she was back? Would he come looking for her?

"Are you worried about my mother? She doesn't care who you are. If I'm happy, she's happy."

Sarah raised a brow at him. "Julien, she's in denial. When you told her I was a governess, she laughed."

"Well, look at you. It is difficult to believe."

Sarah didn't think it was difficult to believe at all. But the duchesse had done more than just laugh. Sarah had expected the duchesse to express shock or disbelief at their story, but she only shook her head. "Do you think I'm a fool? That I don't know what goes on in my own home? I know who she is."

Sarah had blinked in surprise. The duchesse had known she was a governess all along? Why had she never said anything? "H-how did you know?" Sarah stammered.

"You thanked the maid who poured your tea—that first day in the drawing room. It was as though you had never been served before. I knew something about your story didn't fit. I did a little investigating and made my own conclusions."

"Je regrette," Sarah said, reaching out to take the older woman's hand. "I'm sorry I lied to you, and I'm so sorry I pretended to be Serafina."

The duchesse frowned at her. "Sorry you pretended to be Serafina? Child, don't you know?" Her eyes locked on Sarah's. "You *are* Serafina. I knew your mother, your father. You are the comtesse du Guyenne."

"What? No, I—"

But the duchesse had not let her continue. In fact, she would hear no more about it. When she finally realized Julien and Sarah spoke the truth, how would she feel? And the duchesse did not even know the worst—the Foreign Office still considered Julien a traitor. What the duchesse would soon realize was that Sarah was not just an imposter but their enemy.

She glanced at Julien and saw his eyes were closed. He was finally drifting off to sleep. Good. As soon as he slept, she would sneak away to see Sir Northrop. She could not afford to wait until the morrow.

❦

Sarah tightened the cloak around her face and crept silently through the Valères' dark garden. She was probably going to be murdered, sneaking about London in the middle of the night like this, but she had no other choice. She had to find Sir Northrop before the morning.

The back gate was just ahead, but when she reached it, she found that the latch was rusty and difficult to maneuver. She struggled with it until her fingers were raw and then jumped when a hand reached around her and jerked the latch free.

Sarah spun around and gasped at the sight of Armand, standing behind her. As usual, his eyes were shadowy and unreadable, but under the slash of his dark brows, his gaze was focused on her. She took a shaky breath and stepped back. She had not noticed before how handsome he was—the hard planes of his face, the cut of his jaw, the breadth of his shoulders. He was barefoot, his white linen shirt open at the throat. He wore no cravat or tailcoat. And still, his stance, his bearing told the story of his aristocratic heritage. But that was not what would draw women to him. Underneath the trappings of civility, there was something primitive and feral about him. Something waiting to be tamed.

"Th-thank you," Sarah said, willing her heart to slow. "I know this must look strange, my being out here in the middle of the night."

He raised a brow, and she wasn't certain whether he understood her words or not.

"But I have an important task that cannot wait. I have to go see my old employer, Sir Northrop. I'll be back as soon as I can."

She would be back, wouldn't she?

Armand merely gazed at her as she slipped out the

gate and closed it behind her. He did not speak, but she could almost sense his displeasure with her actions, feel those dark eyes burn into her spine. Well, he wasn't going to tell anyone, and she would be back before Julien realized her absence.

She made her way across Mayfair to Sir Northrop's elegant but small home. It was not far from Berkeley Square, but she felt like a different person from who she had been when she left just a few short weeks ago. When she stood in front of the house, she realized she could not exactly knock on the front door and rouse the occupants. Perhaps if she went around to the garden, where Sir Northrop's library was located, she might find a footman to wake him for her.

But when she entered the garden, she saw that a lamp still burned in Sir Northrop's office. She crept to the French doors and quietly tapped on them. There was a long, silent pause, and then the doors were thrust open and she was yanked inside.

"What the bloody hell are you doing here?" Sir Northrop hissed. "You almost got yourself shot. You make more noise than the crowd at Ascot."

"I wasn't trying to be quiet." She shook his hand off her arm. "I was hoping to rouse you. I need to speak with you."

He shut the French doors behind her, locked them, and went to his desk. As he poured a glass of brandy, he said, "Oh, so now you need to speak with me. You didn't seem to feel the need to do so before you traipsed off to France with your lover."

"There wasn't time," she lied.

"No time." He drank heartily. "Was that it, or did

Valère seduce you until you decided to turn traitor as well?"

"He's not a traitor." She looked about the room, remembering the last time she had stood here. Then she had been terrified, afraid of losing her position and searching for the poker in case Sir Northrop accosted her. Now she could hardly believe she was that same girl. So much had changed. *She* had changed. "He's not a traitor," she repeated. She was not afraid to stand up for Julien, for herself.

"Is that so?" Sir Northrop gave her a long, hard look, perhaps seeing the change in her as well. Finally, he set his glass on the desk, opened a drawer, and pulled out a pistol. "A short time ago, you were wiping snotty noses and playing blind man's bluff. Now you're telling me who is and is not a traitor to my country."

"I can prove Julien isn't a traitor. We found his brother and—" Sarah's words died out as Sir Northrop hefted the pistol and pointed it at her.

"You couldn't just do what I asked, could you? All I wanted was proof that Valère had contacts in France, proof that he had traveled there. It was simple, really. Any idiot could have done as I asked. But not you."

"He wasn't a traitor," Sarah repeated, eyes on the pistol. Surprisingly, she was not afraid at all. She was angry. How dare Sir Northrop point a pistol at her! Did he think he could bully her into betraying Julien? "I couldn't lie."

"You didn't want to lie," Sir Northrop boomed, his voice filled with rage. Sarah sucked in a breath and watched the pistol waver. "And do you know the trouble that has caused me?"

Sarah shook her head.

"They're after me now. *Me!*"

"What?" His words made no sense to her, and yet she could see the fear and fury in his eyes. "What are you talking about? You should be glad Julien is not a traitor. Now the Foreign Office can find the real traitor."

He shook his head and gave her a sad smile. "They already have."

Her eyes widened as the import of his words washed over her. She should have known. She should have guessed when The Widow disappeared. "*You.* You're the traitor," she whispered. She straightened, and her gaze flew to the locked French doors. She could not stay here. She had to get away, tell Julien, tell someone. "And you hoped to implicate Julien."

"The Foreign Office was growing suspicious. I needed to point the finger elsewhere. It should have been a simple matter. I've been a double agent for years—long before you were even born. The French simply pay better than the English. King Louis was extremely generous." He was bragging now, sauntering about the room as though he were the king, waving the pistol as though it were his scepter. "But now—now things have changed. Bonaparte doesn't trust me, and that's why I'm working to restore the monarchy. Unfortunately, I was forced to sell information to Bonaparte to fund my efforts. The Foreign office grew suspicious. I needed a scapegoat."

She stared at him, hatred brewing within her. He had used her to trap Julien. "You used me." She clenched her fists to control the anger. "You knew Julien was innocent, and yet you used me."

"And I'll use you again, little fool. You should never have traveled to France with the duc. With his long-lost brother returning, I may not be able to prove Valère is a spy, but you've just sealed your own fate."

She shook her head. "You're mad. Who would believe I'm a spy? I'm nothing more than a governess."

He laughed, and she took a surprised step back. She had expected any number of responses, but not laughter. "I never should have sent you in," he said between chuckles. "I knew you would fail, but there was something too delicious about the irony."

He moved closer, his pistol aimed at her heart. Sarah took a shaky breath, his words causing her heart to race. "What irony?"

"Don't you know? Think, *Sarah*. I believe you do know."

Sarah shook her head, but the duchesse's words earlier that evening played over and over in her head. *You are Serafina. You are the comtesse du Guyenne.*

"I don't believe it." She put a hand to her head, tried to still the loop of words. Was this another trick? Another ruse?

"And that's the irony, Miss Smith—or should I call you comtesse? No. Actually I think Sera is more appropriate. That's what your parents called you."

Sarah stared at him wide-eyed. *Sera*. Yes, in those phantom memories. In those phantom dreams of her mother and father, they had called her Sera.

Petite Sera.

"But how?" she stuttered. "I don't understand."

He sighed, clearly bored. "It's exactly as I told you. Your father, the comte du Guyenne, angered the king.

He made too much noise about the king's spending and the rights of the peasants. It riled up the people, and in those days, even years before the revolution, it did not take much to anger the peasants."

Sarah swallowed and nodded as she tried to digest the information. But even as Sir Northrop's words spewed forth, she easily put them into place. Instinctively, she knew them to be true. Her father had been a comte. She was the daughter of an aristocrat. But an aristocrat who had cared for the people, who had wanted to help them.

She had had a family. She had belonged to someone.

"The king exiled your family, and they left for England. Only, shortly after they arrived here, they disappeared."

A chill ran down her spine at the look in his eyes. "What happened to them?"

He smiled. "King Louis feared they would be a threat, even in England, so I dispatched them."

She gasped, crushing a hand to her mouth. "You—" It was all she could manage.

"I was to have killed you as well, but I felt you might be useful, so I brought you to the best orphanage in London and made a generous donation so I might be apprised of your progress. When you left your last post, I hired you. I found it amusing to have the comtesse du Guyenne as a servant in my home. And then"—he shrugged—"the perfect opportunity arose. You were engaged to play you." He laughed, but Sarah stared at him in horror. With just a few words, he had changed her life, her identity. Everything she had thought was true was false. Her mother had not been a prostitute but the beautiful Delphine, comtesse du Guyenne.

And this man had murdered her. He had murdered Sarah's chance at a normal life and a family.

"And so you see," Sir Northrop continued. "No one would believe Sarah Smith a spy and traitor, but Serafina Artois? Oh, yes, she might have many reasons to aid the French—loyalty, return of her birthright, revenge on the country where her parents were killed…"

"No." She moved toward him, not caring that the pistol was pointed directly at her heart. She did not know what she would do; she just knew this man must be punished. She could not allow this lie, this abomination to go on any longer.

"What are you doing?"

She did not know what he saw in her face, but his hands were shaking now. She refused to answer, continued moving forward.

He cocked the pistol, tried to aim, pointed it, and fired.

But his aim was off, and the charge went wide. Sarah ran forward and crashed into him. They tumbled onto the floor, and she scratched at him, tearing at his face, kicking him wherever she could reach.

She was screaming and thus did not hear the commotion as the doors were broken open and men rushed inside. She didn't look at them, just felt their hands as they reached for her and pulled her off Sir Northrop.

As she was dragged away, she saw his bloody face. He was still grinning.

She screamed, but strong arms engulfed her, pulled

her into an embrace. She struggled to free herself until she smelled citrus and wood.

Then she stilled and glanced up at the man holding her. He smiled at her, blue eyes crinkling in a roguish grin.

"Looks like I got here just in time."

Twenty-seven

As the torrent of emotions rushed over her face, she looked more beautiful than he remembered. Julien saw surprise, chagrin, relief, and finally—yes, that was what he had been waiting for—love.

"Julien?" She reached up and touched his face, his hair, then fell into his arms. "I'm so glad you're here. It—he was horrible."

He pulled her tightly against him, the feel of her body pressed against his like a wool greatcoat in the middle of a snow storm. His heart warmed, and he buried his head in her neck, not caring that the men from the Foreign Office were staring.

She was safe. She was unharmed. His heart could stop clawing its way out of his chest.

She pulled away, put her hands on his cheeks. "How did you find me? How did you know? And who—" She looked back at the men wrestling with Sir Northrop.

"Armand." His brother was standing just outside the French doors, his arms crossed and his expression menacing. If Julien hadn't gone in to aid Sarah, there was no doubt Armand would have done so. "He must have followed you here then come back and woke me. Scared the hell out of me." He smiled at her, stroked her smooth cheek. "But I went with him. These men were skulking about outside, watching Sir Northrop's movements. They saw you go in and were waiting to see what would happen next."

The men hoisted Sir Northrop to his feet and began to restrain him. "That's the traitor!" he shouted, pointing at Sarah. "Arrest her!"

"Ma'am," one of the men began.

Julien grabbed his shoulder. "Your Grace. She's a duchesse."

"Sorry." The man cleared his throat. "Your Grace, we'll need to question you."

"Of course," Sarah replied. "I'll help in any way I can."

They muscled Sir Northrop past her, and Julien had to restrain the urge to take her back into his arms. But he watched as she faced the raving man, showing no sign of fear. "You're going to burn!" Sir Northrop shouted. "You'll burn for the traitor you are, Comtesse!"

He was dragged through the broken doors, past Armand, who looked like he might tear him apart. Julien exchanged a look with his brother, and Armand clenched his fist then stalked away, giving them privacy.

Sarah was looking at him. "He told me something, Julien. Something horrible. H-he told me I'm the comtesse du Guyenne. I really *am* Serafina Artois."

Julien stroked her hair, her face. He didn't care who she was. He just wanted her safe in his arms again. "So my mother was right."

"Yes. And Julien, he told me—" She swallowed, looked away. "He told me that he killed my parents." A tear sparkled on her cheek, and he pulled her close.

"He's going to pay, Sarah. We'll make sure he pays."

"Yes," she whispered into his neck. "But Julien, do you know what this means? I had a family. I was loved. I belonged."

"You've always belonged." He pulled her tightly against his chest. "Right here. In my arms."

"Yes," she whispered, and he felt her fingers dig into his back.

He breathed in her scent, felt her soft body melt into his. And he cursed himself as a fool for ever thinking he wanted a business arrangement for a marriage.

He wanted Sarah—no matter what her name was.

With great effort, he pulled away from her and led her outside where Armand waited for them. "Let's go home."

"Yes." She smiled at him, loving the way his eyes warmed to indigo with desire for her. *Home.* She finally knew where home was.

❧

She belonged. Sarah looked at the Valère town house, at her mother-in-law, even at the quiet, watchful Armand, and knew she belonged. It wasn't because she was an aristocrat, in truth, as opposed to just playing the part. It was because she knew where she came from—and she knew who she belonged with.

Julien.

If only Rowena would allow them a few minutes to be alone.

"We must have a wedding," she said the next afternoon, leading everyone into the dining room and signaling the footmen to bring in the first course.

Julien pulled Sarah into his lap, and she smiled down at him. She could not bear to be separated from his touch right now either. Rowena frowned at the overt display of affection, but then she waved a hand and admonished everyone to eat. Her chief concern seemed to be they all looked too thin.

Armand was at the table as well. He was clean and dressed, his long brown hair pulled back into a neat queue. Rowena saw Sarah looking at him and smiled sadly. "He still hasn't spoken. I think if we give him time, his speech will return." They watched as he pushed away his untouched plate of food then gave the footman attempting to serve him a dagger-filled glare. The footman backed away, and the duchesse sighed. "In time, I'm certain all of his manners will be restored."

"Has he shown any reaction when you mention Bastien?" Julien asked.

His mother shook her head. "Nothing. I'm not certain he recognizes the name."

"I'll speak with Gilbert. Perhaps he knows something."

His mother reached out and put her hand on Julien's arm. "Don't raise your hopes too high."

The table was silent for a few moments, and Sarah could feel the hole Bastien's absence left in the family. But then Rowena smiled and said, "Let's talk more about the wedding plans!"

Hours later, Sarah lay in Julien's arms, in Julien's bed, blissfully naked and blissfully satisfied. Her eyes were closed, but she felt Julien rise up beside her. She opened her eyes, smiled at him, and reached up to smooth back a lock of his hair.

"I love you, Sera," he said quietly. "*Je t'aime*. I don't think I told you before. I should have."

Her heart was pounding so fast and so loudly she feared she had heard him incorrectly.

"You love me?" she whispered, still finding the idea incredible. Still finding the use of her new name—her true name—wonderful.

"Very much. And I like my mother's idea of another wedding. This time we'll have a huge ceremony, the one of your dreams. Make it as romantic as you want. I'll even propose again. I'll bend on one knee and scatter rose petals around the room."

She laughed. "Oh, Julien. I love you so much. But I don't need any of that."

He frowned, the crease between his brows endearing. Why had she never noticed that before? She traced it with two fingers.

"But I thought you wanted romance."

"No." She shook her head, ran her fingers through her hair. "Not at all." She had never needed a grand gesture. She just wanted him.

"Then what do you want?" he asked, and his fingers dipped to caress her bare shoulders. "What can I give you?"

She bit her lip, looked away, then back again. "I want a family, Julien. All my life I've had phantom dreams of a family, but never a real one—never one I could touch. I want that. With you."

He grinned. "Well, if that's all you want, let's

get started on it right now." He pulled down the bedclothes, bent to kiss her breast.

She caressed his hair, but her thoughts were a jumble. "What do you think will happen to Sir Northrop?"

Julien looked up, leaned back. "I hope he's drawn and quartered. He deserves it for all his crimes."

She nodded, and he leaned down to kiss her again.

"Your mother seemed hurt but not surprised that my parents are dead. Do you think she knew that all along as well?"

Julien shook his head. "I don't know. She's resourceful."

She opened her mouth to ask another question, but he put a finger over her lips. "Why don't you ask her tomorrow?"

She nodded, but just as he would have kissed her again, she said, "Armand seemed better tonight, don't you think? He's improving."

Julien sighed and pulled back again. "Yes. He's doing better. It will take time, but I hope he'll make a full recovery."

"And what about you? Are you done with trips to France? Done searching?"

He raised a brow. "Tricky question. I still have one brother unaccounted for. He could be this Captain Cutlass."

"A pirate?" She gave him a worried look, but she had known before she asked the question that Julien would never disregard his duty. It was part of why she loved him. If Bastien was alive, Julien would not stop until he found him.

"Have I ever told you my father's motto?" he asked.

"No."

"*Ne quittez pas*. Never give up."

She laughed. "How appropriate."

"I thought so. Versatile as well."

"What do you mean?"

"Let me show you." He pulled her into his arms, stripped off the bedclothes, and kissed her breathless.

Sarah kissed him back. She could worry about Armand and Sir Northrop and Julien's search for Bastien later. Right now she was in Julien's arms. And that was all that mattered.

He leaned close, whispered in her ear, "Governess, are you ready for me to teach *you* something?"

Sarah smiled. "Oh, yes."

Acknowledgments

I am indebted to Pascale Zurzolo-Champeau and Veronica and Pierre Ramondenc for their help with the French phrases and terms in this novel. Of course, any mistakes in the manuscript are mine completely. This book would not have been possible without the insightful comments and critiques of Linda Andrus and Christina Hergenrader. In addition, I'd like to acknowledge my agents Joanna MacKenzie and Danielle Egan-Miller for believing in me and in this novel, and I'd like to thank Deb Werksman for her suggestions and comments. Finally, much love and thanks to my family for all of their support—my sister, Danielle, and my parents, Earle and Nancy.

About the Author

Shana Galen is the author of five Regency historicals, including the Rita-nominated *Blackthorne's Bride*. Her books have been sold in Brazil, Russia, and the Netherlands and featured in the Rhapsody and Doubleday Book Clubs. A former English teacher in Houston's inner city, Shana now writes full-time. She is a happily married wife and mother of one daughter and two spoiled cats. She loves to hear from readers: visit her website at www.shanagalen.com.

The Making of a Gentleman

London, 1801

Armand shot upright, the sound of his scream still echoing through the room.

He clenched his teeth until his jaw ached to stop the sound, but it was too late. He had roused the house.

Again.

Reluctantly, he rose from the floor where he had been sleeping and stood in his breeches—feet bare, chest bare. He could hear frantic footsteps approaching already, and he had to force himself not to fist his hands. No one was coming to beat him. They were coming to soothe him.

In his mind, he saw a hand reaching out, touching his shoulder, patting it weakly. He shuddered in disgust at himself, at his weakness.

He wanted to call out—to stop them—but he could not.

Somewhere deep in the recesses of his mind, he knew how to speak. He even had a vague recollection of the sound of his voice. He knew what it was to scream, even the joyful release he felt when he did it. But the word to describe this? Even though he could sometimes think it, his mouth refused to curve around the word. For years, his survival had depended on muteness. Now, he could not seem to make his mouth remember how to form syllables, words, coherent sounds.

It was one of many things he could not remember how to do. Or maybe he just didn't *want* to speak. Maybe he feared what he'd reveal—those terrors that hid in the forgotten caverns of his mind.

The door to his room banged open, and his brother Julien strode in. Julien spoke, but Armand tried to focus too late. The words sounded like a low hum, and Armand stared at his brother blankly.

Julien frowned and tugged a robe closed over his bare chest. His hair was tousled and unruly, and his face was peppered with stubble.

This man—tall, imposing, and commanding—did not resemble the boy Armand was beginning to remember. No, that was not quite true. The Julien in those faded, misty memories was also commanding.

But the harder Armand grasped at the memories, the more quickly they blew away. He clenched his hands in frustration, wanting the childhood memories to stay. But he could not choose...

Julien looked about and blinked at the bright light in the room. Armand kept several lamps, the fire, and a half-dozen candles burning at night. He disliked dark, closed spaces and would not tolerate them. Thus, even though the air outside was chilly his window was wide open—the parted draperies flapping in the breeze.

"Armand?"

This time Armand forced himself to listen, to focus. "Are you well?"

Armand stared at his brother and strained to make sense of the words. Long ago, he had ceased even trying to comprehend what others said to him; it was safer, better. Now he had to battle daily to master the skill once again. As a youth, he easily plucked words from his vast vocabulary. Now those same words hung just out of reach.

His brother did not seem to expect a response and was looking about the room as if inspecting it. Armand saw his gaze pause on the open drapes, the candles. But Julien would find nothing amiss. Nightmares did not leave evidence.

Finally, Julien seemed satisfied with what he saw, and he stared at Armand again. "Is everything all right?"

This time Armand nodded. He knew this phrase. He had heard it too many times. He might have spoken, but he knew the words would come out as little more than unintelligible grunts.

Armand's nod answered his brother's question, but it did not eliminate the worry in Julien's eyes. Armand hated that he was the cause of that worry—that he was the cause of these all-too-frequent late-night gatherings. He hated his lack of communication and the way he was often treated as a fool or a child. He was no idiot, and he was no weakling either. Not anymore.

"Julien?"

The image of her came faster than the words. Images were easier for him. *Woman. Soft. Julien's.*

Finally the name: Sarah. Armand sighed. It was going to be another gathering.

Julien's woman appeared in the doorway, her white robe held closed at the throat and her brown hair falling over her shoulders. She was Julien's wife. And the slight rounding of her belly indicated she would also be the mother of his child.

Julien turned to the woman. "He's fine, Sarah." He turned back to Armand. "Another nightmare?"

Armand did not respond, knew no response was expected of him. He was ashamed. Ashamed to bring them here. Ashamed that he could not make it through the night without the nightmares.

He gritted his teeth and felt his hands ball into fists. His instinct was to send them all flying back to their beds. He could rant and roar, punch a hole in the wall. He looked at the other holes he had made.

No, that was the coward's way—the same as hiding.

The woman stood in the doorway and studied Armand, her dark eyes thoughtful and kind. She had always been kind. When he had first arrived in London, she had taken him to see his mother, in this very house. He had thought his mother was nothing but a fantasy he dreamed up in that dank cell where he rotted year after year after year.

The years ran together, and so did the memories and fantasies. Armand did not know what was real, what was conjured. His mind played tricks on him; tricks that kept it occupied and drove him half mad.

But his mother had not been a fancy or a whim. She was real, though not exactly as he remembered.

Nothing was as he remembered.

Sarah came into the room now, her small white hand still clutching the robe at her throat. Crossing to Armand she stood beside him. Armand's eyes flicked to his brother. Julien watched his woman protectively. Armand wanted to tell him he would never hurt Sarah, but his attempts at speech would more than likely scare her.

She reached out and took his hand, and Armand braced himself.

The image of fire leapt into his mind—*Hot. Hurt. No!*

But because Julien was watching, Armand endured the pain and allowed her to hold his hand. He knew this was intended to be comforting, but it made him grind his teeth. Her closeness—anyone's closeness—was awkward and almost unbearable.

"Armand," she said quietly. He darted his gaze to her, then back to his brother.

"Armand, Julien and I have been talking," Sarah said quietly, "and we think it might help your recovery if you had a tutor."

Armand glanced back at her.

Tutor?

The word was familiar to him. He could not remember the last time he heard it, but it was a word he liked. *Tutor*, he said in his mind, rehearsing it as though he would speak it. *Tutor.*

She squeezed his hand warmly, causing another searing bout of agony. "Would you like a tutor? Someone to help you remember how to speak?"

She was looking at him, and he stared back at her. Julien was behind her now, his hand on her white-clad shoulder. Her hair fell over that hand in soft waves, and Armand wondered if it was as soft as it looked. He once had a rat in his cell, and he had made it into a pet. Its fur had been soft and brown like Sarah's.

"Armand, do you remember Monsieur Grenoble?" Julien asked. "He was your tutor in Paris."

Something about the name caused Armand's heart to speed up. He did not know who or what Monsieur Grenoble was, but the memory was pleasant.

Before.

This Grenoble was from before the years of hell. Before the dark prison, the frequent beatings. Before he had been left for dead.

Sarah was smiling. "I think he does remember him," she said to Julien, turning her head to look over her shoulder. "Did you see the way his eyes lit up?"

Armand was aware they were speaking of him. They did this often, and he hated it.

He jerked his hand away from Sarah's, and she turned back to him. "I'll begin making inquiries tomorrow," she said, reaching out to pat Armand's arm. "We'll find someone extraordinary." She lifted on tiptoe to kiss his temple, and Armand dug his fingers into his thighs. This time it was not just her touch that pained him, it was her scent. She smelled sweet, like apples or peaches, and the feminine smell of her was almost more than his senses could handle.

When she stepped back, he could breathe again.

"Good night, Armand."

Julien watched him for another moment then followed her out the door.

The door closed behind them, and Armand looked about the white-walled room. He had paced it and knew it was three times the size of his prison cell— bright and sunny during the day, shadowed but not menacing at night. There were pictures hanging on the walls—between the holes he had punched.

Flowers. Field. Color.

He could not remember the names of all the colors.

Armand considered lying down and going back to sleep, but tonight the sound of the peasants singing was too loud. It echoed in his head, and Armand closed his eyes to block out memories of that night so long ago.

But the song would not be silenced, and even opening his eyes and staring at the flickering candle would not burn the images from his mind. The flame rose and fell, hissed and smoked, danced before his eyes—just as the fire had danced in the night sky so long ago.

The fire had danced as Armand's life burned to ashes.

Available October 2010 from Sourcebooks Casablanca

A *Duke* TO *Die For*

BY AMELIA GREY

THE RAKISH FIFTH DUKE OF BLAKEWELL'S UNEXPECTED AND shockingly lovely new ward has just arrived, claiming to carry a curse that has brought each of her previous guardians to an untimely end…

Praise for Amelia Grey's Regency romances:

"This beguiling romance steals your heart, lifts your spirits and lights up the pages with humor and passion." —Romantic Times

"Each new Amelia Grey tale is a diamond. Ms. Grey…is a master storyteller." —Affaire de Coeur

"Readers will be quickly drawn in by the lively pace, the appealing protagonists, and the sexual chemistry that almost visibly shimmers between." —Library Journal

978-1-4022-1767-8 • $6.99 U.S./$7.99 CAN

A *Marquis* to *Marry*

by Amelia Grey

"A captivating mix of discreet intrigue
and potent passion." —*Booklist*

"A gripping plot, great love scenes, and well-drawn
characters make this book impossible to put down."
—*The Romance Studio*

The Marquis of Raceworth is shocked to find a young
and beautiful Duchess on his doorstep—especially when
she accuses him of stealing her family's priceless pearls!
Susannah, Duchess of Brookfield, refuses to be intimidated by
the Marquis's commanding presence and chiseled good looks.
And when the pearls disappear, Race and Susannah will have
to work together—and discover they can't live apart...

Praise for *A Duke to Die For:*

"A lusciously spicy romp." —*Library Journal*

"Deliciously sensual... storyteller extraordinaire Amelia Grey
grabs you by the heart, draws you in, and does not let go."
—*Romance Junkies*

"Intriguing danger, sharp humor, and plenty of simmering
sexual chemistry." —*Booklist*

978-1-4022-1760-9 • $6.99 U.S./$8.99 CAN

My UNFAIR Lady

by Kathryne Kennedy

A Wild West beauty takes
Victorian London by storm

The impoverished Duke of Monchester despises the rich
Americans who flock to London, seeking to buy their way
into the ranks of the British peerage. Frontier-bred Summer
Wine Lee has no interest in winning over London society—
it's the New York bluebloods and her future mother-in-law
she's determined to impress. She knows the cost of smooth-
ing her rough-and-tumble frontier edges will be high. But
she never imagined it might cost her heart…

"Kennedy is going places." —Romantic Times

*"Kathryne Kennedy creates a unique, exquisite flavor that
makes her romance a pure delight page after page,
book after book."* —Merrimon Book Reviews

*"Kathryne Kennedy's computer must smolder from the power
she creates in her stories! I simply cannot describe how awesome
or how thrilling I found this novel to be."*
—Huntress Book Reviews

*"Kennedy is one of the hottest new sensations
in the romance genre."* —Merrimon Reviews

978-1-4022-2990-9 • $6.99 U.S./$8.99 CAN